NY...
The...

'For me, at all ev...
way in life I simp...

Also available in Star

NYMPH IN PARIS

Galia S.

Translated by Nicholas Courtin

A STAR BOOK
published by
the Paperback Division of
W. H. ALLEN & Co. PLC

A Star Book
Published in 1984
by the Paperback Division of
W. H. Allen & Co. PLC
44 Hill Street, London W1X 8LB

First published in France by
Éditions Robert Laffont, S.A., Paris, 1983
under the title *La Déchaîne*

Printed and bound in Great Britain by
Anchor Brendon Ltd, Tiptree, Essex

ISBN 0 352 31456 7

'You only get to heaven by overindulgence'
Twelfth century heretical saying

I
DISCOVERY

April 8, 1981

Anything can happen in Paris, but today was unprecedented.

Promptly at 11 a.m. Prince Jemal Abdelaziz El Faraoud came into view striding up Avenue George V with 40 camels in tow.

As arranged, Osvaldo and I were waiting at the corner *terrasse* of *Fouquet's* celebrated restaurant.

We sighted the animals afar off as they sauntered past an incredulous public with their noses in the air. His Excellency looked alert enough but you would think the camels had seen it all before.

To obtain a better view, Osvaldo and I clambered onto our chairs. We saw Prince Jemal approaching with the first camel, which was towing the second camel, and so on as far as No. 40. The royal camel-driver halted in front of us and tied the first camel to a lamp-post. He then advanced towards us, took my hand and brushed it with his lips, shook Osvaldo's, and beamed at us in triumph.

'My word is my bond. Here are the camels,' he declared with his palms turned upwards.

Whereupon he spun round and walked briskly to his Rolls-Royce or Bentley or whatever it was at the rear of No. 40, and rode off with a majestic purr.

Osvaldo was thunderstruck. Never had he imagined that Jemal would actually keep his pledge. After all, we had all been pretty inebriated that night. My Italian handed me down from my chair, and glowered at the camels.

A week ago we had sat on the steps of the Pantheon: Osvaldo, the Prince, myself and a redhead whose name escapes me. In the chilly pre-dawn wind, Jemal had risen to his feet and waved the bottle: 'I wish to propose a toast!'

We had come from a deafening smoke-filled nightclub, Jemal had seized a magnum of champagne from a waiter and, cramming a wad of banknotes into his pocket, had commanded four glasses to be brought to the steps of the illustrious Pantheon monument.

There, the swaying Prince turned to me and announced: 'To your eyes, Galia! To your eyes, which are the colour of the Canadian lakes!'

'Canadian,' Osvaldo managed to respond. 'Quite so.'

'So that's it,' I rejoined. 'To my eyes!'

We downed our glasses in one go, and stared at the asphalt desert before us. It was growing cold with the first light of day.

'And now let us talk business,' said Jemal, grasping Osvaldo by the arm. 'We shall return shortly, O beautiful ladies.'

The two men went off, and the redhead threw herself into my arms and wailed: 'He doesn't love me, he doesn't love me.'

The Chanel No. 5 still clinging to her, the redhead swamped my neck with tears and snuffled in my ear: 'Why doesn't he love me?' I patted her on the back and consoled her as best I could. She took my head in both hands, planting a pulpy kiss on my lips. That was nothing to the surprise that

10

lay in wait for me.

The men came back, I delicately shoved the redhead into the princely arms, and drew a heavy-eyed Osvaldo to one side. I was worried about all this secrecy.

'Fixed up your deal?'

'Er, well yes, actually.'

'How's that actually? Bought an oil well?'

'As a matter of fact I have sold you to Jemal for 40 camels.'

'You did what!'

'He said to me "She is very beautiful is Galia" and I said "How true", he said "She's highly sexy", I said "absolutely, highly sexy", he said "I give you 10 camels for her", I said it wasn't enough and he bid 20 camels.'

The concept of twenty camels failed to impinge itself on my mind. I wondered how long a caravan of 20 camels would look.

Osvaldo continued: '"Thirty camels", well I still hesitated and he shouted "FORTY CAMELS!", so I said "Stop yelling, it's a deal, 40 camels".'

My Italian paused, and then told me: 'We shook hands to make it official and he said "You got yourself a contract, a week from now at 11 a.m. outside *Fouquet's* you hand over Galia and I give you the camels. Do not forget, April 8, 11 o'clock!"'

So there we were today at 11.30 a.m. with the camels. They were gazing across at the store windows in the Champs-Elysées as if they were in some Arab *souk*.

Osvaldo was none too pleased, I could tell. He has an in-built dislike of animals, even nice inoffensive ones like cats and dogs and birds. And there he was, the owner of 40 camels who, to make matters worse, were treating him with utter disdain. He began pacing up and down the pavement, scowling at these ships of the desert now berthed on one of the poshest street corners in the world.

People were starting to gather, asking the silliest questions: 'Is it for a film? Who's starring in it? Are they camels or dromedaries? Can we have a ride mister?'

11

Osvaldo was losing his cool: 'Filthy damn things. I'm not touching the beasts. Jemal can take them away again or I'll just leave – Ah, here he is again!'

The glorious Rolls or Bentley pulled into the curb, thus providing a further attraction for the crowd. The chauffeur, impeccably turned out in an ash-grey uniform and peaked cap, got out and opened the rear door to release his master. The Arabian magnate advanced straight at us, looked into my eyes and proffered a huge bouquet of roses.

Twisting my mouth, I murmured to Osvaldo: 'His word is his bond.'

'He can go and stuff his camels ...'

The smiling Jemal took me by the arm: 'My dear Osvaldo, I am enchanted with our little contract ...'

'Now listen, Prince, I think there's been some misunderstanding. After all, it was just a joke. April the First, you know? We always have jokes on April the First, ha ha!'

The other's eyes turned as black as a barrel of crude Arabian Heavy and he pinched my arm: 'I never treat women as a joke. Or contracts either. Come Galia.'

There was no longer any doubt, I had been exchanged for a bunch of camels and there was no going back. I was now the property of Prince Jemal Abdelaziz El Faraoud.

I am now penning these lines in my luxurious room at the Plaza Hotel, in a confused state of anxiety, curiosity and excitement. Apart from Osvaldo, I have known not man, as they say in the Bible. My Prince is out fixing up more deals, and has not laid a finger on me so far. He has been treating me royally and I want for nothing.

Tonight we are to celebrate, he says, just the two of us – alone!

With this new chapter of my life now opening up, I have resolved to keep a diary of everything that happens from now on.

I am trying to picture the expression on my father's face if he ever learns that his 20-year-old daughter has been sold for 40 camels. And what he would say if he could see her astride

12

the bidet in this antiquated palace, soaping herself as she awaits her Prince of Araby for a night of love.

Poor old Daddy, working his fingers to the bone to give his children a decent, strict, catholic and patriotic education all those years.

He so badly wanted a son, two sons even, so that he could hand on the warrior's torch to posterity! Alas, the first child was a girl, and the second another. But he didn't give up and decided the next was bound to be his longed-for Hubert. But Huberte arrived in the feminine, and he had another go. Cecile let him down and after her it was me, Galia. Then he gave up!

Stuck with five daughters, he went ahead and grimly made a living as a stockbroker in the ancient city of Tours. As a result of his chagrin, Mummy is becoming more and more neurotic as the years go by. Daddy hasn't slept with her properly for simply ages, that's obvious. She must be frantic in our provincial town where all their friends are so straightlaced and an affair with an outsider unthinkable.

I know how agonizingly frustrated she must be. She runs a mobile library for the respectable citizens of Tours and its environs: Voltaire, Hugo, Diderot and the 'moderns' like Bazin, Sabatier, Bodard and Tournier. She also helps with the local festival and concerts and recitals. And to cheer her lonely evenings, she translates English poetry.

The fact is that my parents have nothing left to talk about. The five of us have left home, and they spend their evenings on the balcony at the old family house, contemplating the River Loire in silence, thinking their own thoughts, he with a glass of whisky in his hand, she sipping herb tea.

Silence. We were not talkers in our family. At least we discussed nothing of importance. Mealtimes were never occasions at which we really communicated. There was no fun to it at all, just remarks about school reports, a cousin who got engaged, a squeaky tap in the bathroom. Personally I would have liked to know some of the essential matters; for example, for months I wanted to know how boys got an erection. What caused it? I would think about this in bed at night. 'Perhaps they do it like the swimming coach when he shows off his biceps and the muscles stick out,' I would say to myself. 'They concentrate, make it happen by willpower and their thing goes stiff.'

I wondered if the penis was a muscle or perhaps a bone that advances and retracts afterwards. I longed to know, too, why my sisters had hair under their arms and between their legs, and what it was for. When I asked my mother in all innocence, she would look away: 'We'll discuss all that when you are a big girl.' She was quite snooty about it.

I would keep on: 'Please Mummy, when a man and a lady are married, how do they have babies? I don't understand about the seeds. Has the husband got seeds in his thing?'

I had seen little boys with no clothes on when we went to the beach, and I used to imagine their penises full of ground coffee or corn or rice and worry about how it came out.

It wasn't my fault. At the Ursuline Convent where I went to school, the sisters were no help at all. Sex was a forbidden word, and the subject was surrounded in mystery and terror. They knocked three things into us:

1. Sex is the work of the devil.
2. The less fun you have, the more merit you accumulate.
3. Beware of men.

Of course these rules were never actually spoken or put down in writing, but the sisters at the Collège Sainte-Ursule managed to say it in a sneaky sort of way.

So we had to hide what we did, conceal our moments of pleasure and cheat the 'cops in coifs', as we nicknamed them. One of these was dreadful, Sister Marie-Thérèse the geography teacher – her ruling passion was masturbation.

After class she would often get one of the girls to herself, and try to make her confess everything, wheedling it out of her.

'Clotilde, my dear, you seem rather pale these days, are you getting enough sleep?'

'Oh yes, Sister Marie-Thérèse.'

'Of course, but before you fall asleep, do you find your hand wandering?'

'Wandering, sister?'

'I mean do you caress yourself just a little bit?'

'Caress, Sister?'

'Yes, you know what I mean.'

And the girl would gaze at her trustingly with a sanctimonious daughter-of-Mary look. Some of my small friends were genuinely mystified, but Sister Marie-Thérèse with her hole-in-the-corner chats made sure they began their nocturnal explorations very soon afterwards.

I suppose I was rather advanced for my age, because I didn't need her advice. I learned how to do it all by myself, and most nights I would reach down for the tiny magic button so conveniently placed. Hardly needing to move, I could bring on the loveliest tingly feelings with nobody even knowing. Several of us did.

April 9, after midnight

It is certainly exotic, spending the night in a palatial room in Paris so close to my own studio-apartment.

At the moment Jemal is asleep in his room, which connects with mine through the bathroom.

A few hours ago he rather ceremoniously handed me a gift-wrapped box saying: 'This is for you Galia. Let us prepare ourselves.' Naturally I couldn't wait, and tore off the paper and lid to discover the most gorgeous white silk nightdress with spangles and trimmings straight out of a fairy tale.

I duly 'prepared' myself. First a hot bath using three perfume essences, then long and languid brushing of the hair, torrid make-up somewhat overdone by European standards, and then the alluring nightdress that might almost have been an evening dress for dinner downstairs. Underwear was not allowed, and as the silk material was semi-transparent the whole effect was most suggestive. I swayed my hips to see how I looked in motion.

A knock at the door, and I swallowed nervously. My bosom heaved as I sought to remain calm, and my throat released a mere squeak as I said: 'Come in.' I put my arms over my breasts modestly.

The door opened towards me, and there was His Excellency head high and dressed to kill, as it were, in a kind of de luxe thin wrap fringed with *lamé*.

We stood for a while facing each other. I dared not move and Jemal seemed almost as nervous.

At least to begin with. But I already saw that I came up to his expectations, for his shiny garment started to bulge just below his waist.

In a voice deep with emotion he declared: 'O Galia Galia, you are so truly beautiful.'

'So are you, truly,' I whispered.

'We could, could ...'

'Yes Jemal?'

'We could take a glass of champagne together. I will call room service ... Hullo, send up a Dom Perignon, the best year you have! Without delay!'

The strained wrap front divulged his rising impatience, and my own excitement increased. But he came no nearer, made no move to touch me, not even bestowing a first kiss. He remained distant, aloof – and erect. When the waiter came in, quietly efficient, pushing a small trolley into the room, Jemal made no attempt to conceal his protuberance. I was embarrassed. We watched as the man presented the bottle of '48 and slowly released the cork. Like a dancing priest, he poured two glasses and returned the bottle to the ice bucket, delicately placing some napkins on the tray.

By now we were seated in armchairs, some distance apart, observing the ceremonial wordlessly.

The waiter went on and on, and Jemal suddenly rose, dismissing the man without more ado.

'That is enough,' he ordered. 'I will see to the rest. You go now!'

The waiter, paid to do as he was told and submit to a hundred small humiliations daily, left instantly and with practised dignity, closing the door soundlessly.

'Galia my beauteous one, let us drink to our love.'

We took our glasses, they went 'tink' as they met, and when I lowered my face to drink I saw his member lengthening visibly under the wrap. He seemed enormous.

I choked as he suddenly threw his glass across the room. He grabbed me by the arms, pulled me over to the bed and pushed me across it on my back. In a flash he lifted the skirt of my nightie, forced my legs apart, and violently penetrated me.

It was all over in three minutes.

Fighting to regain my breath I told him: 'My word, Jemal, you're not at all the sensual type.'

'Oh yes, Galia, I am. It was so good!'

I am now writing this in the still of the night. As politely as I could, I asked to sleep alone.

He had jumped me like a buck rabbit and it still hurts. How is it possible for a man to make love with so little know-how, so brutally and with so little tact? I do know that in the country it is an accepted thing in many homes for the womenfolk to be 'taken' silently in the dark, stealthily almost, with hardly a kiss. The male covers the female without preliminaries, jabs his implement in like she is some old sow, and gives a grunt. He shoots his semen and they turn their backs on each other, just as her juices are starting to flow. It's not fair, and in cotton nightclothes too!

How lucky I was to meet Osvaldo, to have been initiated by an experienced and sensitive pleasure-seeker, an understanding lover who knows how to woo, win and gratify a girl!

I was just 18 when he deflowered me, highly-principled and prim though I was. I was so terrified really. With my strict upbringing I had striven unyielding against the delights of sexual fulfilment, the ultimate forbidden fruit.

I would titter inwardly when I caught sight of a boy and

girl kissing and cuddling in public. How ridiculous they seemed to me, shrouded as I was in my own immaturity.

I am infinitely grateful to my first lover for patiently vanquishing my reserve, for piercing the heavy armour of my puritan morality.

It was simply marvellous the way it happened the first time. We had been playing tennis all morning on that hot July day at the Rueil-Malmaison Club. The score was 6-1, 6-2, 5-1, to Osvaldo. He is a far better player than I am but he lets me have a few points without me noticing it too obviously.

It was deuce, Osvaldo's service. His first serve went crashing into the net, the second overshot by a couple of yards. He served again from my right, an easy ball and not too fast. I whipped it neatly over to his corner, my point, 5-2, change ends. We sat down for a minute on a bench to wipe off our rackets and take a breather.

'You could have retrieved that, you must be getting past it,' I quipped, trying to control my breathing.

'Sorry, not a chance, I was off-balance. That was a fantastic back-hand.'

'And that second serve, miles out.'

'It happens to us all. My goodness, you're soaked, let me help you.'

He stood over me with the thick towel, patting my face, gently wiping my neck and arms and legs. I let him pamper me and closed my eyes. His mouth covered my open lips and I felt his tongue come inside, so slippery and naturally. Mmmm, it was nice. I had always kept my lips closed when a boy kissed me, but he caught me off-guard.

Exhausted and with the midday sun beating down, I melted.

He went on wiping me and it became a caress. He let the towel drop away and ran his hand over my shoulders, fingering my lips, my ears, and then my breasts so that my nipples became hard. He reached round my waist and in front and I instinctively clenched my thighs.

18

'Don't do that,' he murmured.

'Why?'

Was this the language of desire? I wondered. The 'Why?' had escaped, trickled out of its own volition. Was I asking him 'Why there?' or was I asking myself 'Why should I still resist my natural inclinations, why keep my thighs held tightly?'

Taking advantage of my confusion he moved his hand under my short pleated skirt and into my panties, swiftly pressing his fingers into my sex, now swollen and wet with perspiration.

I caught my breath but made no resistance as the first quiver jolted me. Osvaldo stroked me inside, back and forth, and I willed myself to concentrate on the little waves of pleasure spreading all over my pelvis. He changed to a lifting motion under my bottom, and I wanted him to go faster. My interior was pulsing when he gently halted and laid me on the bench, removing my panties. My thighs fell apart and I jerked several times when he resumed his caresses, the warm sun heightening my appetite.

Then a release of exquisite pleasure-pain seared through me, and I remember my head lashing from side to side. Never could I have imagined such volcanic rapture. Often by myself I had orgasms that left me shaking convulsively, but this was a scorching sirocco of joy.

My darling Osvaldo helped me to the changing room. There was nobody else there and he spread our towels on the long seat. Minutes later he pierced my membrane, causing me to cry out in a near coma.

When I recovered, a glow of triumph enveloped my whole body and soul. I have never looked back, for on that day on July I exorcised the ghosts of the past once and for all.

One of the most evil aspects of the pathological tradition in which I was raised – they call it 'civilization' – is the fierce, dark determination of those who govern and educate us to prevent other people having enjoyment at all costs.

In some countries they cut the clitoris of growing girls, and in others they give them a missal. What is the difference? The significance is the same: women may not have fun, women are not made to gratify their senses.

Clitoridectomy and the catechism have kept women in chains for long centuries.

April 10

Today the Prince took me shopping in the Faubourg Saint-Honoré. We went by taxi around mid-morning, and when it came to settling the fare, Jemal said he carried no small change. He thereupon handed the driver 500 francs and waved his hand. I exchanged wide-eyed looks with the man behind the wheel.

We toured the boutiques, and he asked to see the best of everything. But he never questioned the price.

I must admit that this display of endless wealth made me quite heady; we didn't have oil wells at Tours. Money for Jemal was just continuous stationery, enabling him to satisfy his slightest whim – including me, of course! As Jemal approached, doors opened miraculously, broad smiles appeared, all kinds of people bowed low. His hand plunged again and again into an inexhaustible supply of paper money. I felt like the Queen of Sheba.

We visited a fine art gallery where he acquired a priceless jade statuette. As we left, I could restrain myself no longer. I was dying to knew where the money really came from. It was a tricky moment.

'Jemal,' I said as sweetly as Turkish delight, 'how nice for you not to run short of cash, ever.'

He got the message: 'I work for my living.'

'Yes?'

'I buy, I sell, I buy, I sell. Very simple.'

'How interesting,' I said breathlessly. 'But what?'

'Anything there is: oil, land, apartments, companies – anything.'

'It's nice being very rich, you must be very satisfied.'

'Oh no. The more I have the more I want. I work very hard, I am never satisfied.'

'I see, it's a kind of game.'

'Yes, I play with money. Only the rich can afford to play, only the rich get richer.'

'How exciting.' I ventured to add: 'Are you glad you bought me?'

'Oh Galia! I did not buy you. You are my guest!'

'Was I worth 40 camels?' My voice would have melted granite.

'My dear Galia, I would have offered a hundred camels for you!'

'I – a hundred camels! Oh Jemal, that's the nicest thing any man has ever said to me!'

April 11

I have always been starved of affection. It is my father's fault, he is such a hard man.

I have never been drawn to him, largely because he shows no warmth or tenderness towards Mummy. I shall never forgive him for withholding the love she deserves. He has wrecked a wonderful woman's entire existence.

Mummy had so many qualities: beauty, intelligence, a deep feeling for music and poetry, boundless generosity. She devoted herself unstintingly to us and to this man, who failed to show her understanding of any kind, cared nothing for her as a person. Naturally she became docile and arid. My father has to answer for such waste. Like many men of his generation, and indeed of today's, he thinks he owns her, body and soul. She is there to serve him, to be available at all times.

After five children and a miscarriage, she was dried out and the years started to tell. Father went with other women, and she became old in a matter of months.

April 12

I feel so guilty about missing my Thai language course and even more my dancing lessons which I love. I am sure I shall regret this later.

Too bad, I am in this up to my neck. The telephone is permanently switched to the answering machine and I am just letting myself drift. My Prince is my auto-pilot.

I simply let him decide everything, as long as he keeps on adoring me and treats me right. What else could a girl ask for amid the bright lights of Paris?

It was the *baccalaureat* that earned me Paris. Daddy promised to send me if I passed, and the glittering prospect was irresistible for a young girl pining away in the provinces.

During the final year I worked morning, noon and night cooped up like a nun. And when I passed with a distinction my father could not refuse. I knew he hated letting me off the leash, but a promise is a promise.

When I got off the train and walked to the exit, I felt like Balzac's Rastignac in skirts, or rather jeans as it happened. Alone and free outside the Gare D'Austerlitz, my heart leapt. No more grim-faced sisters in their silly coifs with their dreary prattling, no more dismal boring hours and hours at home. I was in Paris, Queen of all the cities. My mood was euphoric.

April 13

Prince Jemal has had me for three days and nights. It has been a gloriously hectic round of nightclubs, five-star restaurants and fabulous presents. Not forgetting the superb Plaza Hotel that would turn any girl's head.

But I am restless somehow. He is nice, attentive and generous, but the sexual side is disappointing. He makes love frantically, like a goat that's been locked up for weeks. We have no communication, he treats me as his property, his prize, to use how he wants.

It was fun at first but we are playing different games, and I feel the need for something different.

After breakfast today, Jemal took my hand and made me stand in front of him. He looked at me with his marvellous brown eyes.

'Galia, you are worried.'

'Oh no,' I said quietly.

'I know! There is an excellent restaurant at Rambouillet ...'

'Please Jemal, we have been to so many.'

'Galia, my adorable angel, you are making me suffer. What would you like more than anything else?'

'I would like to see the sea,' I whispered.

Within an hour the Rolls (I know now) was rushing us to Roissy Airport. A small private jet awaited us, the pilot standing to attention and a hostess with a creamy smile leading us out. We were off to Cannes, via Nice Airport.

April 15, 4 p.m., on a yacht

Cannes or Paris, it's all the same as they say in Montmartre. If you are with someone who is tiresome.

The Carlton Hotel took over from the Plaza and the restaurants are just as luxurious and sinister. To please me, Jemal has rented a sort of yacht with powerful engines and with all kinds of fancy equipment for deep sea fishing. We go to and fro on the azure blue of the Baie de Cannes, and then Jemal decides to let the engines go full out. We roar off out to sea like a torpedo.

At this speed you really have to hold on for dear life. The boat keeps crashing down on the waves and it is so noisy we can't hear ourselves shout.

I wave my arms like a mad thing, and Jemal slows down. Then he orders the engines to be stopped completely.

Ah, what peace, what bliss! Not a cloud in the sky as the boat rises and falls with the wavelets coming in from the horizon.

We lie down on the deck, rocking gently between sky and sea.

I can feel an immense warmth on my legs and abdomen. I have an urge to make love, to be in the arms of an experienced male.

It is a matter of seconds to remove the top of my two-piece bathing suit and the relief is immediate.

'Oh no,' orders Jemal. 'Please Galia, we are not alone!'

The captain, a young man with hair the colour of corn, smiles imperceptibly. He understands. Annoyed, I obey my Islamic lord and master, replacing my bra. It is noon and so sweaty.

'Shall we go for a swim?' I could not avoid the brittle tone.

'As you wish, Galia, your wish is my command' (Like hell!)

Me sultrily: 'Perhaps the captain, who hasn't told me his name, would like to bathe with us.' I hope I have clicked with him.

'With pleasure, Madame, very kind of you. I'd like to. My name is Yves.'

Jemal lowered the portcullis with a crash: 'You are being paid for your services as a captain. You will stay on board.'

So that was that, a swim in a chastity belt, and ordered with such lack of style. It may suit the Prophet but it's not my ethic, especially at 20 years of age. They can keep their yashmaks and their harems, they're not spoiling my fun just as it's starting to get interesting. I resolve to leave for Paris that very night, thumbing it all the way if I have to.

Later I put in a call to Mummy, suddenly feeling tender towards her. I nearly cried when she answered in her thin voice.

'Hullo.'

'Hullo Mummy, it's me.'

'My little pet!'

'Mummy I – I love you so very much. I just wanted to tell you right away.'

I heard her sob, and jammed down the receiver, biting my lip.

Ah, how I would love to be swept away like that for a man!

When I was a little girl I used to like a big cuddle on Mummy's lap after the evening meal. I can still smell her perfume, feel the wisps of hair tickling my cheek, her warm belly. We were united in a tranquil flow of love, our two bodies.

She used to recite her English poems to me, and I would half doze with my eyelids heavy as she translated the lines into French. That is how I started English, which is almost a second mother tongue for me.

I especially liked Milton. She would think a bit, recall a passage and recite it faultlessly in one go, calmly and softly. Once, the whole of *Lycidas*.

But it was heaven to me.

April 16, Montelimar, by the roadside

I can't get over it. I am 20, and I challenge anyone to deny that this is the most wonderful age for a girl.

At moments I want to hug myself, and frankly I'm worth hugging. I have a clear mind, good eyes, supple skin, I get hungry and thirsty, I love men, I love love, I love life!

Spring is a lovely season, full and radiant, and I am sitting on a lump of rock with a large piece of cardboard reading PARIS.

Trees are in blossom all around me, and for once even the motorway looks pretty.

I hardly slept last night but I am not tired.

Immediately we returned to harbour in Cannes, I knew what I had to do. I could not stay a minute longer with that lousy oil millionaire. I carefully wrapped all the presents he had bestowed on me over the past week and put them in a large suitcase. My personal things, not amounting to much, I stuffed in a beach bag.

I was all ready to go in my jeans and sailor jersey, with my beach bag over my shoulder.

'Come Galia, we shall change for dinner, I have a surprise for you.'

'And so have I, a surprise for you.'

'For me, angel, what would that be?'

'This!!' And I hurled the case at the khaki-faced sheikh.

I did not have to wait long for transport. I thumbed a lift on La Croisette, the main promenade. A breakdown truck stopped, it could not have been more appropriate!

'Where to, Miss?' the truck driver enquired in his lilting *accent du Midi.*

'Anywhere.'

'Anywhere, just like that?'

'Anywhere, that's how it is.'

'Good, up you get.'

We had not gone 300 yards when he pulled up, and clamped his big mouth to mine. I let him have his thrill, and I rather liked it too.

We drew apart, panting like a pair of pigs. He wasn't bad looking and I fell for his local brogue.

'I'm a married man,' he said at length, 'but I've got life in me yet.'

'May I ask you something, please?'

'Go ahead, Miss.'

'Please take me to the motorway feeder, it's not far is it?'

'No, pretty near.' His rough hand was creeping over my knee and I froze. 'Maybe we could find a quiet spot ...' He eyed me lasciviously.

'I'm sorry, you're a real tonic, but I'm in a hurry to get to Paris. Please drive on, just take me to the motorway.'

The breakdown man had other ideas. He flashed a paw to my nodal point, but luckily my jeans are tough and he had trouble. Breathing hotly, he tried to force the zip. Even with both hands I could not push his fist away.

'Listen, please don't spoil it. Please! You were really decent just now, and now you can't control it, and I think you're being silly. It needs two to make love, or it's rape!'

No holding him off. He was getting nasty and kept on trying. The zip was undone and with a supreme effort I forced his fingers back and his hand came away. I broke free and jumped out.

As I stumbled away I could hear him yelling: 'Bloody whore. You're all the same, fucking cock-teasers ...'

I started thumbing again. An oldish man with greying hair took me as far as the motorway. He tried nothing, the perfect gentleman.

Getting lifts is certainly an eye-opener. It teaches you more about people than any textbook.

Next, a call to Osvaldo. He wasn't bitchy, thank goodness. Knew my voice right away and said 'Ah.' This, I assume, means 1) So you've turned up. 2) Are you alright? 3) I've got news.

'Anything you'd like to tell me?' I say, husky with sex-appeal.

'They've accepted my screenplay.'

'Fantastic! We've just got to celebrate that. I'm on my way back.'

'Where are you now?'

'In a motorist's paradise. I can see pink acrylic carseat covers, plastic dogs and cats for dangling in rear windows, cans marked "Regional Dish – Société Renard, Clichy", a line of ...'

'Where in God's name ...'

'I'm at a filling station on the *Autoroute du Sud,* see you soon. Oh I forgot, how are the camels?'

'I gave them away.'

'Who's the lucky fellow?'

'Chap in films. He was doing a low budget B picture about the Pharaohs with plywood palm-trees and everything. Now he's changed it to an adventure spectactular with real camels. He's got camels roaming all over the goddam studio. It's called Desert Caravan or Parched Desert or something like that ...'

Now, cars are hurtling by on the motorway like they are

27

afraid to run out of petrol. I may have picked a bad spot, in line with the sun. It was so easy yesterday, took only a minute for a lift to Montelimar.

It is a relief to be on your own in a small town you have never seen. You are not pressed for time and can do what you feel like.

But you have to keep alert. I went into a bistro packed with men and not a female in sight. I could almost hear them all sniffing at me. It was 10 p.m. and I was unaccompanied. Whatever they were thinking, all I wanted was a coffee.

I sipped it, mulling over the past week. I thought of the camels, and Jemal's face when I threw the suitcase at him, I am not a runaway person by nature, and this little escapade with a stranger, an Arab into the bargain, had its plus points too, I was thinking.

It could be that I am acquiring a taste for freedom. I'm not sure.

(Finish later. Car stopped and coming back to pick me up.)

April 21, Paris

Osvaldo obviously felt I was ripe for a new experience. Otherwise he would never dared to have taken me to *Le Bassano*, a highly private club off the Champs-Elysées protected by a thick oak door with copper reinforcements and a spyhole so that they can keep out the trash.

Within seconds, they whisked us inside, so Osvaldo is certainly a *habitué*. The manager shook hands and led us to the bar, an oldish man in a white silk shirt spread wide to display his hair-strewn tan who inspected me with the creased eyes of the experienced seducer and/or drinker.

I wriggled my bottom onto a bar stool *á la Hollywood* and tried to look *blasé*, registering the scene.

Diffused lighting, black and red lacquer walls, mirrors everywhere – awfully sophisticated. Leading off the end of the bar, a room with the door ajar.

That's when I did my first double-take.

A nude woman flitted by the doorway! At first I could not believe it. All I actually saw was a white shoulder, a mass of loose hair and a pair of heavyish buttocks. But there was no mistaking the fact: a grown woman with no clothes on had run past the opening.

My Italian mentor and the boss showed no sign of noticing. They were arguing about nudist club legislation on the Côte d'Azur, or pretending to.

Anyhow I gulped down some 12-year-old Ballantine to save face. Whisky always tastes like crushed bedbug to me, but at key moments like these it certainly keeps you on your stool.

My insides tingled as I sensed a whole new world through that doorway. A discreet orange light from within fuelled my interest, and I was so enervated I could not help fidgeting.

More bedbug in my glass, the clunk of an icecube, and Osvaldo drew near.

'Alright, my sweet?'

'Oh yes,' I squeaked. 'Just fine, handsome.'

'You look pale, treasure.'

'I feel absolutely divine.'

'You are adorable in that dress ...' I felt adorable, but I was nervous about it.

Osvaldo simply oozes romance. His voice was the thing that first appealed to me, of course. So musical! A sort of blend of Rossini, Puccini and Verdi: irony, melancholy and drama in a package deal. When it comes to charm you can't beat the Italians, I say.

Suddenly, there she was again! This time I heard the woman laugh, too. Rather dumpy she was, and I plainly saw the swell of her rump, her chestnut hair, her well-fleshed calves.

Behind a bland exterior, I was devoured with curiosity, longing to find out what they were doing in there. Osvaldo inched closer, smiled and offered his hand.

'Come, *tesoro,* I will take you in.'

I tumbled off my perch, slipped my hand in his and was

led, heart thumping, into the Holy of Holies.

What I saw there was quite devastating! I shall never forget it.

We were in a large room bathed in this dim orange light, and with a round bed in the middle 10 feet across. Couches heaped with sumptuous cushions lined the walls and on some of them men and women were lounging, most of them naked or almost, though a few still had their clothes on.

People were literally mawling one another. Couples and small groups writhed soundlessly except for the labour of heavy breathing. Then a woman started whispering hoarsely 'Oh, yes, there, there.' Someone was moaning, and I distinctly heard the gurgle of coital juices.

My eyes fixed on a stunning blonde in black satin wide knickers, suspender belt and the sheerest stockings. Her bra was off and I gazed upon two of the shapeliest golden boobies you could imagine; they were swelling and retracting prettily as she slowly caressed a phallus jutting from an open trouser zip. Except for his jacket the man was fully dressed and I was startled to see he still had his tie on.

His woman companion was too engrossed to notice us, and I continued looking at her bosom with a certain envy. Then on an impulse she bent down and her hair cascaded forward as she delicately enveloped the erect member with her lips. I was transfixed.

I pulled myself together and looked about to see a seated couple kissing hungrily, he fully dressed, she in the nude. She had her legs competely open and between them was a second woman on all fours licking and sucking at her cleft in generous motions. She too was naked and she arched her back so that her bottom assumed immense proportions. A rather mean-looking man with popping eyes fingered her between her ballooning cheeks. Once, and then again later the kneeling woman jerked her head round and scolded the man: 'You're hurting, do be careful!' The man would wait a few seconds before moving his hand forward, squirming his finger into her again while she swayed and forced up her rump sensually. I was shocked. The seated couple kissed on inexhaustibly, and I saw a blob of spittle running down the woman's chin. Eyes closed, devoured by two mouths, she groaned something over and over again ecstatically. I could not catch what it was.

Osvaldo took my hand in a firm grip and I grew faint as he set me down on a couch heaving with cushions. I was trembling by now and quite incapable of speech.

Next to us, an athletic young man was making love to a woman, her face buried in his neck. With each potent thrust, she squealed 'Oh yes, more, oh yes, more' in a kind of litany.

The man's wet penis went back and forth in her splayed oval, which was starkly red like a wound. I could see absolutely everything!

Greedily I watched them nearing their climax. But I then forced my eyes away, to enjoy the breathtaking sight of the youth's bottom as it curved and relaxed, his crease spreading and clinching rhythmically. I had never seen this before. He was beautifully rounded and tight, and his thigh muscles pulsated as he gradually went faster.

I became aware of Osvaldo's fingers on my cheek. I shuddered at the touch.

'What about us, *tesoro*?' he whispered. There was something devilish about him.

I was so tense that I released an idiotic giggle, more of a bleat than a laugh. But already his hand had cupped my knees and was slipping under my dress. My own hands were none too steady.

Pushing him down, I blurted: 'Oh no, don't. Please, please!' I arranged my dress, it was awfully embarrassing.

'Come, my *tesoro,* you wouldn't play hard-to-get with your old friend Osvaldo?'

'No, I mean I can't do it now, not here.' But it was immediately clear that I would have to fight him off.

'Relax,' he persisted, 'it's so lovely with lots of people ...'

His hand was across my thighs, snaking up, and in no time at all he deftly slipped his fingers under my panty elastic.

31

'No, I don't like it, please Osvaldo, take me home. Please!'

I thought I could count on him, but I was wrong. In a swift movement he slipped my diminutive panties down to just above my knees, so that I was completely powerless to move. All men are the same.

Now another man was looming over me, more of a boy, taut and muscular like a Greek god. I simpered as his hands glided over my legs, warm and soft, his eyes deep and gleaming with desire. 'You are delicious, he murmured, 'so enticing.' I struggled to free myself from his tightening hold. I was so frightened.

Their four hands were caressing me. I was at their mercy, they removed my panties completely and my entire lower body instantly flamed. I tried to control my feelings but the youth's lips were upon my feet, my knees, nudging between my thighs. His ardent mouth drew closer and my pelvis leapt. With a supreme effort of will, I told myself it had to stop and I broke free, seized my panties and was on my feet, frantically rearranging my dress.

'I can't, Osvaldo,' I whimpered, my face scarlet. 'I have to leave.'

The two men stood back and I could see the youth's penis sticking out hard and thick, his face white with thwarted passion.

Glancing heavenward, Osvaldo turned to him and spread his arms like the Latin he was. 'Incredible,' he laughed with a jerk of the chin at me. The meaning was clear: 'Just like a woman!' The phallocrat!

It was well before dawn when I reached my studio-apartment, still fuming, and slammed the door. Damn the neighbours for once, they could go to hell. I flung myself onto the bed.

Hot tears welled up with the avalanche of recriminations that overcame me: 'Stupid bitch, silly little bourgeoise-schoolgirl-daughter-of-Mary. Afraid of sex, frightened at a prick, spoilsport, coward, scared to have an orgasm with a strange man.' I blubbed: 'And I wanted it so much.'

I was still living the youth's moist fleshy lips on my pubis, the entwined bodies of the couples as they wrestled, the exciting orange glow. I felt so humiliated, what a fool I had been.

He was on top of me, wanting me and I wanting him, I had only to yield. His hands were all over me, lusting for me. And his throbbing male-male-male penis that I was yearning for him to push in, even violently if he liked, vanquishing my resistance. Oh how I ached for it, was still aching for it!

But the poison of Sister Marie-Thérèse had done its work. 'Come along now,' she seemed to twitter, 'stop that now, it's wicked and sinful.' And like a naughty little girl I had blushed and run away, prisoner of purity and convent morality. Lord, what an idiot I'd been!

At length, still angered, I turned on my back. I found the hem of my dress and my fingers sought the moist relief I needed so urgently.

April 22

It was Angèle, our petite maid from Normandy, who really showed me how to obtain pleasure by myself.

She slept in a small room close to mine, and sometimes asked me to join her in her bed. She was afraid of the dark and we ought to sleep together. At least that is what Angèle said.

'Slip your nightie off,' she whispered one night. 'You'll be warm enough in my arms.'

She started fondling me after a while, just a little, and then showed me what she did to herself. I knew somehow it was naughty and I might get into trouble, but I looked at her for ages just the same. Later I began doing it to myself, and then often.

I did not mention it to Mummy until three or four years later, by which time Angèle had been gone for some time.

I was no different from most girls in our society, and even boys. My sexual awareness evolved in an abject way and I

33

always had this dreadful feeling it was sinful.

I am still ashamed about the incident at *Le Bassano* and I suppose the fascination the youth held for me was similar to the curiosity I had towards Angèle. I am wondering if the pleasure you get isn't more intense if it is forbidden. The more 'wrong' it is the greater the excitement.

It seems to me that shutting your eyes to this so-called morality is a healthy reaction. It is the idea of wrongness, the ban on pleasure, that is so deeply morbid. At the same time it is thrilling.

But I am not sure what to think about that. I have not quite worked it out yet.

April 25

I chose Thursday evening for the most daring thing I had ever done. This is the evening when the upper classes tend to go out, rather than Friday or Saturday like the crowds. Thursday's people seem more positive.

The manager of *Le Bassano* peeked at me through the spyhole with a rather bloodshot eye, and I gave him my sweetest smile. The door opened at once, but the boss glanced out left and right to check on the passers-by. It was very secretive.

I hauled in Osvaldo and took him right past the bar without stopping. He was dragging his feet.

'*Tesoro,*' he exclaimed. 'Let's just have a little drink ...'

I tugged him into the orange room, and plonked him down on one of the couches. He seemed exhausted, and a little nervous.

'But my treasure ...'

Within seconds I slipped off my dress, kicked my shoes away, took down my panties and everything fell in a puddle under me. I went straight to the big bed in the middle and lay on my back. I opened my legs wide.

'Come on then,' I bubbled.

Osvaldo was stupefied, frozen into immobility. There was

34

a sudden hush in the room, the couples and groups of people stopped wriggling around and everyone looked at me in astonishment.

I suddenly felt scared. What did I imagine I was doing, for heaven's sake? I had got it all wrong and was being utterly ridiculous, and they all knew it. I wanted the earth to open up, wanted to die, it had gone wrong. The gesture was a complete farce!

I sought Osvaldo's eyes and saw he was grinning. It could still work, perhaps, in any case I had to go through with it now.

'What are you waiting for?' I threw out in a thick voice.

Not a soul moved, and I bit my lip. My heart was thumping, and I was in a state of panic.

I remembered a trick I used to use. It generally works and the horrors disappear and I regain control.

I pinched my right ear, deliberately relaxed, drummed my fingers. Then in this mute and half-clothed temple of Eros I quietly whistled 'The bridge over the River Kwai.' My legs are at 70 degrees, and I don't mean Centigrade!

To my infinite relief a man gets to his feet and begins walking around me. I bless him for it. I catch him by an arm unawares and pull him onto me, so that his whole weight is squashing me. I do not care that it is painful at first. Two more come up and I have all three, defiantly at first but with growing enjoyment. Then a woman's face is above mine, her hair falls over us and she strokes my neck and kisses me passionately. I lose count. They are handling my feet, stroking my hands, licking my ear, kneading my bottom. A large misshapen penis forces its way into my mouth and I feel the man's scrotum on my chin. A finger explores my anus, hurting me.

It is not funny any more and I am worried. I throw a desperate appeal at Osvaldo, but he just keeps watching, the swine! I am a squirming mass of flesh being pummelled, massaged, caressed, rubbed, scratched, pinched, bitten, penetrated again and again. I can feel urine trickling over my torso. I give myself up to this festival of erotica and I am lost in a whirl of bodies, rhythms, colours, acrid smells and semen.

How long I went on I have no idea. All sense of time forsook me. My body lost all feeling, I was drained of energy, flaccid from repeated orgasms. I felt like a sacrificed virgin.

At length I managed to stir and they were all standing around me, smiling down. They treated me royally, bending low to kiss my feet, gently cupping my hands. A man with greying hair, in his fifties and immensely handsome, signalled to me to sit up. I recognised him, he had penetrated me from the rear when I was face down in a particularly submissive posture. With incredible delicacy he took my hand and lightly applied his lips in princely fashion.

'*Mademoiselle*, you were magnificent.'

A woman clasped my face in her hands, and kissed my mouth lovingly through straying wisps of hair.

'You were beautiful, beautiful,' she told me.

The manager advanced, his pride taking years off him. 'Our little princess,' he whispered in my ear.

I was radiant, I had regained my self-respect, I was being worshipped. I was so happy!

'Come now, we're going home.' It was Osvaldo, his face as long as an old dishcloth.

Home in my studio-apartment, under a scorching hot shower, spraying my intimate parts in a cloud of perfumed steam, I yelled out an old French lovesong. The neighbours could go jump in the lake!

I felt like a million dollars. I was making up for lost time, having the kind of men I wanted, kicking over the traces, experiencing thrills and joys beyond my wildest dreams.

And this was only the beginning. The world was my oyster, nothing could hold me back now. I was heady with power over men!

April 27

The phone snatched me from the arms of Morpheus around 7 a.m. today. My face contorting in annoyance, I waded out of sleep and out of an exotic dream apparently in the West Indies. A black man glistening with sweat was kissing me on the beach, boats danced on the waves off-shore, and I was playing with his enormous shaft. It was a dream I was having repeatedly just before waking.

With a groan I reached for the receiver. A noise like the Valkyries in a drainpipe reached my tender ear. Osvaldo, I might have guessed.

'You've run out on me.'

'Huh?'

'You've simply let me drop.'

'Ah?'

'Why are you so stony-hearted with me?'

Bye bye black man, *au revoir* palm-trees, the soft white beach sinks into the ocean and I blink myself into reality.

Gentlemen should never ring ladies before 8 a.m., however worried they are about their rights over us. Osvaldo hasn't got over my little orgy of two nights ago. My lips form into a smirk, at least that's what it is intended to be.

When *he* took *me* to *Le Bassano* there was no difficulty. I was his property, his bird to be shown off, his plaything to be shared with his little friends before he collected me up and took me home from the party.

But on the second occasion, *I* was the one in charge, showing my independence, taking the initiative. His male pride was cut to the quick.

He now lectured me as if reciting from a document. Between the lines it went something like this: 'Sexual freedom is for men only, because we're men. It is not the same for women, it is not in their NATURE to be unfaithful. A woman's genitals are wrapped round her heart, but men are not made the same way. Men may copulate without love, whereas women may not.'

Not our nature, says the old pig! There is no such thing as

nature. There is the tragic history of women's slavery to men century after century, bound hand and foot to the male. In the opening years of the 17th century, an imbecile by the name of Thomas Sanchez wrote: 'It is more in compliance with the nature of things that men should act and woman submit ... The natural copulatory position is for the woman to lie on her back and the man to lie on her belly, ensuring that he ejaculates into the receptacle intended for this use.'

How convenient for men that women's nature is thus.

Oh my sisters, poor weak women, wives, mistresses, concubines! How much longer will your vaginas be the toys of Man? Rise up and live your unbridled desires, do not fear them, they can do you no harm!

Osvaldo, then, is perplexed at my little shindig at the club. The poor wretch is now aware that he is NOT INDISPENSABLE.

As the psychologists would say, I am wondering if his phallus hasn't taken a knock or two.

He is crooning into the phone, pleading on his knees.

'*Tesooroo*,' he coos, 'try and understand ...'

I have had enough and I slam down the receiver. I get as far as the bathroom, and he rings again.

This time he's the Flying Dutchman: '*TESORO!*'

'Mm?'

'Do you love me?'

'I'm not sure.'

'*Ma* what do you mean, you don't know?'

'Love, love, love, I don't know what it is. Maybe it's the ultimate for poodles.' (I don't know what I mean either!)

'*Ma tesoro ...*'

'*Ma* what? What-what-what? Oh shit. *Basta cosi!*'

That's it. I switch the thing to the answering machine and run myself a bath. As I flap my hand about making a big blue foam, I can hear the machine clicking away, recording message after message.

Smugly I realize that he cannot go on all day.

April 28

I cannot help wondering how I came to be emancipated so suddenly. How is it that I found the secret and could free myself of the constraints and seemly behaviour driven into me as a girl?

Few women have done as much. Their circumstances, their duties as married women, their life styles – everything divides us. They have remained 'respectable': I have become 'disrespectful' and I like it that way.

I certainly do not envy my two older sisters with their 'fine husbands', and now sliding steadily into a desperate conventionalism. How could I be jealous of the brilliant career opening up for Huberte after going through the E.N.A. Higher College of Administration? Administrators disgust me anyway. Cécile worries me too. Only two years older than I am, she is in her third year of Medicine, cramming night and day, learning by heart everything she will forget when the exam is over. There is little doubt that she is on the straight and narrow road to conformity, the trap all medical people fall into.

No indeed, I would not like to be in their shoes. There is less and less in common between us. I am creating my own revolution, or at least working out my evolution, while my sisters are battening down the hatches of conformist society.

My social status and mental balance are far harder to maintain than theirs. I am not travelling the smooth track of a career, and have no wish to. I refuse to go from A to B.

For me, at all events, if I am going to find my own way in life, I simply have to be sexually emancipated.

As to financial matters, these are secondary. I cannot throw money around, but I am not complaining. My monthly student's allowance is enough for me to get along with.

April 29

Madame Babarenskaya, my aged dancing teacher who

doesn't miss a thing, has noticed I have altered.

Today after a particularly gruelling session at the exercise bar, she took me aside.

'That was very good, Galia. You have perfect balance now, you possess more energy too. What is happening to you?'

'I can't imagine, Madame.'

'Come now, you are keeping little secrets. You can tell old Baba. You've fallen in love?'

'Oh no, on the contrary.'

'Whatever do you mean?'

'I am liberated.'

'Didn't it work out between you?'

'I am liberated less from a man than from the constraints and hang-ups of the past. I am discovering a new freedom.'

'Well, if it gives you wings, why not?' Very quietly she added: 'What hang-ups do you mean?'

'Moral hang-ups that had my body in thrall.'

April 30

Claude Terrois took me to dinner last night at *La Chaumière des Halles*. An excellent choice, a restaurant with a pleasant intimacy and impeccable service.

Claude's hand trembled when he took mine. I liked that. I do a quick mental recall on the Heymans and Wiersma type-classifications and wonder what Claude is: emotive-active-primary? While he is talking he keeps touching me, timidly with his fingertips, though rather mechanically. He is really rather sweet. His eyes are popping out of his head, he likes me, perhaps he is emotive-active-secondary. I am sure I ought not to keep on pigeon-holing people like this. After all, who cares whether they are primary or secondary? Claude is physically there across the table from me, he's nice, and that is all that counts.

Occasionally he stops chattering, gazes into my eyes, smiles and clenches my hand. I am famished, I feel great, and

I like males to want me, to spend money on me.

A bald penguin deposits a grilled turbot on our table and gives us a little bow. The turbot smells terrific. Another penguin uncorks a Pouilly Fumé with slick virtuosity, the cork making as much noise as a fly breaking wind. Penguin Number Two waves the cork under his nose and bats his eyes for a split second. Wordlessly, he pronounces it in good condition. As if we didn't know.

The dinner is perfect. Claude, whom I warm to increasingly as the minutes go by, has the good taste to discuss neither his work, nor money nor cars. This is rare in a man these days. He is an opera enthusiast. And yet he is not homosexual; my theory that all male opera lovers are homosexuals needs reappraising, I can see.

Turbot and Pouilly make a wonderful match. We are into our second bottle and the world looks more promising as the minutes go by. Strange how wine loosens me up.

It is rather quiet, the place is anything but crammed, and the lights are low. Claude is a good listener too, I notice. I'm the one who is running the conversation now, as the wine takes effect. Claude's cheeks seem to be giving off a mauve hue, and he suddenly declares: 'You know Galia, I find you intensely desirable.'

'Do you really,' say I, demurely.

Pushing off my right shoe with my left toe, I slowly extend my freed leg under the tablecloth, and it heads for the Terrois trouser zip. My brazen foot just reaches, if I slouch just a little in my chair.

The aforesaid Terrois turns a bright strawberry, and I breathe: 'But Claude, I thought men got big and hard. You are still soft, although I am touching you.'

'Oh but I desire you. Absolutely.'

'Show me how much, Claudie, show me you crave for me. I wish I had a thing like yours.' I am being so feminine. I pout and part my lips and signal my admiration for him as I apply the very slightest of pressure, then scoop him up slowly from below. He looks as if he might lift off at any moment.

41

What joy to feel his squashy genitals awakening, his organ swelling and then stiffening into a rod of iron! I feel a sense of power, and think it must be hurting him. If I had his thing I would be touching myself all the time to make sure it was still there; and then stroke it so that it stuck out proudly in front. It occurs to me that perhaps I ought to consult an analyst.

My own little volcano is starting to erupt, and I can feel that my gusset is wet. I hope it will not show through my skirt. Ah, the delectable instant of desire!

The thick white cotton tablecloth is aiding our thoughts, and we stay looking at it for a while. I am wearing cotton but Claude does not know. He would love to know what I am wearing.

Our penguin comes up with a list of desserts and an inscrutable look. 'Something to follow?'

'Oh yes,' I say, trying to frustrate Claude's rising lust. 'Something not too heavy, strawberries and cream perhaps? Lots of cream please, and lots of strawberries too. Do take your time, we are in no hurry.'

It's a lie, of course, we are both as hot as a couple of ants. Instead of waiting there, I take Claude's arm and lead him down to the toilet. He is ashamed of the hump in his trousers, hiding it with a napkin.

The walls are a lovely pink and so are the two washbasins. The mirrors have low lighting.

We can't wait an instant, we are holding each other tight now, our mouths wide open, our tongues fleshy and sloppy within. Our noses are bent, such is our haste. I feel so randy, but I prolong the pleasure! I simply nestle into his whole body for a moment, then I undo his zip and feverishly pull down his zip.

'Someone will see us,' he protests hoarsely. 'Anyone could come down.'

That is part of the thrill and I plunge my hand inside his underpants, and at last I am holding his big burning thing and feeling his testicles. I could pinch them and make him cry in pain. I squat down and take his penis hungrily into my mouth and he pushes it far into my throat. As I suck, Claude breathes faster and faster and I hope he won't come too soon. Another instant of penis-envy when I wish girls could have fellatio, then he seems to grow even bigger, and I lick his bulbous tip voluptuously. Claude is babbling incoherently.

Quickly, I pull him against me and step back against the wall. My cotton panties are down in a split-second and I glimpse the wet patch, but there is no time to lose. I lift my skirt up, with one arm I circle his waist, I spread my knees and with my other hand I guide him into my vaginal entrance. Almost at once we both explode in a frenzy and kiss to hide our cries.

Then we climb the stairs in a rose-tinted haze to eat our strawberries and cream.

May 2, 4 a.m.

The phone jerked me from sleep at two o'clock. It is Osvaldo.

'I am going to die.'

'Nonsense, you have years ahead ...'

'I tell you I am dying.'

His voice does sound weak, and I realize he is not bluffing. In an instant I am genuinely worried.

'Whatever have you done?'

No answer.

'Stay where you are, I'm coming over.'

Prostrate on the bed, Osvaldo is sighing half unconscious. I can hardly grasp what he is saying.

'... rather die than live without you ...'

'What have you swallowed,' I demand. 'Quick, what was it?'

He cannot speak. Horrified, I see dozens of pill boxes in the bedclothes. My God, he must have taken them all!

I call an ambulance, and hold his hand until two white-coated men knock and hasten through the door which I left ajar.

43

'Is this the suicide?'

They took him away on a stretcher. His throat made a rattling noise going down the stairs. My eyes are smarting.

At the moment I can hardly control my hands, they are shaking so much, but I must get this down in writing. I haven't stopped trembling since the ambulance.

He is in the Hôtel-Dieu Hospital, but they would not allow me to stay. I can see him tomorrow.

May 2, 6 p.m.

They have put Osvaldo in a white room in a white bed with white bedclothes. He looks ghastly, but they cleaned out his stomach.

I start crying the moment I see him. I weep buckets, feel guilty, and he gazes up at me with infinitely desolate eyes.

'It's not the end of the world,' I whisper.

'Not the end, *tesoro*. Your hand.'

I place my hand in his and let him play with my fingers one by one.

'I cannot live without you, I can't.'

'And you can't think of a better way to tell me?'

'Perhaps it was the only way to show how much I love you.'

I stayed the rest of the morning. Around noon, I consented to a fortnight's 'trial marriage'.

May 3

Osvaldo is being sent home this afternoon.

Already I am concerned about giving in as I did, even though it is only a try.

I wonder if I am capable of having a fully-fledged relationship with a man, something that lasts and is on firm foundations. I tire of people so easily, my energies are too dispersed, I demand too much perhaps.

True, I like the idea of building a home, of two people as a

44

permanent couple, but I cannot build brick by brick. I don't know how to plan things.

It is true as well that I feel the need for a shoulder to lean on, someone who has the answers to my many questions.

I need a lynchpin, a master. That is what I lack and I am beginning to realize it.

My affinity with Osvaldo has limits, is not well balanced. I am his mistress but he is no longer the master. The prospect of these two weeks fills me with misgiving.

It seems only yesterday that we first met. I was scarcely head over heels. But he was struck dumb when he saw me, or at least that's what he has claimed all this time.

It was at the George V Hotel, at a reception by a publishing house which was presenting some prize or other.

It was crowded, noisy, very Parisian, and people were practically fainting with the heat. Everybody kept moving around, forming small groups for a while, depending on the way the champagne and goodies came in and were placed on the buffet tables. They were writers, journalists, publishing people, radio, television and other personalities in the public eye. They were crying out things like: 'I'll give you a ring ... Let's have lunch next week ... No problem ... Have you read it, a superb book ... Chomsky with a touch of Rimbaud expressed in Alphonse Boudard's style ...'

All very stimulating, except for me.

'You seem abashed, my pretty maid,' a voice said.

He had approached unawares and now towered above me, slim and smiling. He looked old, 45 or even 50.

'On your own?' he went on.

'Ye-es.'

'In publishing?'

'No.'

'Journalism?'

'No.'

'Pirate radio perhaps?'

'No.'

'Legitimate radio, television?'

'No.'

'You don't give much away.'

'Sometimes.'

'Unlucky me. You know, you have the most striking eyes.'

'I know.'

'I-er-would you like some champagne?'

'Yes please. Could you also get me some of the sugary things? Especially the little green ones with chocolate on, and a few cream ice-cakes, and some pink thingamies with chocolate sprinkling, and the currants look good too. Oh, and don't forget some coffee eclairs and a dish of almonds.'

'Is that all?'

'Yes. No. I believe I saw some red ices, raspberry I think, but you'll have to ask, I only want raspberry. Those finger biscuits are nice too, and a few dates. Thank you, you're very thoughtful.'

He was gallant, eventually getting back to me loaded up and pushing through saying 'Sorry, sorry.' We sat down under a sunshade on the *terrasse* outside where it was quiet.

'Allow me to introduce myself. Osvaldo Salvatori.'

'Galia S ...'

'An unusual first name. You yourself are mysterious. You are ravishing, in fact. Tell me how you got into this Noah's Ark.'

'I have a girl friend in publishing, and she got me an invitation because I wanted to meet René Giard.'

'The philosopher?'

'Yes, but he hasn't turned up.'

'Why him?'

'He has brains.'

'He has indeed. But what do you like in him?'

'Those green things please. Thanks. A complete in-depth scrutiny of the entire spectrum of Western mythical theologies ...'

'You are at the faculty?'

'I'm reading Thai for languages. I have dancing lessons too.'

He let me go on, talking about my childhood in Tours, the family, my sisters. He certainly knew how to listen. Most people cannot, they just wait until they can get their sentence in. Osvaldo struck me as charming, warm of character, interested in others. Afterwards he told me his life story, about his children including one older than I was, his divorce, his job as a producer in T.V.

Then out of the blue he took my hand and raised it to his lips, elegantly.

'Are you already in love?' I mocked.

'Yes.' He looked at me openly, eagerly. 'And aren't you in love, just a teeny bit?'

'No.'

'Well, that's clear enough ... Might we meet again, d'you think?'

'Yes.' He had said it with such refinement.

'When?'

'Would you like to take me to dinner?'

'I would enjoy it immensely, Galia.'

'Tomorrow then?'

'So be it.'

'I won't sleep with you, Osvaldo.'

'Oh come, please, I had absolutely no intention ...'

'Yes you had.'

'Galia, you are diabolical. Of course, I want you. You are so very beautiful.'

And he made me believe it, taking me out to plays, to the cinema, playing tennis. But not to *Le Bassano* yet. I was still rather gauche. Soon he was phoning me every day, then several times a day. He would meet me at the faculty.

One evening after a kiss that went on and on, I almost let him take advantage of me, I felt something hard between our bodies, but I was still a virgin and scared so told him it was time he left. I was sorry at once and phoned to apologize. Within minutes he was back! We lay down together on my bed, I let him pet me and I responded timorously. But my

47

defences were strong and I resisted the temptations closing in on me.

Until the great day at the tennis courts, when I became his 'mistress', as they say. He became my teacher, showing me everything about my body, everything I was missing.

Osvaldo had experience, he was a woman's man, and it was natural that he should initiate me. I was fortunate, I have to admit.

He was so patient, helping me overcome my inhibitions, he was kind and skilled, he respected me. He knew the virtuosity of a woman's body, the feminine psychology, how women reacted and what they wanted. He obtained immense pleasure from teaching me.

Other men I encountered seemed so awkward and unsure of themselves and selfish and crude. From the outset Osvaldo showed concern over my enjoyment. It was another victory for him every time he brought on an orgasm. At first when we made love I was slow to rouse, my libido seemed to hesitate. Those awful Ursuline nuns had really got me uptight.

I shall always be grateful to Osvaldo for giving me a comprehensive course in pleasure!

May 4
Osvaldo is his old cheerful self again, and as a surprise he is flying me to Haiti.

To tell the truth, this trip is too much of a honeymoon for my liking. He has obviously forgotten his suicide. I haven't.

'What's done is done,' he says rather too often to be comfortable. He is grinning like a sandboy about the future, but in my case it transpires that things are not so happy ever after.

He means well and Haiti could be quite an experience.

May 5
I am writing this on a plastic tray affixed to the plane seat in

front of me, where a fellow passenger is snoring like a warthog. It is 11 p.m. Paris time, 6 p.m. New York time. We are in the Paris-Miami Boeing 747, all of us holidaymakers.

We have been chasing the sun for hours now. It is sinking endlessly in reddish blue space as we advance on it. It's strange, a sunset that lasts for ever.

Osvaldo is sleeping like a child beside me. Everyone has settled into the routine, dozing and dreaming with their eyes open, music plugged into their ears (choice of 8 soundtracks).

I pity the fatties, there isn't much room in these seats. In fact, it is my opinion that the aeroplane is the most uncomfortable as well as the most convenient means of transport in this day and age. The Air France boffins have counted every cubic centimetre, and try to apologize for it with slick stewards and friendly hostesses. I have a feeling it doesn't actually catch on.

The horizon is now blood red and the setting sun is getting on my nerves. The plane is trying to catch up time, and I am going to catch up on some sleep, hand in hand with my beloved. We are in mid-Atlantic and I am a weeny bit afraid.

May 6

The Olofson Hotel at Port-au-Prince is a splendid plantation-style timber residence surrounded by a botanical garden. Only it's for real.

It certainly gives you the creeps, it's romantic and magical at the same time. It could be the relative humidity or the voodoo or the screaming horrors. When I first set foot on Haiti I knew we were in a spooky triangle.

Christopher Columbus sailed into Ayti (in Arawak language it means 'high wild land') and cried out: *'Es una maravilla!'*

Well alright, it was marvellous. But the Spaniards still conquered and looted it. The peaceloving Arawak Indians, who worshipped the moon, the sun, the stars and the springs of water, welcomed the navigators with armfuls of gifts. They were promptly decimated, and new manpower had to be brought in from Africa. Haiti got blacker and blacker, and erstwhile Hispaniola is now more like Africa than the West Indies.

The official language here is French, but the natives speak Creole.

A kid at the airport asked me: 'You American madam?'

'No, me French,' I replied huffily.

'You madam France. Is good.'

The low-lying land that used to be marshy is still called Limonade and Marmelade. The villages have names like Belle Dondon, Marie-Galante and Saltrou (dirty hole!).

The buses in Port-au-Prince are rainbow-coloured and they carry nick-names like 'Mary's Son', 'Thy Will Be Done' and 'Little Jesus of Paris'.

May 7

I am sipping a Planter's Punch on the edge of the pool at the Olofson, and the aroma is going to my head. Osvaldo has gone to see an exhibition of primitive Haiti paintings. I go more for peace and quiet, for lazing around and voluptuous daydreams.

Occasionally there is a splosh noise when someone dives in, a guest titters politely. The people here seem amazingly respectable, mostly Americans from the world of art. A few homosexuals, I notice. Ten yards from me one of them aged about 25 is working hard at his tan, with a kind of silver drip-plate round his neck to reflect the sun. How he can stand it in this heat is a mystery.

My Planter's Punch is pretty hot and, unless it's the Haiti spirits, it gives me an overpowering urge to make love, to copulate like some wild beast, to go crazy, to (this is my private diary after all) have a damn good fuck. I want a big prick fucking me hard right inside. I'm being vulgar but perhaps just writing it down in this impulsive way will reduce the ache, sublimate the desire. Not a hope, there is nothing I can do about it. The sun is wickedly hot and so am I!

May 7, 6 p.m. with T'i Punch

I am progressing, becoming bolder, the taboos are falling away.

This morning I had to have a man, any man, even a fool, provided he could get a whacking great hard on. I looked around, searching for one. Alongside the pool there were some quite eligible males, at first sight that is. But it's hardly the thing to go up to a deck chair and say: 'Excuse me, please. I simply can't wait to get it off, how about a quickie?'

And what if the deck chair doesn't like girls? What if he doesn't want it? Or I'm not his type? How humiliating! I might even pick a homo without realizing it and he might screech out in his fruity voice: 'Oh how awful, d'you know what she just said to me?'

So I play it clever, I want a fuck, but I have my self-respect too. My eyes stray around the pool, watching for a prick at the ready.

I've got one at last! Just what I need. I rivet my eyes on the bulge in his bathing trunks, and I think he hardens up just a little, enough to show he could be thinking on similar lines. Tough luck on us girls, we can't signal it physically, only with our attitude. Our panties grow moist but it doesn't show. How I would love to stroll round the pool, proud and upstanding, my little slip straining in front, scarce concealing my blood-filled chopper! I might stiffen so much, the purple tip would burst out over the top.

He is a tall blond lad, fairly stocky with a gorgeous tan. But my whole attention is concentrated on his 'cobra'.

Oh Galia, how lubricious you are becoming, how lewd! Not entirely, I tell myself, but I am working on it. These days I am more interested in the phallus than the man behind it, than his soul. But maybe pricks have souls too.

The beautiful cobra is lying in his nest waiting to spring,

only the nest is a tight 75% cotton 25% polystyrene, iron at 80°C max.

I slink over without overdoing it, and see he is reading *Newsweek*. It looks like a dull week by his expression, and I stare at his shiny trunks, telling him as loud as I can: 'You have a superb cobra, you know.'

What he actually hears is: 'Have you been here a long time?' In English.

'Only a week. Are you French?'

'Yes I am.' I am pretty vexed at this, I thought I had a perfect accent.

'Fine, well have a drink.'

We're off on the first straight. But how many minutes will we have to sniff around? I can't wait, but we keep on at it. Yes Haiti is a fascinating island, no it's my first visit, yes I flew via Miami, no I haven't been to Jacmel yet, yes I'd love to see La Citadelle. For pity's sake, it's your cobra I want to see! How long is it, how thick, how often does it strike?

They need a while to turn on, these Americans. Take it easy, take it easy, buddy, OK. But I'm in a hurry, I can feel my vulva gaping. I step on the gas and tell my cowboy: 'I'd like to show you something.'

'Ok,' he says. 'I'll be right back, just gonna put something on.'

How dumb can you get? Do I have to spell it out? Have I roped a bum steer?

He gives me a smile as clean as a church pew and goes into a changing hut at the end of the garden in the shade. I wait a whole 30 seconds and then give a light tap on the door.

'Who is it?'

'It's me, open up.'

'I can't, just a minute.'

'Open the door NOW!'

He eases back the door and I give it a hefty shove. I shut it behind me. I am reaching boiling point, we are alone just the two of us in the blessed cool of the changing hut, and he still doesn't catch on. He looks at me with his doleful eyes, and I

52

see that 30 seconds was just right. All he has on is one sock, but he hides himself like a clown behind his towel.

I snatch off my two-piece, remove his towel and press the whole length of my body against his. It's heavenly, so warm and sweaty, so thrilling that I get it off instantly just leaning against him.

I close my eyes and feel the second one coming. This one I have to have! It's lifting me up like a wave and my vagina is pulsing.

I am wrestling with a bull, I massage his biceps and chest; Osvaldo would weep with jealousy to see his mounds of muscle. I am bringing him on, I grope him and clench him and kneel and lick the longest and thickest and hardest organ I have ever seen. It is purple, jerking frantically. Then it pumps and pumps, the hot semen spurting warm on my face. He is moaning and gasping deliriously. 'Oh you bastard,' he croaks, and I don't know whether he means me or him. I don't care, he loves it!

Words of love, words of hate, poor words meaning nothing as we rush together into the Palace of Pleasure.

'Aw you dirty bitch, I love you, you bastard,' he mouths. Oh the divine language of pleasure!

He has not actually penetrated me yet, and I want that to be my third orgasm. His whopper is floppy now, and I wonder if I can get him up again; there are different opinions about that, but I set to work again. In a couple of minutes I have him ready, I am delighted with myself. It must be instinct, or the call of my own drenched sex.

Incredibly his dark red organ seems even bigger, and I can see only one way we can do it. I turn round, splay my hands against the opposite wall of the hut, and present my rump to him, legs apart. He enters me roughly, and I can feel him coming further and further, I wonder if it will ever stop penetrating, and then he withdraws, then thrusts again and again. In and out, in and out, like a piston, bumping me up and down. My orgasm bursts, filling my whole lower torso, and I sink to my knees heaving and gasping uncontrollably. I can hear the bull snorting wordlessly, and we stay like that in a state of exhaustion.

'What's your name,' I rasp.

'Steve.'

'Mine's Galia. See you later Steve.'

'Be seeing you, kid.'

May 8, 6 p.m. T'i Punch

As a matter of principle I hate telling lies. Lies are for people who will not say: 'It's like that, do what you like about it.' I am against evasiveness and concealment.

I tried to tell Osvaldo about it, but every time I was about to say 'You know this afternoon I made love with an American' he said something else. It could be he suspected something, but was unwilling to face the truth. I gave up. We have no right to inflict truths on those who do not want to know.

We strolled round the extraordinary Marché aux Fers at Port-au-Prince.

The Haitians are inventive because they are poor, cutting out shapes of men, women and animals from old jerrycans. The results can be strikingly artistic.

But the waves of tourists have spoiled this creative process, and what you get can be very cheap. It is still possible to pick up good work, but you need tenacity.

Osvaldo buys me an erotic allegory, highly 'macho'. The Women's Lib people would gnash their teeth in rage; in the foreground is a smiling man with an erection, in the background a woman in the jungle amid snakes and birds.

Painting is fairly new to Haiti, dating basically from 1944 when the official Art Centre was set up. Some 30 painters decided to 'create' a Haiti style deriving from African sculpture and Egyptian art. André Breton, they say, was immensely keen on the work of the best-known primitive painter here, Hector Hyppolite, who headed the so-called Marvellous Realism School.

54

These primitives are rather moving: very simple, full of light, flat and with no perspective.

May 9, 6 p.m. T'i Punch and bird calls

Petit Pierre has the best set of primitives on the island, at his villa-cum-gallery overlooking Port-au-Prince. People come from all over the world to see this legendary character.

He is a fine figure of a man, as my mother would say, in spite of his small stature. His skin is a lovely West Indian brown and he is elegant in dress, speech and movement. His eyes sparkle at the sight of a good painting or an attractive woman.

Petit Pierre showed us some of his best paintings, and a collection of tin work to take your breath away.

We had dinner outdoors in the warm air with exotic plants all around us.

Petit Pierre and Osvaldo found they had common friends in New York as well as Paris. It's a small world, they rightly decided. They meant the world of art; I cannot imagine a tourist from Citroen meeting an Italian and crying out: 'Good grief, you know Arturo from Fiat too!' There is a world of cultural freemasonry.

Of course, Petit Pierre proved vastly informed on the paintings of Haiti. He once lectured the French cultural godfather André Malraux when he visited the island. But I don't think he played footsie under the table with Malraux like he was doing with me.

The three of us went dancing at a place with a round floor, a circle of coloured lights and palm-trees waving against the night sky. We swung our hips to the magical West Indian band. Petit Pierre is an expert dancer, and has a romantic way of holding his partner: viz, his right leg welded to her crotch! He smiles artfully and so do I, his not-so-petit prick rolling back and forth across my navel or thereabouts. He knows I am getting clammy where his leg is, and increases the pressure.

Yes, Petit Pierre is horny enough to sweep any young girl off her feet. I have never slept with a black man.

May 10

La Citadelle Laferrière, built in the early nineteenth century by the 'Mad Emperor' Christopher, is a gaunt fortress perched 2,500 feet above the sea. Lindberg said it was the eighth wonder of the world. Whatever he thought about it, I was impressed.

Christopher, known as the black pharaoh of Cape Haiti, wanted to imitate the court of France's Louis XIV with everyone in fancy dress, sumptuous buildings including the Palais de Sans-Souci (Carefree Palace), bewigged officials, chamberlains, masters of ceremony, even 'Ducs de Limonade'. A former slave, he really weighed into his subjects, working them literally to death. He had the Citadelle built high up on its rock by teams of 100 men each. Once, on his orders, a bronze cannon weighing several dozen tons was hauled to the summit. A hundred slaves sweated blood as they struggled to get this goddam lump of bronze to the top. They collapsed halfway up, and he sent in a squadron of troops to shoot them. Another work-team stood by and was told: 'Now it's your turn.' In all, thousands of men perished in the construction of this stark cloud-ringed fort.

We went up on emaciated mules, by a narrow path. At every turn there were kids trying to sell us flutes, necklaces, bracelets and other things they made. I liked their smiles.

We got there at last and surveyed the grandiose sight. The fort is a stone palace hanging silent and deserted between the sky and sea. Mist wrapped itself round us and we shivered a little. I drew closer to my man, glaring at dozens of guns pointing out to sea. My mind flashes back to a book I read as a little girl. But in the case of the Citadelle, the invader never arrived and the blood and sweat was for nothing.

May 11. Terrasse of the Olofson, Planter's Punch, bird calls, 7 p.m.

For the first time in my life a man made me cry out with pleasure today.

Petit Pierre, clever guy, sent Osvaldo to see one of his fellow collectors at Jacmel this afternoon. In other words he had me all to himself for hours on end, and I speculated on how he would go about seducing me. Jubilantly he unrolled his favourite canvases one after the other, and I tried to concentrate on them.

At length he said: 'That's Marat at his best. What he did afterwards, the stuff at the New York galleries, was nothing compared to this!'

I found he was coming round to the point rather too slowly, and to help him I declared: 'Petit Pierre, I want you too. Let's do it now.'

His bedroom turned out to be cheerfully chaotic: paintings of course and articles of clothing, tinwork, books, newspapers, a typewriter with piles of finished sheets of paper. A mosquito net was draped round the bed, turning it into an old-fashioned cradle. He lowered me into the cradle, and I regarded him meekly.

What followed was a new kind of pleasure. He was electrifying, each of his kisses wherever he embraced me enhanced the intensity of my joy. I mean it. His lips, fingers and tongue explored me between my toes, under my feet, behind my ears, the backs of my knees, inside my elbows, the nape of my neck, round my waist, inside my thighs. He was adoring me, and the sensation it gave me revealed a new dimension in fervour. My sex gradually lost its tightness, and I knew he could do anything he liked with me and I would proffer no resistance. I really cannot put it into words. I remember only that I imagined myself to be a lovely pomegranate, erotic and feminine, opening out as the sun shone upon me. He made me feel so beautiful, and I worshipped him for that.

I spread my legs offering my most intimate self, my soul.

57

With infinite delicacy he gave tribute to my loins and my bottom. He licked me and gave me little bites, caressed me and drank my juice.

I exclaimed my ecstasy, although I tried to be quiet and was biting my upper lip. I can hear myself crying out but can do nothing about it.

I am completely out of control, lifted up in confusion, folly, triumph. I am eternal. I do not even think whether or not I am having an orgasm. It was all one.

We made love a second time, and it was another journey among the stars. Oh, the sheer delight of soaring into the firmament!

I learned now that in my own country across the Atlantic, Valéry Giscard D'Estaing has been beaten in the fight for the Presidency by the socialist François Mitterrand.

Politics have always seemed a silly show to me, but I admit to a certain satisfaction at seeing Giscard's arrogance at an end. At least we shall see some new people, hear some new voices. Everything is going to change, they tell us.

May 12, diary time and T'i Punch time (stronger than Planter's)

I had forgotten about the cowboy. He found me this morning as I lay on my cushions at the edge of the pool. I was reading a book about a hundred years of solitude. He picked the wrong moment, that's for sure.

'Hullo baby!'

'Oh, hullo Steve.' (Where did you spring from? And you're chewing gum too, for God's sake. And you look like a mental defective.) 'How are things?'

'I'd like to show you something, Galia,' he says with a wink straight out of MGM's studios.

He shifts his foot and then the other, and moves his hand past his great American cobra. A little hint that he wants some shooting practice.

'I'm so sorry, Steve. I don't want to – er – move for the moment.'

Good Lord, he thinks I haven't caught on, and repeats it: 'I'd like to show you something, something pretty.' He gives me an Uncle Tom smile.

Look here, buster, I want to say, I've had my dose for a while. Now take your big gun someplace else. Instead I moan: 'I want to be alone.'

Miraculously he starts to get the message. He makes a face: 'No jig-jig today?'

'No jig-jig today.'

'Tomorrow maybe?'

'Tomorrow maybe. So long Steve.'

Like kids they are. He'll just have to find another playmate, or do his own thing. Bye-bye Steve, you have a super cobra, but you are too dumb for words.

I am writing this on the marvellous Olofson *terrasse*. It is like being in a novel. The decor, the atmosphere, the characters, the noises and aromas are all so romantic. This old hotel is magic too.

Osvaldo has come and gone, giving me a touch on the cheek and telling me we are dining with R.A. and the French Ambassador, who by the way is said to be a total cretin. Osvaldo has taste, the tact to leave me alone when I am writing my diary.

Our relationship is calm and without incident. He knows this little birdie is touchy and may fly off if there is too much disturbance. It's one of Galia's bitchy days today.

May 13

The dinner was mortifying, in other words deadly dull. The French Ambassador bears one of our country's most illustrious names, and makes sure everyone knows it.

Poor France, for the man is a pretentious ass, the perfect example of the peevish old reactionary clutching onto his privileges for dear life.

Babies are dying by the hundred in the streets of Port-au-Prince, amid general indifference, and he observes: 'Death is something these people are used to . . .' How does he know, the silly old fool? Life is crystal clear for our Ambassador. On the one side there are the decent people, the aristocrats, the elect (God's, not the voters') the nobility. On the other side is the rest of the human race, also known as horse-shit.

This particular member of the nobility has a face like a pig, a degenerate body, the brains of a sheep and horrible breath. But he also has this name, and that's why other top people treat him like God Almighty.

The meal goes on and on. Like a well brought up young lady I keep still and do not fidget, smiling politely as I imagine myself pouring the sauceboat over his head.

Politeness, decency, cowardice, what's the difference? Osvaldo and I leave the dinner feeling we want to scratch ourselves and take a shower.

It is around midnight and in the centre of Port-au-Prince 12-year-old children are making signs to the car drivers, under the soulless gaze of the bodyguards outside the palace of President-for-Life Claude Duvalier. For a handful of small change, a grown-up can buy a child's body for an hour.

Much of the city's population spends the night in the streets, not for the fresh air, but because they have no home. Haiti is the poorest country in the world. The per capita income is lower than in the least developed country of Africa.

May 14
Petit Pierre shows us some of the best-guarded treasures he has at his house.

While Osvaldo is turning over the visitors book on the *terrasse*, P.P. beckons me down to the cellar where he has stored a mass of paintings and valuables. Naturally, he jumps me while we are there. It is a high-speed knee-trembler surrounded by colourful bric-à-brac. He takes me standing up, which cuts the effort to a minimum for both of us as he is just about my height. We are like a pair of vertical rabbits, it is short but sweet – or rather bitter-sweet as the climax for me comes with a rush and seems to sting me. As always after intercourse, I feel refreshed. The fellow who wrote *post coitum omne animal triste est* was talking through his backside. Another negative moralist.

A few years ago at the age of 16 I would have fallen madly in love with Petit Pierre. Today I am less inclined to equate love and sex. This man has given me more pleasure than any other, he drives me crazy, but I am not in love with him. Just terribly fond of him.

I have never said 'I love you' to a man, even in the whirlwind of close embrace, even when I am out of my mind with excitement. I have never actually said 'my darling' either.

Something is missing, perhaps I am inhuman, but that is the way it is and I cannot help it. One day I may fall completely in love with a man, but this is still only a dream.

One of Petit Pierre's friends took us to a voodoo ceremony.

To the thrum of three drums, a splendid woman shimmies in a white garment. Bells are tinkling. She turns round and round, squats, leaps and sways. Suddenly she halts in front of me and signs to me. I turn to our friend, who signals me to stay where I am. The priestess persists. Distinctly embarrassed, I shake my head. Then she looks around and rushes at a tall heavy man, hits him and he goes down rolling in the dust.

The 'Loa' spirit has taken possession of the woman, or more accurately she has become the spirit. The spirit is riding her body and the 'Loa' laughs, insults, threatens, encourages, reveals the past and the future, feels no pain when walking on coals of fire.

Voodoo is indeed a dancing religion that is practised among friends and often in public. The possessed woman thrashes about in a frenzy, staggers, sweats, gasps for breath, starts it all over again. Then she stops brusquely, gazes around her in amazement, apparently emerging from a dream.

Our friend told us she would remember nothing of it all.

May 16
We left Haiti today and I feel disconsolate. We are turning our backs on the world of magic and returning to technology and all the other 'ologies' of civilized Man.

A short stay on Martinique. Fort-de-France makes me think of a Paris suburb in the tropics. A grim stopover, showing us a clear example of a country being wrecked by so-called civilization.

May 19, Paris
We have been back about two days and I feel awful. Uneasy, without bearings, incapable of thinking, losing control.

The Parisians are strange beings, frowning and scurrying about. Is it me or them on the wrong planet?

I wander from room to room in Osvaldo's apartment, opening the fridge, nibbling odds and ends without appetite, watching T.V. but registering nothing.

I feel depressed, alone.

May 20
I was looking through the magazine *Le Nouvel Observateur* and came across the personal ads. Click! I feel better already.

What a great idea! Meeting new people, making dates with strangers, launching out into the Unknown!

I do three or four drafts, and at last the ad is how I want it:

Girl, 20, attractive, liberated, seeks partners for love, fantasies, affection. No jokers, fogeys or flops. Tel ... photo preferred. Write box no ...

May 23

Already a dozen replies. The first letter I open is in jumpy handwriting and is from a psychiatrist. It is tumultuous, breathless.

Paris, May 22, 1981
Dear liberated friend,
I am 33, good-looking, physically in excellent shape, passionate and enthralling, cultivated, tuned-in when necessary and tender at times, and I am looking for an attractive girl like you!
I am a practising psychiatrist, likable and easy to get on with, without false modesty, carrying out fascinating and absorbing work with adolescents, major research and other responsibilities, and am therefore personally concerned with everything to do with adolescence.
I would like to meet you and suggest you phone 491.32.52 lunchtime and ask for Dr Yves Noroit.
Until soon, I hope. Best wishes.
(Signature like a pile of worms).

The second envelope contains a two-page magazine called *La Gazette Coquine* (The Saucy Gazette), with the sub-title 'The magazine of scandalous ads: hundreds of ads to take your breath away'. The contents include some photos the size of postage stamps.

A 042 – Age 50, virile, seeks women of any age if noisy spicey sluts.

The photo shows him standing nude with a towel over one shoulder. I can't see his face properly, but his appliance is impressive and was probably titivated before the picture to enhance its image.

A 043 – Perverted vicious couple seek sub-

missive male to bow to their demands. (No photo)

A 044 – (photo of stunning appetizing girl standing up). Lovely 35-year-old, refined, curvaceous, hyper-sensitive, managerial position with little time to spare, rich in money but poor in sperm, seeks discreet Paris meetings with men 25–49 strong and healthy, able to make love several times with ejaculations. No mouth caresses. Telephone an advantage.

A 045 – (No photo). Gentleman transvestite with liking for women's sexy underwear seeks men or women so that he can live out his fantasies. Lingerie worn during lovemaking.

A 029 – (Head and shoulders of fine bronzed man, athletic and smiling). Tall, slim and highly authoritarian, I seek willing slave accepting all humiliations and obeying all my commands. He will wash me daily with his tongue. Gentlemen interested write me now for detailed programme of what awaits you.

A 030 – (No photo, no indication of sex). I am 23, have a capricious mouth and lovely posterior. Seek young man my age liking love and laughter. No married men. (It must be a woman!)

A 003 – Is there a man who can make my brunette wife with a fine arched back happy? Priority accorded to imaginative people.

A 050 – Youth, virgin back and front, seeks girl or boy to deflower him.

A 028 – Young woman, plain but expert, likes perverted touching with strangers, accepts all rendezvous in porn cinemas.

A 017 – (Woman standing nude, over 40, heavy with big breasts). Young woman (sic) 46 inch bosom seeks man who appreciates large breasts. I like my nipples sucked for long periods and lovemaking between breasts. I come when you knead my breasts. (Oh, the cow!)

The publishers tell me on the bottom of the page that if I subscribe today for only 60 francs to *La Gazette Coquine* (supplied in plain, highly discreet wrapper), I shall receive a SURPRISE with the hundreds of small ads.

On page 2 I can request for 50 francs a secret map of the BOIS DE BOULOGNE indicating its extraordinary NOCTURNAL ORGIES. The Bois is enormous, I learn, and it is very difficult at night to know WHERE TO GO in order to SEE or PARTICIPATE in PARTIES and EXPOSURES of the most AUDACIOUS kind. The 50 francs buys me a DETAILED PLAN giving the precise location of each SPECIALITY or PERVERSION:

1. RENDEZVOUS and departure point for SEX PARTIES: this is where 90 per cent of the GROUP SEX in Paris begins each night. Stop by, just in case, newcomers always needed and taken care of.
2. LONE EXHIBITIONIST WOMEN: usually young bourgeoise ladies ON HEAT, trying to bring their FUTURE PARTNERS to a paroxysm of excitement.
3. NYMPHOMANIACS SUPPLIED NAKED by their husbands: many gentlemen in a state of fatigue wish to hand over their young

wives to groups of vigorous men; note a pronounced taste for MASOCHISM in these women.

4. PEEPERS: certain men and women exhibitionists generously reveal their MOST SECRET DEPTHS, enabling all peepers standing around to GET WORKED UP and GET IT OFF without FEELING ASHAMED.

5. NUDE TRANSVESTITES: you will see superb breasts, making the most beautiful women green with envy. FELLATIO GUARANTEED.

6. HOMOS: One of the major meeting points and HOMO SWAP CENTERS of Paris.

7. WHORES: almost always NUDE under a COAT, EXCEPT IN SUMMER; they will meet your every DESIRE for a few francs.

8. MALE PROSTITUTES: love-sick women give small PRESENTS to enjoy the virile attributes of horny young men. Try your luck.

9. DOMINATING WOMEN: if you are a masochist, here are STRONG-ARM women who are VERY CRUEL and will submit you to the worst outrages.

Immediately under this line is depicted a huge pair of scissors, but I am relieved to see they are for cutting out the coupon! For 50 francs the Bois de Boulogne belongs to you.

Here follows a SPECIAL OFFER FROM AUNTIE PORN: the 200-page SEX POCKET BOOK, a collection of ultra-perverse and scandalous photos selected by Auntie Porn.

Having perused this attractive journal in depth, I open some more letters. Fortunately they are not junk mail and they are hand-written.

Lovely boy, 30, likes liberated girls and unusual ads, would love to meet you.
Jean-Paul Dessirer, *early morning or late evening.*

Gérard, 38, brown hair and slim, 5 foot 9 inches, bachelor, attentive and sensitive, hungry and passionate, adores Mozart and trees, youth, love, beauty, is unable

*to resist the temptation to reply to you. He is Parisian
like you, between journeys and weekends, and will do his
best to make our meeting richly promising in mutual
wonders.
Hoping to hear the music of your voice at an early date,
he submits his destiny to your pretty hands.
G. Fontenay, 742.21.71.
(Pleasant writing, large and leaning right. Impression of
balance. Very readable signature, vertical not
underlined.)*

The next letter, fast writing, small controlled lettering,
readable signature is very small.

*Dear Unknown,
You seek the ideal man, I am one of them. If we are
speaking of this same Adonis, you are the siren with
green eyes, auburn-haired, slender, tall. (Alas this is not
me at all, but let him draw the portrait.) You know how
to appreciate fine things, your judgement goes beyond
culture, travel has made you an artist, reading makes you
a poet (he has too much gab), you are not content just to
live your life, instead you create it. (what does he mean?)
I am a crazy lover of life, I have no taste for solitude. I
invite you to share the day-to-day, laborious early
mornings and tender evenings (hold on! This
programming worries me). We shall have our own lives
together, calm without excess, sometimes mad, always
tender. Marriage not obligatory (thank goodness for
that!), children are wanted, etc. etc.*

The home I have is closer to the pelvis. This noble lad is
afraid of overdoing it, so he can find a herb lady. Into the
trash-can with *La Gazette Coquine*.

The next missive looks rather promising, it's nicely
penned.

Hullo,
In the garden of my heart there is lots of room to play
and roll over in the wool of my veins (oh boy!) There is
a place for you too, little kitten, I think. A place for
imagination, all improvisations. And a little room for
entrechats and tender frolics. To gambol, laugh and have
fun in life it needs two, and the kitten has to be tender,
the tomcat attentive, and each heart must open with
discretion for the enjoyment of the other.
A meeting, a look, smile, adventure, life – all is possible.
Youth is the most precious of treasures, and alone it
allows everything to be created, everything to be
understood and achieved.
I am passionately interested in Chinese medicine and, if
you are not an adept, you are warned that you may be
converted. The other side of my life... from my whole
body, my aspirations and what makes me happy and
gives me pleasure.
Dear friend, I yearn to meet you if your heart responds
to mine, to exchange or taste each of the sources that
give us life.
I should be delighted to meet you one evening, how you
wish since it is you who are extending the invitation.
Loic Renaud, *aged 30*

In contrast with this polite and lyrical letter, the next
missive comes as a shock.

Dear little liberated cat,
I sniff you through your advertisement, my nose goes
right to its target and my tongue is licking you already
and you are wriggling a bit and you like it and you are
getting moist.
I caress you for a long time and you can stand it no
longer and you tell me 'come'.
I am well-equipped (10 inches deployed) and I know how
to use it. See you soon.
Hubert, *548.30.17*

In the Far West pictures, the boys spin their colts before they put them smoking into their holsters (i.e. vaginas). This expansive cowboy intrigues me. I grab the phone and ring 548.30.17. This I have to see!

'Hullo, my name's Galia.'

'Excuse me, who?' A strong deep no-nonsense voice. The fellow has no time to lose.

'I put the ad in.'

'Ah, little liberated cat! When can we get together? How about six o'clock?'

'Six tonight?'

'Yes, six to eight.'

'Well, I . . .'

'Right, that's settled. You come to my place. Know Rue Christine, 5th *arrondissement*?'

'I think . . .'

'I'm at No. 8, there's an intercom, ask for Hubert. Until then, 6 o'clock.'

Pretty off-hand, that runt, with his 10-inch pistol. It can't be true, 10 inches is a lot of Mars bar, worth going just to see that.

I have a yen to contact the psycho, Yves Noroit, the one who examines adolescents.

'Dr Noroit, yes,' he snaps.

'How do you do, my name is Galia, I'm the girl who put a small ad in *Le Nouvel Observateur* . . .' Complete silence, and I add: 'Can you hear me?'

'Yes perfectly, please go on.'

'. . . and you sent me a letter . . .'

A hushed voice: 'It is rather difficult to say anything at this juncture. Can you call me back in half an hour please?'

He'll be lucky. I wait a whole 60 minutes. His voice is entirely different, warm and friendly: 'I really am sorry. Simply could not speak when you rang. Work and colleagues, you know. Delighted you phoned, when can we meet?'

We fix up for lunch the next day. Meanwhile I spend some

time deciding what to wear for Hubert the crackshot. Nothing underneath, I think, although I'll keep my bra on.

I have butterflies buzzing around inside me. What will he be like, his face, the rest of him? I feel I am going to regret this.

The intercom squawks: 'I'm coming down.'

I feel ridiculous and snort in amusement. What the hell am I doing here waiting for a 10-inch prick? What do I want with a three-legged monstrosity? I can still take to my heels, stroll along the Boulevard Saint-Germain, window shopping, killing time. Oh Lord, here he is!

Hubert may not be all that tall, but he is certainly the tough type. Brown hair cut short, a not unpleasant twist to his smile, and the gaze of a man who can sum up a situation pronto. He plants a quick kiss on my lips, and I think that's honest.

'I imagined you taller.'

'I'm so sorry . . .'

'But I'm not at all disappointed.' (Flattery could save your life, Galia.)

He steps back to take a general view of yours truly. He scans me from tip to toe and back again.

'I've got good teeth,' I declare, opening my mouth wide.

'We're going to be friends, come on let's go up, you first.'

The staircase is narrow and we get to the first floor. I feel his hand on my bottom, evaluating the merchandise. 'Fine, fine,' he murmurs. I have an idea he has done this kind of thing before.

His apartment is so spick and span, I'm astonished. Low style furniture, brown painted walls, halogen lamps picking out three impressive abstract paintings. This cowboy has savvy.

'Did you do the decoration?' I ask nicely.

I hear a rumble that tells me nothing. Evidently it's not the matter uppermost in his mind. He says: 'Want a drink now or afterwards?'

Afterwards! The guy runs a tennis court, a golf course, a

fuck-o-rama, for pity's sake. I've got to slow him down.

'I'd like it now – the drink, I mean.'

'Scotch?'

'Something with less kick maybe?'

'Apple juice.'

'Fine.'

The strong silent type, I can see. I watch him pour out the juice, serve himself three fingers of the hard stuff, and raise his glass with a wink.

'To love!' he says. (This man could rip me apart, he's so direct.)

'To love! By the way, what does it mean for you, love?'

'I'm going to show you.'

'Oh good.'

He starts undressing, laying his things out on a chair: 'What's your name?' How many others has he had today?

'Galia, I told you.'

'Funny name.'

I unbutton my blouse, unsnap my bra, let my skirt fall. We are both as nature intended us and he scrutinizes me with an expert eye.

'Excellent, excellent.'

'What's excellent?'

'Everything. Shapely hips, tight arse, good bosom but on the small side, smooth skin, astonishing eyes. Excellent.'

My turn to give him the once over: 'Not bad yourself. Sturdy body, straight legs, well-contoured face, firm mouth but a little on the thin side. But tell me, that periscope of yours, you offered an outsize version, but it looks pretty standard to me. Could you have oversold it a little?'

'I said, when deployed.'

'Ah yes, deployed.'

'Suck it,' he commanded.

'I beg your pardon.'

'Suck.'

Orders are orders, and I initiate deployment. I kneel down and place his stick of toffee between my lips, holding on to his buttocks for safety. His penis swells instantly like a balloon, but I swear I didn't blow! Within seconds his cock becomes dilated, only a third of it is in my mouth. I take a breather and stare at it.

'What a weapon!' My admiration was genuine, I can't believe it.

'Told you, didn't I?'

'Hold it a minute.' (He does.) 'Have you got a tape measure or something?'

'Go ahead, measure away.'

He hands me a ruler, I apply it along the workpiece, I read nine and a half inches and tell him. He won't accept it.

'Make sure you measure from the base, otherwise you lose at least half an inch. Measure along the underside, not the top.'

I keep to the topside and adjust the ruler: 10 inches precisely!

I shrug: 'Alright, you win. That's some decoration you have there.'

'And I know how to use it!'

We dive for the bed like champion swimmers. I have to admit, this pistolero is the best shot in the West. His whole middle torso pumps massively back and forth like a steam locomotive, tough luck for any cows on the line – redskins run for your lives! Three whistles and it's all over, and with minimum lubrication. I feel as if a hot poker scalded me inside. Hubert the Great rolls over on his back, sets fire to a cigarette and blows smoke rings. He has one arm under his head.

I cup my wounded sex and wait. At last he spits out: 'Well, how was it?'

'I figure you're a real big-shot,' I tell him.

II
FRENZY

May 25

Osvaldo and I let our hair down, but we do not tear it out. I lead him round to the idea that I need to keep my independence, that I cannot go on living full-time with him, that we shall go on meeting nevertheless.

Laurence B. has a studio free because she is getting married. This will be my place from now on.

Quite a few of my girl friends are finding husbands, and I am un-finding one. Who is right? There is no golden rule about this, and every girl must paddle her own canoe, as she can and wants. They chose a husband, I chose freedom. God helps those who help themselves.

May 26

I have time to jot down the extraordinary episode with the psychiatrist. 'I am physically in excellent shape, passionate and enthralling,' he had promised. He certainly has imagination.

For our lunch date he asked me to come to his office, where I learned he was finishing with the last of his morning patients. I waited in a small room the colour of porridge. There were three plastic chairs and a table with a dozen or so cigarette burns and loaded with a mass of dog-eared magazines. They were filthy, and the sight of them was enough to depress any patient. An empty waiting room with *ennui* running down the walls.

At length the 'likeable and easy to get on with' lady-killer appears in the doorway, a little 33-year-old man aged at least 40 in a dark blue three-piece suit. He has a large pallid head, big nose and thick glasses hiding a pair of tiny inquisitive eyes. I gulped at first sight; so this was God's gift to adolescent girls! I decided to play the innocent shy teenager, to give him confidence. The stark truth was that the man revolted me, but I reserved my judgement.

'Hullo, Dr Noroit.'

'How are you?' he says. 'You are much prettier than I imagined you. Come into my office.'

Old books, old armchairs, an old couch, everything old and dusty. Death cannot be far away. A ball of genuine anguish forms just above my navel.

He plops down in the chair behind his desk and studies me pensively, especially my bosom. I breathe in deeply and it rises.

'Everything alright, Galia?'

'Oh yes, I'm fine.'

A further silence. I love to see this disgusting creature wondering how to 'make' me, with his grey drooping head, his small searching eyes, his creepy surroundings. It is claustrophobic.

'So you're alright?' Does he always start like this?

I sum up the discussion so far: 'I am ALRIGHT!'

'Ah.'

He doesn't know which way to take me. It would be so much easier professionally if the patient would just spill out her story, he is thinking. Something like: 'Oh doctor, I simply don't know what's happening to me... I can't face life... I feel nobody cares for me...' etc. etc. He could then tell me to get on the couch and he could go ahead. But I refuse to bewail my lot.

Subsequent to a further silence, he ventures: 'Yes, you are extremely pretty. Tell me about yourself. We'll examine the problem together, shall we?'

'I don't feel like telling you about myself.'

'Indeed, why is that?'

'That's the way it is.'

He frowns and the big lenses take on a neurotic look. He is wondering how he can get me onto the couch, but he is shy.

Then my new Romeo blurts out in a quick mumble: 'I want to lie down with you Galia, you are, you are...'

Overcome, he removes his glasses, wipes them, scratches his nose, replaces his glasses, rubs his hands together and swiftly crosses his legs, banging a foot against the desk. He laughs like a schoolboy and declares: 'Well, I've said it, I want you, you are so... And your eyes are so exciting, so are your legs.'

I pull down my skirt but it won't cover my knees. I continue pretending I am innocent, stare at him as cruelly as I can, saying nothing. He slobbers on: 'Girls, I mean women, like you, and you really are a woman, there are so many. When I saw your advertisement I did not think, I mean I expected something else, someone less attractive if you see what I mean. You never know with advertisements. Last time, a while ago of course, she was quite awful, and you are so... I really did not expect a morsel, a woman like you. Ah Galia, Galia!'

Whereupon he throws himself at my feet, begins fondling my knees and hurting me as he squeezes them: 'Come on, let's make love, I want to so badly, I want to so badly...'

I clench my knees together and push his hands away, get up and scold him: 'How dare you doctor! You ought to be ashamed. Do you do this to all your patients?'

He kind of crumples and grovels as if I am going to smack

him: 'I'm sorry, forgive me, please forgive me...' He falls on his face and whines, licking my shoes straps.

'Let me kiss your feet, I beseech you.' He kisses a shoe: 'I want you, I want you, I want you!' The shoe is wet, he is cringing, he is harmless after all, I decide to play him along.

His mouth sneaks up my leg, and I cry: 'Behave yourself, doctor!' It only excites him more.

'Galia, Galia, oh please I must.' Frantically he unbuttons his trouser front, feeling himself.

'No I'm sorry, you really aren't my type. Your letter was nice, quite promising, but you are different somehow. It's no go, I have to leave.

'Wait, oh wait.'

Panic seizes him, he leaps between me and the door, his little acorn poking out, an awful grey colour. His glasses are askew and he rivets his eyes on my skirt hem.

'Let me leave, please.'

'No, no, no!'

'If you don't let me leave, I shall scream. The whole building will hear. I can scream really loud, your reputation will be in shreds.'

He is rubbing his thing fast and whispering urgently: 'Just wait two minutes, my little Galia, don't be beastly, your knees...'

'Play with yourself as much as you like but don't you dare come near me.'

His eyes are glistening: 'No I won't, I just want you to watch me, yes watch me. Look Mummy! Oh it's coming, Mummy, Mummy!'

As a measure of elementary precaution I take a step back, but when he ejaculates it only goes a few inches, dripping onto the carpet in short spurts.

Dr Noroit gasps and goes limp. He is wanked out, and he collapses onto a chair where he straightens his glasses and shamefacedly buttons up his trousers.

'Excuse me, Galia.'

'Think nothing of it, Yves. We all have our quirks. Now let

me go. Glad to have helped a little, better luck with the next ad.'

Outside, a warm bright sun makes it almost summer. The birds are chirruping away and people are thinking it's good to be alive. I take a deep breath and another and another.

Physically in excellent shape, passionate and tender at times. That's what the man said.

Not for the first time I realize how words can deceive, when you hear them, and even more when they are on a thin sheet of paper.

May 27

The more men I go with, the more questions I am asking myself about myself. I seem to be seeking vengeance in some way, and there is a kind of struggle for power between us.

I try to make myself indispensable to the male, like to see him needing me, I lure him – and immediately put a collar round his neck. I run along with my doggie on the leash, until I lose interest and look for another doggie.

Today I feel very feminine. I am scampering all over the place in search of the Ideal Man. He must be hero, sage, saint and perfect lover.

The ones I am meeting leave me crestfallen, and I suppose I try to obtain my revenge on these poor drips. I cannot find my Ideal Man. Meanwhile letters replying to my ad come pouring in. Whether the Dream Man is or is not in one of the envelopes, I decide to let them all out.

One of the suitors cannot spell, but that is not the aspect that worries me most.

Mademoisell,
Having read your letter and found it interesting, I have decyded to reply. Let me introduce myself. I am 24, imployed in an ofice, I am rather gay, stand six foot tall, people say I am presentible, my leasure taste are simple, cinema and modern music. Hopping you will reply to my

*adress which is France Remann, 12 rue de
Ménilmontant, Paris 75011.*

Sorry, Frankie boy, you make a curious prince charming.
There is a postcard from Istanbul showing the sunset over
the Bosphorus.

I am a French teacher in an Istanbul lycée *aged 32. I
love life or at all events I think I like what deserves to be
liked (what does that mean?) I cannot visit France as we
are allowed to quit Turkey once in three years. I invite
you to Istanbul where I live on my own, where I can put
you up easily. We can travel around, particularly along
the Aegean coast.*

Next, a letter in miniscule, regular, vertical script that I
can hardly see.

*I am 23 and in search of adventure and fun with
someone who is neither a submissive envious person or a
shrew who constantly shows me how wrong I am.
I am not a hearty male, but am convinced I am on the right
path. I offer all my resources to someone worthwhile, if I can
find her.
Can we work something out? Please reply, it might be worth
the try.*
Patrick *(address supplied)*

Another letter, written by a spider, it would seem.

*Mademoiselle,
This train is rocking along, but I hope you can decipher
these lines.
I am an engineer aged 35. I do not think I am an old fogey,
but that is a matter for you to decide at our first encounter,
and I hope you will write back.*

80

I could be the companion you are looking for! Awaiting
a word from you. Best Wishes.
Pierre
(Zig-zag signature, poetic and wild)

Next gentleman please!

Dear Mademoiselle,
I am a new man who would like...
(Photo enclosed – No!)
Greetings beautiful Unknown,
In the garden of my heart lies...

Next please!!

Now I am looking at the photo of a killer with a mustache,
cauliflower ears and eyes like steel shafts.

Mademoiselle,
In response to your advertisement, yap yap yap... I shall
arrive at Saint Lazare station at 1952 hrs and stay at a
hotel in Rue Campagne 1er, Montparnasse. The enclosed
photo will enable you to recognise me and approach.
I arrive Sunday Saint Lazare 1952, or Tuesday same time
same place...

Press on.

Unknown Miss 853 6 A,
I am neither joker, nor fogey, nor has-been. I will not
claim to be good-looking, intelligent or rich or cultivated
or the rest of it. That is for you to judge.
You can leave a message on my answering machine, tel:
633.75.82. The timbre of my voice should give you some
idea of what lies behind it. If you do not like it, just hang
up, otherwise say where we can meet.
See you soon perhaps.
Emmanuel R.

With the rompings of the erotic film *Emmanuelle* foremost in my mind, I dial Emmanuel's number. The recorded voice I hear appeals to me, a lot. The diction is clear, the tone warm and a tiny bit nonchalant, lazy. I tell him: 'Phone me back as soon as you can, Galia.' I give my number.

He called me this evening, and we are seeing each other tomorrow at his place.

May 28

I think I am falling in love.

May 29

I met Emmanuel today.

The instant I set eyes on him, I knew that something important was about to happen to me.

He lives in a villa in the 14th *arrondissement*. The house is set back from railings as in an old provincial town, and you reach the front door past a flower-filled garden and a neatly-mown lawn. When I got there I found a man in a straw hat trimming the hedge. He has his back to me, of course, and I advance towards him stealthily.

'Hullo Emmanuel.'

He does not look around, and continues cutting away, delicately nipping the twigs.

'Huh, some welcome, I must say!'

He keeps on clip-clipping, and frankly I don't know what on earth to do. What kind of game is he playing? I stay where I am for about a minute, and then make a third attempt.

'Oh well alright, nice to have met you.'

Still no reaction. The fellow just keeps working on his silly hedge. He goes round a group of rose bushes, and suddenly he sees me. He is an old chap with blue eyes and a white mustache. He is clearly surprised. He is also as deaf as a poker.

'Hullo Mademoiselle, looking for someone?'

I take a big breath and yell: 'Emmanuel, it's me, Galia!'

'Of course, of course, Monsieur Emmanuel is behind there, I'll take you round.'

He has the deliberate stride of the gardener, and I fall in beside him as we crunch our way along a narrow gravel path round to the back of the house, which is facing south. My high heels are taking a beating.

A pleasant *terrasse* with lots of flowers. Some apple trees, cherry trees and a pear tree growing on trellis. It is hard to believe this is part of Paris, it's incredible, all that's missing is a cow and a few sheep. A friend who flew over the capital in a helicopter once told me the city is honeycombed with little gardens, old backyards, trees and blossoms. I am quite carried away; how lovely to live here in this enchanting villa.

The scrump-scrump of our footsteps reaches a man in a deckchair. He sees us at the very instant I am toppling sideways on my heels, he jumps up briskly, laying down a book. He moves languidly towards me.

The effect he has on me is startling. He is very good-looking, strikingly handsome and tall.

A curl of black hair curves down untamed, though with a certain elegance, over a finely-structured face. A pair of deep blue eyes are holding my gaze, honest eyes. Emmanuel is exactly like his voice, and I can feel the flush rising in my neck. We shake hands.

'Do sit down, Galia. I'm so glad you could come. What would you like to drink?'

I am mesmerized and I want to say 'you'. I force myself to keep still as I contemplate this superb male. How easy his movements, how naturally he converses. I cannot take my eyes off him, he gestures like a god, and his voice is heavenly music. This must be love, I tell myself, and I want to sob with joy.

'A beer perhaps, whisky, gin and orange?'

'Er-yes,' I manage to peep.

'But you haven't said. Fruit juice, then?'

'Yes please, fruit juice would be lovely.'

I lean forward in my chair, and he sits down on another next to me with the drinks. For the first time I am aware of his aroma. Every man has his aroma; it may be a strong smell or slight, sometimes animal, sometimes unpleasant or even ridiculous.

Emmanuel smells of cornfields, a bronzed body in the sun, a healthy body. A surge of desire courses through me and I am sure it shows.

'Why did you advertise, Galia?' he is saying. 'Surely an attractive woman like you finds no trouble meeting people...'

'I – I don't know really. I wanted the Unknown, I think.'

'Unknown people?'

'No, the Unknown – capital U. To broaden the scope...' For a minute or so I chatter on about the Unknown, new experiences, Otherness. And I realize with horror that he does not seem to be interested. I have lost him already! At that instant I feel an overpowering urge to throw myself into his arms, tell him I am talking nonsense and no longer want to seek fresh fields, want to stay with him, forever.

'Emmanuel.'

'Yes?'

'I'd like to kiss you.'

Oh those eyes, as he turns to face me squarely: 'We mustn't rush things.'

And that's *you* in your place, silly bitch! Mortified, I can think of nothing to say. My throat thickens and I follow the tears as they well up. One escapes, trickles down my cheek. I feel a complete idiot.

'Please don't take it badly, Galia,' he counsels. 'I am simply asking you not to rush things between us. These "things" will happen or they won't. Let them take their course, and let's meet again soon. I'll phone you on Thursday, I promise.'

Thursday May 31

From break of day I stayed within inches of the phone. When it rang I jumped a yard. 'It's him!'. But it wasn't. Another candidate whom I cut short.

The temptation to phone him is driving me mad. I long to hear him just say a few words, to tell him I'm coming over right away. Let things take their course. It's easy for him!

Thursday 5 p.m.

Still no call.

Thursday 8 p.m.

I can't stand this any more. I am making a fool of myself.

Thursday 10 p.m.

Nothing, nothing, nothing. He hasn't rung me, hasn't kept his promise. He doesn't care, that's obvious. I am writing this just to try and reduce the tension, for something to do, something that helps take the pain away.

I even rang him 15 minutes ago, but no answer. He's probably laughing his head off. I just cannot sit still. A whole morning, noon and night waiting for that damn phone to ring. I've had enough, I am going out.

Friday June 1

At 10 a.m. this morning he called me.

'I tried to get you last night fairly late, but you were out. How are you?'

(How am I? I am like a mad thing. Mad over you, mad at you! Oh you wicked sod! My eyes are smarting but I am going to keep my dignity, we are both intelligent people, oh yes indeed!)

'I'm fine,' I say. It came out wrong.

'I was simply too busy earlier this morning...'

'Emmanuel!'

'Yes?'

'Oh nothing.'

'Yes, say it.'

'I would – would like to see you.'

'Good, let's have dinner. Let me see, next week, mid-week, how about that?'

My whole body seems to collapse. How about next week, he says. I can't believe he is saying that, I want it to be now in the next hour. Next week next year sometime never – how about that!

'Hullo, hullo, Galia, you still there?'

'Yes, I'm still here.' Speechless, however, dripping like a wet rag.

'You seem strange, anything the matter?'

Oh no, there's nothing the matter with me. I just want to die that's all, creep under the carpet and die.

'Emmanuel, I want to tell you...'

'Yes?'

'Oh nothing. Next week, then.'

I replace the receiver, and hurl myself at my bed, shrieking in agony, buckets of tears soaking into the pillow, my legs kicking in frustration.

I am not a weeper by nature, but this time I cannot help it.

June 8

It is all over with Emmanuel, before it ever started.

With him I was completely gaga, it was genuine and it was the first time for me. It just wasn't the same for him.

Never before had (have) I been so in love with a man, and he turned out to be the most inaccessible of them all. Maybe it was simply bad luck; all I know is that he never did unbend with me. He found he 'respected' me, I was 'intelligent' and 'highly attractive'. But it went no further. He did not even bother to explain his reservations, did not come clean about them.

I realize there is no point in hurting myself day after day. He probably found me amusing. I am too proud, I don't know.

My beautiful love story had no beginning and no end. My entire existence was transformed overnight, and it disappeared in a puff of smoke.

But life goes on, I won't turn the knife in the wound. I will simply have to forget the episode if I can.

June 12

I badly needed a change of outlook, and I picked out the most jovial-sounding applicant.

I rang him and went to see him on the seventh floor of the old block in Les Halles, the former Paris central markets.

He is a smallish chap with curly blond hair, rather sweet and full of fun. He says he is 33 but looks 10 years younger. It makes a change.

'Poor Galia, you look as though the world's come to an end,' he chuckled rather nicely when he let me in. 'Come on, let's drown our sorrows in a Meurseault '49. Can't get much of it these days. I found it at Fauchon's, it's an offer you can't refuse. Hah!' He fetched a carton of supermarket biscuits.

He went babbling on and it was good for me: 'You know the Chinese Wheelbarrow? I'll show you later. I'd love to play Chinese Wheelbarrows with you. And the Monkey Up A Tree, you know that? I'll show it to you. And there's the Wild Geese Flying Upside Down, doesn't ring a bell? You're so innocent, a little kitten fallen out of the nest.'

'Cat's don't live in nests.' This man is crackers!

'How do you know? I have read Kant, Schopenhauer and Kierkegaard, and none of them deny that cats can live in trees, and can fly. I see plenty of them flying about at night between this window and the tower of Saint Eustache over there. They are asleep now, of course, trying to digest their gloppy food in tins; drugs, that's what those catfoods are. All cats are mortal. Socrates is mortal, *ergo* Socrates is a cat. And here he is, Socrates, my dozy cat!'

I broke in: 'And what's your own name? You haven't told me.'

'Hey, you're a fast worker. I'm not telling you my innermost secrets in the first two minutes, one has one's self-respect.'

Falling in with his flippancy, I say: 'What's the Monkey Up A Tree, and the Geese Flying Upside Down?'

'Those are two classic Chinese positions. In one, we are face to face – don't worry I'll show you – and in the other the woman stretches out on the man and she faces upwards. The whole art of it depends on the way the male, that's me, makes his thrusts during coitus.'

'Coitus!'

'Coitus. Alternate deep and slight penetrations, by magic numbers: 5 deep, 8 slight. You do it on the floor, and some mystical schools of thought say the male should not ejaculate. But on this aspect of the theory, I am a complete dissident. In any case I have no choice. What do you think of my Meurseault?'

'It's super.'

'Cheap too.'

'But tell me, I may not be too keen on your Chinese physical jerks.'

'In that case I shall rape you, which involves us in an entirely different erotic pigeon-hole, more Western. I may even kill you, Western style and not with the refinement of the Chinese tradition: first an ear, then an eye, another ear, a foot, and so on. Slowly and surely. Westerners are so crude, they just shove a knife in and it's all over. Such decadence! What's your preference then?'

'The Orient. Give me lots of tiny deaths, Chinese style.'

Two hours later we are lying on our backs like a pair of pussycats after feeding time.

'I liked it, all those *chinoiseries*.'

'You've seen nothing yet,' he cried in a clipped nasal voice, making his eyes into slits with his fingers. 'We behaved like crude lubricious wild animals, shoddy china objects, instruments of utter decadence . . .'

'Eroticism certainly calls for inventiveness.'

'Everything has been invented already. The sum total of know-how is vast, it's in the National Libraries of Amorous Science. We feeble unrefined missionaries of the West are miles away from the beginnings of erotic science. The ancient Chinese, for example, had an extraordinary way of copulating, and it may still be going on.

'The man and the woman are seated face to face on the floor in the lotus position. They are in the nude, they gaze into each others' eyes, their eyes caress the other's body. And they wait. They are not allowed to touch, but they smell the breath and fragrance of the other, so that their desire mounts to dizzy heights. This goes on for some hours. They hardly know each other, they have never touched, they are deprived of love-making as we understand it. This, you will realize, is an explosive situation. It goes on and on, and the man's penis is like a ramrod for hour after hour, and the woman is steamy too but it doesn't show as much. Then suddenly the man is swept away by the whirlwind of orgasm. He is motionless, yet he ejaculates long hot streams onto the woman, and this triggers the woman's orgasm. After that she throws back her head and swoons. Sometimes she comes first, and this brings on her companion's orgasm.'

He paused and then continued: 'To attain this level of perfection, you need immense expertise, long training, the backing of an entire culture, century upon century of amorous science. So you can imagine the contempt I have for our sniggering compatriots in the bistros telling dirty jokes, recounting their sexual exploits and their next conquest. For 20 centuries Western sexuality has been hamstrung by the concept of sin, and our sexual culture dominated by what is prohibited. The result is that men and women and children and old folk are in a corner, bitter and peevish, trying constantly to extend the law that is written between every line of our loves: thou shalt not come.'

I give a sigh: 'Oh my Chinese Master, thou hast not revealed thy name.'

'My name is Tien Hang Tsu, which means...'

'Oh come on, tell me.'

'My name is Alphonse...'

'Stop that.'

'...and I bounce!'

'Please tell me your name.'

'My name, *femme fatale*, I will tell you. My name... Good heavens, is that the time? I shall have to move fast.'

I raise my voice a tone: 'You're not moving anywhere. I want your name or...'

'Or what?'

'I'll strangle you.'

'Oh transport of delight! Now I won't tell you anything because, my sweetie, strangulation is the *ne plus ultra* of paradisiac ejaculation. Quick, find a scarf.'

I try another tack: 'If you don't give me your name, I won't strangle you!'

'How superbly logical women are, she wants it both ways! Let's just get the strangling over, shall we? My name's Matthieu.'

'Matthieu?'

'Certainly, Matthieu. As in passion, short-arse, saint, boss of money-changers and usurers.' This nonsense was helping me so much, I started to giggle.

And then: 'Matthieu, it's a nice name.'

'Matthieu wants to be strangled nicely.'

And so we went on playing like children all afternoon, and I managed to forget my unrequited love. In this attic in the entrails of Paris I relived my lost exuberance. Perhaps it was doing him good too.

'Matthieu, teach me another Chinese caress. Please, Matthieu.'

'I'll demonstrate the Chinese Fish, if you like, but we need someone to tie our hands together.'

'Tie our hands!'

'The Chinese Fish method consists of Madam Yin and Mister Yang lying down naked and bound on a mattress to make love like fish do, without using their hands.'

'Sounds delicious, much better than Chinese nougat. I'm sure it's out of this world.'

'We'll do the Fish when we have someone who knows their knots. Lie down. Put your glass over there, I'm going to give you the Spring Butterfly. Close your eyes first, no don't cheat this is serious, now relax. You are next to a stream in the province of the Yang Tse. It is midday, your warrior has gone off to work, that is, to fight. Your servants are collecting grasshoppers for the soup and you are in the meadow in the sun among the flowers, naked as a water lily, a brightness in the mist. You are beautiful, you are dreaming of your glorious master and of his strong arms, his beautiful sword; and you are dreaming too of the young lord who lives across the way, of the smooth flesh of his thighs. Suddenly, a butterfly...'

For a long, incredible and marvellous hour, Matthieu makes his butterfly fly. With a very fine silk brush he strokes the most sensitive parts of my body, hidden parts I never knew about: behind my ears, in the bend of my wrist, the backs of my knees, between my toes. The sensations he accorded me were extraordinary, exquisite, tiny electric spasms on my skin. I begin to feel the subtle excitement coming on, I want the caresses to be firmer.

He knows this because he is diabolically clever, but he keeps me waiting. Matthieu takes a small bottle of the oil, yellow and perfumed, dips another silk brush a little larger in the oil, and unexpectedly stops everything.

'Matthieu,' I whisper, 'please go on, please...'

'The butterfly has flown to a branch, but it will return.'

'Matthieu, you are torturing me, let me get it off please, with you.'

'The butterfly is nudging the flower. We must be still and

wait. Ah, there it is on another bloom.'

Then he slowly opens my legs, spreads my own little flower with utmost care, lifts my clitoris with the brush and begins to caress it upwards with the end of the oily brush, and then round and round and round. The pleasure this affords me is unbelievably intense, I am excruciatingly exposed. I am panting as I whisper in a high voice: 'Yes, oh yes, more more, please Matthieu.'

At that instant Matthieu covers me with his body, and I feel him enter me. But we do not move, time stands still, and together our orgasms, our united orgasm, bursts forth in a climactic symphony.

June 15

I cannot help thinking of Emmanuel, and I feel quite dreadful. I am trying to pretend the pain is not there by plunging into a round of activity: I go shopping, clean my windows, tidy the kitchen cupboards – anything to stop the aching obsession with Emmanuel, this impossible love story.

The worst time is around three in the morning, when I have a knife entering my very heart, reminding me of my lost Emmanuel. Hell must be like this. In the still of the night I lie in my bed with my eyes wide open to see his eyes, his hands, his hair, his smile. It hurts terribly.

I cannot weep, I cannot sleep, and I hopelessly resort to Valium and barbiturates. I can't stand the suffering, am afraid of the pain. Sleep becomes a nightly suicide enabling me to keep going for another day.

June 16

Mummy phoned. Daddy has been taken to hospital with a heart attack, but his life is not in danger, she tells me.

The news leaves me indifferent, and all I am concerned about is how she is taking it. I am not ashamed of this daughterly callousness, for I never loved my father. I hated him for not making Mummy happy and still do. He is a stranger for me now and his death would not affect me. I am an ungrateful daughter but that is the way it is, one cannot fabricate love. Even so, I get Interflora to send a bouquet of lilies, though my heart is not in it.

I am unconditionally and fervently tender towards the mother I love. But the time she has herself lost in mediocre love will never come back. My father did not deserve this sublime woman.

June 17

Elisabeth R. sent me some junk mail announcing the opening of a 'College for Women' near the Arc de Triomphe. She describes it pompously as 'a higher institute of erotological research'. To please her I pay the subscription.

It transpires that a former street-walker from Rue Saint Denis, who first tried running a bar in the 5th *arrondissement*, had the idea of a training centre for prostitutes. Later the project evolved and took in some students from Censier faculty.

Together these students set up the College for Women, rather as a joke but also as a challenge and an intellectual game. Its aim is to teach eroticism to women. Madame De Chaussoy, the ex-street-walker's assumed name, apparently takes the venture very seriously. This is no lighthearted enterprise but a genuine school for women in the sexual desert who want to learn the skills of lovemaking. The women who are prepared to pay for this instruction include girl students, housewives, society women, the elderly, young people – all sorts.

Today was the first day of the first term, and the Directress as she calls herself delivered an inaugural address. She is a buxom blonde of nearly six foot, outrageously made up, an Olympic weight-putter by the look of her.

The lecture hall in Avenue Niel is fairly small, and the students (all women of course) took their seats rather timidly under the severe scrutiny of Madame De Chaussoy. The average age seems to be about 40, a time of life when women have the urge to make up for lost time – while there is still time! There are a few girls a wee bit older than I am, but yours truly is the baby of the class. Some of the oldsters keep glancing at me: they give off hostility, admiration, hatred, perhaps desire in some cases. How unfair to be young, they seem to be telling me. But I would like to stare back and tell them: 'I'll be old one day too.'

Madame De Chaussoy calls for silence, which is unnecessary since nobody has breathed a word since we came in.

'Mesdames, Mesdemoiselles,' she declares. 'This is neither a whore-house, nor Women's Lib nor a university establishment. You have come to the College for Women to learn what you have never learned so far: to be a woman. You went to school but they did not teach you what was essential. The universities taught you abstractions, Women's Lib teaches you hostility, the whore-house taught you submissiveness!' Mumbling breaks out in the hall. 'Yes I know you haven't come out of whore-houses, but it's the same thing: you have lived under conjugal fealty for centuries with men crushing you with their power. The reaction of Women's Lib to this defeat has been "Get rid of men and let's live on our own." But you know very well ladies that this is not possible, there is no such thing as a happy homosexual.' Slight mumbling from parts of the hall.

'Man and Woman, male and female, are two complementary forces. Without their encounter there can be no true enjoyment.

'The toughies of Women's Lib suggest you eliminate Man. I propose to you that you find Man again, and win him over.' A pause. The speaker takes a few deep breaths into her mighty chest, scanning the gathering with ferocious eyes.

She continues: 'We love men, we do!' Applause. 'But subjection we shall not admit.' Applause. 'We too have the right to power.' Applause. 'And this power we shall win through men's orgasms!'

Another silence, in case we have not understood. A cloud of uncertainty and doubt floats above our heads.

The Directress breaths again and booms out: 'We have got them by their weak points, ladies.' Prolonged applause at this and stamping of high heels. 'Silence please. Thank you. Jesus said he would teach us virtue, but God is dead. Nietzsche showed us Superman, Freud showed us the Subconscious, Marx declared "workers of all lands unite". The workers united and with barbed wire inside and all around we can see what that has produced. We see that, Subconscious or no Subconscious, people are still in the doghouse and so are their psychoanalysts. As to the Supermen, we have watched them marching in their tin hats and jackboots within living memory.

'But I say to you that I will teach you the pleasure, the reconciliation and the knowledge that comes with love. I will give you neither paradise nor glory, but you will feel better in your women's bodies.'

This afternoon we had Practical, using a rubber man. He was a full-scale painted latex doll with two detachable penises: one limp, one erect. The pricks are unscrewed like hot water bottle stoppers and you work on one or the other depending on the stage of your instruction, while a smiling paratrooper head looks down on the flabby body.

The first lesson was the limp penis. We were asked: 'Your man has come home from work, he is tired and lies down on the bed. You want to make him want sex. What do you do?'

A volunteer is called for. Claudine, a petite brunette from somewhere round Marseilles, says she will have a go. Smiling broadly she approaches the paratrooper, hesitates and then gives him a quick kiss on the lips. She doesn't seem too convinced about it and looks round at us with a sheepish smile. Claudine then grabs hold of the rubber prick, it wobbles about but she manages to pump it up and down, fairly energetically.

Madame De Chaussoy intervenes: 'You're being too

rough, Claudine, in too much of a hurry, you're shaking him like a baby's bottle before he has time to think about it. Softly, sensually. Next!'

Madame has scared everyone off already, but as no-one else volunteers I say I will have a shot at the paratrooper.

'Fine Galia, show us how you do it.'

I move up to the kind of operating table where the male object lies waiting, and pull him round a bit, then put the rubber cylinder in my mouth.

I hope Claudine doesn't have anything catching, although anything is better than syphilis. The prick is all ploppy and yukky and cold, and the man's thighs have that soapy rubber smell. But the insides are slippery too and I feel a little itch beginning inside me. It's sort of naughty. I can see why sex-starved men buy inflatable dolls, especially if the dolls' eyelids flutter. Rubber is nice to handle and my own fantasies start moving in as I speed up.

'Not too bad, Galia,' I am informed. 'But please, ladies, do not forget the object of the exercise. What would you think if your companion immediately started chomping at you? ('He's never chomped at me,' I hear a woman muttering behind me. 'Wouldn't mind it if he did now and again.') Delicately, ladies, fastidiously, like this; I just run my fingers over the whole body, upwards of course, never stopping, never pressing. Very light quick touches along the thighs, arms and chest. Then I move in with a quick flip to the penis, and away again. He is beginning to come alive now. So please remember: Phase I, lightness of touch.

'Phase II, still light, but focusing on the organ with tiny licks using the end of your tongue, like a feather on this side then upwards and ABOVE ALL no oral insertion yet. Let's not run before we leap. Our man is now excited and his work and worries and fatigue are far behind him. He wants sex, so . . .' (She unscrews the limp prick which is now wet, puts it on a shelf under the table, screws on the biggie. The paratrooper is looking more interesting now.) 'More licks, not too fast there's plenty of time, languidly, while you continue feathering your hands all over the body.

'Phase III: alternate licking and insertion. Six licks, and in, six licks and in, 10 or 15 cycles. Our man is now jumping for joy. Ladies, you have him just where you want him!'

She adds mundanely: 'That's all for today. Tomorrow nine o'clock for sexuality in the Trobriand Islands.'

June 18

At the College I have made a friend of Myriam. She is 28, a little on the chubby side, but a stupendous blonde. She is finishing psychology and starting at the Louvre. She is a strange girl, highly independent and bursting with energy. She writes serial love stories for a magazine.

She confides to me that she acts like a man in many ways. It is she who chases men, manipulates them, makes use of them and then discards them. She can't get enough of sex, she says.

'Come along,' she said when we emerged into Avenue Niel today, 'Let's pick up a man for ourselves. Why shouldn't women take the initiative?'

Close by the Arc de Triomphe, Myriam scans the male talent and picks out a nice little chap about to enter the Metro station. She falls in behind, tugging me along.

'He's real cute, don't you think?'

The man stops and turns, visibly astonished.

'Nice, eh, Galia? A juicy piece, I'd say. Yes I mean you, sweetie.' The fellow turns as red as a beetroot, and she goes on: 'Don't be afraid, handsome, I like your eyes! D'you live with your parents? Oh Galia, take a load of that bottom, beautiful, my word I could go for that.'

The poor man looks terrified, as she persists: 'What's your name, Charlie? Lost your tongue? Sulking?'

Myriam moves in and plants a kiss on his mouth. He mumbles 'But, but' and she says: 'There is no but about it. Oh come on, we don't mean any harm, we just want a bit of fun, give us a kiss. Hurry up, round here.' She pushes him against a tree, where he looks ready to be executed. I am definitely roused, if it's as easy as this. 'You first, Galia.'

I hoist my little self onto the tips of my toes and kiss him nimbly. I detect a fleeting interest from him. Myriam says: 'That's more like an accolade, my turn now.' She gathers the man and the tree in a single swoop, somehow manages to open his mouth and twirls her tongue round inside, simultaneously undoing his belt regardless of passers-by. Her hand slithers down his trouser front, and the man closes his eyes. He likes it!

Still smooching, she gropes him for a couple of minutes and stands back with spittle running down her chin. She is flushed and lets him escape.

As we walk away she says in my ear: 'I went right round to the rear entrance.' Myriam is certainly over-sexed.

June 19

Dinner with Osvaldo. He is in love with a girl just over 18. Eighteen is the lower limit under law, and he is scared of the law. She is a smallish student from Quebec with rosy cheeks and that amazing French Canadian accent. He seems keen on Emilie, but I know already that he likes adolescents.

'Do you know what the Canadians say when anyone gets irritated?'

'No.'

'They say "Don't climb up the curtains". And d'you know what she calls a mint-lemonade? "Fast lawn water juice". You must meet her, she is delightful.'

I am genuinely pleased for Osvaldo. All's well that ends well. Things are never as bad as they seems. Life goes on. Dear Osvaldo!

June 20

I have had a rollicking from my sisters. They say I should have gone with them to see father at Tours. I let them prattle on, I cannot be bothered to argue back.

I am in another world, the only real family tie I have is with Mummy. I simply cannot raise any interest in the others. I must be quite monstrous, morally speaking, but at least I do not pretend to be a little angel.

Even if it is hard going at times, I shall never give in and conform. If my four sisters want to continue the tradition of respectability, that is their affair.

I find life is too momentous a thing, too exhilarating to waste in a standard mould.

Instinctively I believe I am right to be a wildcat. Whatever they think, I have learned more than they ever got from their fancy education.

June 21, first day of summer

Myriam and I feel on top of the world as we trip down Avenue Niel with arms linked in our gaily-swinging 1920s' above-the-knee dresses.

When Myriam perceives a male she likes the look of, she gives him a whistle without stopping to see the effect. I am drawn to her but she is quite a phenomenon and I still haven't worked her out. Today I asked her: 'Do you sometimes meet a man you like and take him home?'

'Naturally.'

'And you make love with him?'

'Sure, if I like him.'

'And keep on seeing him?'

'Not usually. When I've had what I want, it's bye-bye Johnny and no violins.'

'In fact you do like men do: have your poke and walk off.'

She laughs: 'Just like Don Juan without the talk. It's hullo, we go upstairs, I straddle him, we wash it off, cheers.'

'And that's enough for you?'

'It's fun while it lasts, but it's no worse than a man who sleeps all over town without love coming into it. Being in love is completely different.'

'Are you in love often?'

'Rarely. Men have always disappointed me. They are egotistical, always going on about their work, they take themselves too seriously, they don't give their whole selves. Life has turned them into liars and bluffers. And those who refuse to be young turks, greedy for power, end up drop-outs or merely bitter. That's the way men are today. Women are far more interesting, deeper, absorbing.'

Since she is prepared to talk, I go further: 'I find it hard to understand why a girl like you is at the College for Women. You are already fulfilling yourself. Do you just want to become more expert in lovemaking?'

'Hm, expert? I know perfectly well how a man likes it. I do it all the time. I'm at the College out of curiosity, for the enjoying of it, for the company almost. It's an amazing project, launched in the face of prudishness and hypocrisy. Mother De Chaussoy fought for months to open that College, and I felt she deserved backing.'

This morning our Directress was in a good mood. Her athlete's face was almost kind, transformed after 90 minutes of make-up.

'Ladies,' she said, 'I am very pleased with you. You have made great progress.' (Old Ma Chaussoy handing out compliments, whatever next?) 'You are not fully expert yet but you have grasped the elementary techniques. No man will resist you, I am sure.

'So far we have been working *in abstracto*, but from today we start *in vivo*. The models you will be experimenting on now are well and truly alive. Let me introduce you.'

Three lovely men then came in. A tall blond man, the elegant kind you see at the Racing Club de France; a squat stocky man with black hair, obviously highly virile; a slender, brown-haired, delicate looking man with a fine bone structure, almost effeminate.

The sound level rises as we start cooing like doves. The woman next to me bawls in my ear: 'Oh what a hunk of meat!' 'Which one?' 'On the right of course, who else?' She means hairy.

De Chaussoy: 'I would like to present to you: Gérard, Hughes and Cyril.' The three bow nicely, scanning the women like Christians in the coliseum sizing up the lions.

Madame De Chaussoy certainly knows how to pick her stallions. The sportsman, the brute and the nice one. We all can't wait to ride them, but we want to see their livery first. *In vivo veritas*!

Perhaps they are going to do us a striptease. Or maybe go out and come in again naked. We all wriggle in our seats.

The Directress declaims: 'First we are going to see how a sensual woman undresses a man. I want someone for Cyril. Come now, ladies, don't be shy.'

Cyril is so long and thin he looks like a virgin being auctioned in a slave market. He lowers his eyes.

'Reckon he's a nancy boy?' Myriam says in a whisper everyone can hear.

'Of course not, Cho-Cho would never have picked a homo.'

Cho-Cho is getting impatient: 'Instead of yapping like a bunch of 15-year-olds, show a little initiative. Undressing a man isn't going to give you a baby!'

Old Sophie steps up. Actually she is only about 50, and still alluring.

'A volunteer for Hughes, please.'

'Me!' yells the woman next to me. And to make sure of her man she strides towards the dark guy and grabs his arm.

'Now, anyone for Gé...'

'Me, me, me, me!' A dozen voices screech out.

'Oh dear, ladies, let's not lose our reserve. Valentine, you take Gérard. Quiet please, we are not in the infants school. You will all get your turn. The three gentlemen on the platform please, and let's see how we get on. Ready? You can start now, I'm not telling you a thing at this stage.'

A hush falls on the hall as we watch the three heroes divested of their clothing, item by item, by their three females. Almost the Folies Bergère, it's so entertaining.

Gérard acts up, knowing how resplendent he is. Head high, he sticks out his chest when his shirt drops away.

Hughes looks like a chimpanzee in disguise, a bashful one at that, but he submits to his female, who just can't get him undressed fast enough.

Cyril still has his eyes on the floor; he lets Sophie go ahead, lifting his long arms so she can remove his pink T-shirt.

We are now approaching the moment of truth. Gérard and Hughes are in their underpants, but Cyril still has his shoes and trousers on. Sophie takes her time, her motions are unruffled and loaded with suggestiveness, her hands peeling off the garments lovingly. Sophie was born for this, we feel. But Cyril is clearly uncomfortable, there is a bump in there somewhere and we can all see it, and he knows we can see it. Amid a highly-charged silence his trousers fall, and a murmur of admiration flutters through the hall, for his thin turquoise slip is projecting out in front like the bow of an ocean liner. The atmosphere is distinctly clammy, you can smell it.

Cho-Cho starts up: 'Well, ladies, we are now at the nub of our problem. Need I say more? The evidence is before your eyes. Once again you will realize that haste does not pay. Sophie knew that. Right, gentlemen, get dressed and we'll try another three...'

The entire hall lets out a sigh. 'Oh!' Frustration looks like part of Cho-Cho's technique.

June 26

In my fireplace, the whole pile of the letters replying to the ad is waiting to go up in flames. I cannot really answer them all. I have met some of these men and, apart from Emmanuel I wish I had not, although I would not have lost out on Matthieu in Les Halles.

I have been offered all shapes and sizes, every imaginable colour of eyes, I have seen a good many white marks where a wedding ring has been hastily removed, some candidates

have cheered me up and others have told me with a shudder
that life is black except when I am there. Actually it is true
that in the case of some, life had a taste of the sewer.

I came across professional copulators, men with obses-
sions, perverts, hystericals and psychopaths. And I am fed
up with the whole damn lot of them. Every single letter is in
the fireplace, I am a female Beelzebub.

June 28

A phone call from Jemal Abdelaziz Faraoud, Prince of
Araby. He holds nothing against me, and I've nothing
against him. He is staying at the Stella-Park Hotel on
Avenue François 1er, which is reputedly the most expensive
in the world.

He asks me to meet him this evening in the bar of the
Stella. He will introduce me to some 'very important
friends,' he says.

June 29

I must get this night at the Stella-Park down while I can.

Jemal welcomed me with open arms and introduced me to
his friends: a Saudi businessman, an attaché at some
Embassy, an American businessman and an Arab Minister
of Technology or Transport, I forget which. I never had a
chance to check because the moment we sat down everything
started to go crazy.

The bar was crowded with about 100 billion dollars.
Greying financiers out of a picture book, de luxe call girls,
foreigners of all sorts, the Paris-based jet set in action.

My hosts are already fairly advanced with their drinking,
whisky for Uncle Sam and champagne for the others. The
Minister seemed to be most lucid, and from time to time his
personal male secretary came up with a telex, which he
scanned and then blew something in the ear of the secretary
who would bow and disappear.

The conversation was in English except for a few asides in Arab. Probably dirty jokes.

Two girls join us, pretty little things used to hanging onto the world's richest testicles. All they needed was bunny ears and they could have come straight from Playboy. They were cheap, stupid and ravishing. For a moment I wished I had their brazen sex-appeal.

The blonde one was the more professional at first sight, and she immediately sat curvaceously on the Minister's lap. The other, not so striking in appearance, nestled cosily between the two thickest wallets in the group: Jemal ($1 million) and the American ($750,000), I would guess.

I watched the girls' gold-digger faces, their letter-box smiles. It looked like they had got themselves a fat retirement pension. I had to admire them.

We went into eat round a huge table. While the little bunnies swayed their bottoms on their chairs, the men talked of interest rates, women, capital cities, beaches and casinos. The Minister got up twice after glancing at some messages, but was soon back. Jemal, sitting next to me, confided in a low steady voice that he was most upset by my hasty departure from Cannes.

'I can't understand it, Galia, you left so hurriedly and so unfairly.'

'Forgive me, Jemal, I was in a dreadful crisis of emancipation, I was unable to stand the least constraint.' I gave him what I hoped was a sweet smile.

'But I did not impose constraints on you.' It was rather satisfying, after all, having this sheikh pleading with me.

'I really can't remember. I only *felt* restricted, in bonds. It was probably my fault rather than yours. I'm sorry I upset you.' I laid my hand lightly on his arm.

'Do not excuse yourself. You followed your impulses and you were quite right . . .'

One of the bunnies hiccupped over her champagne and broke in with a baby voice: 'No private sessions. Come and sit by me, Jemal.'

My ex-prince was embarrassed and threw me a hopeless glance. I worked my eyelashes to tell him: 'Go ahead and have fun, Jemal. Sure, she's an idiot, but we are not here to rake over the past, and we are still friends, you and I. In any case, she has lovely thighs, go and stroke them.'

By midnight we were all in the azure blue of the Stella swimming pool, with exotic green-leaved plants all around us. The two pink rabbits have nothing on, and their bodies are so superb it doesn't seem to matter how they get their money.

One of them is doing a slow underwater yankee-doodle-dandy on the American who is hooked with his arms to the pool edge, his bathing trunks around his knees. He looks like he is being crucified and is mouthing: 'Oh Gard, it's so good in the water, I didn't know it could be so great. My Gard!' Every 30 seconds the girl comes up for air and then plunges again. The more she sucks, the louder he blows.

The Minister goes back and forth doing the breast stroke. He is smiling and still sober. His secretary comes to the pool edge and shows him another telex, looking out of place in his suit and waistcoat.

I can see Jemal with the super-blonde in the foliage. She is leaning back with her wonderful legs gaping and he is licking her genitalia, his head nodding like an alsation dog. She makes quite a thing of her jerky little motions and is twiddling her toes just a little. She utters whimpering noises and is gasping, and I find it enthralling. She seems to be liking it and it may be genuine; this stirs my own concupiscence. I stealthily move close until I can see Jemal's tongue working repeatedly into her opening and then upwards again and again, sometimes darting into the crease in her bottom. Jemal has progressed a lot, I am jealous a bit.

The Embassy attaché is nowhere to be seen. I thought he looked a little sneaky and may be hiding in a cabin masturbating. The Saudi businessman has drunk bottle after bottle of champagne and keeps laughing.

A nice respectable orgy for the start of the 1980s, I am

thinking. But, although I feel the flesh motioning, I would rather not join in. I cannot honestly say why, this may be just an 'off' day for me. Even so, I won't spoil the others' fun and, when the party moves off towards the Minister's suite, I cheerfully tag along. The pink bunnies move through the hotel in beachrobes dripping with water. A guest comes out of the lift where we are waiting, a typical English duke or something, and with one accord the girls fling wide their robes, revealing everything. His eyes pop out of his head, and he will need a week to get over it. On the other hand, who knows, it may be the start of a whole new fantasy world for him. He must be at least 68. I would love to watch a duke playing with himself.

We get to the Ministerial suite, all of us except the attaché who is probably locked in his cabin. The suite measures 1500 square feet in all, I am told. It has five bedrooms, several balconies, a solarium, bullet-proof windows, electronic bug detectors, telephones and of course the telex, little palm-trees and other things in boxes, television and a video tape recorder, plus bathrooms fitted out with various sexually-inviting aids.

The Minister has about a ton of champagne sent up. At first a waiter in smart black attire came in with six bottles. Above the noise the Minister yells: 'Six bottles, you must be mad, I said lots of champagne, get six cases up here.'

They can say what they like about the Arabs, but they certainly know how to throw a party. The Minister and Jemal empty the six crates, and then empty the bottles – into the bath, where it bubbles. Corks are popping about all over the place, and the music is deafening.

The blonde bunny cannot resist the bubbles, and slides into the bath. The Minister starts splashing the champagne all over her, but the male secretary comes up with a telephone and his boss grabs it.

'Jeddah, Your Excellency.' Immediately after that: 'Los Angeles, Your Excellency.'

The Minister barks his orders down the phone as the

bunny squeals with delight and the rock rhythm makes the crystalware tinkle in unison. Thus are the affairs of the planet decided.

In due course I had to lie down in one of the bedrooms, overcome with champagne and noise. I fell asleep and missed the belly dancer. The party broke up around dawn.

July 1

Money trouble looms. I find I am unable to pay the rent and certain other bills.

I have no intention of taking to the streets. I could ask Mummy, and I know she would give her last sou for me, but I would not do that to her. She has pinched and scraped all her life for us children.

I make a few phone calls to friends. I am decidedly embarrassed about asking them.

Tomorrow I am 21, and wish I could be more cheerful about it.

July 2

Matthieu flings a birthday party for me in his attic. Myriam, Osvaldo, Jemal and Elisabeth are among the guests.

At one point in the evening I can hold back the tears no longer. I weep because I am just as stupid as I was two years ago, three years ago, five years ago.

As a little girl I used to tell myself: 'When I am grown-up I shall understand everything.' I am grown-up and I still don't understand a thing. I am less naive, and it simply makes life more difficult to cope with.

July 3

Today I was asked to play in a hard porn film, 4,000 francs for a week's work. It's not exactly a star's fee but I agree to do it. I am in dire financial straits and in any case it will be

107

something different.

Filming is to take place from 6 p.m. to midnight, which means I shall not miss any lectures. That counts most.

July 4

I have now met the actors playing in *Charlotte Mouille Ta Culotte* (Charlotte Wet Your Panties).

It was Gérard, the dazzling model from the College for Women, who got me the job, and he is playing the principal role. He told me he had done seven porn films already; he is completely *blasé* about it and yearns to play in 'real' films as the star. One problem he has is his diction, but frankly he is also a terrible actor, stiff, melodramatic and unconvincing. Gérard has also done three serials for television, and the other star Nadia told me he definitely will not get any more T.V. work.

Nadia is a small blonde of 22 from Poland, rather on the plump side and with short legs, but she has magnificent green eyes.

I have the supporting woman's role. In fact there are just the three of us in the cast.

The story line could never win an Oscar in a thousand years. A man (Gérard) and his wife (Nadia) seduce a girl friend (me) who is staying with them, initiating her into the joys of triangular sex. And that's it! The producer came up with the understatement of the century when he murmured to me: 'With our budget, we can't really go in for creative work.'

'But why not?' say I in all innocence. The question shook him rigid, and for the rest of the evening I was the bright-eyed 'intellectual' of the party.

The film crew consists of a chief operator (he prefers to be known as the photo director for some reason), an assistant cameraman, a sound engineer, an electrician who seems half asleep most of the time, a continuity girl and of course the producer (he prefers 'director') whose word is law. The producer comes from the wilds of central France but he calls himself John Turner because it sounds more American.

The aforesaid Turner strides up and down the set frowning fiercely. He wears a small black cylinder on a length of cord round his neck. He can look through this and see what the camera sees.

Last night he spent much of the time sizing up the job, and we are all a little subdued. You would imagine it was Cecil B. De Mille planning how to get 20,000 extras up the side of a pyramid.

'Ready when you are, John,' says the chief operator.

'Hold it a minute, I'll be right with you.'

And he goes on with his pacing. The set measures all of three yards by four and everything is going to be filmed in that space. Even this area seems too much for him.

Suddenly Cecil B. Turner demands: 'I want the two kilowatt right away.'

'Ok, it's just above your bonce.'

'I want a back-light on Galia's hair when she comes in.'

'Fine, cock, but it'll take an hour to fix it.'

Turner is clearly annoyed at such familiarity on the set. He stretches to his full height and bellows: 'For Chrissakes, who's supposed to be directing this picture? How the hell we can get anything done in this...'

The electrician snarls through his dangling cigarette: 'Eh, do I shift the two kilo or don't I?'

'Oh leave it where it is,' growls Turner. 'We'll forget the back-light.' He takes up his stance and peeks through his black cylinder, then moves towards the door where I am to make my entrance. 'It'll be alright,' he declares.

The electrician stubs out his cigarette with a foot: 'Buggering about over a bloody two kilo...'

John T. bellows forth anew: 'Right everyone, we'll run through just once. Positions, silence!'

Turner takes me by the arm and explains the first scene. I am to appear in the doorway and exclaim: 'Oh hullo. Sorry to disturb you.'

Turner: 'Quiet! Galia, try it.'

'Oh hullo. Sorry to disturb you.'

'No lovey. Your second sentence comes too quick. Take a pause, look surprised, they're in bed naked, and then you say "Sorry to disturb you." OK? Try it again. Galia!' He flings a finger at me.

'Oh hullo.' Pause. 'Sorry to disturb you.'

'Great! She's got what it takes, our Galia. Positions, you stay at 18, you pan slow right, quiet please, roll 'em.'

'Roll 'em.'

'Title!'

The assistant-cameraman says: '*Charlotte et Ses Pelottes* scene one. Oh shit, wrong film. Sorry Mr Turner.'

Turner: 'For crying out loud, you don't have to say the whole damn title, just *Charlotte*. Do it again, quiet, roll 'em.'

'Roll 'em.'

'Title!'

'*Charlotte* scene one.'

I say my piece: 'Oh hullo.' Pause. 'Sorry to disturb you.'

'CUT!' yells Turner. 'Perfect, well done Galia, you should go far. We'll just do a back-up.'

The whole procedure gets into motion again and I say: 'Oh hullo.' Pause. 'Sorry to disturb you.'

July 5

Events are moving ahead fast at the College for Women. Gérard, Cyril and Hughes are treated by us all like precious objects, mascots, lucky medals.

We touch them, we fondle them, we breath them, we venerate them. They are the Ideal Man in Triplicate, the Erotrinity, the Three-Pronged Stronger Sex!

Gérard plays his part to perfection, Hughes acts like a total blockhead and Cyril lowers his eyes in modesty.

After several undressing cycles, our live males appeared at last in their naked glory. The audience got its money's worth. Their equipment was superb, each with a massive long phallus and a scrawny bag underneath with two well-defined bulges. Our men exuded health and strength. We all stared greedily at their manly credentials.

I was finding it hard to keep my legs closed. We had practised with the droopy rubber penis and with the hard rubber penis. And now we were moving onto the real thing! With real men!! We were positively drooling. The men got dressed again.

Madame De Chaussoy quietened us down: 'Now let us go back to the other day when our companion comes home tired from work and lies down on the bed. You want to rouse him. How do you go about it? We shall now see if you have grasped it so far. Claudine take Hughes, Micheline you can have Cyril, Myriam take Gérard.'

A choke escapes from my immediate neighbour. Her dream chimpanzee has gone to a rival, and the blood drains from her face. She seems likely to break into hysterics.

Hairy Hughes lies down on his demonstration camp bed on the right, Gérard in the middle and Cyril on the left of the platform.

The three women start the undressing procedure again. Myriam giggles a bit, Micheline is all fingers and thumbs with the buttons and zips, Claudine plods along methodically like a little girl playing with her doll. We were all waiting for her, as she carefully folded each article of clothing.

Our men lay naked on their beds, and the entire hall held its breath. I dared to glance around me. My fellow students were licking their lips, panting, shifting on their perspiring rumps, their whole bodies expectant. I had never seen so many randy women at one time.

Cho-Cho: 'Ladies, remember what you have learned so far. Yes, Myriam?'

'Madame, can we go right through with it, I mean can we – er – allow our partner – er – to ejaculate?' Even she was nervous.

'There would be no basic objection to that.'

111

My neighbour turned green. She was about to scream and I whispered urgently: 'Take it easy, you can collect him afterwards. It's a lesson, not real lovemaking.'

Cho-Cho: 'You can begin, ladies.'

Six hands surged forward and began touching lightly, stroking, feathering from feet to head. You could have heard a pin drop. Two of the women had certainly learned their rudiments, for Hughes and Cyril were erect in seconds. Flushed with victory, Claudine and Micheline took the penises in their mouths, removed them again and began licking. By now the men were expectant.

Myriam was in trouble, however. She tried again and again, using every. trick in the book. So much for *her* experience.

'Come on Gérard, be a sport, what's happened to you?' she scolded.

'Nothing.'

'You can say that again!'

She licks more eagerly, lifting his scrotum so that the skin is stretched and shining.

'For God's sake concentrate,' she orders. Gérard sits up and whispers in her ear. 'Well don't make such a fuss about it,' she snaps. She pinches the root of his penis, but to no avail. 'What do you want me to do?' He whispers again and she says: 'Well why didn't you say so in the first place!' Myriam resume her tongue work and sneaks a finger into his bottom.

At last his member springs to life, she envelops it with her generous lips and her head jolts several times in a swallowing motion. She stands back choking, and scurries off the platform looking neither to left nor to right.

July 7

We did some more filming in the sweltering heat. The air-conditioning has broken down, but fortunately we are

112

wearing almost nothing. These scenes start with the classic preliminaries.

My opening greeting is answered by Gérard: 'Not at all, we are delighted to see you, come right in.' Mickey Mouse would have said it better.

Nadia adds: 'Why of course, come and sit down.' Nadia is more of a professional but the action just doesn't come across. It's not my problem, and I sit on the edge of the bed. They both start pawing me and undressing me.

The dialogue is unbelievably crummy:

'Mmmm, your pussy is lovely!'

'Yes, yes, yes, yes.'

'Oo, I'm all sticky.'

'Me too, ooh, ooh.'

'Put it in, *chérie*, put it in.'

'I'm going to, I'm sliding it in!'

This is easier said than done. We girls have Myriam's trouble on our hands, and we hear John Turner bawling out: 'Hurry up Gérard, get a hard on, any way you like, but get a hard on.'

Nadia knows her business and gets to work on him, and I lie spreadeagled on the bed. Gérard exclaims: 'I've got it in' and I cry out 'I can feel it sliding in!' Indeed I can and I get ready for the climax. It's taking longer than I thought and the sweat is pouring off us: 'I'm coming, I'm coming!' He's a good bluffer anyway, he couldn't ejaculate to save his life right now. He works too hard, I am thinking. 'I'm coming, oh it's spurting!' I hope he's right.

'CUT!!' We all fall back exhausted. Turner says blandly: 'Not too bad, Gérard. Nadia, give it more punch when you say "Put it in". Quiet roll 'em.'

'Roll 'em.'

'Title.'

'*Charlotte* 27.'

'Put it IN, *chéri*.'

'I'll put it in, I'll put it in!'

'CUT!' John leaps out of the shadows: 'How the hell can

you put it in when you can't get it up. You're shrivelled! Fix it, Nadia.'

Gérard looks like a character from *Les Misérables* but within a minute we are into *Charlotte* 28 and the scene ends with us all thrashing around gargling: 'Ah, mmm, ah...yes, yes...there, there...mmm, *chérie chéri*...I'm coming... Ah Charlotte...'

'CUT!!That's great kids. We'll take 30. I want you all back here in half an hour sharp.'

At the bistro four doors away we order a beer and *croque-monsieur* (what else!).

The male star is disconsolate: 'It's no good, I'll never make it to the end of the picture. I'm flaked out.'

Perfidiously I say: 'But you don't even ejaculate, so you ought to be springy. You tire yourself out too early on.'

'It's the College for Women, they are all sex mad there, they've cleaned me out. And all for a pittance. I can't go on like this.'

Nadia says: 'Ask the Directress for a few days off.'

'She'd never have that, the dragon! You ought to see her, she'd pull my balls off.'

'Go on sick leave, think of anything, say you've got the pox.'

A bright light flickered in the eyes of our weary stallion: 'Hey that's an idea, the pox! Great! Galia, promise you won't let on. You won't split on me?'

I tell him he can count on me, and Nadia says he's got to complete this film.

When we get back there is a power cut.

Turner is tearing his hair out: 'I don't believe it, I don't believe it, who is this damn fool of an electrician they've landed me with?'

The damn fool takes it in his stride, fiddling with his cables, a cigarette stuck to his lower lip.

The boss chides him: 'Come on buddy, get your finger out, we got a take on our hands. Oh for crying out loud!'

The electrician: 'Listen buster. Just keep it low, eh? I can't

114

stand noise. Second, just let me get on with it; there's a short and I'm finding it. Third, if you want me to walk off the set just keep on shouting and I'll go and take a wander 'cos I've had a bellyful.'

Mr Hollywood from Brioude, Haute Loire, buttons his lip. He concedes: 'Forget it, we're all boiling over. Let's leave Paul with his short-circuit and run over the material. There's a candle on that shelf over there. Now, we're coming to close-ups and close-ins, Gérard on his back, Galia on her back on top of him, he is stuck into her' – this is starting to worry me – 'Galia opens up and Nadia moves in with plenty of action.' Nadia gives me a wink, I'm even more worried.

'What do we say?' I murmur.

'There's nothing written down. Do your own thing. Ah! The lights! Come on kids, positions. And you Gérard, a nice fat beat – see.' He signals to Nadia to handle it.

We are right into the hard stuff now, the camera is two feet from my vaginal entrance, I am sandwiched between Gérard who is mumbling, 'What a lousy job, what a lousy job' and a sparkling Nadia whispering 'Do you like this Galia, it's turning me on.'

John Turner is prancing round conducting us like he is Herbert Von Karajan. 'Get a beat, get a beat,' he orders Gérard.

On account of the power cut, we do not finish until 1 a.m. and are too tired even for a last drink.

July 8

Rumbles of discontent are sweeping through the College. The men are in open revolt saying they are not animals. Even the kindly Cyril says: 'You are asking too much.'

The ladies are exhausting the lads with their ministrations, extracting the very life from them. But they won't stop, they want more. Fights break out as they jostle for their turn to mount the steeds.

Madame De Chaussoy would like to bring in replacements, but she is worried about her budget, that is obvious. Gérard goes sick, and says what he has got.

'We'll catch it,' several women cry out. The entire project is heading for disaster.

July 10

I am not ashamed to confess that I go over the top in some of the *Charlotte* scenes.

The heat of the projector lamps, Nadia's lubricious lapping, Gérard's thrusts (yes, he can make it!) cause me to cry out in ecstasy. Which is precisely the moment when Johnny boy decides to cut. When I play-act and screech like a demented goose he keeps the cameras rolling. He's kinky.

July 11

The men have gone on strike at the College, and as with every strike the public are angry.

Some very fierce arguments break out, and I am amazed to see these extremists transformed into blind Furies calling for blood.

Cho-Cho does her best to quieten them down with lectures on the general theory of sexuality and its history, but the students won't have it.

They are haggard with frustration, they want their men back.

July 13

Charlotte is finished and we have seen the rushes.

We watched them in a tiny dust-laden room stinking of stale tobacco smoke, and I was absolutely horrified at what I saw. The picture has been synchronized but not edited. Turner says there will be hardly any editing.

The result is appalling – alignments quite amateurish, flat lighting, inaudible speech, washed-out colours. And there

116

simply isn't a story.

'Well, what do you think?' says John Turner when the lights go up. Even he looks a little shamefaced.

'Looks great to me,' says Gérard. 'Fast pace, plenty of rhythm, should go like a bomb.' Pity there wasn't a bomb under him, I'm thinking.

'Nadia?'

'I think it's really very good, yes, very erotic. The scenes with Galia are terribly exciting. She has a wonderful body.' Nadia is actually leering at me.

'And you Galia, how do you feel?'

'I think it's a disaster.' Nobody says a word, and then John waves for me to go on. 'Everything is hopeless: camera work, soundtrack, decor, the whole shape of the thing. We are not people but just ridiculous mechanical fucking machines. There's not an ounce of imagination in the picture, not a grain of humour, not a glimmer of life. It's like a butcher shop with the meat jumping around. It's not even shitty, it's merely devoid of any interest.'

A glum silence. I can see my 4,000 francs disappearing over the hill; pity I did not ask for an advance. Ah well, too bad, but I refuse to cringe.

'So that's your opinion of my picture?'

'Yes,' I pout, and then slip my top lip over the other.

The boss scratches his head pensively, looks at us one after the other, and slowly fetches a bottle of whisky over. He hands out glasses and we drink in silence.

'Galia is right,' he says quietly. 'This picture is a wash-out. And I've made 15 other wash-outs. The only reason I go on is that I have no choice. I have a wife, four kids and a house to support. I have always wanted to direct real films, with real decors, outside shots, action, something with life to it. I would have done Western pictures, crime stories, adventure, Robin Hood, exciting chases, suspense, with hundreds of extras, big names. I never had the opportunity and I haven't the talent. So I do porn. You've noticed sometimes I have faith in that silly little set and I play at film-making too. But

117

I'm no fool, I know we produce crap. I agree with you Galia.'

I get up and walk over to him, giving him a big sloppy kiss on his forehead: 'Sorry John-John, I didn't want to hurt you . . .'

'You can call me Léon, that's my name.'

July 15

The College is in an uproar. A disgraceful incident occurred today when a minority group of the women tried to force the three men to halt their strike action. Not for the first time. And again it was to no avail, for the lads are demanding fixed hours and improved conditions, not more than one woman per hour, and beer breaks.

'You sort it out with the management,' the women scolded. 'You have been taken on to do this specialized work, it's a contract, you can't hold us to ransom!' Hughes gives them a two-finger sign.

'We'll go back when we have written undertakings,' Gérard said. Cyril fluttered his eyelashes in agreement, and even his doe-eyes have a militant look about them.

'We'll see about that,' Valentine snapped. 'Get back to work and stop messing about.'

A group of three seized Gérard and started tearing off his clothes, he fights them off with a few back-handers and more women move in. Hughes and Cyril stand by Gérard but the men are losing ground fast.

Then they started dealing out punches. Fists are flying from both sides, and the noise is infernal. Cho-Cho barges in and grabs the women one after another by their necks.

'Stop this, the lot of you!' she roars.

The punch-up subsides and Cyril is spitting out blood from a cut lip. Gérard's clothes are in shreds and Hughes cannot open one eye. Some of the women are pretty dishevelled too, and they stand back glowering at the three men and rubbing their wounds.

Myriam and I are horrified. We are disgusted with the

turn of events. The yapping dies down and Madame De Chaussoy walks onto the platform, she surveys the extremists, some of whom are locked in battle with the moderates. But the pushing and shoving comes to an end, and we prepare for the masterful Cho-Cho to put us in our place. But she does not shout this time.

She says in an even voice: 'As the result of this unruly incident, the College will be closed until further notice.'

The entire hall freezes. The news sinks in and suddenly some women begin patting the men, wiping their cuts with their hankies, kissing them better, crying and sobbing and trying to make amends.

'I'll run out for some iodine,' a middle-aged lady says. 'Let me heat some water, that needs a poultice,' moans another.

The three males allow themselves to be pampered, the women are back in their element, looking after their menfolk, unstinting in their duty. It's all lovey-dovey again.

Myriam and I exchange astonished glances. The women have all turned into nurses, and there is no sign of the hideous shrews of minutes ago.

Which goes to prove what I have always contended, that, for women, sex is a thing apart.

July 17

It is true that I have just had my 21st birthday, but I am as agitated as ever, dissatisfied physically, constantly on heat. It's terrible.

I have this powerful urge that I cannot control, I need the Great Unknown, I have an irresistible longing for debauchery. A bell seems to tinkle inside me and I am a Pavlovian dog.

There are millions of women, men too probably, who immediately snuff out any desire in themselves, especially if they think it is wrong. They keep control, sublimate it, argue it out in moral terms, avoid risk like the plague.

I am exactly the opposite. Temptation, the fire in my

entrails, the torrent of bestial desire – all this I love. Oh, how I adore the craving when it comes! It's a drug and I have to have sex.

It happened last night during dinner with Matthieu, Myriam and Gérard.

'I say we go on to *Le Bassano*,' I announced. Already I am breathing heavily and a sensual huskiness accompanies my statement.

'*Le Bassano*, where's that?' Matthieu asks.

'You don't know?' says Myriam. 'Never heard it mentioned? But my dear old fellow you've spent too much time in your Chinese cooking. You should live with your epoch, take a refresher course.'

'What about *Le Bassano*?'

'It's a sex club,' I tell him. The very thought of it is turning me on.

'A what club?'

'S-e-x.'

'What's that mean?'

Myriam is annoyed: 'A place where people fornicate!'

Matthieu: 'You mean they need a club for that?'

'Oh come on, you'll see. Coming Gérard?'

'I'm off my form at the moment, and in any case it's too expensive, 400 francs a glass of whisky. Sorry there's a limit.'

'Be my guest,' Myriam coos, obviously as sex-starved as I am. It must be the wine.

'Sorry, another time.'

So we eventually leave, just the three of us: Matthieu, Myriam and I.

At *Le Bassano* the eye of the manager is even more bloodshot than ever. So is his nose, in fact I think he must have cirrhosis of the nose. People have a horror of suicide, and the bottle is less forbidding than the gun. But the result is just as awful.

'Ah Galia, our little princess,' he growls. He has 70° proof coming out of his ears, but he remembers names. He leads us to the bar, and I experience a surge of nostalgia at this return to my starting point for Big Sex.

I hoist myself somehow onto a stool. These ones are designed for tall men with thin bottoms, another phallocrat trick as we spread when sitting on the stools and our thighs are forced apart. Myriam and I don't look too bad, almost rivalling Marlene Dietrich.

'Haven't seen you for ages, Galia,' says the blue nose. 'How's your friend from Italy, so charming: Eduardo or Octavio isn't it?'

'Osvaldo, he's just fine. He's with a Canadian girl about half my age, and he loves her.'

'And you?'

'Oh me . . .' I wave a hand in a gesture that says I'm alone, not in love, I adore men but not just one, and Emmanuel was my last chance.

'How about a starter?'

'Something nice and strong, but not whisky. Business looks thriving by the look of it.'

'Plenty of action, that's true. But plenty of cops too. They are calling now every month, they must be underpaying them. It's a real scourge of our times, this inflation. But we survive.'

I am delighted to see that the place is nice and full, and it seems like the orange room is overflowing. As we sit there, we see several rear quarters flit past the doorway: big ones, little ones, droopy ones (ugh), round ones (mmmm!) belonging to who knows? Civil servants, secretaries, captains of industries, priests, call girls, generals' wives . . . It may be seeing them, or perhaps the Armagnac, but my tummy is getting mellower minute by minute.

Then I can wait no longer: 'Coming in Myriam? Coming in Matthieu?'

My companions enter slowly, but I commandeer the bed in the middle. The male fraternity catch on quickly as I lie prone, kicking my legs invitingly. Some recognize me, and before long I am surrendering myself to their every whim. Some take me on my back, others when I am on my tummy, others force me onto all fours and we play doggies. One middle-aged man rips his veined and full-ridge penis into my anus and I cry out, but at the same time he pinches a nipple and rubs me hard just above my clitoris and the pain becomes exquisite. I feel I am one huge sore, and that my anus is going to burst.

At moments I can see men waiting, masturbating like monkeys as they prepare for their turn. Little is said, but a young man protests: 'Excuse me, I was before you.' The other retorts: 'Pardon me, I've been here nearly 10 minutes!' He has trouble keeping his thing hard, and I quip: 'Too much of it makes you deaf.' He should know, he looks about 70, and when he mounts me he puffs and blows in my ear, concentrating for all he is worth. At last he utters a long groan and collapses on me like an eiderdown. I am shaking uncontrollably by now and rolling in a sticky pungent mess. I choose that moment to whisper: 'I didn't dare tell you, but I have syphilis.'

I am past caring, my sex is twice its normal size, I have had orgasm after orgasm and the craving has gone. In a dream I gather up my dress, my bra and G-string, someone hands me my shoes amid thanks. I stagger over to Myriam and Matthieu who are near the doorway and collapse into Myriam's arms.

'It was wonderful to watch,' she tells me bright-eyed. 'Sodom and Gomorrah was never like this. I came just looking.'

'It's purely physical.'

'Confucius here was explaining that the bacchanalia of ancient times achieved quite another dimension. He finds it rather sad, this club.' Her words underscored one certain fact: Matthieu was not really with us in spirit, and as she spoke he was looking at the fish in a tank next to the door.

I sat by him: 'We have to make do with the bacchanalia we've got. It's hardly our fault if we live in a society of decadents, whose idea of adventure is to drive up and down highways. You can criticize the people here as much as you like, but you will never convince me that these places are not necessary. Whether it's a knocking shop or a private sex party, we have to have it. Where else are we to let off steam and get back to normal? Our civilization will not accept sin, the diabolical, the incongruous, the abnormal, the non-standard. That kind of moral environment creates a huge build-up of tension and so you have to have places like this.'

Matthieu slowly raised his head: 'I don't need to let off steam. When I want to copulate, I copulate. If no-one's available I wait.'

A surge of anger went through me and I snapped: 'You're lucky, you're not abnormal like me. I need sex and sin and being naughty. I was born with a love of forbidden fruit, and that's how I get my thrills. I'm not saying it's right or wrong, but I have to have it. You can laugh, but I am really rather proud of the way I defend my pleasures.'

July 20

I am obsessed with sex, I think about it and want it all the time. I must have a new experience that is more daring than the last.

Yesterday I went on the rampage like an alley cat. In a small public garden at Denfert-Rochereau I egged on two total strangers in leather jackets, leading them behind a fence. I let them take down my knickers, I stood with my hands forward leaning against a statue, and let them have it off with me.

Later in the apartment block where a boy friend of mine lives, I got him to do it in the lift. Every time someone called the lift, I pushed the red emergency button to stop the lift. The danger of being discovered or the lift going wrong made it so much more exhilarating. Lifts are wonderfully secret and erotic places and they sway about too.

Last night another boy did it to me standing up inside an entrance porch in broad daylight. At any moment someone could have found us.

Myriam is as insatiable as I am, which is how we found ourselves today in a highly roused condition inside a sex shop in Rue de la Gaité in Montparnasse. We wore thin semi-see-through dresses and nothing underneath. People could see everything. I could feel every fibre of the material as it fluttered and wedged itself between my legs.

We went in slowly and found three or four men leafing through the literature. I glanced at some of the titles: *Schoolgirls On Heat*, *Toss Me Please*, *Vice Girls*. The men looked up as we sauntered in, and their tongues were almost hanging out. We were giving them something in the flesh to fantasize with. It would not have been half as fascinating for them had we been in the nude. Women know instinctively that desire can be infinitely more inflaming than the *fait accompli*!

Myriam and I approached one of the staff. I said in my cuddliest voice: 'We so wondered if you happened to have any – er – vibrators.'

'Vi... Yes of course, certainly *Mademoiselle*.' He can't have many bourgeoise customers.

The man fumbled behind the counter in a carton: 'These are ba-ba-ba-battery models.'

'Oh how nice, and how do they work?'

Fingers trembling, he showed us how to put the batteries in: 'You press the ON button and it works, it vibrates, you see.'

'Yes, but where is the best place to put it?'

'Pu-pu-pu-put it?'

Myriam helps out: 'Why don't you show us?' And she demurely drew up her dress with agonizing slowness, stood with her legs slightly apart and said: 'I hope it really does give relief.' She reached down and presented her genitals more prominently. The salesman had the machine in his hand and looked around at the other customers. Myriam said: 'Well come on, if we're going to buy one...' One of the bystanders had his hand in his pocket, and I saw the bump in his trousers moving.

A broad grin split the salesman's face: 'You're having a little joke with me, I can see, ha ha ha!'

'I am not joking, this is a serious matter, I need relief and be quick about it. Oh please!'

With calculated lasciviousness, but still pretending to be naive, she rolled her haunches ever so slightly, then said: 'Perhaps the other way round.' Myriam turned and bent forward a little, lifting her hem. She showed a beautifully rounded bottom, and I wondered how any man could resist her.

One of the customers saw his chance and grabbed the vibrator, trying to introduce it between Myriam's legs.

'Oh,' she sighed. 'But do be careful, lower down. Push the button, yes that's just right. Oh it's lovely, Galia we must buy it. Oh, it feels delicious.'

The salesman's mate is now guarding the door, and Myriam has ceased all pretence. She holds onto the counter and grits her teeth, throwing her head to right and left. We are all touching ourselves when she has her climax.

A few minutes later we left with our packet. We did not actually say it, but we both knew why we had done that in the shop. It's nice being a woman when you can tease. And it is so easy, because there are so many frustrated men, and most women won't dare make advances to men even though they want sex just as badly.

July 25

The vibrator has roused us both to fever pitch, Myriam and me.

Today we were in the Metro, and between Chatelet and Les Halles stations Myriam whispers to me: 'Do you think we are normal?'

'What's normal?'

'I don't know, like other people.'

'Then we're not normal. Look at the women in this carriage, they go out to work, have a husband, a fiancé or a

125

friend. They end up faithful spouses, good housewives, they have kids, build a home.'

Myriam giggles: 'We just have a hot stove, and you know where.'

'Do you envy them? Their fire is out, they spend all day doing their duty, conjugal or otherwise, getting meals, cleaning...'

'There's something to be said for a loving man who gives you reassurance. Is ours the next station?'

'No, two more. You know Myriam, I am keeping a diary, a sort of notebook.'

'Yes?'

'I write down everything that happens. I started it when I began to be sexually emancipated, when I was with Osvaldo. I thought it would help me work things out.'

'And are you keeping it going? Am I in it?'

'Of course, Myriam.'

'What do you write?'

'Everything that happens to us. The College, *Le Bassano*, the vibrator, everything.'

'Ooh! Has anyone seen it?'

'Oh no, you're the only one to know.'

'Darling Galia, I want to kiss you. Kiss me.'

We clung to each other in the swaying carriage, and kissed tenderly, sensually, desperately.

As we come out of it, a smart guy says: 'Another pair of cunt-suckers.'

His pal returns derisively: 'Lesbians, they're everywhere, what with Women's Lib and all...'

We flash loving messages to each other with our eyes, as we step off the train, holding hands.

III
DEBAUCHERY

September 2

After a long gap, I have decided to resume this diary and relate the *Roi-Henri* episode.

This is a villa perched on a hill in the snooty Western suburbs of Paris, right next to the Parc de Saint-Cloud.

The host and his wife receive guests in a rather dignified style. The old timbering gives the villa the appearance of a hunting lodge.

And hunting is indeed what the rendezvous is about. The huntsmen are numerous and not all hale and hearty. The 'game' is not always easy to find, and the males are famished.

The host lacks the friendly haze of the boss at *Le Bassano*, and is more like Alain Delon, the film star, in appearance. This sort of man has always attracted me and made me afraid at the same time.

I felt terribly vulnerable as soon as I was in the room. All eyes were on me, there was no standing on ceremony, not even a drink for the 'prey'. The female, that's little me on this occasion, enters the ring and the huntsmen size her up. There is a rich masculine odour of wild beasts, shirt sweat, leather, sperm.

The men standing in the shadows look at me crudely. I arrived with a man friend but he fades out at once, free to run riot if he wants with the hunters' own females. 'She's nubile... marvellous eyes... lively... what's she like from the back?' The comments are to the point, everyone knows why they are here.

Then suddenly, two steely-eyed men with slit mouths take my dress off, quickly but politely because these are distinguished people. And immediately several pairs of hands are pawing me, lightly pinching my bottom, thighs and breasts. I look this way and that, and they know my fear is half-genuine. I see several men unzipping their trouser fronts, but they keep their trousers on, so that they do not lose their dignity, maintaining their superiority over the female. They take out their penises, and most of them are already gorged and hard. Then the first one comes at me, two colleagues hold me down by my arms and the man sires me brutally. Then there is another and another. There is nothing romantic about it, and I feel humiliated. Even when a woman submits to being ravaged, she likes to be treated as a human being. This was too close to real rape, it was sadistic.

I left with my escort soon afterwards.

My legs were like cotton wool, I felt a wreck, I was still soggy, but I said: 'Let's walk a bit, I need air after that.'

There was a keen breeze on this early autumn evening and the woods were redolent of newly fallen leaves and of the good earth. I leant on my man, a friend but no more than a friend. I wanted to cry but I held it back.

I still feel uncomfortable about the *Roi-Henri* incident, and he is reserved.

September 3
Myriam is worried about me, and told me about a sexologist

a girl friend of hers heard about. To tell the truth I am running a little scared myself.

'He's called Dr K and he practises in Rue de Vaugirard. Why not give him a call, go and tell him about your problems? He may be able to help.'

I phoned for an appointment with Dr K and he fixed up to see me the same day, which was yesterday.

He is about 50, has thick black eyebrows, seems nervous and speaks in short rushes.

As soon as we are alone, he orders: 'Take your clothes off, I will examine you.'

Shocked, I blurt out: 'But I have not come to see you for any physical trouble. That side of it is perfectly in order.'

'Organic, psychological, everything is linked. Undress please.' He is extremely grumpy and I am not sure I like him.

Truculently I observe: 'If you think you can find my life-style problems in my vagina, you are an optimist.'

'Get undressed!'

I decide to dig my heels in, after all this is a genuine consultation: 'I'm sorry, I don't see the necessity.'

'As you wish,' he growls. 'Well, what's the difficulty?'

This is not an easy question to handle on the wrong side of the desk from an irritable man who keeps tapping the desk and shifting in his chair.

'I would like to know what is normal and what is not in the matter of sex.'

'Can you be more precise?'

'Well, for example, is it normal for a woman to want sexual relations with a lot of men?'

'How many?'

'Well, I don't really know, I haven't kept count. Sometimes I go for three or four days or even a week, and then make love in a day or a night with, say, 10 men.'

'I beg your pardon?'

'With 10 or 12 or perhaps 6. I mean, almost continuously.'

The consultation lasted about five minutes. Then Dr K wrote out a prescription in a rapid hand and thrust it at me:

'That will be 200 francs.'

I read what he had written down: *Two tablets Tranxène 5 three times daily. During crises one Valium 10 tablet. Relations twice weekly maximum.* My face dropped.

'Come and see me again in two weeks' time.'

'Certainly not! Here are your 200 francs, but I'd like to ask you a question first.'

'Yes?'

'In your view... Hey, are you listening?'

'I am.'

'In your view, is it dishonesty or stupidity that drives you on?' He is nonplussed and I add: 'I would guess it is stupidity. But you've got your 200 francs just the same, haven't you?'

September 5

Osvaldo phones, inviting me out for a party flung by 'a famous and remarkable and enthralling friend.'

I retort: 'Why don't you take your Canadian girl?'

'I couldn't do that, it's not the sort of evening for her. You know what I mean, she hasn't the style, the experience...'

Huffily I rant: 'You feel better with your old flame for a saucy evening, is that it? You don't want to contaminate your nice tender little girl with the barbarians. But you still want to have a dirty evening once in a while, and old Galia will suit just nicely!'

'Oh Galia, don't be silly, you...'

'I'll come on one condition: it must be good entertainment. If it's another miserable routine gallop, count me out.'

Osvaldo switches on the honeyed Caruso voice I know so well: 'Galia, I promise you'll love it, real entertainment, I'm not joking. Say you'll come, I need you.'

'Alright then.'

'Oh wonderful! Galia, I'll love you for ever. You are the most stupendous, the...'

'Don't climb up the curtains, as they say in Quebec. What do I wear? I'd prefer jeans to a ball gown.'

132

'You'll be wearing a peplum.'

'A what?'

'A Roman peplum. It's a flimsy white thing with a hole for your head and one for each arm. Nothing else of course.'

'And where am I suppose to acquire a peplum, if you please?'

'Everything will be supplied on the spot.'

It was well organized, and for an excellent reason. When Osvaldo introduced me to the host, I blinked and blinked again.

I recognized the creased laughing eyes of this 50-year-old personality known to the whole of France. In less than a split second my mind wrote out the story of his life: baby's bottle, potty, fingers in the jam, snatching small brother's toys, kicking nurse, giggling at nurse from the bath, touching his little penis for the first time, kissing his cousin under the apple trees, spluttering with a cigarette, sucked off in the Bois de Boulogne as a teenager, first real girl friend, she dumps him, second girl friend, and so on. Yes, I knew him! It's R. D., the T.V. and radio joker who runs the 'Musk and Truth' show on the radio.

'Delighted and honoured to have you with us,' he beams, taking my erotic temperature with a flick of his eyelashes.

'I listen regularly to your programmes,' say I. (My God, Galia, what a liar you are. You heard it once in a taxi stuck in a traffic snarl. The 'Musk' programme, of indescribable banality, consists of openings by fatty R.D. on the lines of 'And for you, what is happiness?', 'And for you, what is Man?', 'And for you, what is love?', 'And for you, what is wealth?'. He must have done about 5,000 programmes, all as pathetic, treacly and alienating as the one before. R. D. is the unctuous confessor of the French nation.)

'Come right over,' he croons. 'You must meet everyone.'

He takes me over to a third rate pop singer I recognize, one willing to flirt with anything risky as long as it sells his latest album: 'Galia, but she's bee-ootiful!'

A young neuro-psychiatrist, charming, twisted face and

133

probably nymphomaniac.

Next a ginger-haired fellow with a curl that keeps falling forward. I would like to lend him a hair-slide and wonder whether he runs on wind or sail power or both.

A blessed relief, I shake hands with a girl student aged 18 or 19, pretty and likeable at sight, obviously the carefree kind.

A businessman, ugly like most of them. The job makes, or deforms, the man, and in this case the result is grisly.

Another businessman, not quite so grisly no doubt because business is bad, with his lawful wedded spouse who keeps tittering and nattering about the weather in the park.

After that I am presented to a curious moon-like creature with a grey complexion seeping through her make-up. She has saucer eyes of a deep black. I am not surprised to hear her named as Stella.

Finally, there is the pearl of the evening: a tall striking beauty with natural grace. Large blue eyes, chestnut hair and a truly superb pair of legs. I gather she is our host's partner, for this evening at least.

R. D. then takes Osvaldo and me to our room, where the first thing we see are two immaculately white peplums. (Pepli? Pepla? I should have looked it up perhaps.)

'Well, I'll leave you to get changed,' says R. D. in his impeccable bronze voice. A round-the-clock professional is our R. D.

Dinner by candlelight with all of us in peplums, served by two adorable English girls disguised as Napoleon's grenadiers, which seems tough on them. They are wearing black trousers and golden jackets with frogs and loops, and have mustaches crayoned under their noses so that they look like twins.

'May I help you to some more consommé?' they ask in their delightful cross-channel accent. We can hear the question go right round the table in a sort of cotton-wool tone.

'I could eat grenadiers like that any day,' says the uglier of the businessmen, trying to get the party going.

'So would I,' shouts the pop singer, but then he would do anything as long as it sold another cassette.

'And you, Galia, how about two little grenadiers for you?'

The joke is already thin and I simply reply: 'I have a horror of anything military, but I think these two soldiers could change the views of any pacifist.'

And so it goes on for a while, with everybody well-behaved and respectable. I wonder when the perfect subjunctives will give way to the perfect whoop-up. The film of good manners seems fairly thin.

The answer comes with the grilled lobsters. The salient feature of the peplum is that it has gaps and the wearer is semi-bare on each side; and the thing about lobsters is that you have to wave your arms about as you tug, crack and gouge out the beasts with a variety of implements including fingers. Inevitably the garments ease open to reveal the ladies' breasts, and from that point onwards there is no holding back the men. Or the women. Wine flows freely as male hands insert lobster nippers into our yawning garments and fingers accidently press our nipples. Arms advance around our shoulders to help us with our lobsters and lose their way in our folds. The women make a fuss of being embarrassed, but it fools no-one, and in less than no time the pearl of the evening is squatting on her haunches, peplum round her waist, calling for offers. Needing no further encouragement the neuro-nympho sidles over to the pop singer and gropes him generously. The less ugly of the two businessmen makes a dive for me and massages my breasts as his wife looks on breathing 'Ah, ah, ah.' Osvaldo is working on the girl student and the ginger fellow buries his head in Stella's orbs muttering about cybernetics.

Then everything stops as suddenly as it has started, and the dessert is brought in.

All in all it is an excellent dinner with stimulating wine and efficient service. Added to that, we have the promise of more licentious events to come.

Logs crack in the huge fireplace as the toy grenadiers clear the table. Everyone is bourgeois again. The men shift the table to one side, freeing a large area in the centre of the room.

Our host advances and, as solemn as an archbishop at his own enthronement, unhooks a cord that works a pulley system.

Unusually excited, Osvaldo murmurs to me: 'I promised you entertainment.'

A pregnant hush descends on us as the English girls stand to attention next to the rope. R. D. emerges with a whip and whirls it round and round over our heads. He leers at the girls and strokes their faces.

'You are she-dogs, aren't you?' he says.

'Yes, we are she-dogs,' they recite like schoolchildren.

'You are little bitches.'

'We are little bitches.'

'And you have lost the war.'

'Yes, we have lost the war.'

'And you deserve to be punished.'

'Yes, you must punish us.'

The whip circles again and we cringe.

'What shall we do, ladies and gentlemen, to punish these wicked she-dogs, so that they do not forget it?'

'Thrash them,' says the ugly businessman.

'Ah, ah, ah,' squeaks the silly wife.

'We shall give them the whip, beat and thrash these naughty she-dogs.' He reads strip cartoons in bed, I am sure. 'First we shall take their clothes off.'

Osvaldo assumes a sickly grin and advances to remove their clothing. He loves anything to do with teenage girls. He is showing his teeth like an overgrown boy scout who has won a badge.

The fancy tunics come off first, and we see the girls' white breasts, two little apples adorned with pink cherries. They tremble as Osvaldo bends down and takes their shoes off. He undoes their belts and slowly slides down their trousers with

136

their little white knickers inside. They step out of them and are completely naked. Osvaldo's eyes are shining.

The radio confessor lifts up their arms and ties their wrists together. They are prisoners back-to-back.

R. D. scowls and walks round the girls, threatening with the whip and licking his lips. He looks genuinely cruel.

He gives the whip a sharp crack, and the silly wife goes 'Ooh.' They ought to gag her, or she is going to spoil everything. We need complete quiet now.

Thwack – thwack – thwack the whip goes, and the two girls jump each time, their breasts shaking. I notice something else now, there is a bulge in the whipman's trousers. His eyes are glistening, he is sweating, twirling the whip faster and faster. He is in earnest and the cracks are getting louder. I look at Osvaldo's trouser front and see that he has a bump too.

I lean over to him: 'He won't really hurt them, will he? There'll be trouble.'

'I don't think so. He's done it before, and so have they, and the whip makes more noise than anything else. He got it in Japan.'

The dishy tall girl appears from nowhere, she stands in front of a spotlight, in her peplum, and we can see her curves outlined through the thin material.

'Have pity on them, please have pity on them,' she cries, loading on the emotion by the shovelful. She has a lovely voice.

R. D.: 'They are bitches, whores...' He really believes it. He is into strip cartoons up to his scrotum, and the make-believe lashes crash down. Lasciviously, I imagine I am a man and can turn this fantasy into reality, thrashing the girls so that they scream with pain. R. D. could do that and get away with it.

But the older girl rushes up to the English pair and hugs them. She flings off her robe and rubs her mound of Venus against one of the girl's pubic areas, then she does it to the other. What delicious bodies they have! But there is no time for me to ogle them, for the host has dropped his trousers and thrown the whip aside. He walks awkwardly towards the trio, his phallus hard and shiny. The veins are standing out.

At this turn of events the rest of us leap up. The men cast aside all attempt at courtesy and we of the feminine gender stand by and watch as the pop singer forces his penis into the vagina of one adolescent and the businessman pumps the other like a crazed bull. The poor mites, they are not fully developed and it must hurt them terribly. A whipping would have been better. I notice the idiot woman wrestling under a man, but we others are frantically trying to pair off now. We are all naked and can't restrain ourselves.

The show goes on until dawn, or rather the sideshows do. It would be easy to mock us. We could be dismissed as mentally unhinged, completely deranged, the scum of civilization. But we do no harm, and everyone is unhinged in some way, and all are sexually obsessed. If you are to make a distinction it should be between those who are obsessed WITH sex and those obsessed AGAINST it. The latter are the silent majority and they have won the battle so far.

Dawn comes at last, salmon pink and with its message of hope. The guests are eking out the last of the night's pleasure, but I go off on my own in the grounds of the house, away from the dirty glasses and cigarette butts and the garments strewn on the floor. I watch for a while as the sun comes up.

I am calm and I reflect that, in the realm of pleasure, anything is permitted provided it does nobody any permanent harm.

September 8

I am seriously worried about myself, anguished about the future. Last night I had another big session with a man I know, lasting hours and hours. Increasingly I need sex and I want it raw. I become frenetic, demanding multiple orgasms any way I can get them. Afterwards I flop around as if drunk. What does it signify? Am I mad and don't know it? This is no

138

joke, being a slave to my racing libido.

The anguish takes on new urgency at the moment, because Myriam has actually started with an analyst.

I phoned her: 'Myriam darling, what's good for you must be good for me, because we are alike. I feel out in the cold. What's your chap's name?'

'He is a woman, she's called L. C.'

'Would you mind if I call her?'

'Of course not, *chérie*, how super to have the same analyst.'

Yesterday evening I put in a call to L. C. She was rather stuffy, saying she could not possibly treat us both, in view of our intimate relationship. It would upset the analytical process. To cut a long story short, she told me to look elsewhere.

I am getting desperate, so I do what she says. By chance (the experts in this field claim there is no such thing as chance) I come across someone in the ad columns of *Le Nouvel Observateur*, my old hunting ground. 'Analyzed by Lacan, fee depends on client's situation, ring 732.85.19.'

My appointment is for tomorrow at 4.30 p.m.

September 9

I have seen him. It was close by Vincennes Metro station, on the fourth floor, with the door stating simply 'R. Psychoanalyst'.

I rang the bell and the door opened to reveal a short man who waved me into his office. He's about five foot tall, not much more.

Her perches on his chair and flaps his hand at a seat on the other side of the desk. I slip into it and our conversation goes roughly as follows:

R: 'You wanted to see me.'

Me: 'Yes I saw your ad by chance in *Le Nouvel Observateur*.'

R: 'Perhaps it's not chance.' (Aha, I was right!)

Me: 'Well anyway, your ad reached me. I think that's the term.'

R: 'Say it how you like.'

Me: 'How would you say it?'

R: 'It's not my problem.'

Me: 'Alright then. I called you because I am wondering whether I ought not to start some analysis.'

He looks at me with every appearance of thinking. I am thinking he is pretending to.

Me: 'What do you think?'

R: 'About what?'

Me: 'About my idea of undergoing analysis.'

R: 'And what do you think?' (I am now wondering how long this little game is going on. Why do these people always answer with another question? Answer: why not?!)

Me: 'We could stop swapping questions maybe. It's too much like a fight.'

R: 'Why do you say "fight"?'

Me: 'Because it's like an indoor game where the winner is the one who gets in most questions, and the one who gives most answers is the loser. It's too easy playing that game and giving nothing away. I saw your ad, you are the one who took the first step, not me. So I'm the one to ask the questions, OK?'

R: 'That's not a question, it's a proposition.'

Me: 'It amounts to the same, don't be funny. You used this ad to fish for clients, patients or whatever. Why?' (If he says 'why not' I'm leaving.)

R: 'Call it fishing if you like. I am a psychoanalyst, my job is to listen to patients. I merely announced that I am here.'

Me: 'Why didn't you use a big display ad? A full page spread with the headline PSYCHOANALYST SEEKS PATIENTS? I want to know why you set up as an analyst. You could be a dentist, teacher, dancer, grocer, poker player or a stockbroker. An analyst, why? What does it achieve for you? What does it mean to you?'

R: 'What do you think?'

Me: 'That's enough! Enough questions and answers. I am making inquiries, I could become a client, I know nothing about analysis, I need to know what it is, how it works, what you do. You are in a specific job, and I want to know about it, what I am letting myself in for.'

R: 'If I explain what analysis is, I would lead you along a path you would not perhaps take on your own. Every analyst has his own way of helping the analysis along. It's not for me to say what psychoanalysis is, strange as that may seem.'

Me: 'So you are asking me to jump in blindly, into the unknown. Like Pascal said: "Kneel down and you will believe." You are saying: "Lie down and you'll see." I like to know where it's heading.' Especially the kind of couch where I shall be laying my head and resting my bottom. 'I need to know who you are, what your story is. All I know is that you have been analyzed by Lacan. So he's a big name. May I ask why you mentioned that in your ad? A quality reference perhaps? Meaning you've been properly analyzed yourself, lain on France's number one couch? What does that badge mean, "analyzed by Lacan"? What plus point does it give you that he's analyzed you? Extra know-how, super-power? Answer that!'

R glowers at me, I repeat the last question or rather the demand. He keeps on glowering.

Me continued: 'You stated it in writing "analyzed by Lacan" and that must mean something. I have a right to know what it means for you.' He remains tight-lipped. 'Good God, are you going to answer? Your pitch is too easy, you keep quiet and the patient fends for herself. Well it won't work with me. I have a right to know all about you as a practitioner.'

R: 'You have a right.'

Me: 'So you haven't lost your tongue. What's it mean "analyzed by Lacan"?' Renewed silence. 'What's it mean?' Silence. 'I demand a reply. Huh, so you won't reply.'

R: 'What would you like me to reply?'

Me: 'Ha, so we're back to the pussy-footing! Well you can

find someone else to love you, you and your question-answer game and your wise old neutrality, your small ad and your chocolate medal. You can stuff your couch, you cut no ice with me. Find some other victim in *Le Nouvel Observateur*. And good hunting!'

September 11

I am still mad at the dwarf analyst during the evening and I need to get him out of my system.

I have bugs in my panties and I show up at *Le Bassano* where the boss gives me a great big smile.

'On your own?'

'Yessir.'

'But...'

'There's no but. I ain't alone because I'm here. Dribble me out some of your firewater. I want to take off, fly round the world, be nice with everybody.'

He gives me a quick glance: 'I've got some good grass, if you're interested. Let me roll you a joint.'

'That's nice, but no thanks. Give me a brandy, and then I want to be laid. Any good stallions tonight?'

'It's a little early, people take a while to warm up. But there's a hot gringo from South America looks like he'd shoot at anything that moves.'

I down the brandy and stroll into the orange room. The first thing I see is the gringo playing at humpty-back with a large squashy woman in her mid-forties. The South American has a neat mustache across his mouth and plenty of not-so-neat hair everywhere else. Except on his head which is slicked down like Rudolph Valentino's. He is a big man, this is going to be quite an experience.

I can smell leather, the fragrance of raw skin, and I throw a husky 'Hullo hombre' at him. Slowly I gather up the skirt of my dress and lift it till I judge my lace curtains are just showing. (I felt like frilly things tonight, and it looks like I chose right.) He stops wallowing in the swamp and stares at me open-mouthed. I close my eyes, swivel left and right, I have him in my power and I like it. I strip in professional style, and he gets up and rushes at me, fingering the lace on the only remaining article of clothing.

I goad him: 'I'm a better heifer maybe? Come on picador, show me how you do it. Let's see if you can ride me too.'

He really goes for this tarty act, and rides me in the customary position for a while with his jaws clamped firm, his black eyes shining.

This boy sure has muscles and he turns me over like a flapjack.

'You play bitch,' he croaks.

'I play bitch, *si signor!*'

He jams one hairy arm over my back, the other under my neck, so that my back arches to breaking point. His phallus edges between my vulva and goes on entering, he withdraws and then thrusts and thrusts repeatedly. I am entirely his and I can't savour enough of his meat. Never have I felt so raunchy. He is indefatigable and I want it to go on for ever. He doesn't come and I am glad. I glance about and now see a whole circle of spectators admiring our performance.

I wave a small pink-faced young man over to me: 'Please help me, bring me a triple brandy.' This he does and wafts it near me. 'Let me have it, let me have it, don't be afraid, I won't eat you.'

The picador releases me and I drink the brandy in one go, then he enters me again. The brandy sets me on fire and I imagine myself being sired by a donkey.

The young man is in front of me and my hands find his belt. He lets me undo it and I pull down his trousers, then his underpants. His little penis is pink too but limp, he puts it in my mouth and I make it harder, sucking and sucking and loving my power to make it harden. The two men are penetrating me, my mouth and my vagina. The brandy has rendered me frantic, and I can feel the gringo getting to monster size. This time I am at their mercy, being buffeted, and then they ejaculate together as I thrash about with my head wildly. I go into a pleasure-pain coma.

I can remember little of what followed, although it was only yesterday.

I do know that a naked man aged about 60 with a fine bronzed body put his head beteeen my thighs and that I jerked again and again. Others threw themselves on me and violated me. I remember seeing men masturbating and spurting over me. An auburn-haired woman with ginger fur laid back and showed me her sex, and I got up and put mine against hers imagining I had a penis, and we both came. I rolled my haunches forward and back pressing my clitoris against hers and rubbing and rubbing, and got off again.

I was completely drunk and lost count of the males who took me. One smelled putrid, probably hormone trouble. I provoked them and insulted them, and one protested: 'Not so loud mademoiselle, you can have us all but you must keep your manners.'

Mad with rage I got up and staggered against him, enveloping him in my arms. I got him on the floor, forced my tongue between his teeth, then grabbed his thing and chewed it. Then in a final gesture of defiance I stood over him with my legs apart and pissed all over his belly. Then I suppose I collapsed.

Never had I behaved as outrageously as I did last night. I lived the ultimate in sin and debauchery with every fibre of my body. My whole being was a red raw sex. I was going to hell and I did not care. I was in a state of despair.

September 14

Today I made another attempt to fix up an analyst.

This time I went to see a sober-looking man in one of the high-class avenues in the 17th *arrondissement*. The time was 3 p.m. and he had me shown into his office where I felt humble, almost contrite.

Below I give the conversation word for word, partly because I recall it clearly but also to cheer me up when I am old and grey.

'I asked to see you because M. L. gave me your name. I am wondering whether I ought to undergo a course of analysis.'

'The fee is 300 francs.'

'I beg your pardon.'

'Three hundred francs.'

'You mean each session costs 300 francs?'

'Quite so.'

'I'm afraid that is more than I can afford. I am a student and my father gives me a monthly allowance, but ...'

'It's 300 francs.'

'So I understand. And the sessions last how long?'

'Why do you ask that question?' (Oh for pity's sake, we are into pat-a-ball again.)

'It's so that I can fit it in with my work, other activities ...'

'Sessions are short ones, lasting no longer than 15 minutes.'

'If I come at 2 o'clock, can I be sure of getting away by 2.15?'

'Certainly, it's 300 francs.'

'I see. How many sessions a week?'

'Three.'

'Making 900 francs a week.'

'Quite so.'

'In other words 3,600 francs a month. That's more than my monthly budget. So with you I shall have to stop eating, buying clothes, and sleep in the open. How do you think I can manage that?' No answer. 'Could you arrange for a reduction, at least at first?'

'It's 300 francs.'

'Strange, but I was told that psychoanalysts adjust their fees to match their clients' incomes. That's why I'm asking for a reduction. The fee seems on the high side.'

The shrink glares at me, he does not move or speak, and we stay like this for a while.

I volunteer: 'At 300 francs per 15 minutes, you should be a rich man. Social security doctors don't even ask 60 francs for

15 minutes.' No reaction. 'Supposing you work eight hours a day, which would be the normal thing, you make 9,600 francs a day.' No reaction. 'With that kind of money, couldn't you take on some impoverished patients? Do you absolutely need nearly 10,000 francs a day?'

Calmly he replied: 'I am afraid our conversation is turning into an argument. I have said all I have to say. It's 300 francs.'

'Not for me. I prefer to remain neurotic than pay money to a crook. Good day to you.'

Setpember 15

I'm trying so hard. Another shrink, a woman.

About 30, brown hair, big doleful eyes that still missed nothing. On her desk a large photo of Freud with piles of his books including the *Gesammelte Werke* along with the English and French translations. A complete Sigmund library. And around stood his friends, disciples, pupils, traitors and renegades: Jung, Ferenczi, Rank, Groddeck, Adler, Abraham, Klein, Winnicott, Lacan and the others.

Hélène W. offers me a seat, and I sit on the edge of a couch. She comes over and sits by me.

'So you are thinking of starting analysis?'

'Yes.'

'Why do you feel the need?'

'I want to sort myself out, learn more about myself, try to put right some things that are not right and make me feel awful. I want some of the ache to go away and to feel better when I am fine. I want a better existence.'

'You're unhappy?'

'No. Yes. I don't know.'

'Perhaps you don't feel you are loved enough?' (Crash, the first wrong deduction!)

'I feel I am loved enough, loved too much in fact.'

'Are we ever loved enough?' says Hélène W., fingering back a long wisp of brown hair that is tickling her nose. A silence follows. All analysts without exception have the irreplaceable quality of knowing the value of quiet.

'Men, it's men,' I whisper. 'That's why I need analysis.'

A new interest appears in her expression: 'Do they do nasty things to you?' (Crash, number two error.)

'No, that is not the problem.'

'Tell me what the difficulty is, then.'

She seems disappointed. Her gaze is now tragic, and she reluctantly clears it away with fluttering lashes. It would certainly have suited her better if I had been beaten up by men, raped, sodomized by force, tortured or strangled. Unfortunately they have always been so nice to me.

'There are no difficulties,' I gulp.

'But you mentioned a problem.'

'I? Never!'

'Yes you did.'

'Oh no.'

'You said it was because of men that you needed analysis.'

'That's certainly true. But it's not strictly a problem.'

Actually I am not being quite honest with her, because I sense that it is not with her that I want to lay myself bare.

'You want sessions because of men...'

'Yes, because of them.'

'Why's that?'

'Because I despise them.' She falls to reflecting on this, linking facts, kicking them around, looking for symbols.

'Do you know why you despise them?'

'That's the trouble, I don't.' Her eyes are soft and tender, she smiles at me, moves a bit closer.

'Don't worry too much, we can sort all that out together...' (Crash, third error.)

Then I pour it out: 'I don't want an analyst who reassures me. Even before you start, you are crushing me with kindness. You want to help me and that in itself means you are not helping me. When I need comforting I go and see my friend Myriam, when I want to be petted I go with a male friend. I don't need tenderness, I need clear facts. You are very kind, responsive and sympathetic, but I feel that if I started analysis with you, myself on the couch and you in the chair, we should soon be changing places.'

My lips expand into a sweet smile: 'I believe *you* are the one who needs lots of love, but I can't help you. Let me give you a big kiss, you are so nice.'

September 17

At 1 a.m. today, when all respectable people are in their own beds, Sylvain and I went in his car to Porte Dauphine on the edge of the Bois de Boulogne.

Sylvain, who has made love to me just once, has a small electric car. He drove slowly with about three thousand other cars with headlights on, round the main traffic island and then along the dark roads lined with hookers in net stockings, showing their breasts and beckoning to the drivers. This night as on so many others they sway their hips, blow kisses and heap scorn on the transvestites. Here the law of the sex jungle holds good, each animal defending its territory tooth and claw.

My escort slows the car alongside a sumptuous girl with long hair drawn back, superb lashes and long legs that peep tantalisingly through her brazen red slit dress. Her breasts are uncovered, firm, round and full. She has a perfect body, except that *she* happens to be a *he*, one of the many Brazilians who have been operated on. We stop and I wind down the window.

'Fifty for a suck, hundred for lovemaking,' he says in a melodious voice straight from the Sertão.

'Do you go with women too?'

He freezes a moment, leans forward to get a closer look at us. This is something new for him, a woman customer.

I extract myself from the midget car and take the 'girl' by the hand. She is taller than I am.

'Come on, Sylvain.'

'Er, sorry Galia, not my kind of trip.'

148

'Well wait there till I come back.'

Sylvain throws his head around left and right, worried. Shadowy figures move furtively from tree to tree, illuminated briefly as the headlamps show the woods.

'Alright, I'm tagging along,' says my companion.

'Afraid of the Big Bad Wolves?'

'Frankly, I'd feel better at my place or yours with the lights on, a drink, cushions, music.'

'Oh don't be silly, learn to live dangerously, it's something new. Hurry up, I can't wait.'

The Brazilian leads us under some branches and we reach a small deserted clearing. I fish out some banknotes and the Brazilian switches on a little torch to check them. He smiles broadly, it's more than enough.

'You want lovemaking?' You bet I do. He has an honest face, a gaze soft as velvet. I am longing to see the rest of him and I tell him.

'I want to see you strip, and then we'll try some improvisations.'

'Provisions?' The angel hardly understands French, and I squeeze his hand: 'Don't worry, we are nice people.'

He is so utterly erotic that I catch my breath. He unhooks the dress and lets it slide off languidly. He moves exactly like a real stripper, and even Sylvain releases a low whistle of admiration.

His panties are white and show up invitingly in the half-light. He keeps them on and moves his belly and hips sensually. My mouth is watering as I watch his dark body in its undulating dance.

He slows to a halt and theatrically whisks off his pants, throwing them a few feet away. The Brazilian stands still, with proud breasts heaving as he recovers from the dance. His penis is sticking out exactly horizontal in a semi-erection. The effect is sensational and Sylvain and I are unable to comment, such is our emotion.

Excited beyond measure, for this is really something bewitching, I feel the bitter-sweet desire in my loins. I take

149

two steps forward.

He does not move when I touch him, caressing his whole body, avoiding his breasts. I kiss his right arm and play with his golden bracelet, drawing the hand past the elastic round my hips and placing it on my mound. The transvestite pulls his hand back in an instinctive gesture as his fingers make contact with my moist vaginal lips. I enclose his hand and try to show him how to fondle me. I realize then that he has never done this before, and my heart melts for him. It is like being teacher to a 10-year-old boy.

'How old are you?'

'Nineteen.'

'Where are you from?'

'Sao Paulo.'

'Have you ever made love with a woman?'

He shakes his head. Oh bliss! I want him, I want him, I want him.

I pull down my own panties and open my dress. I must go slowly and not frighten him. I kiss a shoulder the texture of moleskin and work my way to his breasts, taking a nipple hungrily into my mouth. I feel his penis and find that he remains half-cocked. This increases my desire. I want him to possess me, the urge is frantic and I gently rub my orifice against his sex in quick movements. But he remains in weak turgescence, his unruly member is exasperatingly uncooperative. I am desperately trying to get him up, thinking how marvellous it would be if I could get it off myself with this man-woman with the appeal of both male and female. I yearn to be penetrated by this bisexual as our breasts press together. I began fondling him more subtly, titillating him as I have done to men so often, but the more my desire increases the less he is stimulated.

'Don't you ever get hard? Concentrate! What's it for, what do you like?'

'Please men, not women,' he says.

'Sylvain it has to be you, come here.'

'But . . .'

'Stand here and let him do it.'

My escort opens his zip, the Brazilian kneels down and takes him into his mouth. Soon the transvestite's phallus stiffens and rises. I throw Sylvain aside and pull the man's shaft into me and it keeps firm. I ride it wildly, clinging to him hopelessly.

September 18

My head is a rushing torment of noise. Am I normal or beyond help? What is to become of me?

I know now that only treatment can save me, can give me the answers I must have.

Setpember 24

My debauched condition is worsening.

Close by Réaumur-Sebastopol Metro station two evenings ago, I walked the street clad in an outrageous miniskirt and a see-through blouse. I have laid my make-up on thick, my lips are two red weals. Men fall in step behind me as I saunter along. The regular girls eye me with hostility, and I am scared of pimps. But at last a man comes up to me.

'What's your price?' He may be a pimp.

'Five hundred francs.'

His mouth turns down, I am obviously not worth it.

'Two hundred, in the car,' he mutters.

'What car?'

'Mine.'

I nod and follow him. In the passion waggon, he pokes me hurriedly as I lay sprawled diagonally on the back seat. I feel no emotion but grit my teeth, then leave him to look for another client.

Later in a nightclub in the 17th *arrondissement*, I shock everyone by starting a striptease act. I am groggy with drink, and they take me out. My male companion starts an argument over it, but we cannot get back inside.

I get as far as the *Katmichou*, where only women are allowed. I play the clown and appeal for partners. I remember attaching a celluloid penis to my loins, and going round the tables asking girls: 'Would you like it?' One or two nod, I walk forward with the thing and they help me introduce it.

In the early hours I stop a young couple in the street. I go straight up to the man and put my tongue into his mouth. They are flabbergasted, so I kiss the girl too. 'How about the three of us going to bed?' They march off briskly.

Then yesterday in the Luxembourg Gardens I sat on an iron chair in the sun, the metal hurting my bottom through my muslin dress. After a while I spread my legs and keep the material taut, I am wearing nothing underneath and people can see my sex. A group of men go jogging by, I beckon to one and take him behind a clump of foliage.

September 30

This cannot go on much longer, I have few illusions left, I am willing to have any man, any phallus, a woman. My head is whirling, I have sunk low, anything is good for an orgasm. I am a wild animal permanently on heat, I have lost all sense of control. I shall be picked up by the police soon, I can see it coming.

October 2

Thank God, I have found my analyst.

We exchanged a look, shook hands and within minutes I knew this was the one. I did not even harbour any sexual designs on him.

He is oldish, of sturdy build, slow in movement, and the reliable type. I trust his limpid blue eyes, he is attentive, I know he is going to understand.

He is not icy, tense, stuffy or play-acting like the others. We sat in armchairs and chatted away. I told him how I

wanted sex all the time, how I kept swinging between elation
and gloom, how I was full of contradictions, how confused I
was.

'Do you think I can possibly pull out of this?'

He could have been evasive, replying 'What do you think?'
or not even bothering to answer.

All he said was: 'Yes.'

It seems absurd but that little word filled me with
happiness. I threw myself onto his lap and gave him a great
big kiss on the cheek. He showed no surprise but took it
naturally. He is my real daddy.

October 5

Today I went on the couch for the first time.

It is a leather couch, low in height, with a rust-coloured
piece of material on it. There were two pillows, one on the
other, and a small carpet thing for the feet, in case it was a
rainy day!

In accordance with Freud's method, I could not see the
analyst and faced away from him, but he could watch me.

At first I was uneasy: 'This is not very convenient for
speaking.'

'Why's that?'

'You are sitting and I am lying down.'

'That's the usual way it's done.'

'But why must I lie down? I could sit too, or stand up even.'

'People think in a different way when they lie down.'

'How do they think then?'

'That's not for me to say, you'll see how you get along. You
can always get up if you really want to.'

'No, let's keep it orthodox. So fire away, I am lying down.
Where do we start?' Silence. 'What do we start with, what
shall I tell you?' No comment. 'The first thing I remember,
my childhood, my first disappointment, what do you want to
know? Please tell me, what should I say?'

He speaks: 'There is no must about it, you know. You are

153

not being interrogated. Say whatever occurs to you, without sorting it out, let it come on its own.'

'That's not going to be easy, my ideas are often all mixed up, they come in waves simultaneously. Take that painting over there, when I look at it I think of several things at once...'

'Tell me one of them.'

'Well, a horse. I don't know what the painting's supposed to be, but it makes me think of a horse...'

I stop, aware that he is almost touching me, waiting and listening. I think of horses in the Camargue country in Provence, a white stallion with an erection, with a fantastically long member. I don't talk, I let the pictures go through my mind.

My analyst interrupts with a quiet 'Yes?' and I realize I ought to say something: 'I was thinking of horses, in the Camargue, about a horse I saw as a little girl. The stallion was on his back legs and he put his tummy against the mare and I was fascinated by his thing, his big organ, and I felt funny. I think I must have dreamed that...'

October 8

The analyst has fixed up two appointments a week, and I asked him how long the sessions would probably go on for.

'Two years, perhaps 10, perhaps longer.'

'I can't believe it, I couldn't possibly carry on for 10 whole years, or even eight or four.'

'That is very positive of you, wanting to move ahead quickly.'

'Let's say two years, three at the most. How does that look to you?'

'Just fine.' I want to cry on his shoulder in gratitude.

I feel exalted, a great adventure is beginning, I shall attempt to become the person I really am, the person I don't know yet. Obstacles will be swept away, pretences thrown aside, I shall be getting closer week by week to reality.

I can honestly say that today I began a new existence. I am not sorry about the eventful past months, no doubt I had to go through that. No doubt too I shall see things in better perspective as a result of the analysis.

I am entering this new life such a happy person. I am so full of joy at the prospect. Everything's going to be alright.

October 10
On the couch: 'I had better start with the day Osvaldo and I were sitting at the *terrace* at *Fouquet's*. We had arranged to meet Jemal there and suddenly I saw him coming up Avenue George V ...'

LUST IN PARIS

Mireille opened the door. She was wearing a mauve negligée. It revealed two round breasts which looked firm enough, for all their years of being fondled and sucked. Florian tilted back her head, she pulled his down, and they kissed lingeringly. She was a tall woman, blonde and somewhat marked by alcohol, sun and the general wear and tear of life, but still attractive. Mireille was hot. Exceptional. She would do it anywhere, any time. And probably with anyone, thought Florian with a trace of bitterness.

Also available in Star

LUST IN PARIS

Antoine S.

Translated from the French by
Celeste Piano

A STAR BOOK
published by
the Paperback Division of
W.H. Allen & Co. PLC

A Star Book
Published in 1986
by the Paperback Division of
W.H. Allen & Co. PLC
44 Hill Street, London W1X 8LB

First published in France by Editions Robert Laffont under the title
Florian ou le savoir-jouir

Copyright © Editions Robert Laffont, S.A., Paris 1984

Printed and bound in Great Britain by
Anchor Brendon Ltd, Tiptree, Essex

ISBN 0 352 31654 3

In memory of the master, Henry Miller

'Greatness of character does not consist in having no passions. On the contrary, one must possess them to the highest degree yet hold them in check.'

Nietzsche

1

FLORIAN AND GULLIVER

Florian always slept naked, whatever the season, the circumstances or the bed.

That morning he woke up early, tugged awake by Gulliver, which sprang to attention as it invariably did at the start of a new day. The lively creature's fiery, sensitive head was enjoying itself, rubbing against the linen sheet which scratched and tickled it simultaneously, giving rise to a delicious sensation.

His eyes half open and his desire on edge, Florian allowed himself to wallow in the pleasant sensation of this gentle awakening. Thoughts and ideas gradually began to take shape, then darted off like butterflies. Where was he? Whose bed was this? With whom had he spent the night? He stretched out his right arm, then extended the left: no one else on either side.

The mists of the night cleared and the world resumed its familiar contours. He was surfacing, gradually. He recognised the window, the ceiling – with its long crack rather like an aerial photo of the wall of China – the room and all its familiar contents were there, everything in place. He was in his own home.

He checked out the assortment of scents which assailed his nose as it ventured over the edge of the sheet, and sniffed at the air with a series of little inhalations similar to those of an animal emerging from its burrow. When wine-tasting, only very small mouthfuls are required, after which the tastebuds themselves go into action.

In much the same way, Florian was inhaling small measures of air through his nostrils, respiring and exhaling with a subtlety acquired only by many years of olfactory practice.

The predominant aroma at present – the orchestra's big bass drum, so to speak – was that of coffee, a mixture of Robusta and Arabica apparently. Yes, that was it: Arabusta 60%, medium quality and medium ground, imported from Africa. Over this vacuum packed powder had been poured water insufficiently heated.

The robustly Arabic effluvia had climbed three floors and infiltrated beneath four doors before finally reaching the fifty million olfactory neurons nestling in their velvety mucous. Some of the neurons – specialists at detecting alkaloids – transmitted their infinitely complex signals to the brain, after amplifying them a million times. 'Coffee, yes! Arabica, Robusta, filter-style, made with ordinary tap-water, .02% fluoride content.'

But actually Florian was none too bothered about the coffee. While aware of this effect upon his nasal passages, he turned his attention towards a very much subtler odour, that of the day itself. Nostrils aquiver, he evaluated the quality of the air, the atmosphere of a fine spring day. For it promised to be fine indeed, the atmospheric pressure around 1025 millibars, and dry too, hygrometry between 60 and 70%. Florian opened his eyes wide. The sun was filtering through the wooden shutters.

Gulliver however chafed with impatience, head rearing with displeasure at this bachelor's reveille.

'Relax old fellow,' Florian muttered, stroking the warm rounded tip with his fingers casually. He did not linger thus, reserving such pleasures for later. 'Keep calm! The day's just beginning. You'll have your fun today – more than once – if not several times! Pretty girls await us, women are everywhere!'

Each day he would marvel at the thought that every other person in the world was of the female sex. What a wonderfully gluttonous prospect! Hundreds, thousands of trim little buttocks just asking to be caressed, and myriads of lissom legs waiting for one thing only – to dance and kick to the frenzied jig of as many bucking Gullivers.

'Who will I seduce today?' wondered Florian Nazulis, 33, b. Paris, father: clarinettist, mother: maternal; *address*: 69 Rue des Saints-Pères, Paris 6; *height*: 1.74m; *weight*: 72 kilos; *blood group*: A Rhesus Positive; *hair*: light brown; *eyes*: blue; *nose*: aquiline; *status*: twice divorced, 12 times separated, engaged 20 times; *profession*: wine writer and columnist for *Gourmet Magazine*; social security no: 1.51.03.75.129.0014.2; *birthsign*: Scorpio with Leo rising; *astrological characteristics*: problems with women, chiefly sexual instability, hyper-energetic; *psychological aspects*: prone to neurosis, calls his genital organ Gulliver, apparently converses with and listens to it. Case history gives cause for alarm. Does not look after himself properly.

'Who'll I seduce today?' Nazulis wondered, stretching out his arms in a languorous imitation of a javelin thrower, accompanied by a lengthy yawn that turned into an Indian war-whoop.

Now he was wide awake. Today, Tuesday 24th April 1984, latitude 48°N by longitude 2°E, what new pleasures lay in store? What wines, culinary delicacies, music? And, primarily, what women?

2

THE NEIGHBOUR, SCHUBERT
AND MIREILLE

Out of the darkness, a stunning female body, toffee-coloured and stark naked, appeared in the doorway to the bedroom. Nazulis, his eyes wrinkling in astonishment, recognised her.

'Oh, Lea!' he exclaimed.

A long silken mane of hair cascaded down past the small of her back, as far as the tiny golden-brown buttocks. Black eyes sparkling out of the darkness. Curve of shoulders, diminutive youthful breasts jutting proudly – yes, it was Lea, the Eurasian, with her languorous liana-like suppleness. And that tongue of hers: a nonchalant rasp! A strange smile played upon her moist lips. She drew closer and opened her mouth slightly. Her little pink tongue flickered like a serpent's . . .

Gulliver quivered in an electric surge, hoarding all the ardour of the morning hard-on.

Then suddenly replacing the vision, there followed another, this time strong and strapping, right in front of Florian's astonished nose. Here were the magnificent haunches of the young German girl: the real rump of a natural blonde – pink, with flaxen down. What was her name? Greta, Hilde, Martha? Florian wracked his brains, but he was bad at remembering names. A splendid, imposing athletic bottom that had been, in the Teutonic tradition of the Valkyries, with ample cheeks in whose centre blossomed the hairy bouquet, that fine golden sheaf.

It was the type of rear at which he loved to thrust, bucking and battering vigorously, with Martha or Greta or Birgitta or whatever her name was, lying spreadeagled, face down. She would part her legs somewhat and raise her arse and he, foraging through the blonde thatch, would thrash his way into her, working away with ever-wilder cudgelling blows. 'More, more, more!' she would groan, gasping gutturally and interspersing the command with moans of 'Ach!' or 'Noch!' which might turn into 'Nein!' and finally 'Ja! Ja! Ja!' The latter exclamatory triad formed the three final steps of that orgasmic staircase she was squealingly climbing while she bit the mattress, ground her teeth and dribbled over the sheets.

Deeply embedded inside her, and on his knees, he would regain his breath, gasping like a marathon runner. On filling his lungs once again, he would resume, Gulliver by now quite demen-

16

ted. He gripped her firm, rounded bum, accompanied by trumpets, tubas, horns and Wagnerian trombones in an endless crescendo, a wild Germanic gallop towards the yellow and black clouds of a Valkyrie sunset which finally faded out altogether in his memory.

Then everything became silent and peaceful again. A drop of water rolled along a leaf and fell on to a stone, then another followed suit. Beatrice's dazzling features swam into view, that ambiguous, fascinating green-eyed inquisitive look of hers: ah Beatrice, gentle redhead whose milky skin was sown with freckles! She too promptly disappeared, vanishing somewhere in her land of dreams. (In fact, she had ditched Florian Nazulis for an Italian she had fallen in love with, a rich exporter of pasta.) And now, making her appearance on stage, was the perfect body of that Negress, whose particular aroma was of musk and warm pastry, and who had been exquisitely baked by centuries of solar cuisine. She it was who brought him swiftly to the vertical, with her peppery scent and her woolly-tufted oxters into which he loved to sink his nose and indulge in an olfactory truffling full of savour, thence downward to the coarsely-haired nest, which he opened with the tip of his tongue, thus flushing out the scarlet fledglings . . .

His eyes smarted with these images. Florian

got out of bed and placed his feet on the threshold of a new morning full of a host of possibilities. How good it was to be alive! And how strong desire is!

He uttered a sort of joyful growl and with a single rapid motion flung open the shutters, which banged against the wall, making the whole building vibrate.

His eyes dazzled by the sudden sunlight, and Gulliver still stiffly in evidence, Florian casually waved hello at the silhouetted figure framed in the window opposite. Startled by the noisy clatter of shutters, this silent form was now motionless. Florian gradually distinguished its outline, shading his eyes with a hand like a sea-captain scrutinising the horizon.

It was a woman.

With one hand to her mouth in her astonishment at seeing this muscularly naked man flourishing a spectacular erection.

The sun picked out the prick extended like a veritable hammer so that it cast a huge shadow against the pale yellow background of the bedroom. It resembled some projectile, a missile of sorts, a demonic vision from which she could not avert her gaze.

'Good morning neighbour!' Nazulis cried.

She did not answer.

Her eyes looked extraordinarily round and her attractive features were fringed by chestnut curls which fell on to the collar of her blue quilted dressing gown. She was indeed delightful.

'Hello, good morning, dear neighbour whose name I don't know,' intoned Florian.

'Good morning, Monsieur,' she replied in a clear but not loud voice.

Blushing and embarrassed, she turned her back as if to retreat.

'Wait!' Nazulis shouted. 'Don't go! You're my nymph of the morning, the radiant visage of the dawn . . . The charm of . . . of . . . well, to be honest, I like you.'

She was looking at him hesitantly.

'Come and have a cup of coffee,' he suggested, pulling on his dressing gown. (Curtains for Gulliver, for the time being.) 'What a lovely day! Ah, spring!' This with an expansive gesture towards the sky.

She made as if to shut the window.

'Wait, wait! Coffee, tea, chocolate, alcohol, hashish, sweeties . . . Anything you like, so long as you call by!'

She bit her lower lip, indecisive now.

He took a deep breath, bowed his head, put on a hangdog air and, staring hard at her, repeated in a very serious tone: 'Do come over.'

She rang the bell very lightly. When he came to open the door she had half turned as if ashamed at her boldness.

'Come on,' Florian said, politely taking her arm, 'don't be shy. There's no harm in popping over for breakfast with one's neighbour . . . This is my hovel. Make yourself at home. Sit down. No, not the chair, you'll be more comfortable there. Tea, coffee?'

'Tea would be fine, thanks.'

While he was busy in the kitchen she was looking round the room. There were books up to the ceiling. Plants, erotic paintings, musical instruments – a saxophone, a South American bandoneon, a transverse flute . . . A Japanese wood carving of a horse's head on the wall. On the floor lay Schubert scores, paperbacks, a solitary sock. A stuffed monkey grimaced in a corner, wrinkling up its nose. In the opposite corner there was an opaline vase of the Louis-Philippe period, the exact colour (this she was soon to notice) of Florian's own eyes. On a table rested a bottle of Château Haut-Brion 1973, three-quarters empty.

'What do you do?' she asked him.

He answered her from the kitchen but she did not catch what he said.

'What did you say?' she inquired.

'Oenologist,' he declared, returning with a tray stacked with tea-things, *petits fours* and assorted cakes. This he set down on a low table. 'And yourself?'

'Studying Classics.'

'With a view to teaching?'

'That's the idea, yes.'

He pulled a face.

'Teaching, God, what a pity!'

He sat beside her on the small settee. She had a pretty face and wore no make-up. Nice blue eyes and a friendly expression enhanced by her brown curls. Vivacious, open features. Her full, rounded mouth turned up at its corners in an impish grin. He liked her a lot.

He sniffed her scent and that pleased him also. Gulliver reared its head. This was how Nazulis liked women to be – natural, no make-up, no doubletalk. He leaned over her neck and indulged in a series of tiny inhalations. She recoiled momentarily, unused to being sniffed in this way.

'What's the matter?' she asked. 'Don't I smell nice?'

'You smell fine,' he murmured, leaning further across her.

He nuzzled forward and sniffing very precisely

21

progressed along her shoulder, moving on up to the neck, then her hair, which he barely brushed with his lips. She smelt of dry straw, the open air, good health. A natural scent of wholesome skin. She must be, he estimated, in her early twenties. Nazulis' nasal guesswork indicated that she probably came very easily, in uncomplicated fashion, first time out. It was anyhow clear that mind and body were in fine fettle. This was a healthy girl.

'Do you shave your armpits?' he asked brusquely.

'Why do you ask me that?' she said, uneasy.

'There are two sorts of women,' he explained. 'Those who shave their armpits and those who don't.'

She suppressed a giggle by pinching her nose.

'In the latter category,' he continued imperturbably, 'there are two sub-groups . . .'

She listened to him, chin on hand, unsure whether or not he was joking. But Nazulis was quite serious.

'One of these groups is comprised of those who simply let themselves go. They aren't bothered one way or another. And then there is the other group, the one which interests me. For them the hirsute oxter represents one element in their physical hyper-sensitivity and sophistication. Thus they look after the armpit, trimming its hair just a little, with scissors, to form a tiny silky island into which the nose enjoys delving during intercourse.'

He drank a cup of tea, replaced the cup, and went on.

'Do you remember how a few years back nearly all women plucked their eyebrows, leaving only a thin line above the eyes? Those lunar faces were a bit offputting, I always thought. Today there's been a big swing towards the New Hairiness: eyebrows are allowed to grow. Sometimes fashion displays glimmers of intelligence.'

While he was talking she stared at his hands, which were fluttering about like birds.

'Underarm hair,' he concluded, 'is sensuality to the ultimate degree.'

'I don't shave beneath my arms,' she whispered, smiling.

Delighted and appreciative, he pecked at her cheek, which was as velvety as a peach, then he refilled their cups with the passion-fruit scented blend he had bought in London. He wondered what colour her armpit-hair was and what shape the tufts took: rounded little islands or wedge-shaped thickets? Were they long or short, bristly or scratchy foliage?

'What's your name?' he asked her.

'Clémence,' she said.

'Florian Nazulis,' he announced, kissing her

just beneath the ear.

He relieved her gently of the cup she held and began stroking her hands – slender, distinctive, ringless fingers. Continuing to stroke her along her arm, whose delicate down he savoured, he reached the curve of her shoulder. It was smooth and warm, but the dressing gown hindered his caresses. He started undoing the buttons.

'No, no!' she protested.

'Yes, yes!' Gulliver insisted heavily, down below.

He leaned over and there was something of a struggle. Gulliver was in full cry. She was smiling and this made him want her all the more. Her half open dressing gown had revealed firm, round breasts whose pink nipples were now hard. He tried to undo the garment completely but Clémence was putting up some resistance. Holding her tightly by the wrists he succeeded in getting her onto her back along the settee. Then he wedged himself against her, lying full length on top of her, leg on leg, belly to belly, quimlet to Gulliver. 'Get on with it!' the latter urged him, his head battering at that delicious warm mound whose silky hair and disturbingly attractive scent were clearly evident through the material.

'You really are . . . passionate,' gasped Clémence.

Florian, atop her, was feeling too lecherous to

laugh or talk. His mouth found those sensual lips of hers and soon gave him her tongue; then both flickered, lingually conversing awhile. Her eyes were shut as she uttered a little moan of pleasure, a sort of slow, low recitative based on a single note. Gulliver continued his thrusts at the downy hillock. Florian's loins surged weightily and deliberately to and fro, and this relentless urgency gradually forced the adorable body beneath his own to part, open up to him. Gulliver, like a ploughshare, dived downward at the female furrow.

'Let's undress,' Florian breathed.

'Wait,' she said.

'I can't any longer,' he insisted.

'Wait, wait . . .'

The motion continued. The two bodies, linked yet separated by the barrier of material were coupling in an urgent frottage. The young woman's monotonous aria turned into a raucous panting deep in her throat.

'Ooohh . . .'

'Come on,' he repeated.

'Oh, oh, oh!' she burst out, astonished and overwhelmed by the orgasm which was swelling like a tidal wave.

Her body went rigid and she grabbed the man's shoulders violently. Head flung back, eyes closed, she let herself drown in sheer pleasure.

She had not even taken off all her clothes and there she was, coming already! Relaxed, looking happily flushed, she regained her breath. Florian was perturbed.

'What about me then?' he exclaimed.

'Another time,' she said. 'I have to leave now.'

She got up, kissed the young man perfunctorily, opened the door and disappeared.

For a long time he remained seated on the edge of the bed, head bowed, thinking. He didn't understand. He went across to the window. His beautiful neighbour had closed hers and drawn the curtains.

He put a record on the deck and began running the shower to maximum heat. Under the scalding jets his skin turned scarlet. Alfred Brendel meanwhile played Schubert's *Impromptus* with exquisite tenderness. Nazulis turned the tap towards blue and an icy spray covered him. He too began to turn blue and withstood the shock throughout the *Impromptu No 3 in G Flat*. When Brendel embarked on the first part of Opus 142, he turned the arrow to red again, almost suffocating in the steam while the pianist's dexterity, intimate and lyrical, recreated the despair of the composer of *Death and the Maiden*. The Prelude ended on an F Minor chord. He cut off the water for a moment and turned on the cold again, as Schubert calmly reaffirmed all the melancholy melody in that strange, inaccessible world of his.

Nazulis, skin glowing pink, emerged and donned a dressing gown. Gulliver, penitent and shrivelled, had been transformed into a ridiculous spigot whose sole, doleful function seemed to be that of purveyor of urine.

Revived by the vigorous shower, he seized the phone and dialled a number, whistling the *F Minor Impromptu* excruciatingly.

Somewhere in Paris, at the far end of the enchanted line, a woman answered.

'Hello?' a rather singsong voice replied.

'It's me,' Florian said. 'Has your husband gone?'

'Ah, good morning Lucie dear, how are you?' the voice then cooed.

Florian got the message.

'Call me back,' he said, before hanging up.

A few minutes later the phone rang, tickled into action from the other side of Paris by a dainty, delicate forefinger doing its sly work on the dial.

'Gorgeous one, it was quite impossible to get rid of him this morning. First he wanted to jump on me. Then he discovered he'd left behind a file . . . I thought he'd never go.'

'Can I see you?' asked Florian.

'Oh yes!'

'Now?'

'Oh yes!'
'I'm on my way.'
'Oh yes!'

When Florian set foot outside he stopped at once, as if paralysed. He swayed from one foot to the other, hovering and hesitating in the doorway of his apartment block, expectant, yet unable to plunge into the city's maelstrom. He stayed where he was for a while, indecisive.

A bus passed, grimly grinding by in first gear, and making the grey walls of the buildings bounce back echoes. Opposite, level with the third floor, a sander was scraping at the stonework, throwing up a fine white dust which then sifted down a little further on, ageing the unwary passers by. Further away the noise of a demonstration was audible: car horns blasting out slogans in morse. Something to do with somebody's resignation. In any case the march went on repeating its particular scansion of long and short blasts, while a helicopter covered the whole district with its rotor din. In the neighbouring streets those other cars held up by the demonstration played irate horn concertos.

Assailed as he was by noise, the various simultaneous commotions and that throng of assorted aromas which seemed to strike him full in the face –

Florian could not make up his mind which way to turn. Then like a gust of breeze a woman swirled by, close enough to brush past him, and wafting a cloudlet of perfume in her wake. He followed hot on her heels, captivated by the scent of Miguchi, which brought back some delightful memories. She walked swiftly, swaying enticingly upon heels so high that her progress seemed a very marvel of equilibrium. Her legs were superb: trim ankles and slim yet muscular calves. He had not been able to see her face. Black hair gently bobbed in rhythm as she swept onward. Led, as it were, by the nose, Florian let himself be drawn along by the mingled odours of cypresses in the sun, pepper and nutmeg, which he recalled all too clearly: the beautiful Emilia from Turin had worn that very scent! But that was ancient history now: why dwell upon these Proustian madeleines, these olfactory titbits which titillated his nostrils so long after the event, remembrance of clings past? He half-turned abruptly and cannoned into yet another woman.

He lived in a smart part of Paris, filled with furriers, shoe-shops, boutiques and the like, and where the number of pretty women per square yard broke all records for the capital. She bestowed on him a dazzling smile as if the young man had actually caressed her. Her eyes were grey-blue and the vermilion lipstick she wore had smeared a fraction over her top teeth. Florian's hand instinctively shielded his eyes against the reflections flung from newly-cleaned plate-glass – the shop window of a particularly opulent and fashionable designer's HQ.

Florian took refuge in the doorway of a block of flats, trying to collect himself and keep calm. He then plunged into the crowd and made for the Métro, head down and hands jammed into his pockets. Just as he was crossing the Rue de Rennes he walked into a strong gust of *Diorissima*. He turned towards the perfume's purveyor but the blonde head had already vanished. Gritting his teeth he forced himself not to be diverted from his objectives, pedestrian crossing, Métro stairs, corridors . . . Borne on the wind were drifts of *Apple Blossom, Shocking You*, and whiffs from a man's shirt whose owner had bad BO. A group of yelling schoolchildren jostled him. He bent his head towards one of them and was reassured by the wholesome adolescent aroma thence exuded. Their teacher-in-charge looked at Florian suspiciously, but then the crocodile broke ranks and the hapless pedagogue had to rush to reassemble it.

Florian vaulted the Métro turnstile: this was one of his favourite exercises. One foot crashed into an empty beercan which clattered down the corridor. He retrieved it and tossed it assiduously into a litter bin. A little further on a tall, goodlooking violinist was busking, a saucerful of small change at his feet. He played the last few bars of an 18th century composition, emptied the saucer into his pocket and replaced it on the ground leaving a couple of one franc pieces in it. Then he slowly chinned his violin and thought for a while, an intent expression on his face. People funnelled down towards him, rushing for the train coming in with a dull roar to the platform below them. Florian stood expectantly in front of the busker, who winked at him before launching into Bach's *Partita for Solo Violin*.

The throng thinned again and the corridor was once again nearly deserted. The soloist played on as if in the concert hall. He must have had a Conservatoire training, ten years' practice at the least. Not a fault in phrasing, intonation or taste. The *Partita* with all its fugal and contrapuntal complexity unravelled effortlessly, with geometric precision . . . A circle of listeners had formed, enthralled by the virtuoso performance. The various musical paths of the *Partita* finally coverged in a resonant G Minor chord which reverberated throughout the corridor. The travellers bestowed their largesse and departed. He got it right, thought Florian, dropping his biggest banknote, folded into eight, onto the plate. He avoided the musician's gaze, since being charitable invariably embarrassed him.

Mireille opened the door. She was wearing a mauve negligée. It exposed two round breasts which looked firm enough, for all their years of being fondled and sucked. Florian tilted back her head, she pulled down his, and they kissed lingeringly. She was a tall woman, blonde and somewhat marked by alcohol, sun and the general wear and tear of life, but still attractive. Mireille was a hot piece, an exceptional fuck. She would do it anywhere, any time. And probably with anyone, thought Florian with a trace of bitterness.

While he concentrated on devouring her mouth, Florian worked his right index finger into her slippery snatch, exploring that honeyed grotto. Mireille uttered little simian yelps.

Their favourite game together was playing monkeys. They would spend much time – when her husband and children permitted – aping gorillas, mimicking chimps and being baboon buffoons. They'd scratch their armpits, pull faces and emit jungle cries, leaping at and on each other in mock delousing rituals.

'Come on, you monkey, you,' said Mireille.

Florian followed her down the hallway,

absently sniffing his index finger: yes, all was well and healthy down below, on the evidence. Mireille was a scrupulously clean woman who visited her gynaecologist every couple of months, maybe even more often. (Florian wondered whether there was no ulterior motive in that; some additional, unacknowledged sensual excitement.) The kingsize marital bed was still unmade. Florian frowned.

'What's the matter darling?' asked Mireille.

'That smell of tobacco . . . Please open the window.'

'There you are, my apeman, that's it.'

'And do remove that ashtray . . . Why this mania they all have for sucking their cigarettes like deprived infants?'

'It's only mild tobacco, dearest . . .'

'Just as well, otherwise it really would be intolerable . . . Are the kids at school? OK, are they? Still behaving themselves?'

'Yes, darling. Quick, come on,' she said lying on the pink sheets.

'Listen . . . I'd rather you pulled the bedspread over if you don't mind. It's embarrassing to make love in a bed that's still warm. I can feel your husband's presence.'

'As you wish, my darling.'

After rearranging the bed she took off her nightdress and lay down on top of it.

33

'Come on,' she said to him, holding out her arms. 'Come on, my sweet monkey.'

Florian let himself be examined and turned over, and had his back scratched and ears nibbled. She flicked her little tongue briskly over a drowsy Gulliver.

'Just look at the little lollipop,' she crooned. 'My liquorice-stick, my dear little dolly, my sweet little bit of candy . . .'

She crammed in the tender morsel and began a subtle to and fro motion. At once Gulliver, delighted, started to stir.

'That's better,' mumbled Mireille as she darted her tongue-tip along the moist sinew. 'Ah the brute, the burglar, the slyboots, you naughty little beast you . . .'

'Mmmm,' said Florian, who was getting excited by now.

'Oh fuck me, fuck me quick!' cried Mireille, suddenly crouching on all fours and presenting him with her pink posterior.

'At last!' exclaimed Gulliver, plunging head-first into the blonde thicket.

'Oh yes, yes! Harder, more!' she was begging him.

Florian, standing over the bed, in the clutches and throes of love, abandoned himself to sensations.

'Yes, yes, oh, aaaaaahhh!' yelled Mireille, who

had by now lost every vestige of sophistication.

'Mmm?' he asked her.

'Oh yes, oh yes, fuck me harder! Again, more! Deeper!'

'Uh, huh, huh,' Nazulis panted.

'Split me, fill me, shove, fuck, more, more!'

'Ugh, ugh,' he groaned.

'Oh, I'm coming, I'm coming, I'm going to come, I'm coming . . .'

'Go on, go on,' a glassy-eyed Nazulis gasped through clenched teeth.

'I'm coming now . . . Yes, oh, I'm coming now, now, now, God how I'm coming, now, *now*!'

It was no bluff. Mireille being one of those women who get an enormous kick out of sex, which becomes all-engrossing, completely over-powering for them. She collapsed, demolished utterly, as if dead. Lying stretched out on the bed she resembled some great newly-felled African tree. They regained their breath and wallowed for a while in a contemplative calm.

From a deferential distance, Gulliver gazed at his master. A clock chimed. A lorry passed, gently rattling the windows.

Several minutes later they were at it again, this time in the missionary position. She was stammering 'My chimp, my ape, my sweet monkey,' with her hands pressed into the small of his back.

35

She had lifted her long legs aloft so he could penetrate her more deeply. At that moment the phone rang.

'Oh no,' she said wearily. 'Not now!'

'Don't answer,' said Nazulis, continuing to work away at her.

'Perhaps it's the school . . . I'm always worried something might happen to the children . . .'

'Don't worry,' he gasped.

Gulliver, turgid, imperious and sleek, grew ever redder and more taut, on the verge of his apoplectic apocalypse.

The ringing persisted. She lifted the receiver, while still connected to her Siamese twin, who would not be separated from her.

'Is that you?' she exclaimed. And then, her hand over the mouthpiece, she whispered: 'It's my husband.'

'Tell him he's disturbing us,' he puffed, continuing his seesaw.

'Yes, yes . . . I understand,' she was saying.

Finger up to her mouth, she was smiling at Florian, who took the hint. She covered the telephone again, whispering conspiratorially: 'He says he loves me and wants to fuck me . . .'

Nazulis, goaded – as a horse by a fly – began thrusting ever more vigorously and silently.

'Mmm . . . Mmm . . . Yes, darling . . . I understand.'

Suddenly Florian grabbed the receiver, winking at his lover, as if to say 'I won't give the game away', and with Gulliver in seventh heaven still buried deep inside her, he heard the nasal voice of the husband. That husband – the good father, worthy worker, and promising computer programmer who was still in love with his wife – the ideal husband, in fact, was expounding upon the hardship of being so far from his beloved little squirrel . . .

'Can you hear me all right?' inquired the uxorious voice.

'Mmm,' Nazulis answered, with a sort of upper-octave whine.

Then it was Mireille's turn to shake with a mischievous belly-laugh which sucked her lover into an irresistible ground-swell.

'You realize,' the husband went on, 'that I want you all the time, but I can't help it, as soon as I start thinking about your legs, those long blonde legs of yours, I get all randy . . . You know what I mean? Are you listening?'

'Mmm, mmm,' said Florian.

'My dear sweet feather duster, my tickly quim, you're always so hot and wet . . . Oh God, I'd like to come back home right now. How about you, are you in the mood for it? Go on, tell me.'

'Mmm, mmm,' Florian agreed.

'I'm really steaming now . . . I can just see your

furry snatch, as though I were right there beside you . . . Oh yes, I can see you all right!'

Nazulis winked at Mireille, who was now sitting astride him and fervently enjoying her belly-dance.

'. . . If you could see *me* now. There's a pile of files on my desk, stacked up to the ceiling. Fascinating stuff about our new subsidiary, for instance . . .'

'Mmm,' Florian responded, gripped by that muscular cunt which was sucking him in, snatching, squeezing him then bulging outward to force him back, before ingesting him ever more urgently. Gulliver was truly in its element.

'Well, you can bet I've forgotten about those bloody files, I'm thinking so hard about you! You're so close . . . I'm thinking about your arms and your hair . . . Then your mouth, your tongue, your teeth . . . your . . . ah Mireille my love, my dear little wife, I love you!'

'Mmm, mmm . . .' Florian repeated.

'Say something, though!' begged the voice.

Florian turned the receiver towards his lover.

'Ah yes, I sympathize, I really dooooo . . .' she at last gasped.

SANDRA – THE FUNDAMENTAL THESIS

Florian left his Number One lay (yes, fidelity in long-term relationships is a traditional virtue) late that morning. Mireille had to prepare the children's lunch while he was off to meet the ravishing Sandra, she of the gorgeous physique, who had so often posed nude for a variety of magazines. He scarcely knew her, but he could still clearly see her enticing adolescent body which had recently made the cover of *Him*.

He descended the staircase two steps at a time, sated and elated, inhaling from his fingers the fragrance of Mireille, that fresh and lingering scent of her recent pleasure.

There are those – and they usually qualify themselves as 'right-thinking people' – who would claim that Florian was a sex-maniac. The term would have given him a laugh or two. 'It's they who are the sex-maniacs', he'd maintain. 'They're the true obsessives of the sex war, the legions of killjoys, the anti-sexual mercenaries, always screaming 'Death to Sex!'

For Florian, lovemaking was no obsession but a constantly renewed pleasure which always changed and always began again, just like life itself.

Copulation calmed him, bestowing him with a joyous surge of energy. He and Gulliver existed in perfect harmony.

That had not always been the case. In his youth, Nazulis had wrestled with heavy bouts of conscience and angst. Those days, they tried to instil in him a sense of sin, a reaction of disgust against pleasure, an aversion to desire itself. The natural pulse and impulse of his uncomplicated libido had had to be misleadingly or mysteriously diverted or simply suppressed.

But he had come a long way since then, and had lost patience with neurotic priests, teachers and phony psychologists and other poisoners of the life-force. Gulliver, the modest, much maligned childish spigot had become a trusty companion-in-arms and an ever-ready confidant.

Florian had become perspicacious in the course of mocking established morality. He had learned to listen to the dictates of his naturally strong and healthy body. He knew how to understand and respond to his physical needs, to the inmost hints of his body's private language.

For example, sometimes his organism might say to him: 'Milk!' Then he would rush to buy a bottle of fresh milk. On other occasions his body would shout: 'Woman!' He would seize his raincoat and charge down five flights of stairs to go out on the rampage.

Sometimes the physical demands were more precise: 'Blonde!' He'd riffle through his address book, hunting for those numbers marked with a yellow cross: Mireille, Florence, Sophie, Laurence, Carine. Then he'd pick up the phone. Or his body would transmit a more specific message: 'Brunette, on the hairy side!' He would thereupon loiter in the vicinity of the Portuguese Church in the Rue de la Convention. He knew that a plentiful supply of nice young chambermaids and *au pairs* awaited him, shy and invariably hirsute, even to the occasional moustache.

These physiological summonses drove Florian into a manic state of well-being, for what better can befall a man than a wave of desire and its satisfaction?

It could also happen that surfeit — too much food or excessive indulgence in wine and women — brought in its aftermath the need for a rest. Nazulis would then go on a 24-hour diet (herb tea or vegetable broth or total Gulliverian abstinence) – time enough for his system to recuperate.

His body was not only sapient but also available. Whenever a new or unexpected pleasure presented itself, he would follow it and every inch of his physique would gleefully surrender to the sensation.

Florian, his body and Gulliver formed an inseparable trinity.

Thus it was that a few days earlier, strolling by the Square du Vert-Galant on the Ile de la Cité – the very heart of Paris – he had found himself in close proximity to a delectable creature. It was the early afternoon of a bright but mild day. At that hour the garden, surrounded by the waters of the Seine, was almost deserted apart from two or three *clochards* lounging on a patch of grass and sipping their rotgut.

Florian was not on the lookout for women. His body was well content after two early morning orgasms. Gulliver, snugly coiled in his cotton pouch, dozed tranquil. Meanwhile his master was contemplative, savouring the reflections of those ancient stones in the grey and yellow swirl of the Seine.

She was sitting on the actual prow of the islet

itself, propped against the stone parapet of the quay, gazing at the river. Her legs, slightly parted, allowed a glimpse of skimpy, skyblue-edged white panties, for her skirt had ridden up above her knees.

Nazulis's heart missed a beat when he saw this deliciously immodest display. She had glanced up and said 'Hello' in friendly fashion. He'd mumbled a sort of 'Good Afternoon' back, fascinated by her smooth tanned legs which, when one's gaze worked further up them, allowed a distinct and tantalizing glimpse of a downy mound that the tiny panties could not quite conceal. Eyes riveted upon this intercrural area currently being exhibited, Florian enjoyed a sublime moment of voyeurism. He was unable to utter a sound. The enthusiastic Gulliver at once twitched. And she had noticed, too, that sudden bulge through the thin trousers. Time stood still. Only the sparrows seemed to be carrying on as normal. His lips dry, Florian stood motionless, as if petrified and indeed resembling those aged stones everywhere about them, which had wit-nessed battles, revolutions, guillotined heads, and governments overthrown . . . She slowly ran her tongue over her lower lip and looked up at this silent man standing over her and staring at her with his blue eyes.

'Good God!' Florian murmured to himself.

She moved a fraction, shifting the position of her legs.

'Oh no,' he pleaded silently, 'don't you move, not yet, I want to look. Just stay as you are . . .'

But it was not the motion of closure. She had spread her thighs even wider and continued to stare back at him, smiling. Obviously she found this wild-haired man with the intense stare attractive. She had splayed out her right leg and tucked that same foot under her buttocks. Pulled taut by the change of position, the stretched cotton panties became even more revealing. He tried to discern the outline of the secret lips but the blonde thatch was too thickly furred for that.

He remained silent, standing there. Her eyes never left him. A serious expression had replaced her smile. She continued licking her lips, while her hand gently slid along her thigh towards her panties.

'Good God,' Florian repeated in fascination.

She inserted her middle finger past the embroidered hem of the garment and kept staring at him. Her mouth was half-open and traces of saliva glistened on her lips.

An American, surely. Her multi-coloured sneakers and checkered tee shirt, quite apart from her physiognomy, were not at all French. She was probably eighteen or nineteen. Her unabashed gaze quietly quizzed the young man while her finger worked on in slow, rhythmic rotations. The noise of water purling past over the stones of the Quai was clearly audible. The general hubbub of the city seemed a long way off. They were alone in the very centre of Paris, at the far end of this garden facing the Pont des Arts opposite, and further on, the Louvre.

She beckoned to him.

'Come on,' she said.

He drew very close to her.

'Isn't it just great here?' she opined in a distinct New York accent.

She laid her hand on Gulliver without ceasing to caress herself.

'Really good, huh?' she commented.

Then, still using her left hand she unbuttoned Florian's fly, fishing out a flushed and heated Gulliver. She bent her head, opened her mouth wide and swallowed. Immediately Florian felt a warm tongue lap him, back and forth in a steady tidelike rhythm. Her lips were clamped firmly around the jubilant Gulliver and her tongue was folded into a natural groove along which slid the tricorn tip of the tool and the underside of its shaft, thus procuring for Florian some wild sensations. He had grabbed the young girl's head with both hands. Her hair felt soft. The American girl was an expert in the tricky field of fellation. He soon felt the rising flood of orgasmic flux, welling up in an irresistible surge.

'Mmmm!' he murmured, closing his eyes as he sensed the imminent paroxysm.

'Wait!' she insisted, abruptly abandoning him.

Keeping him at arm's length she began to increase the speed of her own masturbation so that she too could reach a climax.

Frustrated by this sudden abandonment, Florian thrust Gulliver straight back into that wet, juicy mouth, thus obliging her to service him again.

'Wait!' she urged, pulling back to leave the electrified Gulliver stranded once again.

With furious self-absorption, her hand vibrating in an ever-accelerating momentum, she reached the very threshold of the spasm so long desired. She began breathing very heavily, then her head slumped and she came so violently that she was completely unaware of the man beside her – and now quite beside himself.

She regained her breath and treated Florian to a dazzling smile.

'That was wonderful!' she said.

Florian, his palms against the American girl's temples, pulled her face to the extended Gulliver. She began sucking at its head with tiny licks then, seizing the man's buttocks with both hands, she let herself be orally penetrated. Gulliver, sheathed to the hilt within this tender mouth, pulsed in rhythmic ecstasy . . .

Another day Florian had been sitting in the starry night of a Champs-Elysées cinema, seeing *Barry Lyndon* for the fourth time. On that occasion too he had not been in a deprived state: the previous night and the following morning had been filled with embraces and delightful frolics. Two women had succeeded each other in his bed, and what was more, the evening brunette and the morning blonde had been followed by a short siesta at Mireille's full of stimulating exercise.

Body and mind at peace he had felt like seeing Stanley Kubrick's masterpiece yet again. In order to take his seat in the middle of a row he had negotiated the obstacles of half a dozen rather bony knees and finally found himself apologizing to his immediate neighbour for treading on her foot.

'Oh I'm terribly sorry . . . Excuse me.'

'That's all right,' she'd replied frostily.

She was an impassive if handsome woman, with black hair pulled back in a businesslike style. He settled himself comfortably, knees propped against the seat in front and the nape of his neck supported by the head-rest. The lights went down and the film began. As soon as Handel's famous *Saraband* resounded, with its martial and solemn air, he had felt the pressure of an arm against his own. He paid it no heed, again captivated by the scene where Barry seduces his cousin. The pressure became more urgent. He recognized the keen sensual signal and, moving his arm lightly towards his neighbour, responded to it. He loved those somewhat dubious situations in which desire takes advantage of darkness and anonymity to find its expression.

The female hand started softly exploring his arm and then found his own hand and was still. Barry Lyndon was serving his military apprenticeship. The adjoining hand led Florian's towards a warm and quivering thigh. Giovanni Paisiello's *Cavatina* accompanied the nonchalant decadence of powdered faces bent over the card tables. Nazulis loved the music. Completely absorbed in watching these eighteenth century duels, he started unzipping her jeans. His fingers infiltrated to find the warm nest, which his index and middle digits then delicately parted. She was sopping wet. He masturbated her to the strains of *The British Grenadiers*. Then, as the English army's guns opened up in a thunderous bombardment he felt her come. All this time the woman's head had remained motionless and utterly impassive.

The duel scene followed, orchestrated to the doleful beat of Handel's drums. She undid his fly-buttons and with her left hand jerked him off until he too came. She was even fastidious enough to wipe him with his handkerchief. Then, her eyes still fixed upon the screen, and indifferent to her neighbour, she watched the conclusion to the film. She left during the credits, respectable and anonymous to the end.

Yes, the three of them – Florian, his body and sturdy Gulliver – were in perfect harmony, making hay while the sun shone, and cheating death for as long as they could. Because, as Florian was well aware, it was by no means certain that there was paradise or even another world awaiting them. Florian had had plenty of time for reading and reflection on that particular score, not to mention considerable trials, errors and experience of life. One had to seize any moments of happiness here and now and in this world, before they disappeared.

In the movies, the streets of the city, the garden of the Vert-Galant or the vineyards of Bordeaux, on the Greek islands or wherever, Nazulis nosed out the various nooks and crannies of Paradise.

There are those who always lose the toss, as if fated. For his part he always called, and came up, tails.

If a young girl should decide to leave home in search of adventure, it was Florian she would run into outside the Gare Montparnasse. And guess who that delectable wife would meet upon the stairs of her apartment block, only moments after she had slammed the door in her estranged husband's face?

What about a certain February day on the ski run at Val d'Isère and those skis which came to a sudden halt right in front of our hero? Their owner was the sexiest, most sought-after Italian actress, by herself just for that particular day of days, without her 'constant companion', a macho type away shooting a movie at Cinecitta. She was alone, had beautiful blue-green eyes, and her famous arse was in the snow. Florian did not believe in God or destiny, but he was convinced some god or other was with him, Ah, that wonderful and cautious descent down the icy slope to the ski resort, her tiny hand firmly clasped in his as he guided her . . . And that come-hither look, the small curvaceous body which melted, writhed and clung . . . 'What memories for my old age!' Florian told himself. He'd also be able to tell his grandchildren a thing or two! 'Yes, my little lad, she was the Number One Box Office Star in Italy. Wonderful eyes she had. And I've led quite a life, laddie, I can tell you! Lots of wine, women and much else besides. I've enjoyed life to the full.'

Florian Nazulis was always ready for the unexpected bonus, the happy accident, the weird and wonderful encounter.

He was a true libertine.

Nazulis and Sandra were due to meet at the cocktail party celebrating the 1000th issue of *Gourmet* magazine. He knew that lovely body of hers from top to toe, and all its highways and byways too: firm, rounded bottom; curved slim thighs; little girl's breasts. Her anatomy held no secrets for him, nor for the readers of various pin-up and fashion mags, who would often find this nymphet-model plastered in all poses, in every degree of dress and wanton undress, across those glossy pages. There had also been that celebrated cover shot which had caused something of a scandal among all right-thinking burghers. In fact the capital had been covered with huge coloured billboards reproducing that same richly suggestive cover, and these turned every head. Parisian walls had never before sported such a provocative photo. Never had Woman so shamelessly exhibited herself. The Salvation Army itself was reduced to choosing between salvation or apoplexy. That was Sandra, all over!

At the party Nazulis spotted her immediately.

He elbowed his way towards her, rescuing her from the Managing Editor's inane witticisms, much to the young woman's relief, and dragged her over to a quieter corner. En route he had tucked a bottle of champagne under his left arm, filched from the tray of an aghast and beleaguered waiter. She worked her way rapidly through half a dozen glasses and he had soon had to find another bottle. He whispered all sorts of things into her ear and she kept dissolving into hysterical laughter. The guests turned in surprise, disconcerted by the raucous note that had intruded upon those serious topics under discussion in hushed tones. 'Crisis . . . Yes . . . You think he'll sell his shares? . . . No chance of election . . . No, definitely a new committee . . . Seven and a half per cent, no question about it . . .' Sandra continued laughing helplessly. Only one thing for it: Florian knew the most efficacious remedy. He pulled her towards him and started flirting. She let him do so, purring with pleasure then. Unfortunately they had to stop when Sandra's steady appeared, looking for her. As they left, she managed to tell Nazulis half-hiccuping and giggling into his ear: 'Come and pick me up Wednesday at the studio – you know where. We'll have lunch.'

The studio of the men's magazine in question occupied the entire top floor of a building on the Champs-Elysées. Its ceiling was dotted and hung with large spotlights which garishly illuminated a dais. On the latter were three straw huts, two palm trees and some sand. A huge backdrop blow-up of an azure sky and sea constituted the remainder of the decor.

Sandra was lying on the sand, nude, her arms flung out and legs wide apart, offering her private parts to the probing eye of a Nikon. The motor whirred and clicked on, taking shot after shot in quick succession.

'Great, fine, sensational,' the photographer intoned. 'Look up, higher, back, yes, again, turn your head a bit . . . no, right, that's it . . .' *Tchakaclick, tchakaclick*. 'Lift the knees, spread, wider for God's sake.' *Tchakaclick*. 'Now put your hand on it as if you're wanking . . . No, just one finger . . . Natural, be natural.' *Tchakaclick*. 'No it looks fake, do it properly, do it for real. Go on, that's it. Yes, fine . . .' *Tchakaclick, tchakaclick, tchakaclick*. 'Now turn and give us a bum, that's it darling . . . spread the cheeks . . . More, more . . . Let's see both holes . . . yes, right, fine . . . Tchakaclick, tchakaclick* . . .

On all fours, arse in air, Sandra managed to discern Florian silhouetted against the arc-lights. She winked in his direction. He gave her a discreet wave.

'What a job!' She confided, when she had dressed, giving him a tiny peck on the lips. 'What a crappy job. Where are we eating? Are you hungry? Do you think I'm sexy? Come on, let's go.'

In the lift she kissed him properly, deeply deploying her tongue. Florian was happy. He'd slid his hand under her flowered dress. She was not wearing a brassière. Her breasts were small and firm. Gulliver began to stir but the lift stopped and they had to get out.

They lunched at the Plougastel, in a nice quiet corner. The next door table was taken by a couple with thick Provençal accents. The man was a paunchy fifty year old rather reminiscent of the great Raimu. He wore a light grey suit brightened up considerably by a splendid scarlet and white tie – obviously brand new. She looked disapproving, her expression tight and menopausal as she repeated: 'Mind you don't spill it. You're bound to make a mess all over your nice tie and that'd be a shame . . .'

He continued eating in silence.

'Watch out or you'll spill it,' she would repeat whenever a waiter brought another course.

'I won't. I'm not about to spill anything,' he protested.

'I just sense it. I just know you'll make a mess *somehow*.'

After a while the man, utterly exasperated, bent low over his plate, took hold of his tie and dunked it comprehensively in his gravy.

'There's your mess, you were quite right,' he said, all but choking with rage, 'that's it. Another fine bloody mess I got you into!'

Florian and Sandra first ordered oysters and a Pouilly Ladoucette. They were hungry.

Quite soon they ordered two dozen more *Belons* and a second bottle. From time to time their hands and fingers would meet and tease. They were feeling content, knowing they would make love in due course. This prelude enchanted them.

'How old are you?' said Sandra.

'Thirty three.'

'Ugh, you're *old* . . .'

'Weell . . .' he said thoughtfully.

A waiter arrived to take their order. Beef and a Beaune.

'And how about you?' Florian asked. 'What age are you?'

'Twenty exactly.'

'You seem even younger, I thought you were about sixteen.'

'That's what everyone tells me. It's useful, sometimes. I can play the nymphet. I tell some guys I'm fourteen. It puts the wind up them, they're worried about my being under-age. To others, I say sixteen or eighteen. People I like, I tell them the truth – twenty.'

'What do you want more than anything in the world?' Florian inquired.

She thought for a moment and announced, 'Some roast beef.'

'No, don't put me on, tell me. What do you want more than anything?'

'Your cock.'

'Oh come on, seriously. I'd really like to know.'

She took hold of the Pouilly and refilled their glasses. 'I'd like all this to last,' she said, waving expansively, 'as long as possible.'

No longer was it a Nikon poised above her but a rubicund and swashbuckling Gulliver, rearing his pink head, ecstatically exploring that youthful, supple, plump body and its intimate aromas.

Lying naked on Florian's vast bed as if on a beach, with her arms and legs akimbo, Sandra, somewhat tipsy, was giving herself unreservedly, letting herself be penetrated again and again. Then she almost purred, sated. Florian suddenly passed out while making love to her and had begun snoring. She too gave way to sleep. Gulliver was also curled up taking a nap, cuddled snugly against the brownish downy mound pillowing his tip.

They all awoke, dazed and contented, after two hours deep and dreamless sleep. And began a celebratory romp. Sandra's warm and nimble tongue toyed with Gulliver. Florian, for his part, played with his tongue and lips upon the miniscule Gulliverette, that pretty cherry sweetmeat always so full of surprises.

Sandra's skin had a dark glowing tan.

'How do you get so brown?' asked Florian, wiping the lovely girl's elixir from his chin.

'In the West Indies. A modelling job. The photographer was goodlooking but he was absolutely impotent. He could only get an erection for a couple of seconds. And that was after working at it, I can tell you. 'Erection' isn't the right word for it either; despite everything I did, he just couldn't keep it hard and horizontal. Zap, it'd collapse, just like that. He never did succeed in putting it up me with the necessary member. Mind you, he compensated for that by all sorts of nice and effective alternatives, but for sex there's really nothing to replace the vital organ.'

'Do you often go on that sort of assignment?'

'Oh yes. The magazine likes my little arse. They sent me off to the Seychelles, the Bahamas, the Virgin Islands, India, the Philippines . . .'

'Always with the same photographer?'

'No, luckily. I've had Helmut, Roberto, Peter . . .'

57

'Do you always fuck them?'

'Nearly always. I like men. And sex. I don't go without.'

His eyes looking at the ceiling, head cradled in his hands, Nazulis was dreaming of distant isles.

'I like you a lot,' he said. 'You're a really . . .' He searched for the right word.

'Really what?' she asked him as she crouched to impale herself upon Gulliver's head.

'A girl who's really . . .'

He couldn't find the phrase he wanted. She began a motion up and down the swollen shaft which she could feel dilating within her.

'A really healthy girl,' he said.

When Sandra had left to continue her modelling session amid the coconut palms of the Champs-Elysées studio, Nazulis sat down at his desk and started writing.

For several months now he had embarked upon a weighty treatise concerning Bottoms. A quite serious, well-documented study, too. His thesis was fundamentally as follows: a woman's character revealed itself via her bottom and vice versa.

The researcher indicated how the shape of the female buttocks was the key to character analysis, and inversely, psyche. To this end, Nazulis had established a very full and detailed typology. There were groupings and sub-divisions of big bums, flat arses, perky podexes, jutting rumps, curved cans, dimpled cheeks, apple anuses, rosy rears, pinchable posteriors, droopy derrières, bony backsides and so on . . .

'The arse is a cultural phenomenon,' he wrote, 'which implies that it is by no means static but subject to change and development. As with all human organs, the arse changes according to use. Without erotic activity, it softens and spreads, the flesh becomes flabby, the muscles atrophy and it loses skin-tone, firmness and even colour.' ('None so vast as a respectable bum,' was one of his pet slogans. The oxymoron pleased him.)

'On the contrary,' he continued, 'libidinous activity and erotic athletics shape up the arse and give it suppleness and a streamlined appearance. Here are features which evolve over centuries, just like those of the human face . . .'

Nazulis supplied examples to which any unbiased observer could attest.

'There are sad bums and cheeky cheeks. Mischevious tails and dull dumplings. Sinewy and sinuous shit-holes, muscular meatballs, large lard-lumps, alas . . . Certainly too many slack, unhealthy sad mountains of adipose tissue and pitted with cellulite . . .'

In the Métro, Nazulis often amused himself by cataloguing the trim and the gross. He would compare their contours, assess the correct category, then move on to their owner's character. Sometimes he took notes. On other occasions he made a cautious approach, initiated a conversation. He frequently got short shrift, but now and then the woman might accompany him to a bar and, over a drink, the researcher would compare his notes with the psychology behind his interlocutor's line of chitchat. He would, in the most interesting cases, take his specimen back home with him for further, more detailed fieldwork. If he was particularly lucky, the woman might permit him to measure as well as pleasure her, and such statistics invariably enriched his dissertation.

One day, Nazulis told himself, he would receive the Nobel Prize for his pioneering work in this area.

The theory was not yet fully developed. There were, to be sure, exceptions. Wonderful women with wizened buttocks, or frail females with splendidly lunar, strapping posteriors. As with every exception, these only confirmed the general rule: each woman's character is inscribed on her arse.

After two or three hours' work, Florian visited his cellar and retrieved a bottle of Nuits St Georges 1969, which he brought to room temperature while going through his notes for the next day.

He put on a new tape in the Uher, checked its batteries and took the tiny capsule out of its case. This tiny microphone, as big as an aspirin, could adhere to any smooth surface. He tested for sound, fixing the capsule to the outside of one of the shutters. Everything was in order. He carefully replaced the machine and accessories into its container and poured a dash of burgundy, turning the glass and admiring the wine's fine, rich colour.

He raised the glass to his nose and delicately sniffed it, his eyes shut. '69 was definitely a mystical number, a miraculous year for burgundy after the disaster of '68. It was also the number of his flat in the Rue des Saints Pères; and, composed as it was of those interlocking curls, its fine numerical symmetry symbolized of course that other form of tasting which he so loved to practise.

The Nuits Saints Georges had such a delicious bouquet that Florian could barely suppress an exclamation of voluptuous surprise. For him it was similar to what he felt when appreciating a new and nude female body to which he was about

61

to make love. 'The girl born the same year as this wine will be fifteen now,' he fantasised, letting the first droplets of the Premier Cru, called Clos des Forêts, slide across his tongue.

It was a full-blooded wine, quite lively for a burgundy, and though on the robust side, full of flavour. Florian smacked his lips and half-filled his glass. He held his glass up to the light, admiring the dark coloration of the liquid and trying to imagine its attendant twin or nymph. 'She'd have a sturdy physique, broad hips but firm arse, a steady yet soft look in her eyes, rounded breasts . . . Wouldn't shave her armpits, naturally . . . So young that she wouldn't yet have been brainwashed: no mania yet for keeping 'clean', i.e. depilated and deodorized . . . She'd still be a virgin and she'd have the scent of a young girl who revelled in the fresh air of Burgundy. Her hair (and pubis) would be luxuriant, sleek and black . . .'

He drank another mouthful, still dreaming about the girl, and letting the fine wine refresh his tongue.

The telephone rang. He rushed to cut off the call and leave the phone off the hook.

He did not want to be rung up. He wanted to be alone. For him the supreme happiness was to be able to choose his moments of solitude – not to have others choose to disrupt them.

He picked up the glass again, swirled the liquid within it, and continued examining its lustre against the light. He went on drinking, savouring the wine upon his tongue. Then he put on Schubert's *Sonata in A Major*. Alfred Cortot's version was a re-mastering and the original master had been rather crackly, but what an interpretation!

'Poor Schubert!' Nazulis thought. 'To compose those phrases, such musical intensity yet such simplicity, so every note seemed to strike the heart – he must have sweated blood! And he must have really loved women, that poor old ogling timid chap!'

Nazulis ran a bath, scattered a handful of *Youth Dew* salts and lowered himself luxuriously into the hot water, still holding his glass. The music had stopped. Only the trickle of the bath taps disturbed the silence.

After a moment he began wrinkling his nose with annoyance. 'No, that won't do at all,' he muttered angrily.

He got out hurriedly, dripping, and placed the precious glass of burgundy in the other room.

'That was damn stupid of me. What a thing to do!' he grumbled. He sank back into the water redolent of *Youth Dew*.

'Drowning Nuit Saint Georges in bath salts – what a bloody fool I am!'

4

CLÉMENCE AND THE CONFESSIONAL

At eight a.m. Gulliver woke his master. The creature was straining at the leash, so swollen that Nazulis was all but in pain.

'Hey, hold it, you're going crazy!' Florian exclaimed. Gulliver bobbed assent, full of gusto.

Nazulis scratched his head as he hobbled over to check his gadgets once more: tapes, mike, wires, machine. All set.

She was there in her blue dressing gown, leaning over her blacony, smiling.

'Aha,' said the drowsy oenophile, 'you're bright and early, aren't you?'

'Tea?' she suggested.

'Come over,' he said.

'Let me make it,' she announced on walking in, 'I'll sort it out.'

'All right, fine,' Florian said. 'The tea is on the . . .'

'I'll find it, don't worry.'

She returned with the tray. Florian had donned a dressing gown. Gulliver had relaxed somewhat. She put down the tray and without further ado knelt down in front of Florian, parted the garment and took the warm brute into her mouth.

'Hey, but . . .' the surprised Florian exclaimed.

She worked on with tongue and lips. 'Does that feel good?' she asked.

'You bet . . .' Florian said.

When Gulliver, now fully rigid once again, began to jerk and buck his head demandingly, she lay down on the bed.

'Undress,' Florian instructed her.

'No, wait. Kiss me, come on . . .'

Her breath smelt of peppermint. She had recently brushed her teeth with an American toothpaste — in all likelihood Crest. Her tongue darted with soft, swift, eager flicks around his. At times she would swallow his tongue ferociously before once again thrusting her own down his throat in a determined buccal onslaught.

'How about me?' Gulliver was protesting, beating his head against that melting pot still covered by the protective panties.

'Get undressed . . . I'll undress you then,'

Florian was insisting.

'No . . . wait, press against me, I like to feel you all hard against my stomach.'

She started moving her belly up and down, making rythmic undulations like a ship at sea, up and down, to and fro . . . He could feel her fill with salty fluids. But that damn gown, those quite unnecessary panties! He tried to rip them off. Gasping for breath, she defended herself, her body stiffening.

'Squeeze me,' she repeated. 'Rub against me.'

He made Gulliver lunge back and forth, ever harder, against her protected proffered loins. She herself was virtually on the brink of orgasm. She was breathing very heavily, clutching at his buttocks fiercely. 'She's going to come without me,' Florian thought and made a renewed effort to tear down her panties. He pulled their elastic which snapped but she still resisted, tense-jawed now. It was both struggle and embrace.

She delivered several culminating lunges before plummeting into climax, uttering a sort of strange, strangled gurgle which seemed to well up from somewhere deep in her larynx. Nazulis watched her regain her breath; she was close yet far away.

'God, that was good,' she smiled.

'How about me?' he asked petulantly.

Using her thumb and forefinger, she endeav-

oured to extricate a hair adhering to her tongue.
She shrugged.

'How about me?' he repeated, he all but
shrieked. 'Do you always get your kicks like
that?'

'Like what?' she retorted.

'Swiss style.'

She shook her head, laughing now at him. Her
hair flailed about her face, wafting that womanly
odour, the incomparable scent of skin whose
pores have recently oozed pleasure. Gulliver was
giving Florian a hard time.

'I'm not on the pill,' she said.

'Oh,' he said worried. He got up and headed
for the shower, Gulliver still stiff with unreleased
tension.

'Come back,' she said.

He returned then, half hesitant.

'Lie down here,' she said, patting the bed
beside her. Her tongue made about forty trips to
and fro, from Gulliverian tip to scrotum. Very
gently and deliberately at that.

'Oh, oh,' Florian began to gasp.

The tongue became more caressing, lingered
longer, then turned rapid.

'Oh, oh! Ohhh . . . too much!' he groaned.

After a long teasing exploration, Clémence
took the entire shaft in her hot mouth and waited.

'I can't take any more!' moaned Florian.

She remained motionless.

'Oh no . . . listen . . . Woouuu . . .'

She felt him dilate, contract and grow harder still, but she stayed absolutely immobile.

'Aaaouh!' he wailed, crazy with desire.

Then she sucked in her cheeks and bobbed back and forth again, forcing the rampant Gulliver to travel even further, before bursting at last with a white tide which pulsed and throbbed in nine steady spasms. Seconds after the ninth and final spurt, Nazulis, eyes still closed, took a deep breath, filling both lungs. He then exhaled equally deeply, emitting a voluptuous sigh of satisfaction.

'It might be a good thing if you did go on the pill,' he remarked.

'I don't often have sex,' she said.

'That makes twice in as many days.'

'Which is unusual for me.'

'I'd like to come in your arms, deep inside you,' he said.

'I'll start taking the pill next month, just for you,' she promised.

'You're a good neighbour,' he said, kissing her.

She stretched. One firm breast appeared as her dressing gown slipped open also exposing that delightful dark oxter patch which had given Nazulis such olfactory thrills. Her armpit tuft, seen from that angle, seemed quite long, its hair a deep beige.

'It's my turn: I'd like to suck you off too.'

'But you'd only want to fuck me afterwards, though,' she said.

'I promise not to.'

'I'm anti-abortion,' she added.

'I wouldn't fuck you afterwards.'

'Not even if I wanted you to? Not even if I begged you?'

'I promise. I'm against little accidents – having babies as a form of Russian roulette.'

She undressed and he finally saw her naked. She had a lithe, soft body, delightfully curvaceous, but not an ounce overweight. Her limbs were sleek and plump. Her breasts full and tilting slightly upwards, were crowned by hard, brown nipples. Under each arm there was that thick thatch, undergrowth enough to entrance the explorer. And beneath a wide yet flat stomach, lay a delta of fine foliage which he approached purring like a lovesick cat, drooling gluttonously.

He made her lie down with her legs apart and a pillow beneath her hips. Delta became promontory. The brown fleece, also raised aloft, opened into a pink, dripping ravine. A lukewarm liquid had trickled down it, past the arsehole, to form a little puddle upon the coverlet. 'Reminds one of shellfish', he thought. 'They all smell of the sea, mussels, clams, cockles, whelks or whatever . . .

A nice scent, I like it . . . Women are magical, marine delicacies . . .' He started lapping at the tiny bud that kept appearing and disappearing, tantalizing, elusive, yet real enough.

'A bit lower down,' breathed Clémence.

He had positioned his hands beneath his neighbour's buttocks. His tongue, plunging inside the aperture, worked to a regular, deliberate rhythm. She began breathing heavily through her nose, in a series of urgent inhalations and exhalations.

'Is that it, there?' he enquired.

'Yes, go on. Ah yes, right there, exactly like that. Don't stop.'

He enjoyed giving pleasure this way. His heart was beating hard and he was anticipating her paroxysm with a kind of awed impatience. To witness a woman's orgasm was a pure form of joy to him – the best illustration he knew of that injunction to love one another, so deformed and misrepresented by the Church. In that moment he did indeed love his neightbour, and with all the altruism of which he was capable. In this caress there was nothing for him: it was all hers, for her. And he thought only of her mounting pleasure, of how her excitement now inexorably increased. Mouth to that other mouth in all the heady intoxications of love's most secret kiss, he felt those preliminary throes which heralded her final seismic seizure.

'Yes,' she gasped. 'Go on!'

At that moment there was no need to alter at all the pressure, rhythm or quality of the caress. It was the very instant of paradox, when the clitoris coyly retreats as if to avoid the supreme and imminent pleasure. A final tickle and the eruption would follow. Here was one of nature's own contradictions: the clitoris shrinking to sheathe itself, as if renouncing the extent of its bliss! Nazulis, who had loved many women, knew that at this crucial moment a man must never let up or let go, tracking the trickily reticent and burrowing bud . . .

'Ah yes, oh yes!' Clémence shouted.

Her whole body was rigid, overwhelmed by the onset and intensity of her ecstasy.

Florian felt the breakers of bliss surge over his tongue. Completely carried away, he had a violent temptation to climb on top of her, clutch her, and ram Gulliver home, deep into the dripping cleft. She even flung her legs up to receive the thrust. He burned to solder his body to hers in a blaze of bliss. But remembered his promise. And contented himself with sliding his tongue as far up the receptacle offered as possible, to the very lingual root.

Florian too was adamantly opposed to the use of abortion as a form of contraception.

'Do you have to go to work? the pretty neighbour asked him a while later.

The pair of them were lying naked and relaxed across the huge bed, just like good friends should. They weren't in love. The situation was quite straightforward. The love they had just experienced – that great wave of human warmth – they would have for any other man or woman, under the circumstances. They had indulged their mutual attraction. Clémence and Florian had not chosen each other, they had met by chance. They'd excited one another, nothing more. They weren't making plans to live together nor hearing violins. They liked each other a lot and that was it. (Sometimes, Florian would remind himself, there was nothing more miserable than a woman who flung her arms round your neck after a fuck and tried to keep them there for ever . . .)

'No,' Nazulis answered. 'I don't "have to" go to work. I work in my own time, whenever I choose. Every day I can hardly believe my good luck – no clocking in, no boss, no office routine.'

Clémence hung over the bed and took her dressing gown off the floor. She rummaged in its pockets.

'What are you looking for?' he asked her.

'Cigarettes.'

'Oh no, not that, please! Anything but that.'

'Are you allergic to tobacco?' she said.

'You could say that, yes.'

Nazulis did not need to smoke: he was not nerve-wracked enough for that. He felt no desire to inhale a futile and deceptive substance which would anyhow have ruined his sense of smell. He was happy to live the other side of the smoke curtain, aware of subtler aromas. Such abstention from that poison so freely available at every street corner meant that his tastebuds were spared, preserving their remarkable sensitivity.

'What's all this oenologist business involve?' Clémence asked, her forefinger tickling the drowsy Gulliver.

'I travel round the main winegrowing regions, the Burgundy and Bordeaux areas, the Loire and Rhône valleys and so on. Various vintages are obviously superior, certain years better than others – and I do the selecting for a number of French and foreign buyers. My function is to act as a sort of middleman-taster, the intermediary between the wine producers and the retailers.'

'Does it pay well?'

'Well enough, though I've no job security. Any day I might find myself out of work. Luckily I have a sideline which is also rather interesting: I write a monthly wine column for *Gourmet*, a gastronomic and travel magazine. This regular article means I have to get opinions and criticisms down in black and white, which otherwise I might never have formulated. A good exercise, since few things are harder than trying to classify and describe a wine. You have to find "correspondences", as that masterly word-connoisseur Baudelaire put it.'

Clémence listened to him as she toyed with the Gulliverian bush, teasing its hairs into tiny curls.

'Are you married?' she blurted out.

Florian looked at her warily.

'Why do you ask?'

'I don't know . . . I don't know you well. I'm trying to understand you, find out what makes you tick. You don't have to answer if you don't want to.'

She was experimenting with a pigtail effect, but the pubic hairs were too short to plait. So she placed a kiss on Gulliver's empurpled head, which no longer twitched.

'Marriage is the end of a couple,' Nazulis declared.

'Ah!' she said, almost as if assenting.

'It's the death of the couple, the institutionalization of love. It means social security, the suppression of adventure. Yes, it's the beginning of the end.'

'But there are successful marriages,' claimed the young woman, who had now found a comb and was carefully combing Gulliver's fur.

'How many? What percentage?' he demanded.

'I – I don't know.'

'Ten per cent. If that. The remainder, after the first six months of illusion, sink into mediocrity, boredom, frigidity, compromise and charades.'

'You're very harsh.'

'Marriage constitutes the biggest social con-trick going.'

'But . . .'

'It's a rat-trap, a fool's ambush.'

'Have you ever been married?' she inquired.

'Twice,' he replied. 'Each time for two years. The two experiences were worth having, so in that sense only, each was a success. Both times, as soon as things started going wrong, we separated. The greatest personal illusion and social hypocrisy is proclaiming "I'll always love you". There's no always. It's a snare. You only love once: that's true of most people. The individual evolves, everyone changes in his or her own way. The day inevitably comes when the two people involved are no longer complementary or mutually supportive. That's the day the couple should separate, quick, before things get even worse and they reach the final stage – hatred.'

'What about children, though?'

'Ah, children! That's the great argument invariably produced by defenders of the institution of marriage.'

Clémence went on doodling with Florian's

golden fleece.

'One last word,' he persevered, 'and then I'll stop making speeches. We've better things to do than talk. Ouch, you're hurting! What was I saying?'

'The children.'

'The children, yes. Very important. It makes me sick when I see how they're brought up. What I want to say is this: happily separated parents are better for their children than parents who persist in living together despite not seeing eye to eye.'

Clémence let go of Nazulis's thatch, thoughtful now.

'Nothing's worse for children,' the oenologist went on, 'than being caught between their parents' mutual hate or indifference.'

'Right,' she agreed.

'I could tell you a thing or two yet to put you off marriage, but I don't want to play the wise old uncle. After all, people are free to do whatever they like, and to make their own cock-ups too.'

'I certainly don't plan to get married,' she affirmed.

'You never can tell. One fine day you might just get the urge – it's catching. You think you're starting with a clean slate and the odds are even. This time it's the real thing! You're starry-eyed as the ring slips on your finger. Then the weight drops and the trap snaps shut. There's no longer a way out. You're trapped, the pair of you, married!'

Florian waved both arms emphatically.

'Marriage, oh what an illusion! What an abominable insitution!'

The Church of St. Honoro-d'Elée, Place Victor Hugo, was one of the most fashionable in Paris's 16th *arrondissement*.

For a priest to be appointed to this particular parish signfied something of a rise in the religious hierarchy. Such a worthy would be working in a district with a God-fearing, conservative tradition. He would speedily adapt to this genteel environment and himself strive also to acquire an unctuous yet elegant style of speech.

The good *curés* of St. Honoro soon became (in the words of their flock) all too 'proper', very models of 'good taste', dispensing advice that was invariably 'discreet' or 'well-bred'.

At St. Honoro-d'Elée, everything reeked of the odour of sanctity.

Florian parked his car in front of the side entrance in Rue Mesnil. He glanced momentarily at the main door, where several nuns who smelt of

78

Marseilles soap were busily dislodging a peaceful spaniel asleep on the front steps. They also shooed away a flock of pigeons which fluttered off into the blue. Chiselled into the yellowish stonework of the vaulting was an inscription that had faded to grey over the years. Nazulis deciphered it: D.O.M. SVB INVOCATIONE SANCTI HONORATI EPISCOPI. He blew a raspberry. The formula was, he thought, more than somewhat stale. There had been all too many fine resounding phrases in Christian history . . . Above the Latin words the big bovine eye of a rosaceous plant seemed to stare over the Place Victor Hugo. Above it dangled the pendulum of the church clock, and that was surmounted by a bronze casing. To top the lot, a stone cross. So much for the entrance to St. Honoro-d'Elée.

Florian reached the porch. Just as he was pushing open the church door, he had second thoughts, turned round and dashed across to Lasavin's shop nearby.

There he knew he would find the finest chocolates in Paris. 'Life's not at all bad,' he told himself as he selected an assortment of goodies, loading one of the tiny trays provided. Pockets bursting with sweets, he entered the church.

Along the silent aisles reverently shuffled the devout, sometimes overtaken by the whirring flurry of a soutane busily going about its business and characterized by muffled, scurrying steps.

A little old lady, moustached and muttering, approached a wrought-iron multiple candelabrum on which flickered holy candles of varying sizes (2, 5 or 10 francs' worth). She looked anxiously around her, first left then right, then vice versa and over her shoulder. She slipped some small change into the wooden moneybox and drew back again to make sure no one was looking. With a flourish she seized the largest candle and skewered it into place. Thirty days' indulgence. She hadn't wasted her time. Thirty days, a whole month's absolution! Oh no, she hadn't wasted her time in the least . . .

Florian extracted the mike from its case and entered the deserted confessional. A notice on the front door read: *Confessions from 15.00 to 17.00*.

The dark wooden cage ensured that you could only squeeze in upon your knees. Groping, he located the sides and corners of the cabin. He then took the capsule mike between thumb and forefinger and secured it high on the right hand side. There the sensitive apparatus could pick up every whisper.

Suddenly, with a sharp click the little communication hatch opened.

Florian had not heard the priest arrive. The latter was now silhouetted against the grille, mumbling in a voice so low that the young man could not tell whether he was talking French or Latin.

Ready to flee, Nazulis hesitated. The priest's voice was suddenly very loud and clear.

'Well, my son?' inquired this man of the cloth.

'Well, M. le *Curé*,' Florian echoed, not knowing what to say. I certainly haven't come to confess my sins, he thought, since God died years ago, and this infamous Church blighted my youth quite enough, what with all its mumbo-jumbo and lies . . .

'Well then, my son?'

Through the grating drifted the priest's aroma: he stank of boredom, along with an old man's odour of encrusted sperm and dried urine, of unclean underwear. His breath was heavy with constipation and tobacco. Florian had nothing against the poor sod personally, be it noted.

He decided to leave and made as if to do so before abruptly changing his mind. He leaned nearer the grille and stammered:

'I've masturbated five times today – no, six – in front of the image of the Virgin Mary. I found her exciting, you see. A virgin is always provocative, and what with her little blue veil . . . I fantasised that she hoisted her dress over her legs – she has really nice bare Mediterranean legs – and exposed her little knickers, the sort they used to wear in

81

those days, made of transparent papyrus . . . It really got me hot . . .'

Silence. Nazulis the Blasphemer listened to the priest's breathing. It was the priest's wretched dogma, not the man himself, which Nazulis resented: the rubbish that had poisoned the best of his adolescence. They did me quite enough harm, he thought, for me to be entitled to a bit of revenge.

The silence continued interminably.

'Yes . . .' said the priest, softly.

'And then I raped a small girl, the day before yesterday, a girl walking through the school gates with her satchel under her arm. I offered her sweets. She got into my car and I took off for the suburbs. On some waste ground I raped and buggered her. Did everything. I beat her up until she didn't move any more. I took out my knife and cut her . . .'

'Hm,' said the *curé*.

'What? Did you say something?'

'I'm listening to you, my son.'

'Last week I poisoned my wife with arsenic. She was ill and running a fever. Flu. She'd become very ugly. Her face all pinched, bad breath and so on. I'll make you some tea, I told her. She drank her cup, staring at me with abnormally bright eyes, full of gratitude. You've just drunk arsenic, I told her calmly and she laughed feebly, thinking I was joking. I slapped her face and went out to pick up a whore. I took my time, and when I got back she was dead.'

The priest turned his face towards the grating.

'My son, don't you think you're laying it on a bit?'

'Not at all. There's worse to come. Three days ago I held up a . . .'

'Why do you take pleasure in telling me all this?' the man said, coolly adjusting his chasuble.

'That's what you're here for, isn't it? To listen to people's confessions. And what about my penance? You haven't given me a penance!'

'As penance, you must come back and confess your real sins . . .'

'I don't believe in sin!' Florian shouted furiously. 'What you call sin is a devilish invention created by moralists, cops and people like yourself, designed to turn people into sheep, and society into a huge flock for the greater profits of those masters you've always served. Army, Church and the Banks: there's your Holy Trinity.

'You ruined the best years of my youth with your ideas about so-called sins. You wrecked my childhood and now you louse up kids of the new generations. As well as adults naive enough to swallow your syrupy or threatening speeches and your pseudo-pieties. You're all the same – illusionists without real faith – because you don't even believe it yourselves . . .'

But the priest had left the box and was heading towards the sacristy, his shoulders hunched.

Nazulis made sure that the mike was securely fixed above his head. He came out of the confessional, left the church and got into his car. He switched on the recording apparatus, which was now set to pick up and record anything over a decibel rating of only ten. In other words, as soon as anyone began talking quietly or even whispering. Thereafter, the machine would automatically stop after 30 seconds of continuous silence. And of course the device also allowed for listening-in only. All one had to do was press a small green button.

This Nazulis now did. The amplifier transmitted only a vague hum, the generalized church noise comprised of murmured prayers, sniffles, coughs, stealthy footsteps, doors creaking, curtains swept aside. From time to time there would be a louder sound: the scrape of a chair across the stone flooring. For the time being the confessional was unoccupied.

He waited, enjoying his mastication of a peppermint chocolate. Then he chewed another, followed by a third.

At last the sound quality improved, due to the presence of someone entering the confessional box. A human body installed itself inside, knees against the wood, which creaked slightly. Florian waited for a while.

The click of the confessional door made him jump. There was the mumble (was it French or Latin?) of the priest, then a very young voice which became more distinct after various phlegmy clearings of the throat.

'I haven't been to confession since last Wednesday,' the little sinner launched forth. 'Since then I – well . . .'

'Well?' said the priest.

The child hesitated then gabbled his confession in a rush, without pausing for breath.

'I stole a box of nougat. I didn't do my maths homework. I said shit to my mother.'

'That's really sweet!' Florian exclaimed delightedly in the car. 'He's cute, this lad!'

And he crammed a *griotte* into his gizzard.

'Hum,' said the priest, 'that's not very good, not good at all. Anything else?'

'Um . . . nothing.'

The child was obviously wracking his brains – and quite sincerely too – in order to see what else might rank as a sin. But he had remembered and listed the lot, even before kneeling, so no, there was nothing in particular, nothing more.

'Really nothing else?' the cleric insisted.

'No, honestly,' replied the kid.

Florian was fuming. Was the old bugger going

to keep trying for his pound of flesh?

'No . . . impure thoughts?'

'No,' said the little boy, clearly confused by the priest's insinuations.

'No . . . fondling?'

What a shit, Florian seethed: I'll soon sort him out, and his cesspit too!

'No,' said the schoolboy, still quite unable to see what the confessor was driving at.

'How old are you, my young friend?'

'Ten, sir.'

'No impurities then, you're sure? As penance, you'll say ten Hail Marys.'

The kid, cockahoop at getting off so lightly, rushed off even before the absolutional claptrap had finished. The nougats had particularly worried him. It had been a big box and the shopkeeper hadn't seen a thing. Ten Hail Marys seemed a bargain, under the circumstances.

There followed the timorous snivelling of an elderly crone who had arrived late for 8 a.m. Mass that morning, having yielded to gluttony the previous day. Three helpings of cake, at that. The usual soothing reassurances, then a respectable citizen of fifty, the tight-arsed, tight-lipped type who had come to confess yet another wet-dream. This Holy Joe was succeeded by another sanctimonious female and a Portuguese maid who blamed herself for not working hard enough. Then there was a house-owner who confessed to exploiting her servant. ('But I pay all her Social Security for her, she costs me a lot . . .') After this microcosm of society Florian at last heard a voice which did not actually jar: what a wonderfully melodious voice it was, too! He turned up the volume control and listened.

The voice belonged to a young woman. After several venial peccadilloes she dared to get to the point, stammering slightly. For several days she could think of only one thing. It was obsessing and tormenting her. Nothing she did could dispel the thought, the picture of this . . . thing. Finally she had given in, and had taken to entering her bedroom, locking the door, lying down on the bed and pleasuring herself.

'This . . . thing, my child,' the priest said, 'which so obsesses you, what is it?'

She would not reply. Nazulis heard the noise of knees shifting uncomfortably against wooden planks.

'What is this thing?' the priest persisted.

A fraught silence.

'You can tell me everything, my child,' he snuffled.

87

The confessional was cracking apart, judging by the deafening racket of knees on wood. The priest's heavy breathing was also much in evidence.

'You must tell me everything, my dear child,' he insisted.

'Father . . .'

'This thing . . . Well?' he murmured unctuously.

She plucked up her courage.

'A prick!' she blurted out, bursting into sobs. 'I just think about it all the time, night and day. Being, um, penetrated, with deep thrusts of a prick!'

'Mmm,' said the priest.

'I know it's terrible, Father. What am I to do?' she sobbed.

'But what about your husband?'

'Oh *him* . . .'

Florian leaped out of the car and dashed into the church. As he charged towards the confessional he congratulated himself on having the knack of being in the right place at the right time. He reached the repentance shack just as she was emerging, her eyes red and with handkerchief to nose, on her way to kneel upon a suitable hassock.

Her penitential stance was the perfect position for posterior observation, and Nazulis was jubilant. Beneath her demure dark blue dress there was a superb, rounded arse – the sort of wind-breaker which, he was convinced, would work wonders in bed. Always assuming one knew how to go about it: i.e. getting it there in the first place!

Sitting three rows of chairs behind her, Nazulis composed his hands in a posture which a casual onlooker might have mistaken for one of piety pure and simple. Actually, a myriad lubricious pictures were racing through the young man's mind as he continued his contemplation.

He saw her get up, and himself rose to follow her.

She had a very slight limp. Each step she took she swayed a little to the right, with a barely noticeable awkwardness of that hip, though the movement in no way detracted from her manifest charms. On leaving the church she walked along Avenue Victor Hugo. He still had not seen her face to face. She took short, quick strides despite her limp. He loped along in pursuit.

Just as she was about to cross the street he caught up with her.

'Excuse me, Madame.'

Poised on the kerb as she was, she looked somewhat surprised and glanced askance at him as if unable to decide whether he was collecting, skirtchasing or conducting a market research survey.

She was very attractive and on the small side. A great quiff of blonde hair hid one of her hazel eyes as she turned her head. The other eye, however, was bright, intelligent and filled with curiosity.

'What do you want?'

'I was in the church just now.'

'And?' she asked.

'I was in the confessional with you. The other side.'

A moment of hesitation. The 82 bus passed, punishing its first gear as usual.

'So?' she said drily as the bus moved on.

He stood right in front of her and looked her straight in the eye.

'I heard everything.'

She turned pale. Her mouth opened and closed noiselessly like that of a stranded fish. She reeled, tried to regain control of herself, but promptly blushed a deep scarlet.

'Don't worry, Madame,' he said in a jovial tone, taking her arm. 'Nothing to get steamed up about. Your so-called sins are trivial enough – the odd fantasy, some mild masturbation, dreams of a big dick . . .'

'Oh, please!' she gasped.

'Come on then!' he blithely urged her. 'Don't be upset, my dear little lady. Fantasies are only natural, after all. And quite healthy. A big hard prick, eh? No, no, don't argue, don't worry: relax, come on. Calm down.'

'Where are you taking me?' she all but whispered.

'My place,' he said.

He bent over her for a moment and surreptitiously took a couple of sniffs. Guerlain's *L'Heure Bleue*: he liked that one. A mellow, flowery, spicy scent.

'Your house! Oh no. Out of the question,' she protested.

She was pleading with him, he could see it in her eyes. Her pretty face, still flushed, was lightly made-up: a daytime foundation cream with an apricot aroma he had distinguished at once; a touch of Rimmel around the eyes; a trace of pink eye-shadow.

'No no, I beg you, I – ' she was repeating.

'Come along,' he said, smiling broadly.

He looked as if butter wouldn't melt in his mouth: a young man of neat yet distinctive appearance, with an attractive and open face, obviously honest. He was dressed in British style, what was more – silk scarf (doubtless from Hermès) and dark green tweed jacket with leather elbow patches. Yes, Florian was clearly well-dressed, well-bred and well-educated. Hadn't she met him at St. Honoro-d'Elée, after all?

'No, no,' she went on protesting feebly, but she let herself be walked to the car.

He opened the door for her, carefully stashed the recording equipment and turned the starter. All aboard for the bed of pleasure!

'It's not possible, just not possible,' she repeated.

Her voice had a definitely upper-class intonation but was lilting enough to delight the ear. God how he wanted to make her yell! How she would scream with pleasure at the thrusts of that long-desired prick . . .

Florian drove well, smiling. He placed a hand on her warm thigh and she jumped.

'Come on, don't be childish – you're a big girl now. The time has come to live like an adult, according to your desires . . . 'Deep thrusts of a prick' was how you expressed it.'

'Stop it!' she sobbed. 'I'm ashamed . . .'

He stopped the car at the far end of the avenue and took her in his arms like a father cajoling a young daughter, stroking her hair and holding a handkerchief to her nose.

'Don't cry any more . . .'

'I'm so ashamed . . .'

'Nothing to be ashamed of. Though it's time you became a free, independent individual. They taught you to reject desires, repress your feelings, mortify yourself. You have to sweep away such crap. Relax, for God's sake!'

'But . . .'

'Fantasies like the ones you mentioned are *good*! That I promise you.'

'Stop this! I want to go back home . . .'

He put his arm around her, stroked her cheek and brushed away a tear. Her big eyes were staring at him with a lost child's expression. He tilted back her chin and gently kissed her lips. She no longer protested. Her eyes closed. She did not fully open her mouth but then she didn't close it either. He massaged her a little before sliding a hand under the top of her dress. He could feel her brassière with his fingertips. A sad mistake, at her age, he thought . . . Then he cupped her whole breast with his hand. She uttered a tiny moan. He began ferreting around her belt and undid the dress. She did protest at that, and struggled a bit. He persisted and managed to insert two fingers inside her panties. The hair they felt was soft, warm, silky. She struggled again, but he slid one finger against her vulva. She was wet, absolutely sodden with desire. Which illustrated the Christian neurosis, Florian reflected: the mind saying No while the body said Yes.

'Oooh,' she said, surprised to feel such pleasure rise in herself, as successive waves of emotion threatened to overwhelm her.

She sprawled all loose and relaxed across the

confined space of the car seat, her legs wide apart, as if his for the asking. He continued caressing her, and his finger worked inexorably to and fro, prompting a series of puppyish yelps from the young woman.

Then he took one of her slim hands and laid it on Gulliver. The latter had been straining under Florian's trousers for what had seemed an interminable time.

'Dear God . . .' she gasped, amazed at the firmly cylindrical bulge.

'That's what you wanted, wasn't it?'

'Oh . . . my goodness . . . oh . . .' she repeated in fascination.

'That's what you needed, wasn't it?' he remarked, his tone now slightly brutal, though she did not seem to notice or care.

'Oh yes, yes,' she murmured.

'Let's go, then,' he said, turning the starter key.

While he was driving her fingertips shyly stroked that 'thing' of her dreams and fantasies.

'You can do that harder, you know. It won't break,' he commented.

She did not dare. With a swift movement he unzipped and the animal's head popped out of its pouch, glistening and shamelessly scarlet.

Her eyes goggled in astonishment. She was temporarily speechless.

Had she never examined her husband's (Lilliputian?) Gulliver close to? It seemed as though she were discovering the prime male organ for the very first time.

The passengers in a car beside them at the red light were craning over, all agape. Florian burst out laughing and waved, half friendly, half mocking, as the lights changed to green.

They travelled along the Boulevard Saint-Germain and the Rue de Rennes, to Place Saint-Sulpice, the heart of the 6th *arrondissement*, full of trees and strolling pedestrians. It was a cheerful and lively scene, despite the preponderance of creepy little religious shops where old folks from the provinces could buy rosaries, missals, and assorted edifying and devotional paraphernalia.

On this square dominated by the ugliest, most lumbering church in Paris, a veritable sacred bunker, children were roller-skating round the monumental fountain which sprinkled frothy sprays of water over the stony shoulders of Fénélon, Bishop of Cambrai; Bossuet, Bishop of Meaux; Eflechier, Bishop of Nimes, and Manillon, Bishop of Clermont. Four bland old boys sitting unperturbed amid the deluge, guarded by four roaring lions. Four worthies, well and truly out of it, far removed from the world and its realities – kids, roller-skates, birdsong and lovers on benches.

Florian parked the car beneath a plane tree. Her head was still lowered, she was still staring at that dream pistol of hers, on whose rubescent tip twinkled a jovial teardrop of clear liquid.

'Desire,' he said. 'I get wet too.'

She dabbed it with one finger to collect a drop of fluid and raised the finger to her nose. Odourless. Next she tested it with her tongue.

'Sweetish,' she said.

He turned towards the young woman. Her expression had about it a beautific, expectant intentness.

'I want you so much,' he said.

'I want you too. I've never felt quite this way before,' she said, running her hand through Florian's hair.

'Have you ever been unfaithful to your husband?' he asked, playing with her platinum engagement ring set with diamonds.

'Never,' she said.

'Did you have any other men before him?'

'Not intimately. One or two flirtations at the most.'

'What do you mean by "flirtations"?'

'Amusements. Nothing below the belt.'

'So you were a virgin when you married?'

'Yes.'

'Incredible!' he exclaimed. 'So it still happens,

even in 1985! This bloody religion really does poison people's minds, to this day. And what does your husband do?'

'He's quite high up in the Ministry of Defence.' Florian suppressed a grimace.

'Does he love you?'

'Sort of.'

'What does that mean, sort of?'

'He's certainly very fond of me. He's a thoughtful, affectionate person.'

'Does he make love to you often?'

'Once or twice a week.'

'What?'

'Once or twice . . .'

'I heard you all right. It's dreadful – a woman like you, beautiful, young, sexy . . . Once or twice . . . What a waste! What a sod he must be! How sad!'

She snuggled close to him, so near and so lonely. She was looking at him with those distinctive pale eyes. All at once Florian felt like weeping, like having a damn good cry. The world was full of strange anomalies quite beyond his comprehension. Sometimes he no longer understood anything.

He took her hand and pressed it to his lips, sensing that what was happening to them in that transient moment was far beyond desire. Between them, between their spoken or unspoken words, between the lines, there was something invisible. Quite simply, it was love. A moment of love without calculation or conventions, without past or future. Absolutely gratuitous as only real love can be. He sought nothing from her; she had her life and he had his. Their paths had crossed. Perhaps they might never see each other again.

'What's your name?' she asked.

'Florian,' he said.

'Fancy,' she said, 'our names are almost the same. Mine's Florence.'

She laid her head on his shoulder. They stared up at the pinnacles of the church of Saint-Sulpice, those formidable and lofty bastions.

'Moments like these make life worth living,' said Florian. Certainly there was desire, for they both knew that they were soon going to fling themselves on to a bed in a few minutes, and be shaken by the Great Earthquake, but just then they were beyond desire. Love itself goes beyond desire. Gulliver too had relaxed, as if instinctively understanding that love goes beyond sex. Indeed he waited confidently in his nook, knowing all too well that the young master never passed up an opportunity. Just for now, the master himself was in love. It wasn't the time for frisking and frolics. Gulliver waited.

Ah, they were getting out! he realised happily after a period of silence. A rush of excitement filled Gulliver, which reared readily at the thought of plunging headfirst into that wonderful well so redolent of womanly desire.

Gulliver all but crackled with erectile electricity.

5

FLORENCE AND THE MIRACLE

Florian was right. Florence revealed herself to be a fantastic lover.

How, though, was it possible to prove so adept at amatory arts after so little practice? She must somehow have learned from all those amorous orgies she had never actually experienced, imaginatively recreating every sexual encounter hitherto forbidden.

She certainly knew how to compensate for her inexperience and lack of confidence.

'Shall we get into bed?' she asked her abductor timidly.

'We'll get on to the bed. I want to look you over from head to foot, my beauty.'

She started to undress methodically, like a schoolgirl, folding her dress with care before laying it across a chair.

'Wait,' he told her. 'I'm the one who'll take off your clothes.'

She allowed him to do so, showing traces of embarrassment, unused as she was to these sexual rituals.

'Am I hurting your leg?' he asked as he was removing her white silk petticoat.

'No of course not. Why?'

'I noticed you were limping slightly. Did you have a ski accident?'

'No, it's the sciatic nerve in my hip . . . I'm not really sure, but I've been in pain for two or three months. It hurts when I walk. I've seen several specialists, to no avail.'

'Doctors, well yes . . .' Florian said with a sceptical dismissive frown, continuing to slide a pair of tiny embroidered cotton panties down her long, slender legs.

As soon as she was naked in his arms, trembling and quivering with desire, Florian slipped down so that his head was poised between her legs, ready to render the initial homage, for play and foreplay, of the oral embrace.

'No,' she gasped. 'Do it quickly please, inside me, quick.'

She parted her legs, raised her knees a little and held out her arms to him. Her slim, warm body still had the remnants of last summer's suntan. Two small firm breasts tilted in youthful pride. Her legs were trembling.

He gazed at her with momentary apprehension.

She wore an expression of such intensity, such concentrated passion – a crazy look, in fact – that he was dumbfounded, motionless. She grabbed his shoulders with immense strength, and he felt her nails sink into his back like an eagle's talons gripping its prey. She pulled him abruptly onto her stomach and was penetrated at a stroke.

Only then did she relax. Her hands released their grip and her muscles too unclenched. Her eyes lost their demented stare.

She undulated her belly in a slow, supple grind, linked now to her lover's own loins. Propped somewhat uncomfortably on his elbows, he thrust downward at her and could thus observe her too, fascinated by her absorption, by the fervour of her lovemaking. He had fucked many women (he was one of the most notorious womanisers in Paris), but he had never yet witnessed such ardour during intercourse.

'It's even better than I dreamed,' she murmured.

'What would you like now?' he asked. 'What would you like me to do?'

'I used to have one particular fantasy. I'll show you what I mean.'

She uncoupled and knelt on the bed, her head bent, leaning forward like an animal on all fours.

'Like this,' she said.

Admiring the superb curvaceous rump thus

raised and proffered to him, Florian let Gulliver's round tip truffle at the moist mound.

'Strike as hard as you can,' she said.

Florian hesitated for a second. What did she mean by the odd verb 'strike'? Spanking those lovely, plump cheeks with whip or cane, crop or switch? Beating of buttocks till they bled and she came? He fervently hoped it was not the case and she didn't get her kicks that way. He'd never been one for SM games. He liked to stroke not strike. Loved love, not violence.

'You want me to beat you?' he inquired anxiously.

'No, no. Not strike *me*, just to go deep, drive into me hard, as hard as you can, into me from behind.'

Florian had further misgivings: what did she mean by that last phrase? Did she want him to bugger her? Why not? he asked himself. It really wasn't his speciality, so to speak, nor did he rate sodomy as a more pleasurable option than any other (though there were plenty of anally-fixated characters who would disagree), but if that was her desire he was ready to satsify it.

He pressed his finger against the alternative entrance and felt the taut elasticity of the puckered membrane.

'It needs some lubrication,' he suggested, 'otherwise it's not too easy. Might be painful.'

He put out his tongue and tenderly and conscientiously accomplished the manoeuvre dubbed by erotologists *feuille de rose*.

She began laughing and her whole bottom shook. The sight was irresistibly provocative.

'When I said "from behind",' she explained, 'I only meant the position, not *that*.'

'I see,' said Florian, with relief.

There were no further misunderstandings or reciprocal agreements. Gulliver to the fore, he penetrated her by the more customary highway, which was sleek and hot. His poker stoked her ever more vigorously.

'Aaaaaoooooaaah!' she was wailing interminably, her mouth jammed against the mattress.

Every time he sensed her nearing climax, he accelerated his rhythm and dug deep between those firm cheeks which slapped against the skin of his inner thighs. When he felt her beginning to come, he pounded away faster still, like an express train going flat out. She was coming. He could feel orgasmic contractions around Gulliver's glans, and that telltale sprinkling increase of moisture. He slowed pace accordingly and counted aloud: 'Four!'

Then he recommenced, panting and sweating like a woodcutter, and counted out a new series of strokes, concentrating upon a mass of foliage flailing in a high wind before crashing spectacularly to earth.

'Five!'

'How can you keep hard,' she managed to gasp between two loud groans, 'and stay like that for so long? My husband goes soft straight afterwards.'

'That way he's got time to spare for his weapons and wargames . . .'

Florian resumed his pit sawyer's regular rhythm. 'Six!'

'Why are you counting?' she asked, her face still pressed into the mattress.

'Hoarding pleasures . . . Woodcutter's pride . . . Trying for the record . . . I don't know.'

'I can't take any more,' she moaned, against the sheet, her voice muffled.

'Wait! Go on, go on!'

He worked on, driven by obscure forces of which he was merely the instrument and Gulliver but the instrument of an instrument. In – out, in – out, more, more, deeper . . .

'Seven!'

'Stop, Florian, I can't go on . . .'

They collapsed in a heap, breathless, sweat-drenched and drunk on orgasms.

'How can people who don't make love exist?'

said Florence, her toes toying with Gulliver.

'I often wonder myself,' Florian said.

'One feels so at ease. You seem to understand things better, with heightened perception. The world looks brighter.'

'The world belongs to those who fuck,' he affirmed.

'But how do you manage to stay hard for so long?' she asked.

'Whenever I feel myself about to come, I hold back. I slow the rhythm, stop or wait. There's a sort of friendly rivalry between Gulliver and myself; he wants to shoot off and I'm trying to restrain him.'

'Gulliver?' she said.

'My best friend, loyal companion and inspirer of my keenest pleasures . . . Down there,' he pointed.

'Ah, that – "the thing"!'

'Yes,' said Florian. 'Whenever I keep him well under control, so the old rascal's straining at the leash, in fact, I can start up again in a flash. The pleasure is more overwhelming, far greater if orgasm is delayed. Desire increases in proportion to the delay in satisfaction. The keenest ecstasy is that of the sharpest desire. The big mistake in lovemaking is coming when the desire is too weak. Most neuroses stem from that. Very often people feel dissatsified afterwards because they haven't given their desire enough time to grow. They come too soon, too lightly, and they are discontent.'

'So you haven't come yet?'

'Not yet, no.'

'And that's why you were able to make love for so long, so much?'

'Yes.'

'I've never had so many orgasms, one after the other. It was incredible. It was . . .'

'My method,' he said.

She gazed at him in admiration, bright-eyed. He wasn't being vain about this ability of his which so often astonished women. Prolonging the enjoyment was quite natural for him, tension adding a necessary, voluptuous edge to pleasure's urge.

'But you must want to come so dreadfully, don't you, after holding back for so long?'

'Yes.'

'Do you know what I'd really like to do?'

'No,' he said. 'I don't.'

His lips were teasing at the down on Florence's nape, just where the hairline proper begins.

'I want to do everything I haven't done so far.'

'Tell me then.'

'My husband doesn't think I'm interested in certain things.'

'The turd,' said Florian.

'He's only ever had me in the missionary position, mechanically and too fast.'

'Doesn't surprise me.'

'I'd like . . .'

'Anything you want,' he promised.

'It's sort of greedy of me but . . .'

She hesitated.

'It might seem odd to you,' she said.

'I've done plenty of fairly odd things myself, in this field,' he admitted.

'I . . . I . . .'

She couldn't bring herself to put it into words.

'Look, get one thing straight,' Florian said. Then he continued, very slowly and deliberately: 'Everything is permitted.'

Finally she plucked up enough courage to blurt out:

'I'd like to make you come. With my mouth.'

'A delightful wheeze,' Nazulis said approvingly.

'I'm not sure I'll be very good at it, but I'd like to try.'

'It's soon learned,' Florian said.

'But I've never . . .'

'I'm sure you've a talent for it. The main thing is, be very careful with the teeth. Use only the lips – the lip muscles are ideal for the purpose – and the tongue.'

He lay on his back, tucked a cushion com-

109

fortably under his head, and let her get on with it.

'Like this?' she asked.

Over-eager to perform well, she accelerated the osculation, almost knocking Gulliver flat in her zealous onslaught.

'No, that's not it,' Florian informed her. 'Too abrupt. You have to go slower, start gently, rhythmically, sensually . . .'

She gripped the Gulliver tube in her right hand and lapped with her tongue in circular sweeps around the violet head.

'That's fine!' Florian exclaimed. 'Go on. Oh yes, oh yes, oh, you've got the knack all right . . .'

Giving her instincts their head, Florence in a series of serious licks moistened the bulbous tip which swelled and hardened, about to explode.

'Oh yes! Yes, yes!' muttered Florian, who had almost taken leave of his senses.

He was seeing fiery abysses, sulphurous craters where incandescent lava boiled. Molten stones shot upwards like rockets, spattering the night with comet-trails . . .

She had engulfed the glans gently, taking care it did not touch her teeth, and was moving it to and fro between her lips.

'Oh, oh, oh,' he murmured. 'Listen, when I come, don't stop that movement, keep me in your mouth to the end.'

The doorbell rang. It made Florence jump.

110

'Don't worry,' he gasped. 'A salesman or a survey or something – who cares . . . Go on.'

She continued her embrace, lips and tongue attentive, assiduously increasing his pleasure.

'Wwwwwaaaaoooouuuh . . .' Florian moaned.

At the crater's rim, vast showers of sparks burst, scattering skywards in an enormous firework display. The surface of the crater, lashed by a storm originating from the very depths of the planet, flung gouts of earth, lava and white-hot metals into space.

She felt the engorged organ dilate still more until it was burning hot and rock hard.

Nazulis, fists clenched like an angry baby, eyes closed, muscles contracting, remained motionless.

She received the first spurt on her tongue, hot and sticky, then a second. Then it was her turn to count, as his spasms succeeded one another. Three, four, five, six, seven . . . There, she told herself, we're even. But an eighth jet swamped her throat and she waited for the next. Nothing more – that was it.

'Ye Gods,' he said. 'You did that like an expert.'

'I've been wanting to try it for so long,' she said contentedly, curling up in the young man's arms.

For some time they did not say a word, like spaced-out junkies whose heads are full of private clouds and lights.

He was flying above the dark green, endless tresses of the Amazon forests. Then there was the sea, that tranquil expanse of bluish-white reflections . . . A dove flapped its wings, fluttering momentarily in the azure sky and tracked by the inner eye of a bedazzled Florian. Florence had placed her hand over the drowsing Gulliver.

'Moments like these, too, make life worth living,' Florian murmured.

The doorbell rang again. Nazulis pulled on a dressing gown and in a split second – for he had the feeling of walking on air – had opened the door.

'Awaken!' chorused two characters, each clad in blue caps with earflaps and chinstraps. These females were brandishing booklets on which was depicted a bilious-looking sun.

'I beg your pardon,' he said, rubbing his eyes.

'Wake up, wake up!' gabbled both these girls of indeterminate age, their tone joyously hectoring as they waved their brochures under Florian's nose.

Both wore khaki army-surplus tops and dark red, nearly heel-length skirts. Clumping ethnic sandals shod their large white feet, while their

112

faces, brightened only by occasional flashes of yellow teeth, were a pasty hue.

'God is with you!' they announced reassuringly. 'He can help. Business success. Shine in society. Overcome shyness. Making money. God is with you! Wake up!'

'You've got some nerve, I must admit,' Nazulis said crossly.

'God is everywhere. Awake . . .'

'All right, I heard you the first time,' he said. 'How much for all this bumf of yours?'

'You can give whatever you like,' they said in unison.

'Whatever I like,' he repeated, scratching one armpit and then the other and automatically sniffing his fingers. 'Whatever I like?'

'That's right,' they confirmed. 'A hundred francs, for instance.'

'Or maybe more,' suggested one of them eagerly, with an avid yellow smirk.

'Or maybe more . . .' Florian echoed. He suddenly adopted a regretful look.

'Yes?' they said in a tone which was the prelude to all sorts of special bargains.

'There's a threefold problem,' he said.

'Ah – a threefold problem?'

Their eyes became shifty and they shuffled about uneasily.

'Yes. This is it. 1. I'm quite awake. 2. God is

dead. 3. You're beginning to cramp my bollocks.'

'Oh!' They exclaimed in horror. Their eyes were goggling now, their mouths pursed tight as chickens' arses.

'Don't you believe me? Look!' he shouted, pulling his dressing gown wide apart. 'See what you're doing to my balls?!'

They took off down the staircase as if pursued by the Furies, losing various pamphlets en route. These fell open to reveal brash title pages: APOCALYPSE . . . GOD'S WRATH . . . ANGRY WITNESSES . . . AWAKE!

Florian flung their prose down the lift shaft. The threatening literature fluttered between floors.

'And if you ever come back,' he yelled, using his hands as a megaphone, 'I'll bugger the pair of you!'

Florence was sleeping like a baby, a wisp of hair over one eye. Hands limply oustretched. Arms akimbo. Her armpits were shaven, but he forgave her that. She still had so much to learn!

He lay down gently beside her and discreetly sniffed at her. The animal aroma of the post-orgasmic female mingled with the scent of L'Heure Bleue. He kissed the curve of her shoulders and her lips. She awoke.

'My God,' she murmured, 'I fell asleep . . . What's the time? I must be getting back!'

She rose and began picking up her clothes. Suddenly she froze in astonishment. Her eyes widened and her mouth fell open soundlessly.

'What's the matter?' asked Nazulis.

'Florian, it's amazing!' she cried.

She was holding her head in both hands and uttering a sort of sob or laugh which she evidently could no longer contain.

'What is it then?' he said worriedly.

'Florian, Florian!' she stammered.

'Darling, tell me what is the matter?'

She bent her head and her eyes filled with tears. 'It's quite extraordinary,' she said, unable to believe the undeniable evidence. She walked around the room, naked, radiant – and upright. She no longer had a limp. 'It doesn't hurt any more! I can't feel the pain in my hip! Unbelievable! Miraculous!'

He went over to her and kissed her ear, beneath the tiny ringlets scented with L'Heure Bleue.

'It's no miracle,' he said calmly, 'it's just love, that's all. The only real therapy. But that is something the doctors will never tell you.'

'But how could the pain vanish like this? So completely?'

She paced back and forth, crying quietly to

115

herself, walking with a triumphant relish.

'The body is a single entity, all of a piece from head to toe, thyroid to anklebone, from intestines to imagination. Paul Valéry used to say: "The greatest poet is the nervous system".'

Florence continued to flex her legs and muscles. She was ecstatic.

'The body can be overwhelmingly content, to the very peak of its powers,' Florian went on. 'It opposes psychic or somatic disorders with all its strength. If it doesn't get its fair share of sexual pleasure (the intensest human fulfilment), the body just starts falling apart. So does the mind. There then follow all kinds of problems: the individual punishes him or herself with illness, as psychiatrists point out. Lack of sexual pleasure, or not enough of it, leads to serious disease, ill-health of one kind or another. Abstinence makes you ill. And chastity – whatever the priests and moralists say – is not a virtue but a sickness.'

'How does that apply to my hip trouble?' Florence asked him.

'Your desires ran into a brick wall. Your body had to confront the ban placed on its deepest desire. And in one sense it rebelled.'

She was examining her hip as if it were possible to perceive some cog which had been jamming the mechanism.

'Your body, for very complex reasons it might

be a wise idea to analyse, chose a precise spot at which to show its resentment: your hip. From the exact time your organism rediscovered its satisfaction, the rebellion ended and the pain disappeared.'

'It's extraordinary!' she exclaimed.

'It's normal,' he added. 'The only real antidote to illness is the complete satisfaction of one's desires.'

'I get the impression that I've just made love for the very first time,' Florence announced.

She was blooming, voluptuously thrusting out her arms in a huge stretch. Her small, youthful breasts jutted pertly. Florian admired her figure once again, finding his desire for her renewed.

'My husband doesn't think I'm sensual,' she said, abstractedly running a finger over a slight scratch on her shin. 'He thinks "all that sort of thing" doesn't interest me. We make love hurriedly, without saying a word, and then goodnight, that's it!'

Florian was intently stroking her buttocks. She was purring like a cat.

'As for myself,' he said, 'I have a friend called Agnes. We're not all that close, one might say. She thinks I'm impotent. With her I just can't get a hard on. It's not that she's unattractive, but there's simply something about her that – in my case, anyhow – inhibits or prevents erection. We've tried to make love on several occasions, but every time it ended in failure. She likes me a lot, she feels a sort of tender compassion for me, thinking I'm impotent with all women. It's never occurred to her that desire is selective.'

'My husband has such little interest in me,' Florence went on, 'and does it so perfunctorily that after . . . sex, I have to satisfy myself, on my own.'

'Is it then that you fantasise?' Florian asked her. He was sucking her nipples alternately. They hardened under his tongue.

'All those images which run through my head,' she said dreamily, 'when I give myself pleasure.'

'Tell me about them,' he said, excited now.

'Until today I used to think it was wrong. Forbidden images which had to be dispelled. So I'd go along to confession. I never felt at ease.'

'And you limped.'

'Yes. Inside myself I felt that something was not quite right. Now I know what I was missing. You've suddenly shown me my true self. I have an urgent need to be loved. I'm a sensual person.'

'Tell me your fantasies,' he said, dallying with her pubic curls. 'Describe what's showing in your erotic cinema.'

118

'First of all, that long, rigid, solid cock pointing at me . . . How often I dreamed of that! There's also a male torso, a muscular suntanned body which goes with it and comes to take me in its arms . . .'

Her eyes stared up at the ceiling, as if gazing at distant yet distinct pictures.

'Is that all?'

He had introduced the three middle fingers of his left hand into Florence's moist vagina and was moving them in a slow circular motion.

'I'm looking for your G-spot,' he said.

'With me,' she laughed, 'it's everywhere . . . Oh yes, go on like that . . . Oh that's good, that's good . . .'

Gulliver had sprung up hard as a poker. Florian positioned himself over Florence so that they could enjoy a variety of delightful pubic tickling and rub against one another.

'You brought me bliss with your mouth,' he said. 'Now I'd like to come deep inside you.'

'Oh yes!' she said.

She spread her legs and lay ready for him.

'I'm right with you,' she whispered as he gently sank into her.

They remained a while motionless, savouring the exquisite experience of penetration. A beatific Gulliver felt its sensitive head held by Florence's pulsing clonic clutch. From time to time she would contract her muscles, nipping and gripping the firm, rounded tip.

'Oh that's great, I love it, it's marvellous,' Florian blurted out, thinking that yes, all was well with him . . .

'Move inside me,' she urged.

He worked Gulliver's piston to and fro, deliberately, driving to its full length.

'Oh,' she said, 'I think I'm going to . . .'

'Wait for me,' he asked her. 'I'd rather we came together.'

They set up a gradual, perfectly synchronised rhythm. Florian's thrusts probed Florence's depths. Belly to belly, breast to breast, mouth glued to mouth, they went at it, driven by a force greater than themselves yet emanating from themselves. This was the moment, Florian knew, when the body simply took over. He was no longer in control of his – simply content to follow its intense journey. 'The finest stroll any human being ever takes', he told himself.

He let go completely.

The lower half of his body seemed to move of its own volition, pleasing itself, finding its own cadence, and Gulliver's head was swollen, its shaft dilated. Florian's heart doubled its beat. The blood seemed to congest yet throb powerfully below Florian's skin. All this strength sprang from some mysterious logic and all this

120

instinctual energy converged to hasten the over-whelming seesaw into climax.

Florian felt himself surge forward, on the brink of overflow.

'I'm about . . .' he gasped.

'Yes, yes . . .'

'Together?'

'Yes . . . me too . . . with you,' she stam-mered.

Borne on their frenzied dance, they clung to each other wildly, bodies soldered together.

He clutched her hand as if she were on a death bed and about to take the final journey. Then the Great Earthquake seized them, hurling them onto the bed's furthest reaches before flinging them ashore once more, inert and stunned, their tongues tasting salt and in their ears that elusive shell-diffused sound of the sea.

6

ANGELS AND DEMONS

Florian's bag of equipment was ready. Transmitters, miniaturized aerials, batteries and all he required to install sensitive listening devices inside the four confessional boxes. Four systems fitted with the most sophisticated electronic gadgetry would allow Nazulis to gather at source everything our moral guides call 'sin' — uneasy whispers, stammered outpourings, furtively embarrassed admissions included.

This all-pervading notion of sin perturbed our oenologist considerably. The way most individuals would accuse themselves at the drop of a hat, solemnly prepared to repent of trifling or even imaginary offences, and assume what psychiatrists term culpability, both baffled and worried Nazulis.

He himself had escaped from this guilt syndrome donkeys' years ago. He'd come a long way since then. Now he would have to try hard to understand the subtle mechanisms of constant self-blame. How could intelligent twentieth century people still behave in this way? What thoughts went through their heads? How did this creeping sense of guilt spread to choke their pleasures and desires?

In order to find out, he had to listen to them. To listen to them he needed hidden mikes, and to place these he had to get himself locked inside the church overnight. Then no one could disturb his bugging activities . . .

His bag also contained assorted sandwiches, two bottles of Châteauneuf du Pape, one of Vieille Prune, and various other treats – to keep up his spirits during the night.

He arrived just before the doors of St Honoro were shut, at eight p.m. Hidden behind a pillar he waited until the verger turned off the lights one by one. Transept, roof, main altar, chapels, side rows, the saints in their niches – all entered the dark in turn. The ecclesiastical factotum took a last look round. Had he forgotten anything? He scratched one ear, then his arse, then aligned a chair that was not quite straight. It squeaked on the flagstones.

At last he pulled the heavy door behind him. Inside the deserted church now plunged into darkness the sound of the huge key double-locking the door was resoundingly audible.

Florian was alone.

For a long time he did not move. He was thinking of Florence, seeing once again her lovely face transformed by ecstasy, feeling her body blaze in successive orgasms.

All around him the thick, black night was unbroken save for one tiny luminous dot in the distance: it was the small red lamp burning above the shrine. When he was a child they'd assured him that while that red lamp shone it meant that Jesus was there.

'What if someone switched it off?' he'd asked the old woman who was coaching him in the Catechism. 'Does Jesus go away?'

'The lamp is always burning,' she replied sternly.

'What if there's a power cut?'

'Florian, when will you stop asking silly questions?'

'But if the lamp . . .'

'Be quiet. I don't want to hear your voice any more.'

The Catechism, he told himself, was like the Army: you didn't question it. You had to march, obey orders and shut your trap.

He laid his bag against a pillar and opened a bottle of 1970 Châteauneuf – a great year for Côtes du Rhône. The cork made a satisfying *plop* which seemed to echo through the entire building.

This was a wine high in alcohol content, probably even 15%, made from grapes ripened by the scorching sunshine of the Midi. Hardly giving his nose a chance, Florian gulped it down – almost the whole glassful, which was scarcely the wine buff's way. He was thirsty and needed sustenance.

He quaffed a second glass and a third in quick succession. It was a rich, fullbodied wine, but how it hit home! The church all at once seemed warm to Florian. He flashed his torch here and there. St Christopher, holding his staff and with a lamb swathed round his shoulders, was smiling at him.

He gnawed at a sandwich but he wasn't really hungry. He was still thirsty.

The Clos Saint-Jean was truly superb. He polished off the first bottle and opened the second, whose cork again resounded if anything even more welcomingly.

The deep red wine swilled down his gullet. He was enjoying its bouquet, its redolence of vines ripened in the furnace of Provence. He got up unsteadily and shone his torch again.

'The Church has its good points,' he muttered to himself euphorically, illuminating each niche with its saint. The statues held out their stone arms in friendly fashion and seemed to be smiling at Florian.

'What did I actually come here to do?' he wondered.

He could not remember. Meanwhile, now for the Vieille Prune. Excellent. Another glass. Better still: this was a most fortifying and inspiriting beverage indeed.

Suddenly his head slumped. Florian fell over, and into a deep sleep.

There was a shout which filled the whole church.

'Come and see, come and see!' St Christopher was yelling. The saint was floating twenty feet above the ground.

'How do you manage to fly?' asked Florian.

'I put down my staff and my lamb and flap my wings like the angels. Quite simple. All you need do is move your wings to and fro!'

Florian raised his wings and took off without difficulty.

'Good heavens!' he cried. 'I'm flying!'

The two men swooped from one corner of the church to the other.

'Shall we take a trip?' Florian suggested.

'If you like.'

They opened a window and ascended into the starry night. The Place Victor Hugo dwindled in the distance and was soon no more than a luminous dot among all the others on the earth.

The two celestial cosmonauts soared like birds

through the firmament.

'I'd like very much to meet the female angels,' Florian said.

'Don't you know that angels have no sex?'

'Not even a little one? Not even the merest vestige of a working one?'

'No. Nothing. There's just a smooth expanse.'

'But then how do they – ?'

'They don't,' said St Christopher. 'They play music.'

'Music. What music?'

'In front of God they sing Bach. Among themselves, Mozart.'

'What about Schubert?' asked Florian.

'They play Schubert when they're sad.'

'Are we going to see God?' Florian inquired.

'God?' said St Christopher. 'What God? What God? What God?'

His voice faded. Suddenly, with a wingbeat, he vanished.

Nazulis woke with a start. He looked at his watch. It was seven a.m.

Someone had opened the church doors. Footsteps could be heard.

He hastily gathered up his things and concealed himself behind a pillar. A group of nuns were heading towards him. They passed very close, their coifs like great white birds astride their heads. The last in line, slightly behind the others, filed by Nazulis, so near him that he felt a waft of air from her hat as she scurried past.

She caught sight of him.

They looked at each other for a second, eyes wide in mutual amazement. She was very young, a novice of no more than twenty. Despite the severity of her habit, she could not altogether disguise her natural beauty. Nuns as beautiful as that, thought the astonished Florian, were only usually seen in the movies . . . The whites of her eyes reminded him of porcelain, the pupils a bright cornflower blue. Her full red lips contrasted with the pallor of her skin. Her mouth amazingly resembled that of Monica Vitti. It was not the odour of sanctity she exuded but an extremely alluring fleshly charm.

'Sssh . . .!' said Florian, his finger to his lips.

There was in this young beauty's glance something dazzling. Her sisters' procession had now moved considerably further on. Florian had a sudden irrational urge. He lowered his head and lunged forward under the starched bonnet, a wing of which brushed his forehead lightly. And he kissed the young woman full on the lips.

She was so stunned that she stayed where she was, incapable of any reaction. The kiss lasted a second – an eternity. Did she recall Baudelaire's phrase: *A minute's bliss for an eternity's damnation?* Of course not! Baudelaire isn't read in

129

convents.

While the clock was about to register a second second, the nun's lips trembled and left Florian's. He had had time (for his hunter's instincts were acute), to run a hand over this angelic Eve's breasts and to feel how they had been flattened by some tight nunnish cummerbund or probationary bandage. What a waste! he thought.

She fled and left the young man walking on air, in a sort of mystic levitation, upon his tranced lips the taste of wonder. At least just once in her life – Florian mused, on coming down to earth again – she'd have had a fleeting glimpse of human experience to give her something to conjure with, during those long lonely nights.

Nazulis returned home jubilant. He took a shower and shaved to the strains of his beloved Schubert's *German dances*.

'Life is great!' he murmured, dabbing two drops of Acqua di Selva behind each ear. The scent of pine wafted to his nostrils. He went over and replaced the record in its sleeve. Then he pressed the *Messages* button on his answering machine.

'So what's up?' a female voice cut in. 'Are you out of circulation or something? Ring me back then. Here's a big kiss.'

'Who's she?' Florian wondered, racking his brains. But he could not place her and meanwhile the next message was delivered in loud, well-spoken masculine tones.

'Hello, brother dear. I'm off tomorrow for Acongagua. Look after Mother, she tends to worry about me. We'll see each other in two months. Cheers!'

Florian's brother was a mountaineering freak. He had taken part in the first French expedition to conquer Everest, led by Giscard's former minister, Pierre Mazeaud. Whenever the opportunity arose, he would go off to the Himalayas or wherever else there were new summits to be climbed. Whenever he left for these remote mountains (and Florian himself would go to the ends of the earth to meet Javanese, Guinean, Brazilian or any other exotic examples of femininity), their mother would arrange on one mantelpiece photographs, locks of hair, items of clothing and so on. This sort of primitive shrine was to protect the traveller throughout his expedition, and so far the ritual had always worked.

After a new tone beep on the tape, he heard a familiar voice.

'Darling hello, it's me, Ariane. The Lambertinis are throwing a big party tomorrow evening. I'd love you to take me along as I don't like going to their kind of do all on my own. So call me back, lover!'

The message had been recorded the previous evening, which meant the party was that evening. Florian dialled Ariane's number.

'Hello, it's me,' he said.

'Delighted you called, poppet. Are you coming to the Lambertini's party? All the best orgiasts in Paris will be there – movie people, singers, media celebrities . . . Toledo's going . . . .'

'Sabrina too?' asked Nazulis.

'Sabrina Ducelli? Oh yes, and Poppy, Mado, Ricou, the River-Berthoux couple . . . All the trendy partygoers . . .'

'I couldn't give a shit about the River-Berthouxes. I'll come along as soon as Sabrina arrives.'

'But you will look after me just a little, won't you poppet? Mmm?'

'Mmm.'

'I'll call by to pick you up tonight at ten . . . Ah, I almost forgot – the theme of the party is Animals. Fancy dress disguise, masks, the choice is yours. I'm going as Mickey Mouse.'

'I don't like fancy dress,' said Florian.

'Just this once,' she pleaded, 'do make a bit of an effort.'

He pondered for a moment. 'I'll come as an elephant,' he said.

It was an imposing Avenue Foch flat, only a stone's throw from the Étoile, and with its own immaculate garden. The three or four prostitutes whose particular beat covered the hundred yards or so of pavement opposite, watched incredulously as a veritable Noah's Ark of brilliant creatures began to arrive at the Lambertinis'.

Beasts of the jungle, lions, panthers, tigers, assorted birds, ostriches with flower-decorated rumps, big furry bears, several apes — masks gaping in grotesque surprise – and even a little plump chap wearing a pink piggy mask.

Hugo Lambertini, the famous Italian millionaire and Europe's clothes-chain king, had one of the finest apartments in Paris. There he liked to throw parties which were in turn sumptuous, riotous and orgiastic. He would invite the capital's most debauched set – the best-looking women, the most perverted girls, the craziest men and the smartest caterers.

A raucous and joyful din filled the main reception room: friendly greetings, mutual compliments on costumes, popping of champagne corks, squeals of women being groped, laughter and loud conversation . . . Things were warming up.

In a corner musicians in white satin uniforms were playing jazz: a quartet comprised of tenor sax, piano, bass and drums.

133

The hosts welcomed Ariane and Florian with their native Italian exuberance. Hugo was wearing a splendid mask of a horse's head with a mane of silky white hair which trailed over his shoulders. He doffed his mask to greet his guests, kissed Ariane's hand and shook Florian's, then resumed his equine metamorphosis.

'How nice to see you?' he exclaimed volubly. 'Ariane or should I say Mickey, you're always so beautiful . . . Do you know my wife Giulietta?'

Giulietta had contrived an amazing head-dress of multi-coloured feathers which turned her into an exotic macaw.

Florian kissed the bird's hand. With a connoisseur's glance he appraised the creature's shape –which was in no sense disguised. An attractive, well-preserved body, recently tanned by a sun-lamp or a tropical trip. Giulietta certainly knew how to move that figure of hers to best advantage – and she had a roving eye.

'Make yourselves at home. Eat, drink and be merry,' the Italian stallion urged them excitedly.

Then he left (*Scusi, scusi*) to greet a doe accompanied by a deer with an impressive spread of antlers. The pair seemed to have just emerged from a thicket: they had the uneasy, startled look of forest animals listening for human footsteps.

'Pity you're not in fancy dress,' said Ariane as Florian led her towards an opulent buffet heaped with gastronomic delights.

'Not in fancy dress?' he said, delving into a plate of caviare. 'You'll see, soon enough.'

They went for a walk in the garden, where there was another buffet table. Florian quaffed another glass of Dom Pérignon and helped himself to another Beluga canapé. Yes, he thought, feeling the tiny eggs dissolve against his teeth, life was treating him well.

They sauntered through the vast apartment's many rooms. Half naked creatures pursued each other down the corridors, giggling. Under their disguises the women shrieked and squealed, stirring up the surrounding jungle. They jostled, goosed each other, embraced and kissed.

In one room illumined by a pale blue light a Mickey Mouse ('Another!' exclaimed the ir-ritated Ariane) lay on the floor, dress hitched up, being fucked by the little pink piggy-man. The latter was out of breath and straining to satisfy his partner, who wore big black ears which joggled in time with his buttocks. He was failing, however.

'Go and try someone else!' the other Mickey, irate and frustrated, screamed at him.

He pulled up the laughing hog's mask which then stayed perched on his head. Like that he presented a strange, doubly porcine picture: the false – grinning and pink, and the real – miserable and pink.

In another room, beneath a seven-branched candelabra frolicked a calmly copulating couple.

On all fours on the white moquette, the woman had thrust out her splendid, chubby buttocks. She was virtually naked, wearing only a flimsy panther skin, and Florian felt sure he had seen that arse somewhere before. It was being offered to the thrusting prick of a very hirsute man kneeling behind her. Over his head was a bull's muzzle, whose glass eyes shone with an odd yellow glow. It was an extraordinary spectacle, bull covering panther, the thrusts slow and regular.

Her weight on the palms of her hands, legs splayed, the woman let herself be fucked in silence. The fourteen flames of the two chandeliers flickered. From the sitting-room filtered the sound of the quartet, starting in on a Thelonious Monk number. The man's breath sounded wheezy beneath his taurine headgear.

'Florian, it's you!' the panther exclaimed.

'Sabrina, darling!' he cried.

He leaned down to peck the fair Sabrina on both cheeks, while she maintained her position – glued to the minotaur. The latter had not yet finished and was plunging to and fro with metronomic regularity.

'Oh, I'm really glad to see you!' Sabrina said.

Florian made the introductions, ignoring the

bovine fucker, who went gasping on.

'Ariane, this is the divine Sabrina! But maybe you already know each other?'

'Not really,' Ariane said with a thin little smile.

She instinctively held out her hand and at once recognised the absurdity of the gesture. To regain her composure she adjusted her round mouse-ears, tugging at each in turn.

'How's your work going these days?' Sabrina enquired. 'Your arse-essay, your wines, and those articles . . .?'

'Everything all right with you?' Florian said.

The horned beast continued thrusting, quite excluded from the conversation.

'Is Poppy here?' asked Sabrina, her bottom aloft and still being poked to a steady beat: one stroke, two strokes, pause; one stroke, two strokes, pause; one stroke, two . . .

'I haven't seen her yet,' Nazulis said. 'How about you, did you come with your husband?'

'He's over there,' the panther indicated with a nod of her head. 'Right now he's being absolutely awful to me, really horrid . . .'

'That's marriage for you,' said Florian authoritatively.

There was a silence. The candles flickered. Piano and bass were now embarking on an old Louis Armstrong tune. A waiter with a tray passed round glasses of champagne.

'Can you put a glass on the side for me?' Sabrina requested, turning her head towards Florian. 'For the time being I'm . . . busy.'

The metronomic bull suddenly stopped pounding away and snapped his fingers for the waiter. Then he took the bull mask by the horns and ripped it off his head, emitting yet another sigh.

'What a wanker!' exclaimed Florian. 'That's Jean-Pierre Soudard, the Channel One presenter,' he whispered in Ariane's ear.

Still on his knees, still plugging that pert pink posterior, Soudard did not deign (or did not dare) turn towards Nazulis and Ariane. Looking haggard and dishevelled he stared glassily in front of him, with something of MacEnroe's determinedly vacant expression during a change-over.

Soudard seized a glass from the tray offered, knocked back his drink and replaced it. Then he pulled on the massive head again. He had not once looked at Sabrina's friends. He needs to hide his identity, Florian thought: has to preserve his image!

Protected by his mask the bull resumed his relentless motion, his hands gripping the beauteous panther's hips. In – out, pause. In – out, pause . . . He had a sturdy, medium-sized pizzle protruding from a black thicket from which swung the bollocks, one large, the other somewhat smaller.

138

'He's better than on telly,' Florian whispered in Sabrina's ear.

She chuckled, still propped on her forearms.

'I mean,' Florian went on, 'that here he's a bit more forceful.'

Soudard was the most deadpan newscaster (and the most quickfire, come to that) on any current affairs programme on French TV. His huge hairy hands would rest on the news-desk, on either side of the microphone, and with his staring eyes riveted to the autocue, he would talk down to the whole of France every weekend. As he droned on, reducing every item to a self-important newscast monotone, Soudard seemed to embody that relentlessly false impartiality endemic to the tube.

Horns lowered, the taurine personality ploughed on, obsessed with his incessant grinding to and fro.

Florian winked at Sabrina.

'Here at least,' he concluded, 'he keeps his mouth shut.'

Nazulis was thirsty. He headed for the buffet once more. Ariane followed suit, never letting him out of her sight.

'Don't you want to . . . cut loose and enjoy

yourself a bit?' he asked her.

'How about you?' she inquired. 'Do you?'

'Right now I've got quite a thirst. I'll show you my fancy dress after we've had some champagne.'

They passed through the flat again. The atmosphere of sexual heat was rapidly being fanned into flame.

An orang-utang lying on his back in the middle of a corridor was having his organ oralized by a slimly built antelope, whose lyre-shaped horns bobbed about as the caress progressed. Meanwhile this same ape ate, through his mask, an attractive blonde who squatted over him. She herself wore only a black mask which concealed the top half of her face. Crouching over the simian snout, she had adopted the normal posture of female urination, but at that particular moment she seemed to be deriving considerably greater pleasure. Then the animals changed places, the blonde on the doe and the ape upon the blonde.

'Delightful!' Florian enthused.

Further on, inside the large room which adjoined the sitting room, the carnival of the animals was in full swing. A score of couples were entwined in all sorts of positions and groups, kissing, sniffing, sucking and fucking, then taking turn and turn about in a constant sexual exchange. Nearly all of them had removed their masks and fancy dress.

Florian recognized a Minister, another television personality, a well-known comedian and an eminent media doctor who looked like a cowboy. The jungle was flailing about in a state of extreme agitation. Rustles, bestial noises, gasps, sobs, slitherings, lapping sounds, sometimes a brief grunt, but never a word spoken.

The oenologist's nostrils quivered; his nose wrinkled in distaste. Florian pulled a face: male odours, more than anything, tended to put him off. He stayed cool, however, resolving to ignore these animal aromas.

He needed to get in the mood. He went off to find a bottle of champagne which he had concealed in an ingle nook. After drinking three glasses in quick succession, he undressed.

'Look at my outfit,' he said to Ariane.

He dropped his trousers. Ariane's jaw dropped with them. She stared in stupefaction.

'But . . . but . . .' she managed to splutter.

CARNIVAL OF THE ANIMALS

'Not bad, is it?' Florian said.

'But . . . It looks incredibly realistic!' she exclaimed.

'Yes, doesn't it. A whopper of a chopper.'

'Where did you . . .?'

'It's from Hong Kong. Present from a friend. I've never tried it on before but I think it suits me, don't you?'

'As fancy dress it's a bit excessive, I'd say,' the young woman reflected.

'Moulded in special plastic and covered in some very supple organic material . . . Feel!'

She could not bring herself to do so. It was too enormous. Finally he put it in her hand.

'You'd think it was the genuine article,' she said in amazement. 'The texture, colour, even the pink tip . . .'

'Only this one is knee-length! That's the main difference!'

After several more glasses of Dom Pérignon, he strolled around the couples to see what effect his elephantine appendage would have upon them. He sauntered about, stark naked and quite at ease, swaggering exaggeratedly.

As he passed, couples stopped to peer and stare at him, often even pulling apart in order to do so. The guests nudged each other, incredulous.

Silence fell upon the room.

Florian cleared his throat as if to make a speech. All eyes were fixed upon him. Only one middle-aged man continued screwing, well into the alluring charms of a redhead nymphet who looked distinctly under-age. After a moment even this absorbed satyr realised that everything had gone strangely silent. He turned his head and saw in astonishment Nazulis, virtually standing over him, staring scornfully at him, to boot. The arrogant pendant quivered threateningly like a truncheon.

At that the grizzled orgiast grabbed his Lolita and dragged her out of the room, both in considerable disarray. I must have triggered off his complexes, thought Florian – amazed by such a reaction.

His trunk dangling between his legs he went off to refill his champagne glass. He staggered slightly but kept his head, and his tail too, as it were, for the latter had been slipped over, and firmly affixed to, the luckless Gulliver's head.

The pendulous device had a devastating effect.

Word went round that 'there was a man who . . . a stud with a . . . yes, as big as your arm . . . phenomenal!' People drifted in to see for themselves, and all eyes were mesmerised by what they saw.

Nazulis was rather pleased to be the cynosure. He looked regally around him. A crowd had gathered to view the prodigy. The men were especially miffed, becoming almost physically ill at the sight. Wracked by shame, they tried hiding their more modest dongs behind their hands, making nests of their nervous fingers so as to protect their own sensitive fledglings.

The women, by contrast, were wide-eyed and almost drooled. Incredulity and/or lust were clearly evident.

The silence had become suffocating. The musicians too had been informed of the miracle and they also were craning for a glimpse. You could hear the proverbial pin drop.

Nazulis climbed onto a chair and raised his chin in a Mussolinian motion. The crowd had formed a circle, respectfully keeping its distance.

'He's going to say something!' someone whispered.

The Elephant-Dick-Man cleared his throat and

began his speech.

'Ladies and Gentlemen, a brief word only, because I don't want to interrupt your pleasurable activities. Your silence and surprise, surprise *me*. It seems my splendid appendage arouses in you some very strong, confused and secret emotions. All small boys have friendly cock-contests, the largest winning most respect. Do you think the same applies to adults?

'Everyone's fascinated with the phallic. Regal sceptres, military swagger-sticks and cannons, menhirs, obelisks, and missiles of every variety . . . Who has the finest war-head?

'What, ladies and gentleman, does this general veneration for the masculine projectile or projection and its symbolism *mean*?

'I crave your attention now because we have reached the very nub of the problem. I see here some analysts and medical men. I doubt if they'd contradict what I'm saying . . . The rogue you see between my legs hypnotises you because it is the symbol of human power.

'And here's the rub. This is the mistake everybody makes: THE SYMBOLIC IS NOT THE REAL. Gigantic pricks do not necessarily imply enormous power. Sometimes extremely potent men are equipped with quite modest weapons. As that great writer Colette, who knew a thing or two about men, remarked: 'Better a lively little one than a dozy big one.' Napoleon, that notorious fucker, had a bauble of barely ten centimetrcs, a child's willie. By comparison, you see village idiots, abulic thickos and impotent morons trailing things thrice as long around with them.

'Look at all those bodybuilders with bulging muscles, pumping iron. Are they really so strong? Take any contest or sport you like, they're no match for any opponent with so-called 'normal' muscles. They're puffed up windbags, full of bluff.

'So, ladies and gentlemen, this mighty weapon I've enjoyed showing off tonight – since it is, after all, an animal fancy dress party – this engine you find so fascinating, this too is all a bluff. Look!'

Nazulis twisted a valve and tapped at the tube. There was a slight suction noise and the audience suddenly gasped as if in relief.

Gulliver, tried and tested, normal Gulliver reappeared. The show was over.

Murmurs of satisfaction could be heard now, and the room's occupants returned to their previous pursuits. Couples, trios and foursomes re-formed. The jazz quartet once more took up their instruments. The champagne corks popped as frequently as before. The wind of panic had blown over.

'You ought to be in politics. You speak well,'

Sabrina said, resplendently naked under her fur.

Florian replaced the chair which had been his soap box.

'Certainly not,' he replied. 'I value my soul too much. Come on, let's have a drink.'

Ariane followed them despite her wretched Mickey Mouse rig, which seemed glued to her head; its huge ears never remained in place but would keep flopping over, first one then the other. They all found the buffet in the garden deserted. The night air was cool and Sabrina pressed shivering against Florian, who was still stark naked.

'Come on,' she said. 'Let's get warm.'

With Ariane-Mickey dogging their footsteps, they found a cosy corner back inside the apartment – an empty bed. Sleeping or embracing couples lay on the floors, scattered here, there and everywhere. Nearly all of them had shed their masks and fancy dress outfits. They caught a glimpse of the bull-headed Soudard who was shafting the lady of the house in the main sitting room, with his usual rhythmic verve, as if powered by a diesel engine.

'What stamina!' Sabrina marvelled.

'Is he good at it?' Mickey asked.

'Very mechanical.'

'Anyhow he's setting some kind of record,' Florian observed. 'He's preserving his anonymity to the bitter end. I'm amazed he hasn't suffocated himself yet.'

Someone else, too, had kept on his mask, doubtless believing he might be marginally more seductive thus: little Mr Piggy. With his leering porker's snout he was wandering from room to room, looking for love. But his small, paunchy and wrinkled body was finding no takers.

'Poor little chap!' Mickey murmured.

'He should have disguised himself from head to foot,' said Florian. 'He'd have had better luck that way.'

Just then the pig approached them.

'Great party, hee hee!' he squealed in his high-pitched voice, appropriately porcine even through his mask.

He began unceremoniously pinching Sabrina's and Ariane's breasts.

'Shall *we* party? Shall we, then?'

Panther, Mickey and Florian rapidly escaped into the depths of the apartment.

Strewn all over the carpets were what might be called animal-droppings – disguises, masks, feathers, costume, bras, panties, false wings and other colourful litter – while their owners drowsed, snored or flailed and twitched in the last spasms of lust.

A naked girl passed. Her hair was dishevelled and she was vacantly smoking a joint. She picked her way through the recumbent bodies, as if heading for some somnambulists' convention. They noticed a red paper rose projecting from the cleft in her buttocks as she glided along. Was she socialist or poet? Nazulis wondered. At any rate she was keeping a cheekily tight arse to the world, come who might.

The two women and Florian finally found an unoccupied room whose big bed had an enticing multi-coloured coverlet. They lay down, with Sabrina on Florian's right, Ariane on his left.

Gulliver reared its head on scenting Sabrina. Her skin smelt fresh and natural, and exuded an undefinable scent of ozone. Florian had never encountered such an unusual, alluring aroma; it had intrigued and excited him when they had first met. He had never had enough time to appreciate it however.

She stretched luxuriously, writhing sensuously while Florian stroked and sniffed her in delight. He undid the strings holding up her panther skin and took it off. Ariane meanwhile doffed her Mickey Mouse mask and shook out her long dark hair which released its cloud of sleek scents (Lancome's *Magie Noire*). The olfactory organ of Florian was fully occupied with Sabrina though; he himself was leaning over her inhaling in silent admiration. She had a superb, slim blonde body, sleekly muscled as much as conventionally curvaceous. The silken tufts under her armpits had been artfully tended: they were neither too bushy nor too long. How fine she smelt! Gulliver reared in ecstatic fervour, ready for a treat.

Nimbly ducking, Florian tickled Sabrina's stomach with his hair and then his face descended further still, towards that blonde promontory of hers. He was just about to open her when he remembered Soudard – in a sudden vision of that yellow-eyed bull's mask, and that pizzle working its way in and out, to and fro. The small screen filled by that inane smile . . . Those bollocks, the big and the small, swinging about in their pouch to that remorseless pendulum rhythm.

All things considered, he settled for Sabrina's upper lips, kissing these fervently and leaving Gulliver to find its own way through the lower depths.

'Who's kissed you tonight?' Florian asked her.

'On the mouth?' said Sabrina. 'Nobody. I've been fucked by three or four animals that's all. I haven't had a single kiss.'

'Good,' said Florian.

He kissed her in leisurely style. Her mouth tasted of fruit. Meanwhile Ariane, not wanting to be left out, had moved her head downwards: she began licking the drowsy dormouse with little flicks of her tongue. Since she scarcely ever watched television she was not afflicted with

151

Soudardic allergy. Her tongue dabbled amid the golden thatch, prompting groans of pleasure from Sabrina. These reverberated inside Florian's mouth.

Gulliver, still wandering across the blonde scrubland, encountered Ariane's mouth. The young woman's lips left the wet cleft a moment to clamp upon the tense lance whose tip quivered with impatience. Ariane's tongue then worked on the creature's pink bulb, which became harder and redder every second. Florian and Sabrina continued kissing, occasionally pausing to murmur mutual terms of endearment.

'I want you,' he was whispering.

'And I want you too,' she sighed.

'You're lovely, so beautiful. You're an angel. You . . .'

She crushed her mouth against Florian's greedily, devouring it. Gulliver could no longer bear the strain. Somewhere, somehow, the explosion simply had to come. Ariane felt it coming. She accentuated her pressures, speeding up her movements. But Florian pulled away with a wriggle of his hips and plunged deep into the wet, wide-open Sabrina.

She uttered a cry, caught unawares by such an access of pleasure.

Gulliver, like a diver, was moving with long, leisurely strokes through the strange, silent world beneath the delta. Pushed and pulled by Florian, the beast let go, rocked upon the surf which was bearing them aloft.

Ariane, who definitely did not want to remain inactive herself, licked her forefinger and stuck it between Florian's buttocks.

'Hey, take it easy, go slow!' he urged.

He realised that with all this stimulus he could not hold back much longer.

'Sabrina, I'm going to come,' he said.

Ariane grabbed one of Florian's hands and thrust it upon her own pubic thatch, moving furiously up and down. Nazulis promptly worked his middle finger inside her vulva.

'I'm going to come!' Florian repeated desperately.

Sabrina clutched him tightly in her arms and jammed her loins as hard as she could against his.

'Me too,' she gasped.

'Me too,' Ariane interjected.

The three of them came almost simultaneously. But differently, of course. One of the women uttered a series of exclamations, the other emitted a kind of guttural sob, and Florian shuddered in a fiery spasm of pleasure but said not a word.

The actual experience of orgasm is invariably individual, never similar.

'Wake up!'

A hand was shaking the entwined and sleeping troilists: three tangled bodies, half a dozen arms, half a dozen legs, together linked.

'Come on, wake up,' Hugo Lambertini repeated. 'It's six a.m.!'

'What . . . what is it?' mumbled a dazed Florian, frowning himself awake.

'We're all off to have breakfast at R.'s place. Get dressed, everyone's waiting for you.'

R. was a young Secretary of State who was both dynamic and ambitious, a politician who knew which way the wind was blowing and how to bide his time. He lived in a luxury flat near the Bastille. He too had quite a reputation as a partygiver. He had invited all those who had stayed over at his friend Hugo's.

'We're all going to go by Métro!' Lambertini declared.

'By Métro?' Florian said in amazement, rubbing his eyes.

'Yes. A nice democratic gesture, eh? The last time I took the Métro was . . . was . . .'

The millionaire furrowed his brow, delving in the mists of memory.

'Prior to 1981, it must have been. Yes, that's it, it was October 1980 . . . A really fascinating experience . . .'

'Let's get going, come on!' various guests were

urging. They had shed their animal costumes and reverted to human clothing. Long evening dresses, crumpled dinner jackets, and in some cases jeans and plimsolls – the contents of wardrobes and drawers had certainly been ransacked.

The group – forty-five survivors of the previous evening's shenanigans – emerged into the cool morning air. At this hour the Avenue Foch was deserted. Only one elderly whore, her mouth a messy smear of paint, optimistically persevered along her beat. They greeted her with laughter and made for the Étoile, staggering, dancing, singing or fooling around.

From a distance they resembled those processions of bleary dawn revellers in Fellini films. The only thing missing was music by Nino Rota.

They funnelled onto the platform at Étoile-Charles de Gaulle just as the 6.33 train to Vincennes pulled in.

Assorted labourers and factory employees abroad watched the exclusive bunch of merrymakers pile into the leading coach.

'It's terrific!' Giulietta Lambertini was gushing, and she clapped her hands to display sparklers worth thousands of wage packets, glittering

around fingers, wrists and neck. 'Absolutely terrific, the Métro. What a super idea!'

'Don't you think it's a bit rash showing off all
these rocks to the plebs?' Hugo asked one of his
friends, a man who owned a group of factories.
'They're insured, naturally, but . . .'

'Not to worry, old fellow,' the friend retorted.
'At 6 a.m. there are never any pickpockets,
rapists or muggers on the Métro. What would
they have to gain? Just take a look around you!'

The early morning cleaners and shift-workers,
huddled in their seats, their eyes bloodshot from
all the hours of sleep they'd missed out on,
observed these interlopers impassively, indeed
with no reaction whatever.

'It runs on rubber, these days, then!' Hugo
reflected with some surprise. 'The last time I rode
on the Métro it had iron wheels.'

'Well, these people deserve some creature
comforts don't they, even if they are from North
Africa.'

'Oh what fun!' Giulietta cried. 'I adore the
Métro, it's quite an adventure. I find it exciting,
as well.'

She teetered off down the compartment, staring at the workmen and immigrant labourers. She
looked each of them up and down in fascination,
inspecting them as if they were extra-terrestrials.
This was a red-letter day for her.

'It gets me excited, really!' she exclaimed, rolling her eyes.

She went up to Soudard, who had retained his mask, no matter what. He was determined on anonymity at all costs. He alone among the delighted throng of chic ticket-holders stood erect, his hand tightly gripping the vertical bar in the standing area.

'Fuck me again!' she said to him, hoisting up her dress. Her naked buttocks were small and tanned.

'I – I can't!' protested the media-man, shaking his horns from side to side. 'I can't, not here.'

'I want you to,' she persisted.

The train entered the Concorde station. Two immigrant workers alighted quietly, their manner self-effacing, and they went on their way not glancing to right or left. Another got on board: this one had a small moustache, his face was gaunt and blue-jowled and his eyes looked forlorn. On seeing the fashionable crowd in the compartment – their finery, flashing jewels and bare legs, and those hands heavy with gold and precious stones waving champagne bottles – not to mention that character in a bull mask – the new passenger had just enough time to dash into the next carriage before the doors shut.

'Take me!' Giulietta urged as the train put on speed.

She had plastered herself against Soudard, her dress hitched high and her arse pressed into his flies, which she had wasted no time undoing.

'I can't . . .' he kept protesting.

'Yes you can! *Cretino!*' she screamed.

A few feet away from them, various black and white stalwarts of the labour-force contemplated the scene with stolid impassivity, far too tired to react.

'Are you going to do it?' Giulietta complained, wiggling her petite bottom feverishly against the horned man.

Nothing doing. A platonic halfwit.

'Please, Giulietta . . .' he was groaning under his mask, 'not now . . .'

'Imbecile, bullshitter, *filio de puta, ragazzo di niente, paparazzo di merda* . . .'

'I beg you . . .' Soudard duly begged.

They arrived at the Bastille stop. The in-crowd got out. Bullhead charged onto the platform gratefully. One of the revellers had a bright idea involving a bit of bravado.

'Proletarians, workers!' he yelled at the seated passengers.

Some of the latter slowly gazed through the glass at this troublemaker stirring it up.

'Workers, hey, drones!' he again shouted.

Then he very deliberately slapped his right bicep with his left palm. The clenched right fist shot towards them in a sweepingly unmistakable obscene jerk. His friends on the platform fell about, slapping their thighs delightedly. Hugo was helpless with laughter.

The traindriver, who had kept the group in his sights since Étoile-Charles de Gaulle, braked abruptly and reversed. The incredulous Hugo and his companions saw the doors reopen.

'Now we're for it!' Nazulis murmured. Despite his better judgement he had gone along with this charade in bad taste – which now looked like misfiring.

'They're going to clobber us!' shouted Soudard, who was already sprinting for the exit.

The conductor had now stuck his head out of his window, waiting for the punch-up. But nothing happened. No one got out of the carriages. All the workers – immigrants, skivvies and wage-slaves – remained seated to a man, limply and correctly glued to their places, their eyes heavy with sleep. They hardly saw the carousers scattering down the corridors of the Bastille – and thereby hangs yet another symbol.

Florian would have liked to end the night (and start his day) with Sabrina, but it was impossible to shake off Ariane, who clung to him like a leech. So he accompanied them both to the trendy politician's door, where they were easily persuaded to continue partying.

He hailed a taxi.

'69 Rue des Saints-Pères,' he told the driver.

At this early hour Paris was not yet choked with traffic. Pigeons were swooping about. The taxi went along the Quais. Notre-Dame looked lovelier than ever, its stately architecture towering over flowering trees.

'Nice day,' said the driver.

Florian snorted assent. He didn't feel like talking. How beautiful the town looked after an orgy, he thought.

He climbed his stairs two by two, in a hurry to get into a bath. On the landing a man was waiting for Nazulis, revolver pointed at him.

'I'm Mireille's husband,' the man said.

8

A QUICK ONE – AND A TALE OF PARALLEL TRAINS

'Have you been waiting long?' Florian asked.

'Since last night.'

The man was tall and thin, with receding hair. He wasn't bad looking for all his menacing air and set jaw. The revolver he held was shaking a bit.

It was the first time Nazulis had had a firearm pointed expressly at himself. A long, gleaming tubular object that needed only a finger to crook and so beckon you rapidly to the next world. The man trained his weapon straight at Florian's chest. He seemed exhausted.

Florian was not afraid. He was not particularly courageous (he had a generalised fear of violence, madness and duplicity), but he did have self-confidence. He knew things usually went his way: life treated him pretty well on the whole.

He searched his pockets for the key. The man was still aiming his gun threateningly.

'Do come in,' said the oenologist. 'Would you

care for a coffee? I mean, you've been here since yesterday evening, isn't that so?'

'Since eleven p.m.,' said Mireille's husband.

'I'm sorry I kept you waiting so long. I expect you've come to talk to me about Mireille.'

'I've come to kill you.'

'Ah.'

Florian scratched his nose for a moment. Then he pinched his earlobe. He stared at the man somewhat curiously.

'Would you let me make you a coffee?' he asked him.

'I'll follow you in. No tricks, right? If you try anything, I'll shoot.'

Florian found a saucepan, emptied half a bottle of Evian into it and waited till the water boiled. He poured it over some fresh-ground Colombian coffee and picked out a couple of cups and some sugar. He poured out the coffee.

'Here, give me that,' he said, taking the revolver by its barrel.

The movement was so natural that the man did not resist. Florian put the shooter on the kitchen sideboard and passed a steaming cup to the man, who was shaking.

'Why did you want to kill me?'

'Because you're Mireille's lover.'

'Oh,' said Florian in a tone intended to stress the sheer anticlimactic unimportance of such a

162

trifle. 'Among others . . . One of many, if I might say so . . Nothing in that to go over the top for.'

'I love my wife,' the husband definitively declared.

'Fine,' Florian agreed. 'I quite understand. She's a terrific woman. She's charming, attractive, she . . .'

'That's enough!' the man shouted, lurching forward to retrieve his gun.

He was too far from the sideboard to reach it in time. Florian had been too quick for him.

'Tut, tut,' he said, pocketing the revolver.

The weapon was surprisingly heavy. He realised why cops and robbers never keep their guns in their pockets: no trousers could withstand the strain of steel freight for long.

'I wonder if you haven't been reading too many bad thrillers,' Florian remarked. ' "Husband kills wife's lover". That sort of thing is fine for readers of *True Detective*. But we're no longer living in the nineteenth century. Morality is rather more relaxed these days. Women are liberated, thank God. One lover? Three? Why not? Mireille is a free agent, a consenting adult. She knows her mind . . . Anyway, how did you discover she was, so to speak, "deceiving" you?'

'I had my suspicions. I had her followed. A private investigator got me all the details and your address.'

Nazulis burst out laughing.

'This is just like a B-movie! A detective – with magnifying glass and binoculars!' He doubled up with mirth. 'A private eye who slides along walls, hides in bedrooms, sniffs the sheets and takes notes . . . Old chap, you're a romantic!'

'I love my wife,' the man repeated. 'You can't know how much I love her. I never get the urge to be unfaithful to her. I could never do without her. She's the only one . . .'

Florian found such amorous intensity affecting. He remained silent, lost in thought. From the flat below filtered some strains of ragtime. He recognized a Scott Joplin tune.

'And what about you?' the husband enquired. 'What is she to you? Do you love her?'

'She's a good and loyal friend,' Florian replied.

'But – do you love her?'

'Not like you,' he said.

He refilled their coffee cups.

'A love like yours,' Nazulis said, 'is admirable and very appropriate. I can't let myself intrude on it – not any longer. I won't see Mireille any more. I promise you that.'

The man gazed at him in incredulity.

Florian picked up the telephone and dialled Mireille's number. Her familiar singsong voice replied.

'Hello?'

'It's me,' Florian said.

'Oh darling –'

'Listen. I'm with your husband, he's right here. He's been talking to me and I've realised just how much he loves you. I love you too, but not nearly as much as he does. So – I'm taking off and you won't see me again.'

'But – you must be joking,' said Mireille.

'No. Here he is.'

He passed the receiver to the husband, who stared hesitantly at the white plastic, which he at last clamped to his ear.

'Mireille . . .' he murmured.

Florian took back the receiver.

'Faced with love like his, one can't compete,' he said. 'You'll forget me and I'll forget you. So let's forget each other. Goodbye, Mireille.'

He hung up.

'Here,' he said, passing across the revolver. 'Have your toy back. But don't do anything silly, right? We'll call it quits then.'

Florian hugged the man fraternally before he went on his way downstairs.

After a few steps the man suddenly halted, hesitated and came back up.

'Take it,' he said, offering Nazulis the revolver. 'Take it. I don't want it any more.'

Florian had almost run out of Lasavin chocolates. Deciding to replenish his supply, he drove over to his favourite shop on Avenue Victor Hugo. He parked.

The girl was peering into the Hermaphrodite boutique, her nose pressed against the window. She was ogling a low-cut dress with red flounces. Nazulis stopped in his tracks the moment he saw her.

Working from the pavement up, Florian successively appreciated and assessed her slim ankles, the curve of her calves, sturdy thighs, and a waist that was not too narrow but just how he liked it. He could not of course see her breasts, although he imagined they would be rounded and on the small side. Her neck, on which a mass of ringlets and corkscrew curls descended, was entrancing. It seemed designed for lips to kiss. Shortish frizzy hair, chestnut with blonde streaks, crowned all.

'Very attractive from the rear,' Florian reflected. 'Twenty-two or three? What colour might her armpit hair be? And how about her sex-life,' he mused. 'Certainly active, what with an arse like that . . . Not to mention the rest of her . . . Likes to fuck, no doubt about that . . .'

She caught the voyeur's reflection and turned from the shop window with a little smile of complicity. A dimple by the corner of her mouth, and a slight flutter of the eyelashes.

'Even better, front view,' he thought delight-edly. Then, looking downwards at her face, he took in her fringe and the light brown hair bleached almost blonde by the sun. Her nose, small and absolutely straight, was a nasal paragon. Her eyes were not exceptional, but they were friendly and warm – greenish, with a twinkle in them. Mouth enticing. Neck: already inspected. Her breasts were fuller than he had expected. He dwelt for a moment on their nipples, clearly outlined beneath the grey cashmere sweater. She wore a tartan skirt with one of those cheeky outsize safety-pins. Shapely knees. Calves and ankles: previously noted. Indeed, the whole verso-recto inspection process had lasted no longer than three seconds. Life, as Florian was well aware, is all too short.

'Listen,' he said. 'I haven't the energy for a lengthy speech. I like you, life's great and we must take advantage of the fact. God does not exist. You are a form of divinity. I feel I want to caress you, make you come, and share my pleasure with you.'

He paused for breath.

'But I don't,' he added, 'love you.'

He drew closer to her, sniffing her fragrance.

'I do love you,' he went on. 'I mean, no . . . It's all too complicated . . .'

He took her arm. She offered no resistance.
'Your place? Mine?'
'I've very little time,' she said.

Florian looked around him. The Avenue
Victor Hugo was lined with blocks of luxury flats.
He drew her inside one of these. They took the
lift to the first floor. A single door with its bell.
Florian rang.

No one in. He rang again, then raised her
tartan skirt. He pulled down her panties, ran a
hand between her legs in casually exploratory yet
appreciative fashion, and with an equally fluent
gesture took a surreptitious sniff at his fingers. A
very healthy scent. One which immediately had
Gulliver straining at the leash.

She leaned back against the wall, offering her
mouth. He kissed her. Her lipstick had an aroma
of raspberries.

Still keeping her skirt hitched with his left
hand, Florian undid his belt. His pants and
trousers slid down and Gulliver rubbed his head
against that curly, rather coarse mane, which
tickled and scratched simultaneously. The girl
was smaller than Nazulis, so he bent his knees to
work his way inside her. She began moaning.

'Not so loud!' he whispered in her ear as he
glanced anxiously at the floors above.

'Oooh . . . oooh!' exclaimed the girl.

Gulliver was in full swing. Nazulis meanwhile

had slipped a hand under the cashmere and was caressing her breasts. He felt each nipple harden against his palm. He moved up, armpit-wards. Shaved, alas. Still, you couldn't have everything. We won't be choosy about that, he thought.

'Oooh . . . Huuuuh . . . Mmmmm . . .' she was crooning.

Florian's legs were braced wide apart so he could gain maximum penetration. He made no effort to hold back. After all, thcy had to be quick. The girl too was clearly about to come. Her back jammed against the wall, she had gripped the stranger's shoulders and her head was nodding frantically, gasping nonsensical 'No's' of acquiescence to the pleasure beginning to flood her.

He hoisted the girl's thighs, grasping them firmly with both hands. That way his own posture was straighter and more comfortable – his legs had been seizing up. The girl was not too heavy and all her weight bore down upon the stiffened shaft of Gulliver, now churning dementedly into the oiled maw of that generous snatch-patch.

Her mouth opened, this time with no sound. Her expression turned to an intense, preoccupied rictus. She was now in the throes of climax.

Digging his nails with fiercely luxurious delight into her thighs, Nazulis began thrusting even harder. He shot off, joyous jets of jissom inundating the delta.

He set the girl down. They rearranged their clothes in silence and emerged from the building. She gave Nazulis a swift kiss on the lips.

'Bye!' she said. 'That was nice.'

She dashed away, actually at a run. She seemed to be late. Unlike some obsessive cranks Florian was not a great devotee of the quick fuck. It was all right from time to time, though: no need to be too high-principled on that score.

He would have liked to drop into the Lasavin shop, but it was closed. Too bad: life was pretty sweet anyhow. He finally readjusted his belt. What a rush it had all been.

The Victor Hugo pigeons swooped from the clear sky. They fluttered and flapped their wings ferociously as they tried to peck at the crumbs an old lady had scattered over a bench. One of them soon laid down the law and gave the weaker ones a series of vicious pecks. Nature, thought Florian, is definitely not democratic.

The great wheel of the zodiac was turning. It was the month of May, and soon the trees would become even lovelier, the pigeons fly higher still. The girls would wear progressively less. Flowers would blossom everywhere.

Every day Florian felt happier at being alive. He would wake up to find his friend Gulliver invariably erect and sensitive. The latter too derived such sheer joy from existence that sometimes he even shed a little tear.

The train was on its way to Burgundy. Nazulis winked at Florence.

They were alone in a compartment for eight. Florian had closed the door and drawn the plastic curtains, thus insulating them from the corridor.

Florian's destination was Beaune. The oenologist was scheduled to tour the region arranging orders for the Burgundian growers. This trip would coincide with a big dinner for four hundred people, given by the Brotherhood of Tastevin Chevaliers.

As for Florence, she was going on to Mâcon to visit her sister-in-law who'd just had a baby.

Florian and Florence had managed to coordinate their trips. (Travelling together, Florian maintained, was the nearest they got to domesticity.) The lovers had not seen each other for over a week. As soon as the curtains were drawn they fell into each other's arms and embraced passionately. Florian in ecstasy inhaled the scent of the young woman's skin, hair and neck, while their hands eagerly clasped and groped and roved over one another's bodies. He tugged at the

171

sleeves of her silk blouse.

'Take it off,' he said.

'Do you think we can . . . in the train?' she asked.

'Train, car, plane, balloon, troika in the snow, camel's back in the desert, on top of an elephant in the jungle – I'd make love to you no matter where, my love.'

She was wearing a brassière and Florian made her raise her arms. Ah what bliss, the two little thickets had sprouted at last! He breathed their aroma fervently. Like a mother recognising her brats he discerned Florence's own special scent, a freshness of pinewood in sun and various perfectly blended odours he did not attempt to classify. He drank her in, just as she was, high on her fragrance. Gulliver bristled.

'Put your hand on him,' Florian requested. 'He's going bananas.'

She readily complied, placing her hand between the man's legs.

'Don't move,' he said.

They waited until Gulliver calmed down again.

'Take off your bra,' he said.

Right elbow raised, left arm behind her back, she undid the white wisp of material, the fingers of both hands meeting at the mother-of-pearl (or more probably plastic) catch. The bra was removed, and those small breasts, so firm and shapely, displayed.

'Why do you insist on wearing bras?' he asked her.

'My husband's orders,' she said. 'Naked breasts shock him.'

Florian sighed, looking up to the heavens – and yet again appalled by human folly.

'Now your skirt,' he said.

'Do you really think . . .'

'Yes.'

She unfastened her skirt, stepped out of it, folded it and laid it along the luggage rack.

'Tights too,' he said.

She slid them off. She was now clad only in her cotton panties with their pattern of bees.

'And those,' he said finally.

She hesitated.

'But what if the collector . . .?'

'He'd be only too glad to get a glimpse of a body like yours while he was clipping our tickets. He'd remember the 8.50 from Paris to Mâcon and Lyon, and this Tuesday 15th May, for ever. You're an unforgettable woman.'

She took off the panties and Florian gazed at her nude body. She seemed to him even lovelier and more desirable than that first time.

He undressed hastily and flung his clothes into a corner of the compartment in a heap.

They were face to face, both naked and

burning with desire, but they still did not fall upon one another. Florian was savouring the wait, prolonging the delicious suspense. Gulliver resembled the proverbial ramrod.

Meanwhile the train was shunting slowly on. The telegraph posts flicked past one by one. Florian's hand rested on Florence's shoulder. His fingers descended, toyed with a nipple, dallied down her stomach and reached the silky fleece.

'Ye gods I'm randy,' he said.

'Come on Florian,' she murmured.

She pulled him against herself.

'What position?' he wondered. 'The seats are too narrow . . . Standing up? That'd be too shaky . . . I've got an idea. Let's try a variation – we can call it getting into training – if you just face me, on your knees on the seat, yes, like that . . . Spread your legs a bit wider, that's it.'

Knees parted, her heels tucked under her buttocks, and her back straight, Florence seemed to be engrossed in yoga meditation. She turned up her palms and thus it was that Florian penetrated her.

When fully inside her he stopped moving.

'Can you feel me?' he asked.

'Oh yes!'

'Do you like it?'

'Oh yes!'

They remained as they were for a long while.

Nazulis's nostrils did not cease quivering, sniffing, inhaling the various different aromas released as the young woman's excitement grew. He again made her lift her arms so he could brush his nose against her odorous oxter tufts.

A train running parallel to theirs slowly drew alongside. One by one its coaches passed their own. Then the speed of both trains was identical. They ran side by side in leisurely fashion.

A few feet away on the other side of the glass, a woman was knitting with a sort of tight-lipped fervour, her nose deep in her patterns. Opposite her, her husband was reading the financial page of *Le Monde*. Suddenly the woman looked up, glancing abstractedly at the train next to hers. Her eyes goggled in shock and a hand flew to her mouth.

'She saw us,' Florian said blithely, coupled to Florence as he was, with his nose truffling from one treat to the next.

The owl-eyed knitter tugged her husband's sleeve urgently. The man raised his head with the kind of exasperated grimace one makes in the throes of constipation. His wool-piercer nodded meaningfully, causing him to look to his right. His eyes met Florian's.

'Hello! Hi!' waved the latter.

The dumbfounded needle-clicker and her consort were staring at them in a state of utter incredulity.

'Ecstasy is not merely mystical!' Florian shouted at them.

They could not hear him in any case. Florian started fucking joyfully, thrusting with vigour against the kneeling girl. From time to time he would turn towards the other train which stayed more or less directly opposite.

'Pretty nice, eh?' he signalled to their neighbours.

But then the other train began pulling ahead and they found themselves opposite a new window, at which were clustered half a dozen youthful faces aged from seven to twelve. They were elbowing and jostling, leaping onto the seats and waving their arms in feverish excitement.

'Children aren't shocked by nudity or love,' Nazulis declared, pausing a moment. 'They're only upset when their family circle is disrupted. It's the parents' squabbles which disturb the children. That's our tradition. That's what causes the damage, especially at the start of puberty.'

The train opposite them continued putting on speed. New windows whipped past, along with new faces – whether stunned, shocked, admiring, envious or apoplectic. One granny applauded enthusiastically when she spotted them. A young wife smiled even as she blushed.

'Hello!' Florian mouthed.

A sourpuss angrily pulled down a blind. An adolescent hastily slipped a hand into his pocket.

'Hello, hello!' Florian repeated, waving amicably to each as he calmly continued to copulate.

Then came the rear brake van and the mail-waggon. Nazulis mimed a final greeting for all those love-letters lying inside their sacks, within the armoured strongbox on wheels.

Florian alighted at Beaune.

'Don't forget me,' he said after a last kiss.

'Oh no,' she said 'I won't forget you.'

The train drew away. Florian waved goodbye briefly, his heart heavy. Behind the glass Florence, looking like a small child about to cry, waved and signalled back. The train disappeared into the distance. Sometimes, he thought, it was painful to love. Yet you couldn't love without some pain. As he headed down into the tunnel he said to himself: 'All things considered, though, one must love.'

9

THE MAID OF BURGUNDY

A car arrived for him at the station. Paul Michelon, a well-established Burgundy wine producer, and owner together with numerous other growers of several vineyards in the Clos de Vougeot commune, had turned up. Michelon was a white-haired, ruddy-hued sixty-five year old. His nose, true, was somewhat purplish, but he was still a handsome man, whose blue eyes sparkled with sardonic humour. A man full of enthusiasm for his profession and with a corresponding zest for life itself.

He hugged his godson in the Brotherhood: this role he had assumed since Florian's induction as a member of the Tastevin Chevaliers. As the two men greeted each other, Paul said:

'Let's see what shape you're in. Put out your tongue.'

Florian complied.

'You don't drink enough. You're not breathing

decent clean air . . . Ah, you Parisians are all crazy . . . Well, what about the women? Everything all right as far as that side of things goes? Getting enough?'

'No problem there, that's for sure,' Nazulis assured him.

Along the Beaune road leading to Dijon they drove between thriving vines. Between rows of the most famous plants in the wine world men and women were turning over the soil for the third and last tilling of the year.

'May I open my window?' Florian asked.

'Go ahead. Do you want to smell the old place again?'

'Yes,' Florian said.

Sometimes he regretted being born in Paris and not having roots in the soil. His roots, he thought ruefully, were in concrete. Now, nose to the window, like a hunting-dog he scented the various aromas of the region. Aloxe-Corton, north of the Côte de Beaune, followed by the first vines in the Côte de Nuits-Préneaux, Nuits-Saint-Georges, Vosne-Romanée . . .

A Mercedes overtook them. The driver, elbow out of his window, was smoking a cigarette.

'Rothmans Red,' murmured Florian.

'You've still got an excellent nose, I see. Are you sure it's Red brand not the Blue?'

'Sure,' Nazulis said. 'The smoke of the Blue

variety is stronger, more tobacco to it, somehow.'

'What about the most expensive sort?' Paul asked. 'The Venezuelan or Saudi style?'

Florian grinned, pulling a face.

'I like you a lot,' Paul said. 'You're almost a son to me, you know.'

Florian, who kept his deepest emotions discreetly veiled, was embarrassed.

'Do you know that?' Paul went on.

'Yes . . . Look, the vines are really beautiful right now, aren't they . . .'

The wind in his face, he was breathing that pure and noble air from slopes which had once belonged to the Dukes of Burgundy, and before them to many generations of humbler winegrowers. For more than two thousand years without a break father had passed on viticultural lore to son, and whole lives had been dedicated to producing the magnificent wines now exported all over the world.

'Do you see those vines on the right?' said Paul. 'They used to belong to Monsieur Vinca and from them he produced one of the best wines in the entire region. His family had been in the wine business for over five hundred years. Now the son has gone to live in Paris and he's an estate agent.'

'The shit,' Florian muttered. 'Fancy abandoning all this just to flog mass-produced hovels.'

The car arrived at the small commune of Vougeot. Whenever French Army units passed the approaches to these particular vineyards they would traditionally halt, stand to attention and salute.

They drove past several old houses and took a small road lined with trees and vines. Then they reached their destination.

Delightedly Florian re-encountered the special odour of the old house: the ancient furniture still smelled of fresh wax. He climbed upstairs to his usual room, a tiny attic. There he found the same flowered bedspread; those same seventeenth century beams cracked, pitted and blackened by time; and that same wardrobe with the creaky door. Beside the door someone (and he thought he discerned the feminine touch) had placed a small vase full of wild flowers.

Before setting off on his business rounds, Florian swiftly changed his shirt, socks and underwear. Next to his skin he liked fresh clothes at all times. He didn't bother overmuch about the rest – old trousers, a leather or corduroy jacket sufficed.

'Off on your rounds?' asked Paul. 'You can use my car.'

'Yes, thanks. I've a big notebook of orders to fill out. Wine's selling quite cheaply at the moment, despite or because of the economic recession. I have to go to Gevrey-Chambertin and Chambolle.'

'When you get back I'll try you with something you'll enjoy tasting, then we'll have dinner at the Brotherhood.'

'I'm sure it'll be a great evening,' Florian said.

Florian's work was very tricky. He could not afford to make any mistakes and indeed there was simply no room for error. The quantities he would order for his American, German, British or Japanese buyers involved hundreds of hecto-litres, discounts of millions of centimes and so on. It was all basically a matter of buying the finest wines at the best prices.

From the outset of these buying trips, Florian Nazulis allowed himself no lapses, no latitude. He never drank: he tasted. He concentrated only on choosing the wines, forgetting or ignoring women, the flowering hillsides and the multi-farious pleasures of life at large. At these times he played the uncompromising wine-expert, tough and absolutely single-minded – a real profes-sional.

Apart from his professionalism, Florian was the possessor of an olfactory sensitivity second to none and an extraordinary memory. In the Côtes de Beaune and Côte de Nuits areas he enjoyed an enviable reputation. At any blindfold testing he was always sure to excel.

He returned at the same time as the sun's rays have lost their strength and strike obliquely, indirectly, spreading the shadows, buildings, telegraph poles, vines and fences lengthwise along the earth of Burgundy.

He rejoined Paul, who was seated at a chesstable in the big ground floor drawing-room. Facing his friend sat a young girl, lost in thought and with her head in her hands. She rose when Florian appeared.

'No, don't get up,' he protested. 'You're in the middle of a . . .'

'Don't you recognize me then, Monsieur Nazulis?' said the girl.

He had not recognized her.

She was small, almost petite, with long brown hair untidily tumbling over her shoulders. She had dreamy, rather nebulous eyes, which gave her an unfocussed or even inexperienced expression with its own youthful charm. She had an unusual, pouting mouth with extraordinary lips. These were almost negroid – upper and lower lips of equal thickness. Her chin was rounded, and her whole face showed she was abruptly moving from child to adult. It seemed too that the transition – as far as the physical side went, at least – was progressing nicely. The young girl's only blemish was a tiny scar on the right side of her forehead.

'No, it can't be,' Florian murmured. 'It's not possible. It's not little Est . . .'

'It is indeed,' Paul said.

'Estelle!' Florian exclaimed. 'Last time – '

She was smiling.

'The last time I – ' Florian went on in astonishment ' – Well, yes, time flies I know, but this is ridiculous!'

'You haven't changed,' she said.

'So much the worse for me,' he said. 'My God how pretty you've become! Well, well . . .'

He took a step back to have a better, admiring look at her.

'Just watch yourself, lad,' Paul joked. 'I know what you're thinking.'

'Look Paul, she's only a child . . .'

'Not at all,' Estelle protested. 'I'm sixteen and a half.'

'She's been helping out here since leaving school. Filling in before getting some more interesting work. This way she earns some pocket money . . . Estelle, can we adjourn the game, if you don't mind? I'd like to show Florian something. Bring us a couple of glasses and that bottle

I put out.'

'Right, Monsieur Michelon.'

'Amazing how attractive she's grown!' Florian commented when she disappeared – and she had moved like a Burgundian ballerina over those red floor tiles.

She returned with large, deep glasses beside which she placed the bottle Paul had opened in his guest's honour.

'I should warn you,' said his host. 'that this is not just any old plonk.'

'I should hope not,' said the oenologist.

At that hour the room was getting darker and Florian had difficulty checking the wine's colour, but when he raised and rotated his glass, sniffed the liquid and finally rolled it around his tongue, when with his eyes still closed he swallowed the first mouthful – he found himself lost for words. Quite speechless, he simply pointed at the bottle in sheer disbelief.

'Mmm?' Paul said. 'Not bad, eh?'

'Fantastic,' Nazulis muttered. 'Where oh where did you find this one?'

'A mystery,' Paul said, forefinger to his lips.

Florian again brought nose to glass, sniffing with tiny quick inhalations, then after another ritual and reverent swill, he at last drank again.

'Fabulous,' he pronounced. 'A Romanée-Conti. A bottle like this must be worth a fortune.

You're crazy, Paul.'

'What year?'

'At least twenty-five years old. Probably a '59.'

'Correct.'

'It's only the second time I've ever drunk it. Sharing a Romanée-Conti has become an exceptional event. That year the output was infinitesimal, was it not?'

'Hardly two hectares,' Paul said.

Nazulis was moved almost to tears. Paul had to pat his shoulder gently.

'Come on Florian! Here, drink a bit more. You're right, though: we have here one of the great Burgundies.'

'From one of the greatest years of the century,' Florian added.

Estelle had remained discreetly at the far end of the room.

'You really must taste this,' said Nazulis. 'A wine like this – well, you understand . . .'

He could not find words to continue.

'I don't know much about it,' she said shyly.

'Here, drink some of mine,' Florian said. 'First enjoy the bouquet, then try just a little on your tongue and let the wine move around your mouth . . . And savour it! You won't often have the chance to drink such a magnificent wine. It's priceless – and no longer even for sale, I should think –'

'Subtle yet strong, eh?' said Paul, his eyes twinkling. He was holding his glass at eye-level, as if it were a chalice.

'What smoothness and fullness!' he exclaimed after drinking.

'You might say it was a feminine wine,' Florian commented. 'Plenty of body but not brash or sharp . . . what a magnificent vintage! What do you think of it, Estelle?'

'It's really nice,' she said.

Florian refilled his glass and turned it between his fingers. Again he inhaled, assessed, enjoyed, closing his eyes to drink more.

'More bouquet than Romanée-Saint-Vincent,' he said, reopening his eyes. 'And more finesse than the Richebourgs . . . It's truly the king – or rather queen – of all the Vosne-Romanées. A queen of Burgundy.'

On the horizon the sun was poised behind hills covered with flowering vines: it was bidding the earth goodnight.

Florian, accompanied by Estelle, was strolling between two rows of vines on the crest of a hill.

'Look,' he said. 'It's sinking.'

The red sphere slowly dipped.

For a second or two Florian felt a twinge of

something close to panic, as he so often did when the sun was about to disappear from the sky. Then, as suddenly as the anxiety manifested itself, it passed. He took Estelle's hand and they carried on walking.

There was a large stone beside one of the vines and they sat on it and watched night fall.

'What are you thinking about, right now – at this very moment? Don't even pause, tell me quick!'

'That's a secret,' she said.

'A boyfriend? Fiancé maybe?'

'No, not at all,' she smiled.

He clasped her hand and played with her fingers. He realised she was taking a sidelong glance at him but it was too dark for him to interpret that glance. With his other hand he began stroking her long hair. She remained immobile.

He leaned forward and kissed her cheek lightly. Then he kissed that cheek more firmly and still she made no movement. He tilted her chin, drew her towards him and put his lips to hers. Hers were warm and full, and for as long as he was kissing her she let him, remaining absolutely passive.

His need for her was brutally sudden and urgent. He lifted her into his arms and carried her to a grassy patch nearby. This was the very spot on which, centuries past, Gontran, King of

Burgundy, had waved at the surrounding vineyards and announced to the Abbé de Saint-
Bénigne: 'It's a gift!'

'But – ' the cleric had stammered.

'It's for your monks. Your wine for Mass . . .'

As he lay on top of her Florian continued
kissing her, then he began undoing her blouse.
He slid his hand inside and caressed her breasts,
which were well-developed for a sixteen-year-
old. He then undid her blue jeans.

'No,' she said.

'Don't you . . .'

'I can't . . . I've never . . .'

Florian had managed to slip his fingers against
her tufted mound, but it was tautly enclosed by
her panties. He went on trying to remove these,
tugging first at one side then the other.

'No, no!' she kept protesting.

'Why?' Florian asked, his desire becoming
rapidly uncontrollable.

'I don't . . . haven't . . .'

'But listen . . . No! . . . Wait!'

They were rolling over in the grass, struggling,
their bodies tightly entwined. Florian succeeded
in removing her blouse, and despite the gathering
blue-black darkness he could discern the ample
apples of her breasts. He kissed them fervently,
admiring them and weighing, fondling with both
hands.

She tried to evade him but he pinned her to the grass. Lifting her arms he obeyed his olfactory obsession and plunged his nose to her oxters. He sniffed the downy patches there beneath her arms. A piquant mixture of certain odours led him to believe that she wanted to: wanted to, him, it! She was moist with desire, with wanting to make love.

'I've never . . .' she repeated.

'I'll teach you,' he breathed.

'No . . . I don't . . .'

He finally got her zip undone. She was struggling. As she did so, he kept pulling at one leg and then the other, trying to tug off her jeans. But jeans closely moulded to a girl determined to resist are an impregnable barrier.

He managed to slide his hands between her legs, which were flailing and thrashing about. She was sopping wet, oozing a lukewarm liquid, and Florian wondered if she had her period: no, he decided, he would have recognised the scent of that . . . It was desire, no doubt about it.

His hand bore down upon the light fur, maintaining its exploratory pressure despite her efforts to break away.

'No, no!' she repeated.

While she fought him he tried to sink his fingers into the moist folds. Suddenly she no longer struggled. She seemed to surrender and her legs went limp. She allowed him to take off her jeans, then her panties. She was quite naked now, but he could not see her properly. Night had fallen and the moon was not yet visible. A fresh evening breeze blew through the vines and in the distance faint noises could be heard from the various growers' houses.

Florian undressed in seconds and lay upon the supple, resilient body still (so it felt) with its layers of puppyfat.

'I can't make love,' she said.

'Why not?'

'I want to stay a virgin.'

'Why?'

'I want to stay a virgin.'

Florian could feel her chest heave, hear her rapid respiration. Gulliver, squeezed along her furrow, was exuding a transparent oil which trickled down the young girl's sparse pubic fleece.

'Stay a virgin?' repeated Florian in disbelief.

He moved his fingers over the sodden aperture, stroking her expertly with his fingertips and rotating these in a slow, regular rhythm.

'No, no . . .' she murmured.

Under his hand the moisture was so copious that the tops of her thighs were now soaked.

'I don't want to . . .' she was stammering.

He laid his mouth on her vertical mouth, placing his own lips on her nether lips. Her young girl's scent excited him to an unprecedented lustful fervour. He thought he was about to go crazy.

Putting out his tongue he immersed it fully in her cleft. Then he flicked it to and fro, drinking deep of that aromatic fluid which oozed from her like a subterranean spring. He tried to go deeper still, thrusting his tongue forward – but it found the hymen blocking its way. Determined to persevere, he decided to deflower her lingually if need be . . .

'I don't . . . want to . . .' she begged.

Tongue probing taut, mouth clamped avidly over her mound, he was welded to her in an inexorable buccal embrace. The adolescent body suddenly tensed, jerked upwards and remained in rictus, arched off the ground. What luck, he thought, and what bliss too: she was coming.

She emitted a sigh, a sort of sob, then a little puppy's yelp. He felt welling into his mouth the waves of her ecstasy. A new taste mingled with the previous flavour, this time with the scent of fresh-caught prawns.

She thrust her hands through Florian's hair and her body relaxed. They lay there without moving in the darkness of the night.

'Look at the stars,' she said.

He rolled over to lie on his back, pressed closely against her.

'Do you know the names of the stars?' she

asked.

He took the girl's hand and placed it on a Gulliver rigid and slippery with desire.

'It's vast,' she said.

'The night?'

'No, *that*,' she said.

He initiated a gentle motion to and fro against her hand.

'Stroke it,' he said.

'I didn't know an orgasm could be so strong,' she said. 'You made me feel something . . . something . . .'

'Mmmm?'

'Overwhelming.'

'Like an earthquake, was it?'

'Or a tidal wave,' she said.

He repositioned her small hand round Gulliver, her palm cradling his fiery head.

'Yes, use your hand,' he requested her, 'yes, that's fine, like that, go on . . .'

An owl began hooting plaintively far off towards Chambolle. A plane flew by, very high up in the sky now filled with stars. He had a sudden urge to penetrate her. Rolling over, he lowered himself upon her, Gulliver at vulva.

'No, no! I don't want to . . .'

He bore down harder and its tip brushed the soft thicket.

'No, Monsieur Nazulis.'

'Florian,' he corrected her.

She tried yet again to evade him but he held her firmly by the wrists. The oenologist's body was wedged in place between the girl's legs. Gulliver's glans approached the humid gully.

'No, no,' she was repeating.

The head dug in a centimetre or so while Nazulis continued holding the adolescent in a vice-like grip.

'I'm going inside you,' he announced.

'No!' she shouted.

Gulliver half-inched forward. A fraction further and the lips began admitting the rounded stave.

'I'm in you,' Nazulis said. 'Don't tense up . . . Let yourself go . . .'

He advanced again very slightly and Gulliver's tip encountered the elastic resistance of the hymen. The tightness of the passage and the taut membrane were proving obstacles, despite the ample lubrication of the whole area. Florian dug in deeper.

Gulliver's bald pate had now completely entered. The hymen resisted. The young virgin started moaning.

'It's hurting me . . . it hurts . . .'

'It must do,' Florian murmured, kissing her mouth even as it complained.

The owlet again began to hoot. A sudden breeze made the young girl shiver. Florian held himself

195

poised rigidly above her, about to plummet hawk-like down.

'Now,' he said.

10

JANE AT THE CLOS DE VOUGEOT

With a deep, straight thrust he sank into her, his gradual yet firmly controlled advance ensuring that he slid inside her to the very hilt. She uttered a cry. A bird took wing, flapping upward in a sudden rush. A dog began barking in a nearby village and was echoed by another.

Silence again fell on the hillside of Clos de Vougeot.

Florian stayed stiffly ensconced within the young girl and there he remained, motionless.

'Did it hurt?' he asked her.

'A bit,' she said, running her fingers through her lover's hair. She pulled Florian's head down and kissed him passionately. A real, prolonged and fervent kiss – upon the very soil tilled by those monks whom Gontran's royal gift had delighted.

All these vines had guaranteed them a constant supply of wine for their religious services. And what wines! During the centuries which followed, the kingdom of the Burgundians became the Duchy of Burgundy. The various religious orders still controlled the region's vineyards: Chassagne, Savigny, Aloxe, Santenay, Pommard, Meursault . . .

The couple quivering in love's spasms between the vines were merely links in an endless chain. Nazulis devoutly hoped that the soil of Burgundy would go on favouring wine and love forever.

Still joined to Estelle, he was now moving a little, very gently working Gulliver back and forth in the close-fitting scabbard of flesh.

'I'm not hurting you am I?' he asked her.

'Hardly,' she whispered. 'You're doing me good. That's fine now, like that, go on . . . I like it, I like it . . .!'

He plunged slowly and deliberately, to the hilt again, pulled back and almost out of her, then back deep once more, held by those warm, sleek, clinging walls.

'I don't suppose you're on the pill, are you?' he inquired.

They burst out laughing, bumping heads in mutual surprise at such merriment, Florian all but slipping out of her.

'So when – '

'I had a period three days ago,' Estelle said.

'There's no need to worry, then,' Florian

concluded.

Immediately the muscles, nerves and blood vessels hitherto so firmly controlled by Florian relaxed. A pack of ecstatic greyhounds seemed to leap forward, unleashed at last, in full cry.

'I'm going to come,' he murmured.

'Come,' she said.

She was so tight that Florian, on feeling this continuous constriction, had the delectable impression that he was being squeezed by a pleasure-vice, was melting in a paroxysm worthy of the eleventh century monk Aubin . . . And indeed, on that very hummock of grass where Nazulis and Estelle greedily grappled, a fourteen-year-old girl was once tumbled long ago by the twenty-five-year-old cleric.

Aubin had been a bawdy and wealthy monk. In mediaeval times he and his colleagues made fortunes from these vineyards. Certain among them had been seduced by material riches away from the strict monastic regime and had led dissolute lives. Aubin was one of these. He was partial to any young female between thirteen and twenty. Aubin would offer them a gold piece and roger them among the vines. Then he would be off to check his accounts and revenue.

In the twelfth century Bernard of Clairvaux campaigned against the widespread lechery and avarice of the monks. He took over and reformed the monastery of Citeaux in 1112, assisted by his own troop of monks, and thus the Cistercian Order came into being. It adopted the motto *Cruce et Aratro* (By Cross and Plough) and the monks undertook to cultivate waste or overgrown land. They planted new vines and viticulture became the Order's main occupation. The Clos de Vougeot was thus constituted, plot by plot, thanks to donations from noblemen impressed by the industrious sanctity of the monks.

The vine nearest the coupling of Florian and Estelle thrust from a soil tilled 2610 times since the coming of the Cistercians, at a thrice-yearly calculation.

It was as if a gigantic hand had sprouted from the vine-tendrils to seize Florian's loins and force them into a veritable crescendo of relentless pistoning power.

'Estelle,' he gasped. 'I'm coming . . .'

'Yes, oh yes, come,' she said, her legs and whole body now fully open to him.

For the first time in her life she felt the male orgasmic spasms spreading inside her, diffusing a wet warmth deep within. She clutched Florian still closer to her.

'Don't move,' she begged him.

Florian had collapsed on top of the young woman. For some inexplicable reason he kept hearing Schubert's Ninth Symphony – the second movement resounded inside his head, performed by full orchestra while his truffling nose, buried deep as it was in the girl's downy armpit, was ravished by her unique and individual aroma.

'Don't move,' repeated Estelle, feeling the man's seed trickle deep within herself.

BONUM VINUM LAETIFICAT COR HOMINUM! The Latin words, declaimed in unison by the four hundred guests of the Brotherhood of Tastevin Chevaliers, reverberated through the great banqueting hall of Clos de Vougeot castle.

When the guests sat down, the echo still resounded in the selfsame place which five centuries earlier had been filled with the monks' plainsong.

There was a brief silence as each guest took his or her allotted seat in this room whose pillars were decorated with coats-of-arms and with ancient sacks commemorating harvests of long ago. Then, rapidly, the atmosphere relaxed.

The Burgundy Association, one of the best known in France, had invited numerous other wine clubs, connoisseurs and growers. Mediaeval costumes; red and white togas; black, yellow and green head-dresses; multicoloured tunics and facsimiles of original historical designs were all in evidence – a colourful and impressive display.

The Companions of Beaujolais. The Knights of Saint-Emilion. The Council of Cupbearers. The Toastmasters' Association. The Brotherhood of Bacchus. The Gourmet Group. The Worshipful Fraternity of Vintners. The Médoc and Graves Company . . . All these and many others – even the Americans with their Universal Order of the Knights of the Vine of California – were present. Indeed, it was a comprehensive and yet exclusive gathering of food and drink buffs.

Paul Michelon had arranged with the organizers for 'Florian to be seated next to the most attractive woman in the assembly. Good palates are by no means an all-male preserve, and (as well as prominent media and showbusiness folk) the Tastevin Chevaliers had welcomed a select number of ladies with established reputations as connoisseuses of food and drink.

So Nazulis had been placed next to the very vivacious and delightful Jane Kirbin, the Anglo-French singer and actress: she also happened, by a stroke of luck, to be one of the oenologist's own particular showbiz favourites.

She was a slender, almost emaciated woman, whose long brown hair seemed to sweep away whenever her head turned. She was wonderfully blue-eyed and alluring. She had, too, a childish piping voice which wrought some alchemy on Florian's erogenous zones. Usually he preferred better-upholstered women, plumper and more generously endowed about the arse, but Jane had sexual magnetism of an uncommon order and quality.

Florian kissed her hand with impeccable courtesy – they had not met before – and then a young man, a waiter with a red feather on his hat, appeared with the Meursault.

Florian turned towards his neighbour: she raised her glass and they toasted each other. She had such a girlish, entrancing laugh that he felt like climbing up the curtains – thence yelling a wild Tarzan whoop so his Jane would listen to him.

In short, he needed to turn on the charm.

'Do you know,' he asked in a learned tone, 'the meaning of the word "Meursault"?'

'No,' she said.

'Meursault comes from *saut de souris*, mouse jump. There was so little to choose between the white grape vineyards and the adjacent black ones that a mouse could have jumped the gap. Today it's a different story. As you know, Meursault is almost invariably a white wine, apart from a few Noir Pinot grapes here and there . . .'

She listened to him, smiling, her chin resting on her fist.

What, he thought, could he tell her next? He could talk of Chablis, Chiroubles, Moulin-à-Vent, Saint-Amour. But perhaps she didn't like Beaujolais . . .

The *barbillon grillé* was accompanied by a Chablis Grand Cru 1978, a superb wine, then came lobster served with a Pouilly-Fumé, which Florian found disappointing.

'Slightly disappointing, don't you think, the Pouilly?' he remarked to his neighbour.

'You're very particular,' she said, stuffing a lobster sliver between her pretty lips.

'Don't you think it's rather old hat?'

'I beg your pardon?'

'Don't you find it's a bit past its best?'

'I'm not an expert . . .'

'Just trust your instinct,' he said. 'The pleasure your mouth gets from the wine . . . It's a whole world . . .'

He warmed to his theme. He wanted to take her hand and tell her: 'I love you, let's get married and have kids, I'll be faithful, no other woman will exist for me.'

He asked for more Chablis and for the Pouilly to be taken away.

Soon it was the turn of the *fricassée de poulets à l'essence de racines*, and the red-feathered waiter suggested another wine, but Florian preferred to stay with the Chablis.

'Do you mind our sticking to the Chablis before the red wines?' he asked Jane.

'No problem. You're the boss,' she murmured, in that trill that thrilled, her truly prick-stiffening voice.

Meanwhile the great banqueting hall had filled with an ear-splitting and jovial din. Laughter, animated conversations and occasional shouts could be heard the length and breadth of the enormous room.

A rosy cloud floated in front of Nazulis and Jane's beautiful profile blurred somewhat. His head was spinning slightly. Life, he considered, was more than good.

Suddenly he became aware that the President of the Brotherhood was clapping for silence.

'Rest assured,' the latter began, 'that I won't make a long speech. May I simply welcome all the members of the various estimable organizations which have done us the honour of being with us here tonight. We all have a variety of mutual links, but one main common interest unites us this evening – Wine, that right royal beverage, that nectar of the gods, the draught of immortality

. . . It was Bacchus who . . .'

'He's good for at least an hour of this,' Florian whispered in his neighbour's ear. 'It's the same at every banquet: wine is being celebrated but it's virtually impossible to do the subject justice. As with love. How to describe the pleasure of love-making to someone who's never experienced it? What can one say? "This tickles, that scratches, this feels nice, that swells and goes down again"? How does one convey the incomparable sensation of climax? We fall back upon impoverished words which only approximately describe the miracle. These are things one must live, not talk about . . .'

Her big blue eyes were staring at him.

'Do you think I'm an idiot?' he asked.

She shook her head, smiling very genuinely.

'You're an enchantress,' he said, dropping his voice and glancing either side of them to make sure no one heard. 'You're even beyond the *femme fatale* stage . . .'

She suppressed her laughter behind her hands, those slender hands with their long fingers. It would have been bad form to embarrass the President – speechifying in full flow – who was now discussing Dionysiac art, quoting from *The Song of Songs*, touching upon the Grail Legend, and so on.

'You're so . . . such a woman . . . I mean a

woman of such . . .'

He was fumbling for his words, trying to make an impressive and emphatic declaration to this exquisite woman. She interrupted him by leaning across and giving him a kiss. A light kiss, to be sure, but a kiss full on the lips.

'Ye gods,' Florian murmured.

'. . . this modest but profoundly significant shrub of the genus *ampelidaceae*, in a word – the vine . . .' the President persevered.

'. . . she actually kissed me!'

Once again he wanted to give vent to a cry worthy of Johnny Weissmuller in the jungle, to leap onto the table, proclaiming 'Jane! Jane! I love Jane, and, what's more, she kissed me!' But he calmly extracted the bottle of Chablis from the ice bucket and refilled their glasses.

Once again the rosy cloud wavered before his eyes and the room seemed to tremble slightly. Jane had laid her hand upon his own as if it were the most natural thing in the world. Then the speaker ended his oration and was greeted with thunderous applause.

The next course arrived, borne aloft by a host of waiters all looking like Robin Hood and his merry men. It was *perdreaux à la Sierra Moréna*.

Still floating on his cloud, Florian savoured the aroma of Madeira, bacon and cloves. A Chapelle-Chambertin 1970 was served which, paradoxically, sobered him up. The rhyme was generally axiomatic and well-established that ran:

White after red, easy to bed.

Red after white, headache and tight.

– but Florian all too often reacted differently from the norm.

'What do you think of these partridges?' the oenologist enquired of his neighbour.

'I'm full!' she exclaimed, placing her charming hands just below her small breasts – which were slightly pointed but oh so beautifully shaped!

'I wish she meant full of me, and of our ten children,' he fantasised, looking at her slim waist and flat stomach.

She was staring deep into his eyes now.

'I think I love you,' he said.

'Come off it!' she laughed. 'You've had a drop too much!'

'Not at all, absolutely not,' he said. 'And even if I had, would that make it any less true?'

She was scrutinizing this oddball wild-eyed wine-buff with considerable curiosity.

'I love you and there it is,' he reiterated.

'But . . .'

'Come on, let's go, let me take you off to California and we'll plant vines there and I'll give you wines and children . . .'

She burst out laughing again, her laughter so musical that he had to brace himself against the table in order not to float upwards. The waiter refilled their glasses with Chambertin.

'To our love!' exclaimed Florian, raising his glass.

After the various *entrées*, the Robin Hood characters brought in the main course, braised beef garnished with glazed turnips.

'Oh I just couldn't!' Jane cried in her fluting, childlike voice. 'It's simply *too* much,' she went on. Her delightful English accent was fascinating Florian Nazulis.

'I'll eat yours,' Florian hissed into her ear. 'I'm hungry. It's love.'

The waiter was not in the offing, so Florian refilled their glasses with that magnificent burgundy which was Napoleon's usual tipple and which he took on every campaign in huge casks. But the yokel diluted it with *water*! The thought of it made Florian queasy, even in retrospect.

'What do you think of Napoleon?' he asked his neighbour.

'If you ask an Englishwoman that, what sort of a reply do you expect?' she smiled.

'No, no, I'm not talking politics. I was thinking of how he watered down his Chambertin . . . Don't you find that appalling?' he exclaimed. Then he went on: 'Do you love me?'

'But I scarcely know you!'

'All the more reason, then,' he muttered.

He drained his glass.

'The greatest loves are when the lovers don't yet know each other but that spark is there, the essential atom of each person, if you follow me . . .'

She continued to gaze at him with eyes of azure promise.

'You must think me a complete idiot.'

'No, not at all,' she said, putting an arm around him by way of kindly reassurance.

'Oh I can see only too well that you don't really love me as I love you!'

'I like you a lot,' she said, 'but how do you expect . . .? We've known each other only two hours.'

'I can see you don't love me,' Florian said despairingly. 'For once, life's not treating me well!'

He rose to his feet, staggering slightly.

'Where are you going?' Jane asked.

'I don't know. Doesn't matter where. Nowhere.'

He crossed the great hall filled with people, noise, aromas and roasts. Leaving through the main door he found himself out in the fresh night air. The distant sound of a cuckoo greeted him.

'Hello, cuckoo,' he mumbled sadly.

He went and sat down on a low stone wall a short distance from the big house. One of the

Clos de Vougeot watchmen spotted him and came over to him. He had a moustache and a cap whose peak dazzlingly reflected the lights of the chateau.

'Aren't you feeling well, Monsieur?' he asked.

The man was quite used to large banquets with their customary influxes into this garden.

'No. Yes. It's all right,' Florian said. 'Heart, you know.'

'Would you like me to fetch a doctor?' the man suggested, suddenly anxious and envisaging cardiac arrest, angina and the whole works.

'Not medical, heart,' Florian said. 'The other thing, love I mean . . .'

'Ah!' the man exclaimed with relief. 'Ah, well, that's fine then. All right.'

He disappeared into the darkness.

Florian lay down along the wall and gazed up at the galaxy. Two hundred thousand million stars, only a million of them identified, were scattered across the vast velvety-blue void above the vines. He looked for the various planets – Mars, that big red dot up there, Jupiter, Mercury, Venus, Saturn, Uranus, Neptune, Pluto.

A shooting star floated across the sky, briefly imprinting its evanescence. He told himself to make a wish: 'I want her to join me here, now.'

He turned round and there she was, very close by, standing tall and slim in her black dress sewn

211

with sequins which themselves sparkled like stars.

'You all right?' she asked.

'Fine,' he said. 'Looking at the stars. The zodiac signs.'

Still lying full-length on the stone wall he saw her as in a low-angle shot, a star against the backdrop of stars. Yes, it would have made a marvellous shot, and a fine film too . . .

He noticed that the star's face was leaning over him. Her hair fell over his cheeks, tickling slightly, before he felt her lips on his. A kiss of such gentleness he had seldom if ever experienced.

'We haven't finished our dinner,' she said in her lilting tones.

While the young woman led him back indoors, slipping her arm in his, Florian felt like addressing a few words to life itself. 'I apologize,' he wanted to say. 'I take back everything I said earlier. You're always good to me.'

11

THE SIXTH FORM IN THE GYM

For quite some time Nazulis had been observing the Lycée girls running round the track at the Sports Centre at the Porte d'Orléans. In pink, blue, yellow, red or green tracksuits they were trotting past him, their elbows tucked in, breathing heavily as they ran.

Tall skinny girls with long legs; little plump things; some of them pretty, others less so. Blondes, brunettes, one or two redheads and a coffee-coloured West Indian girl – the entire sixth form was there.

Some of them had taken off their tracksuit bottoms in the interests of freedom of movement, thus displaying their bare legs which flashed by with big strides. Their shorts – quite as short as the name suggests – showed off their buttocks, allowing the spectator to appraise their various posterior curvatures. Florian was writing in his notebook.

Little doe-*derrières* propelled by slender legs, or flat bums atop rounded columns. Scrawny cruppers upon such frail tubular twigs that the spectator might wonder how they didn't snap under the strain of racing against the stop-watch and whistle brandished by their gym mistress. This PE teacher was a grim-faced, solid pro who resembled a Soviet weight-lifter: she had a lantern jaw and a beam broad as a barn-door.

Each girl who passed him left in her wake an individual aroma. Florian was also noting these odours. For some time he had been monitoring a particularly interesting bouquet. The scent originated from a wiry little blonde now on her eighth circuit of the track. Her long straw-coloured hair was kept in check by one of those white *bandeaux* that give any tennis enthusiast the professional look. The pretty face, somewhat flushed from the exertion, had just turned Florian's head for the eighth time. But it was her rounded, well-muscled, pert buttocks moving like twin full moons that really caught his eye. A first-class arse, borne along by strong legs: all in all, a sturdy sprig.

The wolf licked his lips and straightened his Electricity Board cap.

The girls were now coming up for the tenth lap. Their respective scents drifted past him, irritating or delighting his nostrils. Each aromatic waft attested to efforts made, to pleasure or discomfort, unhappiness, struggle, recent orgasm or continual frustration. It was simply a question of

214

differentiating between them, if not confusing them. His keen nose sniffed like an animal's, patient and intent.

The diminutive blonde was racing round the slightly banked bend, approaching Florian – her knees high, legs working like pistons, and her pretty brow furrowed from the strain. She sped by like an arrow for the tenth and last time. The olfactory membranes of the sniffer quivered, transmitting millions of tiny information signals to that curious computer the brain.

The formidable gym mistress, her eyes glued to her stopwatch, called out the times and placings, then grabbed the whistle which hung round her neck and blew three piercing blasts to round up the girls.

The electrical wolf moistened his chops and discreetly followed the line of girls into the gym itself. The moment he entered the sheepfold he was assailed by a heady mix of piquant odours. Girls were taking off their tracksuit tops. Some made a beeline for the showers, others were just hanging around.

The gym itself was steeped in maidenly odours and resounded to the incessant racket of the young ladies. One of them, apparently keener than her companions, was continuing her exercises. She was poised across the parallel bars in a posture which made the wolf drool.

She was doing the splits, more or less: one of her legs resting on one bar, the other on the bar parallel to it. The position of her legs accentuated the jut of the pubescent pubis, though the latter was of course concealed by the thick elasticated knickers. Florian, that lupine but bogus electricity man, thought he could detect a split in the material. When he approached he found that the material had indeed given way under the strain, revealing (to an expert eye) the reddish frizz of youthful pubic fur.

'Have you come to read the meters?' the Soviet-style PE pedagogue demanded.

The wolf started, startled from his reverie.

'Yes,' he said, touching his cap.

'The meters are down there,' the instructress instructed him.

'You have some very gifted pupils,' Nazulis remarked suavely, his smile nonetheless predatory. 'What grace and athletic prowess! I really admire that.'

There was much else he was admiring, he might have added but did not . . .

'You should see them on the trampoline, that's really something!' the meaty gym mistress said. She blew her whistle again. 'Right, that's it for today, girls! I'm off now.'

'Goodbye, Mademoiselle!' shouted a juvenile arselicker who already looked as if her juices had run dry.

'The meters are down there on the right,' the electrician was once again informed.

Then whistle at the ready, watch in hand, and face set, she headed back to the Stadium, where yet another class awaited her.

Absorbed in their chatter of fashions and rock-stars, the girls paid no attention to the blue-uniformed employee observing them. This man in a peaked cap was self-effacing and oh so discreet: why, he even had the run of the hen-coop!

The girls were undressing. A tornado of odours was unleashed. Numerous sebaceous glands exuded their scents and drying perspiration impregnated the air. Florian's head began to reel.

Just then he caught sight of an exquisite creature.

Not the little blonde of the track but a willowy brunette with perfectly oval features, big dark eyes and long almost black hair which she was shaking loose with childlike grace. She took off her games things and revealed her superb nudity. Her skin was smooth and her small breasts with their brownish aureoles tilted upwards. Her tufted triangle was small and black.

The wolf from the electricity board sprang from the shadow and leaped into the changing cabin she had just entered.

217

'Oh!' she exclaimed – at once charmed by this surprise intrusion.

She raised her arms languorously in a provocative twirl worthy of a ballerina, ready to surrender her all to this virile visitor, this randy handy-man . . . Her eyes sparkled at him from the cabin's murky recesses.

Suddenly Nazulis' nose twitched: he was getting a warning signal. The nasal alarm almost syringed his sinuses. Florian grimaced and Gulliver, like an aged Buddha, retracted. From the schoolgirl there emanated an unbearable odour, as of rotting rabbit marinaded in week-old sweat.

Florian turned tail, dashing back to his vantage point, gasping. He forced himself to exhale deeply and expunge from his nostrils the rest of that tainted air. How could one look so ravishing and smell so awful? Perhaps her thinking was reactionary, he reflected in a desperate attempt at comprehension: too much morality and not enough ecstasy . . . Even her nymphomania was somewhat suspect . . . He had to admit, with considerable annoyance, that he was utterly at a loss . . .

The girls themselves were absorbed in their endless gossip and were quite oblivious to his presence: only rock groups could monopolize their conversation.

The attractive blonde of the stadium – who had smelt so delightful – at last appeared, wearing a yellow track suit. She slipped its top over her head, then a 'US Army' tee-shirt followed it, then a small bra. What a pity – she shaved under her arms! For a second she sniffed at one armpit and frowned her displeasure. Florian thought: one doesn't necessarily smell bad when sweaty. You certainly don't, anyhow . . .

The girl took off her tracksuit trousers to reveal tight shorts. Once again Florian found himself admiring her rounded little buttocks. He realised how much he wanted her.

She unzipped her shorts and took off those too. The mound, moulded so tautly under sky-blue panties that were almost a G-string, protruded. The panties were removed, revealing a magnificent bottom.

At this point she noticed Nazulis, sitting in his shadowy corner, devouring her with his eyes. She covered herself with a towel in a spontaneous reflex of modesty.

'I've come to read the meters,' Florian said. 'Don't mind me.'

'Right,' was all she said, and she draped the towel round her neck.

She headed for a shower cubicle. Florian glanced to right and left, then charged after her. He got there just as she was shutting the door,

219

and he quickly slipped the bolt, locking them in.

'Hey!' she cried, 'are you crazy?'

'Don't worry, I'm a good wolf. I don't eat or bite, I lick and suck.'

He sniffed her hair and shoulders and got her to raise her arms.

'You're making a mistake, shaving under there,' he told her. 'It's really out, depilation. Same goes for plucking your eyebrows. You really shouldn't. Promise?'

'Listen, Monsieur,' she began.

'Well?' Nazulis said.

She stared at him through wide blue eyes which shone from the humid murk. She was not shocked, but she did seem surprised.

The sniffer resumed his researches. His nose hovered over the (unfortunately) depilated zones – which still smelt good, however – and descended along the curve of the hips.

'Mmm!' Florian exclaimed happily. 'Superb!'

He knelt down and inhaled the tufty blonde shrine, nose tickling at the silken wisps. He turned the girl around as if he were a doctor examining her. His face was now level with her backside.

'Mmmm! Mmmm!' he repeated approvingly, his nose against the fine convex curves.

He slid further down, nasally inspecting the cleft, then the legs, to end at last with her ankles.

He stood up again.

'You're in the best of health,' he pronounced.

Gulliver had naturally risen to the occasion, bucking and twitching in his pouch.

'Are you on the pill?' Florian asked.

'Of course,' she replied.

'How old are you?'

'Sixteen.'

'No longer young, eh? You'll have to slow down a bit, old girl.'

She began laughing.

'So how old are you, then?'

'A few years older than yourself,' he murmured, 'but let's not go into that.'

'Are you really from the Electricity Board?'

'What do you think?'

'Since you ask, no.'

The adjoining cubicle seemed to be shaking apart with girlish laughter. The door banged. Outside, from the cloakroom, the sounds of voices shrieking, jabbering, giggling and swapping gossip.

In their cubicle, Florian and the girl were kissing. It was quite a kiss, deep, passionate and committed. Gulliver meanwhile strained – through the official blue serge trousers – to rub against the student's hirsute hillock.

'Do you want to make love?' the latter enquired.

'What a question! Isn't it obvious?'

'Your place?' she suggested.

'Here,' he said.

'Oh yes!' she said, her mouth moving back into
a firmly exploratory osculation.

Her tongue slithered with Florian's in astonishing ardour. She seemed game enough for
anything, if her tongue was to be trusted.
Gulliver continued knob-frotting against the
adolescent's gorgeous grinder: the girl herself
undulated her hips athletically the while.

Florian doffed his peaked cap and hung it on
the door-hook. While he was unbuttoning his
uniform she perched the pate-warmer on her
head and began pulling faces, trying to imitate a
Nazi.

'Where did you find it?' she asked.

'The Flea Market. Hundred francs and the
uniform thrown in.'

She hung it up again and with no preliminaries
seized hold of Gulliver.

'Not bad,' she said.

Florian was thinking how young people had
improved since his day. True, examples of out-
worn morality still persisted here and there, and
leech-like religionists continued to corrupt our

dear children, but on the whole kids had few complexes!

The schoolgirl inspected Gulliver from as many angles as space and physiology permitted, palping, weighing, lifting, lowering and tugging.

'Not bad,' she repeated.

Florian was momentarily miffed at not belonging to the 'Super' category but no matter, he felt happy as he was – a normal healthy male with a splendid mate.

'Wait!' the girl said.

She knelt and fellated the forward fellow. Yes, thought the delighted Florian, the younger generation was all right by him!

'That nice?' she enquired, looking up at Florian.

'Super!' he attested. 'That's really getting to me. Much more and I'll burst.'

'Do you want to come in my mouth or right inside me?' she asked him.

'Er . . . hmmm . . .'

Even Florian was all but taken aback by such forthrightness.

'Anyway, you haven't got herpes, have you?' she went on.

'No, certainly not,' he protested.

'Shall I wank you a bit, like this?'

She began masturbating him efficiently and with formidable vigour.

'You're really liberated and that's a fact,' Nazulis said.

'Liberated from what?' she asked, never ceasing to shunt Gulliver – gripped firmly in her hot hand – to and fro.

'Listen,' said the almost breathless oenologist, 'wouldn't you like me to do the same for you, perhaps?'

'Oh yeah, of course!' she exclaimed, leaving go of Gulliver. 'Are you OK on oral?'

'I get by,' he said.

'If you like,' she suggested, 'I'll suck you a bit more, unless you'd rather I stuck my finger up you. Do you go for sodomy?'

'To tell the truth – not really,' Florian replied.

'How about dope?' she asked. 'What turns you on?'

'Wine,' he said.

There was a moment's silence. She looked at him aghast, in sheer disbelief. Then she burst out laughing so helplessly that the thin cubicle partition shook.

'Is that you Natasha? Who's in there with you?' a voice enquired from the next door cubicle.

'With the man from the Electricity Board,' she answered. 'How about you?'

'Valerie's here.'

'Are you doing it?' Natasha asked.

'Starting to. Are you?'

'Yeah,' said the schoolgirl.

'Is he any good?' asked her neighbour.

'Not bad,' Natasha said.

The phrase hit Nazulis like a cold shower. He'd forgotten how hard they were, kids this age.

'Want company?' the voice suggested.

'Is that your scene, threesomes – I mean foursomes?' Natasha asked him.

'Well, I – ' Florian managed.

'Open the door quietly, easy now . . .' the neighbour instructed them. 'I'll take a quick peep to make sure the coast's clear!'

Two small naked bodies dashed into the cubicle.

'Great!' Natasha said. 'We'll play sardines, have a real orgy!'

'Hello,' said the taller girl, putting out a hand and shaking Gulliver.

They all began squealing with laughter.

'Hey – what are you up to?' asked a girl in the adjacent cubicle.

'Full up, standing room only!' Natasha yelled. 'Right,' she went on, 'Let me introduce my pal . . . er . . .'

'Florian,' said Florian.

'This is Sophie and she's Valerie.'

'He's not at all bad,' Valerie said.

'I prefer you,' Sophie remarked, giving her a prolonged French kiss.

Encouraged by her example, Natasha followed suit with Florian. The latter was beginning to attain a state bordering upon satyriasis. Their four bodies touched, rubbed, stroked each other. Blonde Natasha, dark Sophie, and Valerie – the only one, Florian noted with pleasure, not to shave her armpits. In any case, he felt considerably attracted to Valerie.

Three women at a stroke: Gulliver scarcely knew which way to turn! Impaling them successively was the logical and pleasurable expectation.

Natasha drew breath, momentarily ceasing her deep tonguing. Her two friends however were still locked in their embrace, grinding their bellies together.

'Do you want me to suck you off?' she asked Florian.

Before he could reply she had dived down and engulfed the Gulliverian glans. A wave of pleasure swept over Florian. The kid knew how to do it, all right. Grasping Gulliver by the root with her left hand, she bobbed slowly back and forth, inexorably and unerringly sliding her tongue along the full shaft, deploying its tip to best effect, and using her lips to grip and squeeze.

'Oh . . . ah . . . oh!' he groaned.

Valerie pulled away from her friend and turned her head towards Nazulis.

'You're not bad,' she said. 'I think you're nice.'

While Natasha, kneeling, on the duckboards, continued her suction, Valerie took Florian's face in both hands and kissed him passionately.

Caught between their two mouths Florian was no longer very sure where he was. Down below he experienced a keen surge of pleasure, while up above the sensual kiss went on and on.

'Tickle my clit a bit, will you Sophie,' said Natasha.

Her mouth busy with Florian and her hand with Natasha, Sophie in turn received a caress. This Valerie, while kissing Florian, managed to give her with one big toe extended. The sighs and moans of the quartet merged into a theme with sometimes languorous, sometimes rapid variations, punctuated by soft cries and gasps.

'I'm taking over,' Sophie suddenly declared. 'I'm going to drain you dry.'

At Gulliver's tip Florian felt the new mouth, quicker and more urgent, breathing feverishly.

'Oh . . . Oh . . .' he gasped.

His kiss with Valerie deepened, continued. Before the culminating spasm, which he sensed imminent, he tried his utmost to hold back, savouring the intensity of pleasure diffused and multiplied. He also had a fierce desire to sniff the schoolgirl's armpits. He tore his mouth from hers and got her to raise her arms. His nose dug into

227

the sparse little tuft of fine hair. The musky aroma heightened his excitement.

'Oh no, oh no . . .' he again gasped. 'I'm coming . . .'

Unwilling to be left out, Natasha knelt behind Florian and with quick flicks of her tongue persuaded him to part his cheeks, until she reached the anal rosette.

It was all too much, this *coup de grâce* to the arse.

Sophie's mouth received the blurted spurts, Natasha's tongue felt his shuddering contractions and Valerie delved on, as if reviving a dying Florian by means of the kiss of life.

A few minutes later Nazulis, resplendent once more in his Electricity Board togs, gave Natasha a folded scrap of paper on which he had scrawled his telephone number.

He waved a brief goodbye to the three girls. There was no doubt, he reflected as he walked out of the gym door, that the younger generation was well and truly liberated.

12

THE WAY LIFE GOES

Rosy-fingered dawn had been caressing Florian's shutters for some time before he woke up. Amazing, he thought, Gulliver was still asleep. That was unusual, since Gulliver always stirred before Florian awoke.

Florian's eyes took in the familiar landmarks of the room, while he listened to the sounds of morning and sniffed the air.

'That's odd – I can't smell anything . . .'

He sat on the bed, turning to point his nose in different directions, like an Irish setter.

'Absolutely extraordinary . . . I can't smell a thing!'

He got up and went over to the window, opening both window and shutters. There was a grey mist outside. He inhaled, standing very still, and taking quick little breaths. He waited, then repeated the process.

'Still nothing? Well, well . . .!' he murmured.

He paced round the room for a while uneasily, quite disconcerted, muttering to himself that it just wasn't possible.

He then located a bottle of 1967 Château-Margaux, opened it and thrust his nose to its neck. Nothing. He rushed to find his bottle of Hautes-Côtes de Nuits, which he was keeping for a special occasion. It was just too bad about that: he wanted to make quite sure now – and if he could no longer smell burgundy, well . . .

With trembling hands he turned the corkscrew and drew the cork. Which broke. He tried to fish out the remaining section of cork but it sank into the wine itself. He cursed through gritted teeth, furiously employing the obscenest oaths in his repertoire. Then he poured the precious liquid into a special wine-glass and tried sniffing it. Again, no result.

Panic flooded through him. He dashed into the kitchen and pulled sprigs of thyme and bay leaves from a drawer. He succeeded in breaking a glass tube containing a vanilla pod, spilt some cinnamon, and then laid out small heaps of pepper and assorted spices . . . He had to admit, in the light of the evidence, that his sense of smell had completely vanished.

He slumped into a chair and stared at the floor as if he were the inmate of an asylum, his mind utterly void and his jaw slack.

The sound of the telephone ringing made him jump. It was Sandra.

'How's life with you, poppet? What are you up to? I'd love to see you! Photo-call till 1 a.m. though. Have to rush because they lock us away till then . . . Yes, it's for a cover . . . In profile, facing the sea . . . Starkers . . . Fix me some coffee, will you, and don't get dressed or anything, I'm on my way over!'

Florian moved like a robot. He poured out some Colombian coffee from the tin, along with Evian water, and plugged in the percolator. He heard the noise the machine was making, but he could still smell nothing whatever!

The doorbell rang and he opened the door to let Sandra in. She looked even more stunning than usual, and her sparkling little teeth were in bright contrast to her deeply tanned face. She flung herself into his arms.

'Ah pet, poppet! Kiss me, then.'

It took only a minute before she was nude and nestling in Florian's arms. Florian was staring at the ceiling.

Sandra's head moved downwards and her lips brushed against the drowsing Gulliver. Her little tongue began working upon the torpid creature.

Still nothing.

'Hum,' Florian said, continuing to stare fixedly at the ceiling.

'What's the matter?' Sandra asked him.

'Hum,' he said again.

'Don't you want me any more?'

She stretched out against him, pressing her stomach close into his. Her lips were warm. She was beautiful, infinitely desirable. Yet Gulliver was shrunken and Florian could no longer smell anything and life was in abeyance.

'Don't you want me any more?' Sandra repeated.

'Hmmm,' Florian muttered, eyes still staring at the ceiling.

Then she began to employ every trick in the erotic book. Not even a Sistine Chapel castrato could have resisted such prolonged sexual onslaughts. Her expertise was that of a professional.

Nothing.

'Wonderful!' she exclaimed with sudden rage. 'If you really don't desire me any more, there's no point in my being here!'

She got up and dressed. The door slammed. Florian continued to stare at the ceiling.

After some time he got up with difficulty, as if exhausted. He dressed and went out into the street. Passers by, cars, shops were all wrapped in a sort of mist and he had the impression of blundering around in fog himself.

He reached the Seine *quais* and gazed for a long time at the water flowing past. Feeling

232

listless, empty and drained of all desire he looked blankly at the dazzling flow of grey waters.

Several hours went by and during the afternoon the sky changed. The wind got up, chasing away the clouds. Beside Florian scraps of newspaper and some dust were whisked aloft by a sudden gust. The sun came out. And suddenly a teasing whiff of Miss Dior reached Florian's nostrils.

He stood up and followed the trail of perfume. It emanated from a gorgeous redhead. She was sauntering along as if in no hurry at all. He drew alongside her.

'You smell nice,' he said.

She looked at him coldly. He was sincere enough. She began to smile as he came over closer to her.

'Do you mind?'

His nose pointed in turn at her hair, neck, shoulders as he inhaled the splendid aroma. He breathed in noisily.

'Have you got a cold?' she inquired.

'It's nothing. The remains of one. I was quite badly affected, but it's over now. Come and have a drink with me.'

After flattering and chatting up this delightful

creature, Florian returned home. He opened his letterbox in the hallway and collected his mail.

He placed his letters on the table and put *The Trout* Quintet, with Rudolf Serkin, piano, onto the stereo. He undressed and took a shower, alternating with enjoyment the hot and cold jets. Schubert's genius all but animated the trout, which seemed to flash and leap through the silvery torrent which toyed with both light and life.

He rubbed down his steaming skin with a towel sweetly scented with lavender: tiny sachets of the fragrance, inserted between stacks of linen, had been a tradition with his grandmother.

When the record ended, he pressed a button marked *Incoming Calls* on his answering-machine.

'Well you dirty rat,' remarked a somewhat adenoidal female voice, 'you never called me back! Louse, swine and cad! You can have a kiss anyway. Ring me.'

Who the hell was that, he wondered.

The tape ran on. There was a tone bleep.

'Darling, it's me, Ariane. The River-Berthoux crowd are having a do on Saturday. It should be a really wild party, so I'm relying on you. It's fancy dress – monsters. You absolutely must come . . . Bye-ee!'

There was another tone signal.

'Sadi's are happy to bring you details of their exclusive Oriental carpets offer at bargain prices with . . .'

He pressed *Fast Forward*, until he heard a distinctive female voice. He stopped short, his heart almost skipping a beat: it was her!

'Good morning. Would you care to come to dinner the day after tomorrow?' said the silvery voice with its English accent. 'I'll cook up something, if you're not put off by the thought of English dishes.'

Jane – inviting him over!

Florian performed a sort of neo-Balkan dance, clapping his hands, clicking his fingers and doing knee-bends. Her place: that sublime woman was inviting him to her house!

It was all finally too much. He had to go and open the window and let in some air.

He filled his lungs with fresh spring air and then caught his breath. Framed in the opposite window was a familiar silhouette. And as the curtains were pulled apart Clémence appeared, wearing only a flowered pair of boxer-shorts. Her breasts seemed to wink at him, and he could see against the glass her lips move. Asking him a question. Florian signalled that he couldn't hear her and she opened her window.

'Now?' she asked.

'In an hour's time, my love,' he shouted.

He returned to his answering-machine.

'... and I don't understand why, you disappear with no explanation and all of a sudden ... I miss you, I want to see you ...' said the taped voice of Mireille.

That, thought Nazulis, was worthy of a Corneille play. My word or my pleasure. Husband or Gulliver. Mireille or no Mireille ... Well, he couldn't break his promise and yet he really wanted to see her ... But ...

'Beep beep, wee! Here's a nice message for you in my nicest voice, right? Well, you dear little answering-machine, when your master returns you can play him this, OK? Sandra to Florian. No hard feelings. Loves him still. Suggests a nude photo-spread in *Penthouse* for the pair of them. Prompt reply appreciated!'

Florian half-turned to inspect himself in the dressing mirror. Had he, he wondered, an attractive bum?

He turned the other cheek, then spotted a letter which had been slipped under the door and which he had not noticed on his return. He opened the envelope. There was a drawing of a big red heart, executed in marker-pen and rather resembling a pair of outsize buttocks. Underneath it was a handwritten line from Florence: *I'm thinking of you, darling.*

Dear, dear Florence of the delectable arse, he

mused . . . Then he remembered the mail.

Feet resting on the table next to the type-written pages of his *Fundamental Thesis*, he slit open the top letter. It contained a sizeable lock of brownish hair. Florian sniffed a few times.

'Little Estelle! My dear, precious little girl!'

The letter was warm and tender and suddenly Florian was back among flowering vines as night fell on the Clos de Vougeot. Again he inhaled, nose pressed against the tuft of hair. Gulliver quivered, recalling that pretty young body as it opened up to orgasm. He reared his head, curious as ever, available and blithe.

'Hey, calm down!' Florian said. 'Plenty of opportunity for that. There's a whole lifetime ahead.'

He opened another window and inhaled deeply. His nostrils twitched, sensing with pleasant surprise a new tang in the air.

'Spring is almost here,' he murmured. 'It smells like spring. Life's not at all bad, at that . . .'

He opened another letter, which the Post Office had forwarded from his previous address.

Grey paper, badly duplicated. The Saint-Honoro Parish Newsletter, rapidly converted to a crumpled ball, described a wide arc across the room before landing slap in the wastepaper basket.

The telephone rang.

A bout of uncontrollable feminine giggles on the other end of the line.

'Hello?' Florian said. 'Ah Natasha, it's you . . . What? Yes, I can hear you . . . Hello Sophie, hello Valerie . . . Yes . . . Tomorrow afternoon, right, of course . . . Yes, that's certainly an attractive proposition . . . What? I can't hear you!'

He pressed the receiver into his ear.

'Girlfriends of yours . . . Well, yes . . . No, on the contrary, why don't you all come along, all six of you . . . What? Yes, right, we'll have a ball, you can rely on me, that I promise you!'

He hung up.

'Bet your life they can rely on us,' he said. 'Isn't that so, my good old trusty Gulliver?'